MAD SCIENTIST JOURNAL PRESENTS

fitting IN

HISTORICAL ACCOUNTS OF PARANORMAL SUBCULTURES

EDITED BY
Jeremy Zimmerman
AND **Dawn Vogel**

Mad Scientist Journal Presents
FITTING IN:
Historical Accounts of Paranormal Subcultures
Edited by Jeremy Zimmerman and Dawn Vogel
Cover Illustration and Layout by Amanda Jones

TABLE OF CONTENTS

FOREWORD

This book started with a game: *The Monsters*, written by Jason Morningstar and Autumn Winters. It had been a bonus reward from a stretch goal for another game's Kickstarter. The premise was simple, drawing a page from *The Munsters* or *The Addams Family*: a family of monsters in a place that doesn't understand them.

The game was meant to be a metaphor for the immigrant experience, and it did its job very well. It reminded us of other stories where the fantastic is used as a metaphor for the day to day. We thought it would be a great seed for an anthology.

The stories that came in included a wide range of mythologies and tones, from the silly to the heartbreaking to the horrific. We hope you enjoy them as much as we did.

This book would not be possible if not for the generosity of our Kickstarter and Patreon backers. In particular, we would like to recognize the contributions of Adam T Alexander, Albert Chai, Alex Blue, Mac Cherry, Andrew Murphy, Andrew Yeckel, Army Vang, Tony Vanags, Chad Bowden, Chris Musgrave, Colleen P Moens, Dave Baughman, David Eytchison, David W. Hill, Drew Wood, eric priehs, Ian Chung, Ian Kelly, Jacob Wilkinson, Jennifer Grier, Jeremy Tidwell, Jessi Harding, John Nienart, Johnny Jiron, Kelley Ross, Kenneth Zich, Kevin Lawrence, Lauren Hoffman, Marco Piva, Mariel Le, Mary Argent, Michele Ray, Michelle S., Mike Vermilye, nohMan, Patrick Monroe, pookie, Rachel "Nausicaa" Tougas, Russell Smeaton, Sara Stillwell, Scott Reid, Simone Cooper, Siobhan Archer-Morris, Susy Hendy, Sydney Stacy, Torrey Podmajersky, Wayward Coffeehouse, Wendy Wade, Will Hodgkinson, and Zedd Epstein.

Yours,

Jeremy Zimmerman

Co-Editor

A VAMPIRE IN THE GARDEN

An account by Patricia Wharton,
AS PROVIDED BY LAURA DUERR

Six months and two days after I was made a vampire, I decided I no longer wanted to murder.

I was out hunting one winter night and wondering why the streets were so quiet. The lights strung on houses, the red and green decorations, the hordes of shoppers, none of it had registered in my single-minded quest for the next human throat at my teeth. Not until I was crouched on a rooftop, poised to ambush a young mother unloading her baby's first Christmas presents from her car, did my long-dormant humanity scream back to life.

Something my parents had always said surfaced in my mind that cold Christmas Eve: *give back to the world whatever you can to make up for what it gives you.*

I had done nothing but take for one hundred and eighty-six days, and all at once, I became reprehensible even to myself. I vowed then that I had slain my last human.

My first step was to figure out a way to survive without killing. The solution I landed on involved stealing blood from hospitals. I stole wantonly, without regard for what type of blood I stole or what its destination was. That worked out for a couple weeks, until I learned that most of the blood deliveries in my territory were destined for a children's hospital.

In my attempt to preserve life, I was actually taking its most precious form, its fullest potential.

I was sort of a mess after that. Vampire books and movies get a lot wrong, but one of the things they get right is our tendency to brood. There's the whole outliving-everyone-you-know thing, the constant killing, the depression that comes from never being able to see the sun... in spite of the supernatural strength, invincibility, and devastating good looks, we have a lot to be depressed about.

Add all those factors to a burgeoning sense of pacifism borne out of guilt, mix in an existential crisis, and you've got me, circa two years ago.

In short, I decided I didn't want to live anymore. But I didn't just go outside during the day and let the sun kill me—I wanted to try to find a death that meant something, a death that could give back in exchange for all the deaths I had caused.

So I left Savannah and headed into the country. I holed up in barns and abandoned houses during the day and traveled during the night. I drank the blood from whatever animals I could catch, mostly chickens. It was nourishing, but it didn't satiate my craving for human blood. I began to worry that being a vampire meant being addicted not to the blood, but to the kill.

I kept traveling, following a neglected country road west. I couldn't find anything to eat one night and went to sleep at dawn famished, curled into an aching ball, in the shade of a collapsed barn. It was the same story for the next night, and the night after that.

On the fourth night, though, I found a man.

He'd heard me under his porch, fighting one of the raccoons that lived there in my attempt to catch something—anything—to eat. He stomped onto his porch with a shotgun and a flashlight. It was the first light I'd seen in days. I froze, blinded, when he shone it in my face, but the sound of the shotgun cocking sent me into action.

When I came back to myself, I was three miles down the road. The man's blood, at first so filling and comforting, quickly made me nauseated. The ease with which I had broken my own vow brought me to my knees in the gravel. I wiped the sticky warmth from my face and clothes and resolved to die as soon as possible, whether or not it redeemed me, before I lost control again and took another life. I vowed to let the sun kill me the next day.

But the next day was cloudy, and the day after that. Depressed as I was, I still wasn't desperate enough to let weak daylight eat away at my flesh for hours, so I kept traveling.

That night, I found the bed and breakfast.

It was clearly a former plantation, all white columns and weeping willows and broad grassy fields. I could practically smell the suffering that still lingered all over the property. Between that and the guaranteed presence of human guests, I was reluctant to hide there, but the eastern sky was already lightening. There was no time left to find a better place to sleep.

Luckily, winter meant the B&B had few guests and plenty of empty rooms to hide in. I slipped in through a window on the top floor and slept curled up inside a mahogany armoire.

Another vampiric trait the media has mostly figured out is the fact that we need to be invited into residences. This is true: we can't go into a house unless the owner gives permission. There's some gray area when it comes to hotels, though. We can't enter through the main door without being invited by the building's owner or someone on staff, and we can't access individual hotel rooms without permission from whoever is staying there at the time.

Unoccupied rooms, though, are fair game. It was from that room on a misty February night that I first saw the B&B's gardens.

The backyard had a knee-high hedge maze, carefully planned

flowerbeds, and all manner of concrete and terra-cotta pots boasting citrus trees and climbing vines. It was easy to see how the gardens had once been beautiful, but they looked like no one had done so much as pull a weed in years. Any garden will look like crap in the middle of winter, but this one showed more than the ravages of the season—it had been neglected for a long time. A few of the concrete planters held no more than bare dirt, and the birdbaths and statues scattered throughout the landscape were obscured by weeds and vines. Not even the camellias were blooming. Bristly dead grass crept over the brick walkways. The trees looked like they were in decent shape, but some of them, especially the fruit trees, needed pruning.

My mother had a large garden filled with flowers, herbs, and fruit trees. She taught me about soil acidity and composition, proper levels of sunlight and water, and how to prevent pests. I was the only one in my kindergarten class who wasn't terrified of bees, thanks to spending my summers helping Mom in her garden. My tenth birthday present was my very own corner of the garden in which I could grow whatever I wanted. I chose carrots (my favorite vegetable), marigolds (to keep out slugs), and Gerbera daisies (my favorite flower at the time).

Peering through the lace curtains at this gray remnant of garden, I began to formulate a plan.

It took a full week of working through the night just to clear the brick pathways of weeds and grass. After that, I alternated pruning the flowering shrubs, replacing the soil in the dead containers, and trimming the entire hedge maze. The dormant trees needed to have their root shoots and dead branches clipped off, and that took another week, especially because I wasted an entire night searching through the B&B's various outbuildings to find the right loppers.

Having a fresh purpose finally broke my hunger for humans. I ate little during that time, and despite the proximity of the owner and her few guests, I never felt the urge to hunt them. I didn't need to see my reflection to know that the squirrels I managed to catch a couple nights a week weren't sustaining me, that I was wasting away.

Oddly, the concept brought me peace. At least my final days would be spent bringing some beauty into the world.

Then, in the middle of March, I got caught.

I had seen the proprietor of the B&B a couple times. She was a portly white lady in her late 60s who exclusively wore floral dresses and answered every phone call with "This is Thelma Jean, how may I be of service?" She had a private suite on the ground floor, and every morning the smell of whatever she was making for breakfast kept me awake while I was trying to fall asleep.

I thought she had no idea what was going on in the garden, but apparently I'd been careless, because one evening the porch lights turned on, the screen door slammed, and there was Thelma Jean with a shotgun standing on the steps. Somewhere amidst my dread, I felt relief: I had no inclination to attack her. My hunger for human blood seemed to have finally disappeared.

However, that could have been due to terror.

"All right, you," she shouted. The shotgun didn't look like it had seen any action since before its owner was born, but Thelma Jean certainly looked like she knew what she was doing. "Stand up slow, now."

I obeyed, letting my trowel fall from my hand. I had found a cluster of wild daffodils growing by a nearby creek and was nearly finished transplanting them to a cleared bed beneath a freshly pruned magnolia. I turned slowly, keeping my hands raised. The paleness of my arms in the porch lights' glare startled me—I looked like an ivory statue, scraped down to its bones.

Thelma Jean squinted at me. "You want to tell me why you been working on my garden in the dead of night?"

I took a deep breath. A shotgun blast at this range wouldn't kill me, but it would hurt like hell. Might as well get it over with. "I have to work at night 'cause I'm a vampire."

Thelma Jean lowered the shotgun slightly. "Smile."

I obeyed, revealing my fangs.

"Huh." The shotgun came back up. "You one of Thomas', then, coming for my house?"

"No, ma'am. I'm from Savannah."

"You come to push him out, then? Come to make me one of your twelve?"

"If I wanted to kill you, I would've done it already. I'm not here to take over anyone's territory, and I'm definitely not here to kill twelve people all at once. I'm not doing any killing anymore—that's why I've been working in your garden."

She snorted. "You silver-tongued bitch. You had me goin' there for a minute. You just give Thomas a message for me—"

I heard the blast and felt the sting of shot as a simultaneous barrage of agony that knocked me onto my back. I blinked up at the magnolia branches. A few dangled from shattered stems, and shredded leaves littered my face.

"Shot my tree," I muttered. I tried to roll into a seated position, but too many of my abdominal muscles were torn. I had to lever myself upright with my left arm; my right was a collection of ivory shards. I tried not to listen to the sounds it made when I moved.

I heard the click of the shotgun and looked up to see Thelma Jean standing before me, starkly silhouetted by the porch lights, the shotgun barrel inches from my forehead.

"The thing is," she said, "I've dealt with vampires. They killed my sister, long time ago, when Thomas killed his twelve and took over the area. Now I know blowing your head off won't kill you, but it will make your existence even more of a living hell than it already is, right?"

I closed my eyes. My stomach burned, my arm ached, and I was just so damn tired. "I fixed up your garden," I murmured. "Didn't get to do as much as I would've liked, but it'll look real nice, come summer."

After a few moments of silence, I risked opening one eye. The shotgun hung loosely at Thelma Jean's side. She was surveying the gardens.

"George was the gardener," she said at last. "After he died, I just couldn't... and I could never seem to afford to hire someone... probably because no one wants to stay at a bed and breakfast with ugly-ass gardens." She began to pace the hedge maze. "You ain't with Thomas?"

"No, ma'am."

"Okay, then. Since you ain't eating me, who you been eating?"

"No one." Talking hurt my abs more, but at least I could feel them knitting back together. "I haven't drunk human blood in four months. Haven't killed anyone in five. Except..." How could I explain my lapse—my murder?

Luckily she seemed hung up on the concept of a vampire who didn't want to drink human blood. "Okay, *what* you been eating?"

"Squirrels, mostly. Chickens, when I can find them."

"Do I need to go count mine?"

"Didn't eat yours." I winced as shards of my ribs and forearm began to settle into place. "Just squirrels ever since I got here, I swear."

"Huh." She paced some more, tapping her French-tipped nails against the shotgun's receiver. She paused to inspect a resuscitated gardenia, already beginning to blossom. Then she laughed, an incredulous outburst.

"Jesus. All right, I can't believe I'm doing this..." She took a deep breath and settled herself on a concrete bench. "Let me offer you a deal. You keep fixing up this garden, I'll get you blood. Don't ask me how—I ain't figured that out yet and probably neither of us will like it much—but if you keep doing what you're doing in this garden, I'll find a way to keep you alive that we both can live with. End of summer, we'll see where things stand. Deal?"

I wasn't sure I'd heard her correctly. It was my first serious injury as a vampire, and I had no idea what sort of psychological side effects to expect. Maybe conciliatory hallucinations were the norm.

"Oh, and if I find out you really are with Thomas—if you attack me or any of my guests—I will shoot you again, and next time I won't be so nice about it."

That sounded more plausible. I blinked and shifted my aching body, trying to process everything she had said, and by the time I looked up again, she was standing in front of me, her hand out for a handshake—her left hand, because my right was still regenerating.

I reached up and took it.

By June, the magnolias, azaleas, oleander, and lilies were all in full bloom. Trellises I had rescued from weeds and invasive vines now boasted fragrant jasmine and wisteria. Thelma Jean had acquired some rare variety of ginger lily, and its spiky sunset-hued flowers could be seen in containers surrounding the maze. The peach trees were heavy with fruit, and the fig in the back corner was just beginning to produce.

Business had improved to the point where I finally had to give up my room. Thelma Jean never formally invited me into the establishment—I never expected her to, and frankly would have been concerned for her sanity if she did—but she never rented out the room I'd been hiding in, nor did she order me to leave. (I found out later that she'd spent the first few nights in the room across the hall from me, her back to the door, shotgun at the ready in case I developed a hunger for her guests. I admit, there were many nights when I felt a craving when I first awoke, but as soon as I climbed out the window and got to work, the craving vanished.)

When the B&B finally sold out during the second weekend of June, Thelma Jean cleaned out one of the outbuildings, sealed tarps over the windows, and rolled out a sleeping bag for me. It was rustic, but it was my own, and it was much more comfortable than sleeping cramped up on the floor of an armoire.

Realizing that I had never seen the fruits of my labor in daylight, Thelma Jean took dozens of pictures of the garden and slipped them under the door one day, carefully sealed in the B&B stationary envelopes. I flipped through them every morning before going to sleep, studying each one under the light of my camping lantern, awestruck by the variety of colors, the delicate shapes of the petals, and the elegant balance between orderly arrangement and wild hues. My favorite showed the hedge maze at sunset, the crimson sky silhouetting the moss-curtained live oaks and casting the entire garden in shades of copper, purple, and rose.

Thelma Jean also made weekly deliveries of blood packs, dropped off in the cooler we'd hidden behind a rusting old tractor. She never told me how or where she got them; she only assured me the blood was always O+, the most common and easily obtained blood type. No one was being put in danger to feed me.

Having a reliable source of surplus human blood in my diet chased away the last of my hunger for the hunt. The blood in the humans staying at the B&B still smelled tempting, but it no longer held the same appeal as a convenient, guilt-free pouch delivered right to me.

Vampires can always sniff out blood, though, no matter how it's packaged, so I shouldn't have been surprised when Thomas himself turned up at the plantation near the end of the month.

He was the first vampire I had seen since I fled Savannah, and his position atop the local hierarchy was immediately evident. He was handsome even by vampire standards, with elegant cheekbones, a mischievous smile, and thick black locks contained in a ponytail thicker than my arm. His sultry eyes were entirely black, with no discernible iris or white, hinting at his age and power. He approached me as I was beginning my nightly work, cutting me off from the garden and the main house. I hadn't even heard him coming, and once I saw him, I felt like I couldn't move. He strolled towards me like a cat approaching a cornered mouse.

I had a bucket full of yard tools in one hand and a sack of fertilizer in the other. Their weight reminded me why I was here, what I'd been doing, and how much it mattered. I stood my ground.

"So," he said with a honeyed Creole accent that melted my resolve slightly, "you're the new girl in town."

"And you are?" I was certain it was Thomas, but nothing winds up these alpha male types faster than pretending you've never heard of them.

"Thomas. Thomas Rivard. Tell me your name, please."

"Patricia, but you can call me Trish. Actually..." I tilted my head, feigning deliberation. "No, you can't."

"As you wish." He strode closer, and I took an unsteady step back. "I have to say, when I heard rumors of a vampire girl working in some human's garden like a servant, I didn't believe it. Now, even though I see with my own eyes, I still don't believe it. You must have some sort of game here, some long con?"

"No game," I said flatly, meeting his black eyes. They chilled me—I'd been turned by a vampire with eyes like those, and I'd seen how ruthlessly she'd ruled her coven. If I had to fight Thomas, I would almost certainly lose. "Just a regular vampire girl, trying to make a living."

He smiled a slow predatory smile, baring his gleaming fangs. "Fair warning: the human and her family are having a party here for Independence Day. My coven and I will be coming through after for... cleanup. You can join us, or you can keep the hell out of our way."

"Fair warning," I retorted. "She's under my protection. If you come here, you'll have to go through me."

He smirked, and before I could blink again, he was right in front of me. He pinched my upper arm with icy fingers, and when he chuckled dismissively, his breath fell cold and musty on my face.

"That shouldn't be too difficult."

Then he was gone, vanished into the darkness as silently as he arrived.

I was on edge the rest of the night, jumping every time a night creature made a sound, pacing the perimeter to make sure I wasn't being watched. The enormity of my lie was beginning to sink in. Of course I wanted to keep Thelma Jean safe, but I couldn't hope to protect her or her family. Even at full strength, I couldn't fight off Thomas, not to mention his coven. This was his territory; he had made the twelve kills to secure it. His coven, comprising vampires who had either failed to claim their own territory or preferred living off the charity of one who had, would be fiercely loyal to him. Their livelihood depended on him holding this territory, and they would defend it.

I barely slept the next day, tossing and turning and trying to come up with a plan. Independence Day was less than a week away. At night, I neglected the garden, choosing instead to search the property for weapons and anything I could use to improve the house's defenses. I didn't eat, partly because the stress stole my hunger, and partly because I was too busy cataloguing the contents of numerous sheds, garages, and outbuildings. All I found were a few old scythes and a couple of old fishing nets. Just looking at the ratty, knotted mess made my fingers itch with the urge to untangle them, so I added them to the pile. Hung from the trees, they might prove distracting enough to slow down a couple of the more OCD attackers.

Of course there were plenty of other possibilities—crosses, piles of rice begging to be counted, holly or hawthorn branches laid across pathways—but even thinking about them made me queasy. So with only two days remaining, I was forced to tell Thelma Jean about Thomas.

I left a note in the cooler, and when I woke up after sunset, she was sitting in the creaky porch swing, waiting for me.

I expected her to jump up and immediately get to work after hearing what Thomas had planned for her. Having known about vampires all her life, surely she had a few ideas for dealing with them, maybe even a few hand-whittled stakes in her bedside table.

What I did not expect was her flippant hand wave. "Honey, that bully has brought his lackeys to my house three times before. Most of my family has known about them since my sister died, and the ones that didn't believe then surely believed when he tried to attack on Halloween of '92. We just get inside the house and wait 'til morning. That's all there is to it. You don't need to worry about a thing."

"But that won't be enough," I insisted. "He won't quit coming, not until he gets what he wants. Vampires are tenacious—if there's something we want, no matter how long it takes, we get it."

She narrowed her eyes. "And this is you being tenacious? About my safety?"

"I… I guess I am."

"So say we drive him off. Happy Fourth of July, fireworks go off, everyone lives, God bless America." She leaned forward, stopping the swing. "What then? What about the fifth of July? What about the week after? How tenacious are you gonna be?"

"I don't need to be tenacious," I said. "I just need to be smarter than him."

By the time Thomas and his followers arrived, everyone was dead. The back door hung ajar, and a smear of blood marked where a body had been dragged out. The guests lay strewn around the garden, one propped up against the magnolia trunk, one sprawled behind a gardenia bed. The feet of another were visible in a pool of blood just inside the house.

I was crouched on the porch next to Thelma Jean's body, wiping blood from my chin, when Thomas stomped up the brick pathway.

"You lying bitch," he hissed.

I shrugged. "Twelve guests. Not my fault you can't count."

"This is my territory!" he shouted.

"Not anymore."

He snapped his fingers. The attack came from both sides, but I was ready. I ducked, letting them collide with each other, then spun, pulling a thick steel screwdriver from where it was concealed in my waistband. I staked the one on the left first, a blonde girl in a black tank top. Her scream cut off as her body dissolved into dust.

The other glanced nervously between me and Thomas. Thomas had obviously told them not to expect resistance. He held up a hand, and my other attacker backed away.

"Twelve kills in one night is impressive, Patricia. I see you were playing a long con after all—and it was well played indeed."

"Enough," I snapped. "I killed my twelve, so your territory is mine now. Do you yield, or no?"

He sulked, his obsidian eyes unreadable. He could probably defeat me in single combat if he invoked it, but according to our laws, he had already lost the contest. Even if he killed me, he'd have to find and slaughter another twelve people in a single night to officially retake his territory, and even if he succeeded in that, he'd be viewed as a sore loser who traded his honor for a patch of land. His coven, which otherwise was obligated to stick with him until he found new territory, might even abandon him in shame.

"I yield," he growled.

I brandished the screwdriver. "Then get out. If I see you or any of your coven around here again, you know what the penalty is."

"I do." And with one last curl of his lip, he left.

I kept still for another minute or two, until I was sure they had left. Only then did I let the screwdriver fall from my hand and help Thelma Jean to her feet.

She groaned. "You know how hard it is to lie on concrete at my age? And I'm gonna smell like ketchup for weeks."

"You're welcome."

Around the garden, the guests were also getting to their feet, making faces as they tugged at their ketchup-covered clothing. We had used five entire blood packs to douse the gardens, walkways, patio, columns, doors, and windows with enough blood to fool Thomas and his coven both visually and olfactorily. The guests had simply been sprayed with ketchup. I had also doused myself in the blood—since I would get closest to Thomas and the other vampires, I needed to look and smell like I had just killed twelve people.

"And you're positive this will work?" Thelma Jean asked. "I don't really fancy the notion of scrubbing blood off my porch every year."

"He surrendered his territory. Doesn't matter whether or not anyone actually holds it... although, I guess technically I do now... anyway, he yielded. You're in the clear."

By now the guests had congregated near the entrance to the maze, whispering between themselves about what they had just survived and shooting me awestruck glances. They kept their distance, though, and I was surprised by how much that hurt. I don't know what I had expected—no way would they view a creature like me as their hero— but the reminder that I no longer belonged in their world, when I had sacrificed so much to protect it, stung.

I pretended not to notice Thelma Jean studying me. It was the first time I had been in a group of people since before I became a vampire. The smell of them, so alive and energized, was intoxicating, especially with the smear of blood still mouthwateringly ripe on my chin—but more intoxicating was the smell of the jasmine climbing the porch railings, and the sweet aroma of peaches, and the knowledge that I had just saved twelve lives.

I no longer belonged among humans, and I had burned all bridges with the vampire community—but at least I had this.

Thelma Jean elbowed me. "You are going to clean this all up, right?"

"Of course. A deal's a deal, even if it takes me the rest of the summer."

"Well… I've been thinking about that." She pretended to be invested in a blob of ketchup on her shawl. "Fact is, I'm just too old to be puttering around out here, and I never did know much of what I was doing."

"Are you offering me a job?"

"Let's just say your probationary period has passed." She held out on a red-smeared hand. "What do you think?"

I looked at my own palm, smeared with the blood I'd used to sell the illusion of my mass slaughter, and held out my left hand instead.

"Deal."

And we shook.

PATRICIA WHARTON used to be a retail manager, until she was bitten by a vampire in 2012. She recently completed her associate's degree in horticulture and is currently working to obtain a BA in sociology. Her gardens can be viewed on the White Azalea Inn's website, and her views on pacifism, vampire law and history, and her ongoing journey as a cruelty-free vampire can be found through her podcast, *Of Blood and Jasmine*.

LAURA DUERR is a writer, social media coordinator, gamer, and reader living in Vancouver, WA, with her husband, a rescue dog, and more cats than she'd like to admit. She has a BA in Creative Writing from Linfield College. Her other work can be seen in *Devilfish Review* and on her blog, *Ruby Bastille*.

LEAD AND FOLLOW

An account by Dana Saltik,
AS PROVIDED BY RHIANNON HELD

Fumes from the bus's ancient gasoline engine stung my nose, and dust made my eyes water as we jounced over the dirt road. Sagebrush scrub extended as far as I could see, ending only at the broken sides and flat tops of mesas in the distance. The brush cast paltry shadows with the sun so high, but the shadow of the bus's roof writhed on the floor. Sometimes a bump would throw us sideways, and the shadows oozed up the corner of my seat, reaching for me hungrily.

I closed my eyes, but not before my heart sped, panicked. Were the shadows getting worse? I hugged my arms over my breasts, tight, holding myself together. I only had to last one more week, maybe two, to accomplish my goal. Then it didn't matter if I lost the rest of my mind before I died. I focused on a deep, gasoline-tainted breath. You'd think the government could have afforded to retrofit their vehicles. But maybe the bus was supposed to remind "beasts" like me of our place in this human world. As if we could forget while being transported to the camps.

I opened my eyes when the bus rumbled to a stop at the first of several checkpoints, layers of electrified fences. I stared without moving my head, to avoid attracting the attention of the two guards in seats behind and beside me. I couldn't let self-pity distract me from my real purpose here. I would free the prisoners. They'd make it to the enclave in Russia, even if I wouldn't.

I counted the guards outside and traced the numbers on my knee to fix them in my mind. It was possible, then. One, two, then four. They smelled overconfident, what I could catch over the dust. If the residents of the camp were lucky, the guards would put too much stock in their silver bullets. The shadow of one guard's sleeve slipped over his gun, caressing it, mocking me.

The buildings, once we reached them, seemed so prosaic. I'd never been to this part of the United States, but I'd seen similarly rundown houses driving in, shacks plopped on pieces of desert land that looked no different than all the other square kilometers surrounding them. The camp had about half a dozen buildings arranged haphazardly in a cluster, all single-story and falling to pieces. A two-story building stood in fenced isolation on the other side of the compound, stucco smooth, tile roof unbroken, a broadcast tower sheltered in the middle of its courtyard. The shadows from its roof clung greedily to its walls.

"C'mon, beastgirl. Out." The female guard of the two stood and motioned me to precede them out of the bus. Dana, I substituted for the epithet in my own mind. I had a name. For all that, the woman hadn't been unkind on the journey. Since I'd let myself be caught, I had learned to spot two types of people. The first thought of the Jews, of the Japanese, of all the times before humans said "never again" as they stared at the camps of their age, and then sincerely convinced themselves that beasts were not only inhuman, but dangerous. Were, I corrected myself. I was a Were, not a beast. The humans couldn't take what my parents had taught me about myself and my people, that was locked away in my mind.

The second kind of people enjoyed themselves, because each kick or jab they gave me was a blow they gave to their fears.

I lifted my hands in acquiescence and rose, silver-cored shackles rattling. My left foot woke to agony as I put weight on it, but the limping was easy enough to disguise in the gait enforced by the shackles. Shadows sucked at my feet with every step, and I tried to ignore them. Not real. Just a symptom of the degradation of my mind caused by the silver poisoning.

I stepped through a patch of comparative cool directly in front of the laboring air conditioner as I exited the bus, then into even worse heat as the sun found my skin without the bus's protection. Even knowing the light kept the shadows at bay, it was hard not to wilt under the glare.

The female guard followed me, silver-loaded gun at my back, and directed me into the building in good repair. I counted guards again as they processed me in, rousing only to repeat my name. I focused on faces as well, to avoid over-counting the complement when I encountered them in different situations. This far out in the back of beyond, they couldn't change people too often.

The female guard snapped a collar around my neck with a finality that matched its lack of keyhole. Not meant to be removed easily, if at all. Both guards relaxed with that snap. When they finished unlocking my shackles, I stood quiet and put my fingers to the collar's cool metal. The stench of silver was ever-present for me, but I still got a shivery sense of the liquid silver nitrate core beneath my fingers. Break the collar, and it ruptured everywhere. A shadow from my fingers slid slippery over my hip and breast and I dropped my hand.

They had me strip and gave me garments like a bikini top and cut-offs, though the fabric was shoddy and thin. I held the fabric against my chest and frowned at the female guard who was watching me all the more closely now that the male had turned his back. Why hadn't they given me a jumpsuit? I swallowed and pulled the clothes on quickly. It didn't matter. It didn't change my plan, which was flexible anyway, since I didn't know the conditions here. The Were who'd escaped at the beginning hadn't lingered to share their experiences.

Back out into the heat. I faked anxiety about the collar to hide my limp this time. The male guard just snorted and prodded me in the back with the muzzle of his gun. "Go on, join the others. Eat a lizard or something, knock yourself out."

Once I'd passed through the gate in the command center's fence, the guards disappeared back into the building. I hugged myself and stared at the rundown buildings. Here was another hurdle. My shadow sneered at me from where it pooled around my feet. What if the other Were betrayed me to the humans? They'd know something was wrong with me. I hadn't been part of a pack, so they had no reason to trust me. My whole plan could end right there, at the muzzle of a guard's gun. Rumors said they executed the troublemakers for "trying to escape."

As I neared, I smelled overlapping Were scents in three of the buildings. I swallowed, gritted my teeth, and headed for the closest, slow and steady in my steps. I wanted to escape this sun as soon as possible, anyway.

The building's interior was as minimal as the outside: a few LED light panels down the center of the ceiling, and a dozen beds without mattresses pushed together to hold a pile of napping Were. There was no fabric to be seen in the whole building. Just the mass of Were cuddled together, women wearing clothes like mine, men wearing just shorts.

My shadow tightened around my ankles like the constriction in my throat. I'd never seen so many Were before. Only my parents. Why would this pack want me, when my whole life had been cowardice? My parents had abandoned their pack, to save the child soon to be born. I'd abandoned my parents to save myself—they'd begged me to do it, did that excuse it?—and even that hadn't mattered in the end. They'd found my parents, gotten their names before they were accidentally killed. Then my name was on the list of those with beast blood. And I'd run again, to save myself.

But I didn't want to keep running. The Were man who'd found me, he'd told me to get to Siberia, that Were lived there secretly, free. I could have gone alone, healthy, and offered that pack my cowardice. Instead, I'd decided to do something more than run. To make a sacrifice to save those who hadn't been lucky enough to stand at the end of a long line of sacrifices, as I had. And here I was, to save them, and the sight of so many Were was almost terrifying. Were my unrealized good intentions enough for them to accept me?

But I had little to lose now. I'd never make it to Russia before I died, so this was my last chance at anything like a pack. I took a step forward.

A long-limbed dark-brown-skinned woman at the edge of the platform they'd created from the beds lifted herself to her elbows. "C'mon in, new girl. We can do introductions after siesta." She settled down again.

I hesitated a breath longer, then climbed onto the platform. I settled on my side, separate, but a broad-shouldered man turned over and flung an arm over my hip to draw me in. "Edmond," he murmured.

"Dana," I said, in the same low voice. I felt him inhale, then his muscles went rigid. "Silver," he breathed. I curled up as tightly as I could, praying that he wouldn't scream for the guards. An image of my parents' Lady didn't come easily to my mind, but I prayed to something. Close enough.

"We should talk, later." Edmond drew closer and spoke into my neck. "After siesta."

I nodded with a jerk and waited. Nothing happened. No one demanded I defend my right to sleep among them. Edmond's breathing returned to the rhythm of a doze, and the stress of the day sucked me under before too long. I drifted off, feeling something I thought might be contentment, even as I watched the shadow puddle under the bed platform ooze bigger.

As the heat eased toward evening, the Were pile slowly separated into individuals, stretching and pushing to their feet. I sat on the edge of a bed and watched them. Here and there I spotted silver scars, hinting at everyone's journey here through a world of humans eager to check for beasts among them.

A shriek sounded from outside and two kids, perhaps six and eight, pelted in, chasing each other. The woman who had greeted me scooped the younger one up, held him out of reach while the girl jumped impotently, and twisted to set him down again, giving him a new lead. They screamed with laughter and slammed outside again.

I stared after them. I hadn't expected children. I hadn't imagined anyone could bear to bring them into a world with camps, but I rubbed the warm spot on my hip where I could still imagine Edmond's arm and the feeling of cuddling up against everyone. Maybe it wasn't a bad childhood, growing up with a pack.

I'd have to add time to my estimate for the escape. Children couldn't run as fast, and they'd have trouble sitting still for me to get rid of their collars. I'd have to warn parents to carry them, when the time came. What to do about the collars I didn't know yet.

Edmond returned from what I suspected was the building with the bathrooms. He seemed to make a point to touch everyone he passed on his way to me, a hand on a shoulder or arm. "The alpha asked me to tell you guys to be distracting for about an hour," he murmured here and there and received nods. When he got to me, he offered a hand to pull me up from the platform. Seen standing, his rugged frame was most obvious, but I saw a touch of what must be his mother in his softer lips, slightly curved now. For a white guy, his hair was dark, but brown beside the black of mine.

"Shall we?" he asked. I nodded and accepted the hand.

"The alpha?" I asked as we crunched over the dirt crust between the bushes outside. The volume of the children's shouts had increased, and now adults joined the game, making the concrete paths and courtyard between the buildings seem a hive of activity. Even when it was quiet, I suspected I couldn't feel alone here. "Who's the alpha here?" That was the person I needed to convince first, I knew that much from what my parents had taught me about real Were society.

"The alpha is a polite fiction. The guards watch for leaders, and they get yanked into another camp." Edmond clenched his jaw, and gestured ahead to a dusty empty space beside the path, enough room for two people to sit without getting prodded by dry sticks or sharp rocks. "Everyone knows I'm not really talking to an alpha, but it keeps everyone's instincts quiet if I play my natural beta."

He dropped to sit cross-legged. I hesitated before following. The only space left was in his shadow, and no matter how many times I told myself it wasn't real, seeing the thing writhe, I didn't want to sit there. I swallowed and did anyway.

"But I can organize everyone if you have a way to get us out of here." Edmond's eyes were heavy on me and I met them in shock. Was I really that transparent? If I was, the guards had to know too. Maybe they were laughing at me, even now. The longer I locked gazes with him, the more I felt the strangest pressure, like hundreds of people were watching me all at once, waiting for me to break.

Edmond broke the contact first, clasping my shoulders bracingly. "Sorry, didn't mean to measure dominance with you. We're all betas here, huh?" He laughed awkwardly.

I shook my head. "What was that? What did you just do?"

Edmond blew out a breath. "You're one of the hidden children, aren't you? Raised after families scattered because packs were too noticeable?"

I searched my memories. Measuring dominance did sound familiar, but my parents had taught me so much, all of it abstract, easy to forget. I smoothed a hand along my forearm, trying to also smooth down panic. In all my worries about a pack accepting me, I'd never considered all the things I might not know. "My father left his pack back in Turkey, when things got bad there, and met my mother in the US. And then her pack broke up, before they had me. How did you grow up, then?" He didn't look old enough to have been born before the humans found the Were.

"I grew up in the Seattle pack. I suppose you're used to how humans age, too. I'm around sixty." He sounded pitying. Jealousy and anger welled up in me, mixed, and curdled. He was lucky enough to have been born in a different world, but I was the one who'd injected myself with silver nitrate, to give myself immunity so I could touch silver in the camp and release him. I was the one who'd traded my ability to shift for his freedom.

I kicked at his knee, he "oof"ed, and then, to my surprise, grinned. "Fair enough," he said, dropping his head in respect.

"How did you know why I'm here?" I pushed the rest of the questions crowding in on me aside. Were society didn't matter, except for how it helped me get everyone here out. For me, it would be moot soon enough anyway.

Edmond reached out to take my arms one at a time, frowning at the smooth insides of my elbows. "I know what an injected Were smells like. If you were injected, you'd heal at human speed, and you could touch the silver they've spread everywhere. You could pass all their tests. Unless they've been able to perfect the genetic test since I was tossed in here?"

I shook my head. "We're genetically human in human, genetically *Canis lupus* in wolf. They haven't isolated the genes for the trigger to switch between the two."

Edmond nodded. "So if they can't find you, you let yourself be caught. And if you let yourself be caught, you're here for a reason."

I folded my arms against my belly. "Because this age has no hero like Silver." I managed a ghost of a laugh at my own joke. Figures of myth never seemed to survive into today's world, when you needed them most.

Edmond gave me the strangest look, almost tangling his gaze with mine again in his distraction. "Silver was my alpha, you realize. She raised me. She was a gifted leader, but I don't know that she was…" He seemed to be struggling to match a description to my tone.

"A saint of the Lady?" In my peripheral vision, a bush shadow congealed into a line and twisted like a snake between a couple of small cacti. They were definitely getting worse. I'd never seen a shadow separate from its original object before. What was to stop them ganging up on me from every direction now?

"My parents always talked like she was a real person. But then I did this, to be like her—" I lifted my left foot and pulled the toes apart to show the needle mark. I assumed that was what he'd been looking for on my elbows. "And instead of gaining the power to comfort the grief-stricken and heal the sick—or at least touch a guard's keys to get us out of here—I start dying by centimeters. I can feel it!" My tone grew strident as I tried to forestall the objection I saw on his face. I lowered my voice again, conscious of the guards. "I knew I wouldn't be able to shift afterward. I thought the sacrifice was worth it to free so many. But I didn't know it would hurt so much." I took a deep breath to press that memory down. "I didn't know the muscles would be partially paralyzed so I'd hardly be able to walk. I didn't know I'd start losing my mind. So now I can only pray I can still free you all before it's too late for me."

Edmond cupped my face. "Look at me, Dana. Silver wasn't a saint. She was injected and lived to be almost *ninety*. Not as long as a Were, but long enough. She died of old age before the humans even knew about us. If you're seeing things—well, Silver said she saw Death."

Not—dying? I could barely take it in, especially while the shadow under his jaw extended a tendril to curl possessively up over his cheekbone.

I heard the crunch of footsteps at the same moment Edmond's head snapped up. He leaned in and slid one of my bikini straps down my shoulder. He spoke in a whisper against the side of my neck. "Forgive me, but they know this is where we come for privacy, since everyone hears and smells it in the dorms. They won't look twice if that's what they think we're doing."

I laughed low in my throat, suddenly punchy with relief from his revelation. Not dying. I was hardly going to argue with the act. Edmond was damn good looking, and it had been years since I'd had the time for any of that. And never with a Were before, either. I slid my fingers into Edmond's hair to add verisimilitude, and the footsteps moved off again.

I was here for a reason, though, as he had said. Even if I had more time than I'd realized, I couldn't let myself get distracted. My plan could still be discovered by the guards. I sat back. "Anyway, since I can touch silver, I can break everyone's collar and not worry about getting splashed."

Hunger flared up in Edmond's eyes so fiercely he must have been feeling it from the moment he'd realized I'd been injected, and kept it banked until now. "That's why we're all half-naked. In the first couple escapes, people popped the collars and used fabric to buffer the worst of the damage. This stuff's so thin, it won't work unless the whole pack goes naked, and they watch the cameras for that." He tilted his head to a flash of a lens mounted on the top of the fenceline.

I tugged at my own collar. The damn thing chafed already. "And I can touch any keys, the gates—get you all out, and on the way to Russia. Like—" I searched my memory for the Were man's name. "Tom said."

Edmond's face lit, chasing a shadow down to drip sullenly over his collarbone. "Thank the Lady, he's still alive. And that the Russian enclave is still safe."

While I'd been watching Edmond, a rock's shadow had crept up to my fingers, fouling them with heavy blackness. I felt as if the same thing had happened to my thoughts. I wasn't dying, so I could join them in Russia—but how was I supposed to escape after opening the gates for the others, when I literally couldn't run? I'd be recaptured for sure. And would the Russian pack really want a Were who not only couldn't shift, she could hardly walk and kept staring at what wasn't there?

I clenched my teeth. If I was meant to be forever alone, so be it. I would free the others first. I was no coward. "Shall I do your collar first?" I was impressed with how even I kept my voice.

His hungry look returned and he nodded, unable to speak past it. I leaned into him and slid a few fingers into the space between skin and metal. "You have to promise you won't shift and take off. I need time to do everyone's collar, and the camp looks set up to hold wolf forms best, anyway. Better to go out the front gate in human."

"Don't worry, I'm not stupid." Edmond reached up and caught my wrists, his grip shakily tight. "Are you sure—?"

I nodded. "Crack it, once I'm ready—" I wormed my hand up so my palm was beneath the collar. No need to mention this was all theory I'd concocted after reading about the collars in the media. There was no reason it shouldn't work. "We want it to drip out at first."

Edmond's throat muscles worked under my hand, then he reached up. He tested the strength of the metal first, fingers on either side of my hand. Then he grunted and the internal latch cracked. Silver nitrate leaked onto my palm.

Shadows skittered toward me along the ground from every direction, bush shadows and lizard shadows and the heavy smothering weight of a building shadow that made it hard for me to breathe the moment I saw it.

I bit the inside of my cheek to force my attention away. I wasn't dying. I had a job to do. I angled my hand so the silver nitrate dripped into my other palm. I scattered those drops harmlessly onto the dirt every few seconds. Edmond was shaking visibly, but he kept the movement from more than vibrating against my hands. At last the trickle slowed, then stopped. I sat back and rubbed my hands in the dirt, then rolled the dust and silver and sweat into little balls between them. I brushed those away and lifted my hands to sniff them. They smelled safe to touch other Were. The shadows boiled over the spatters of silver on the earth and seeped into them, leaving me alone.

"You can take it off," I told Edmond when I noticed he still hadn't touched the metal. I opened the collar and shook it over the dirt to get rid of any drops lingering inside.

Edmond drew in a shuddering breath. "Lady above. Do you know how long I've been here, with that on?" His muscles twisted and his back started to arch.

I snapped the collar back on, keeping my hands there as an extra reminder. A wolf neck was too thick for the collar, that was the point of the things, to keep Were from shifting forms. Even empty, it should remind him. "You can't. They'll see." I bit my lower lip. Maybe should have given him more time to prepare, warned him better. I'd remember that for the next Were I freed.

"You're right." Edmond checked the collar to make sure the ends were seated firmly together. He stood. "Thank you. I wish there was something more than just words I could offer you."

I started to wave that off, but then an impulse took hold of me. I stood too and kissed him. He kissed back, leaning into me. I closed my eyes and sensation reached down deep into my core and took firm hold. I pulled away first. Too much left to do. I needed to count how many Were this camp had, how long it would take me to break all the collars without being noticed.

Later, I'd pick up where I'd left off with that kiss. I promised myself that.

"They'll be serving dinner," Edmond commented as he followed me back to the buildings. He looked a little disappointed, but the suppressed excitement of knowing his collar was a dummy remained in his scent. I savored that scent. If the others felt as he did, I could be part of his pack for a while, before they escaped and left me behind in the humans' hands. Maybe that would be enough.

The more collars I broke, the bolder the shadows got. By the time I'd finished forty of the approximately fifty residents, the shadows dogged my footsteps in a roiling carpet that extended chill tendrils up my ankles whenever I stopped moving. It was as if the shadows were reminding me that soon, I'd be dragged away from the bone-deep feeling of security I'd discovered in this pack. Though I knew even that feeling had a falseness to it. Here, no one else could shift either. Here, there was little enough room to run. Outside of this prison, things would be different. But for now, I had the other Were. I had a few stolen hours with Edmond.

Things all went wrong the morning of my fifth day at the camp.

They fed us two vegetarian meals each day, morning and evening. The guards had no wish to stand out in the midday sun either, handing out lunch. Breakfast today smelled like macaroni and cheese, but I caught a whiff of something else as I approached the cart in the control building's gateway. The shadow of the cart's upper level shrank down to a single foil-wrapped tray on the lower shelf and oozed over it as if searching for a way in.

The woman I had met first, Lizzie, was directly in front of me in line, her son pressed against her hip. When it was Lizzie's turn, the female guard glanced at the child and reached for the tray the shadows loved. As she offered it, the shadows sprang for the boy, covered him so only his face showed.

I jerked a step forward, then cut off my protest. The food didn't smell like poison, it smelled like fried chicken. And the female guard's expression held only concern for a child who looked plenty human enough to stir her protective instincts.

The second guard, a red-haired man, frowned at his partner and shoved my tray at me without looking. "What are you—?"

I jerked my tray from his hands. Had he noticed something wrong? I needed to distract him. "I'm fucking hungry, here," I said, but he still didn't look at me. He nodded for the third guard to move closer, covering them all with his gun, and then strode to the boy and jerked him around.

The boy clutched the tray and screamed when the red-haired guard tried to take it away. The sound shattered the shadows. They formed wolves on the ground, running wolves, dappling the dirt as far as I could see. Frozen.

Then the shadows moved again. One surged up to the catch the broken collar Lizzie tossed aside. She shifted, leapt, and tore out the red-haired guard's throat in a gout of red and choking stink of blood.

No. No, Lady, no! I dropped my food and myself on top of it, because the third guard was shooting. Someone shrieked, the sound full of the rage of someone who lived on, and someone else gurgled, all too final.

But growls grew, and I lifted my head to see the female guard go down. The shooter was already hidden beneath a pile of wolf shapes, like my shadows but painted with color and warmth.

"It's all on the cameras, they'll already be coming with more guns. Everyone who can shift, to the command building." Edmond was still in human at least. He didn't sound confident enough, without the power of the imaginary alpha behind him, but apparently he didn't need to. More collars thumped into the roiling surface of the shadows and more wolves streamed toward the building.

I shoved myself up and looked around wildly. Who was left? Could I possibly open their collars before the guards arrived and shot them all?

No, no time for that. I needed to open the gates. "Go, go!" I directed those I saw still in human, but they were already running. Probably hadn't even heard me.

The shadows licked at the dead guards sluggishly like fire at wet wood, so I could still see what I needed, keys on the red-haired guard's belt. Real, mechanical silver keys, because humans had found that with beasts, silver and simple, strong bars were better than any electronic locks. I clenched my hand around the keys with a fierce pleasure that they didn't hurt me. Perhaps the price I'd paid for that immunity had been too high, but I'd paid it all the same. I tried to breathe through my mouth so I didn't smell what I wasn't looking at: the ruin of the guard's throat.

I tried to at least jog for the series of gates leading out of the compound, but the shadows made my footing seem treacherous, and my bad foot kept turning under me. Shots rang out in the command building, shots and screams. I couldn't do anything about that, though. I had to get to the gate.

My focus narrowed, ignoring the wolves, ignoring the shadows, all my attention on the lock I needed, glinting in the sunlight. Then pain, shocking enough to gray out my thoughts and my vision. My leg collapsed—too much pain, too high. Blood.

I'd been shot. I rolled to clamp my hands over the wound, keys growing slick with red because I wouldn't drop them, not when lives had been lost to get them. I sacrificed my top to make a pad to clamp over the entry wound—no exit, but I couldn't think about anything more than getting up and making it to the locks, now.

I made it to a seated position, then to my good knee, and then someone scooped me up and held me standing, so my vision grayed into sparkles from the pain once more. "Dana." Edmond's voice. "You can make it."

I could make it, damn it. I wasn't going to die of silver poisoning, and I wasn't going to die of a Lady-damned bullet. I staggered forward, got the key into the first gate's lock. Edmond got me to the next. The third and last seemed so far, just a short jouncing ride in the bus, but an eternity walking as my leg bled. I held the pad as best I could and prayed to whatever kind powers existed in the universe.

The shadows were everywhere, raging around my ankles like the sea and splashing up to paint the horizon. Only I and Edmond and the lock remained. Then wolves began to collect behind us. Another Were in human supported my other side, and the lock loomed up. I couldn't match the key with the hole at first, but I pressed until it scraped along and slotted home.

I pushed the gate as much as I could, and the wolves streamed out, disappearing into the desert of shadows. No, that wasn't how it was supposed to work. "Wait!" I called, voice too weak to convince even myself. "They'll hunt from aircraft, you have to leave as humans, in uniforms, confuse them—"

No one listened, even when Edmond raised his voice to repeat my points. Just a couple of betas, shouting at the tide not to go out. My second prop disappeared after the others, and I slumped down to the ground before Edmond could rebalance me.

"We're fast, faster than they realize. We have time before backup arrives," Edmond said. He tried to pull me up. I couldn't muster the strength to help him.

This was it, then. I'd done what I could. "Go, hurry up," I told Edmond, and dredged up a smile for him.

The shadows on Edmond's face were all metaphorical, born of worry. My shadows left him bare and thus the only bright spot in my vision. "Dana, no. Get up."

I tangled my fingers in his to squeeze, and stop him pulling at me. "I couldn't run anywhere, even before I was shot. It's all right. I succeeded. I got you out."

"No!" Edmond clung to my hands. "Promise me, Dana, that you'll follow us when you can. At your own speed. You'll follow us to

Russia, no matter what you have to do. Promise me!"

I laughed weakly, tears welling in my eyes. They refracted Edmond's brightness onto the shadows. Hysterical humor took hold of me. "You're no alpha to make me."

"Promise!" Edmond's voice grew desperate.

He needed to run if he was going to. "Promise," I said, because that's what he needed to let me go. He eased me down. I turned my head to watch as his collar thumped down and four wolf feet ran away.

I drifted for a while, slumped on my side, watching the shadows and holding the pad clamped to my leg. Alone. Slowly, the sunlight drained most of the shadows away, beat hot and hotter against my skin. The remaining shadows pooled beneath me, pillowing my head.

The shadow of my own body stretched itself across the sand, formed my standing silhouette, a wolf beside it. The wolf wavered and disappeared, leaving me alone.

I supposed I was. Just human, no wolf left.

And there was my answer, in the sheer irony of it. To save the other Were, I'd become too human, and now being too human would save me as well. And I didn't have to run anywhere.

Energy flooded into me, hope kindling a fire that pushed strength into my remaining limbs. But I hoarded the energy, saving it. I lay there, skin burning to red banked beneath the brown as the day dragged on, until the clean-up crew arrived. From my angle, I couldn't see if they'd gathered any Were bodies, and I didn't try. I lay still, only breathing, until one of the medics bent over me, checking for life.

I turned my head slowly, eyes searching much faster. There, at the neck of the woman's uniform. I lifted my hand and pulled at the loop of chain, dragged the silver cross out from under the shirt. I clung to it like it was my lifeline.

Which it was, I supposed. "Human!" I gasped, letting tears free into my voice. "I'm human, there was a mistake, the beasts forced me to... I'm human!"

The medic made a soothing noise and carefully pried my hand off the cross to see my unblemished skin. "Don't worry. You'll be just fine."

I would be, I agreed silently. I would heal, and I would follow the other Were to Russia. Follow as a human, to finally find my Were pack.

DANA SALTIK was born a nonhuman in a small town in central Oregon. Her parents had left their "pack," fleeing Registration, and continued to move often over the course of her childhood. In her second year of college at the University of Idaho, her parents were killed in an unfortunate accident when resisting enrollment in the Federal Nonhuman Relocation Program. Dana lived off the grid for a period, but she was eventually tracked down by brave federal agents, and successfully joined the Relocation Program.

RHIANNON HELD is the author of the *Silver* series of urban fantasy novels. She lives in Seattle, where she works as an archaeologist for an environmental compliance firm. Working in both archaeology and writing, she's "lucky" enough to have two sexy careers that don't make her much money. In her proverbial copious free time, she sings in a community choir, games online, and occasionally enjoys betting on the ponies.

CATACLYSM CHILD

An account by Jack,
AS PROVIDED BY VILLE MERILÄINEN

The hammer smashes her frame, time and time again, bending a malformed skull further out of shape, cracking ribs still far too tender. The metal skeleton eats each blow, flinching only from force. What hasn't lived yet cannot hurt. My face is wet; sorrow, anger, and emotionless perspiration all taste the same as they roll in beads onto cracked lips, drawn out by the forge's heat and the weight of the tool and the task at hand. There is too much silver in her, too soft to enclose and secure everything she must hold.

When the furnace turns wan with hunger, the hammer thuds from my grip, and my rage at failure subsides. Too much silver, not enough steel. She can rest here, while night cools my workshop and sleep my thoughts, until I melt her and begin anew tomorrow.

The workshop is deep below ground, and the stairs creak under my weight. The man who built the house fostered chaos, but was well-liked by his neighbours; I seek to build a child whom I can love and cherish, yet they fear me. In me groans a devastating loneliness only she can silence, the gift of my father's ego.

At the top of the stairs is a window. The houses are dark, but the old aunt from two doors down is coming around on an evening walk, quarrelling with her nephew. The boy notices me, tugs his aunt's sleeve until she turns, catches my wave, and quickens her step. They are gone from sight when I've fetched my pipe from the kitchen and come out to the porch, but their spiteful whispers linger.

Everyone here is so damn small. They're scared I might rot the skin off their bodies, or maybe they mistake the frustration on my brow and behind my beard for anger. If anyone stuck around long enough to see cognac smoothen the grooves or, hell, joined me for a glass, they might learn I am a gentle soul, better worth knowing than the bastard whose wine they drank before I saw them rid of him.

After I've smoked and my glass is empty, I return inside and head upstairs to bed. The sea is grey with coming rain when the doorbell takes my dream.

It's not often I get visitors, less at this hour, but it is Sunday, and so I have a suspicion of who it might be. Penny, the preacher's widow, stands behind the door with a steaming pie in oven-mitted hands. She flinches when I appear to loom over her. Though she shows me more courtesy than others do, even kindness, few are comfortable in my presence, and she is not one of them.

Still, she puts on a smile braver than necessary and says, "Good morning, Jack. Would you care to keep me some company?"

"Are you sad again?" I rumble. This is how I speak: in tones so low they become imposing no matter how pleasant my intentions. There is too much steel in my chest, not enough soft metals. When I build my daughter right, I will give her a voice that is sweet even when she is mad, so people will never fear her.

Penny knows I mean no ill, but averts her gaze nonetheless. "Lawrence so loved these grey mornings we get. I thought to treat myself to his favourite breakfast, but—" She gives a little half-laugh, half-sob, and blinks away tears. "It's so silly of me. Almost a year later and I still can't eat it alone."

"It's not silly at all."

Penny's smile grows less brave and more genuine when I let her inside. It is as though she wonders if I'll attack her whenever she visits but chooses to trust me time and time again. She pities me, I think, and that is fine. I pity her too.

That is not to say she doesn't also miss her husband, and I do like Penny. She is as disturbed by my efforts as everyone else, but I have striven to prove myself a kind creature, and so she tries to put aside her prejudices and wants to know how my work is going. In return, I let her talk about the preacher and give her cognac when she starts to cry. It's early, and she doesn't like to be seen drinking, but no one looks my way.

"Sometimes I wake up and reach to his side for a kiss," Penny says, swirling the drink in her glass, "and I swear his ghost holds my hand before I remember he's not there."

She laughs at that, and the sound goes down as sweet as the liquor. I pour her more until her eyes are swimming and she smiles absently. "May I ask you something personal, Jack?"

"Of course."

"Do you feel things? Do you… think you will love your kid?"

"Would you come to me for empathy if you thought I didn't?"

She purses her mouth, takes a moment to think about it. "I don't know if I do. It's as with Lawrence's ghost. I know he isn't there, but for that moment, it feels real. When I talk to you, you're so caring, but once I leave, our conversations seem… ethereal. As though they couldn't have happened like I believe they have." She frowns, looks up with an apology in her eyes. "After all, you aren't—and I truly don't mean to offend—"

Penny bites back whatever she planned to say, trails off into a hum. I chorus it, and we let the discourse come to a closure. She cannot find a way to phrase her words, though I wouldn't have taken offence at the bluntest manner.

The people here are damn small and so are their hearts, except Penny's. It's a shame she's built of flesh and meat and passion. Sometimes, in moments of weakness, I open my chest for guidance from that terrible man, to see how he created my heart and lungs. Mine are more complex than I could hope to create, but they've also combined to birth a being that is detached and clinical—thus, I wouldn't want to replicate them in my daughter. I would like her to be more like Penny, but her I cannot open, even for a purpose so dear. I would rather have two such creatures near me. If my daughter wants to grow her hair long, I will ask Penny to show her how to braid it the way she does.

Rain rattles the windows, and five minutes later we have a downpour. Penny stares outside for so long her food goes cold. "I think I've prattled on long enough," she says, after a spell. The liquor sloshes in the pot of my belly when I stand to help her up. Her gait through the house is wobbly, but rain will hide it from judging eyes. "Thank you for the talk, Jack. I hope you don't think poorly of me for my babbling. You really do help."

She leaves, and I retreat to the basement.

These days are all the same. I come down, strike metal until my limbs ache and my strength drains. Sometimes Penny visits me, when she has heard a song the preacher liked on the radio or dreamed of him, and we drink together. On other mornings, children come to taunt me for dares. Maybe no one comes knocking and I get to sleep in, but even then, only details change. At the end of the day, my child remains in the workshop instead of resting in the bed I have made beside mine.

It's raining again when Penny has drunk too much and needs my help getting home. Maybe people are looking at us, but they won't come outside, and we are shadows in the torrent. Penny has an umbrella, but I am much too tall for us both to fit under it, so she keeps it folded out of sympathy.

"Jack," she mumbles, shivering with cold. "When your kid is… not born, but—"

"Complete."

"When your kid is complete, will you stay in the parish?"

"I have not thought about it."

"I suppose you won't, given how cool everyone is." Her teeth chatter, making the tone difficult to read. She might've sounded disappointed.

"My child will be easier to like than I am. She will be small, like you are, and can smile and laugh."

"Are you skilled enough? I don't want to be rude, but Otto was a genius, and you can do neither."

"Father didn't care what you thought of me."

She looks up at me, winces when a raindrop gets in her eye. "It's strange you still call him that."

"He gave me no choice. I may not hate you anymore, but I cannot stop loving him."

Penny's gaze falls onto the puddles at our feet. "Will you make your kid think of you the same way?" She curls her lip to suck on it. The gesture of uncertainty tags another question to her voiced one: will I make her think of me as I do of my father, and of them as I used to?

"She will be dearer to me than Father ever was, but I will let her think for herself."

Penny muses on my answer until we come to her house by the church. "What if she won't see all the good in you?"

"Then I hope she sees it in someone else."

"Why should you not build a wife? Then you would know your love will always echo in another heart."

"I may not be skilled enough to create a child. An adult would be impossible."

"I see." She unlocks the door and turns. "Would you like to come inside for a minute? I'll light up the hearth so you can dry yourself until the rain stops."

"Are you still sad?"

She sighs. "I do hate how quiet the house is."

"For a minute, then."

Even with a fire, the living room is gloomy. Penny leaves to change out of her wet dress and returns bearing a tray with a teakettle and pastries. She lays it on the carpet between us and sits, but does not look at me. In the glow, the thinness of my skin is evident. Her arms are folded across bent knees as she stares at the flames.

"Penny, may I now ask you something personal?"

"Sure."

"Why do you not have children?"

She gives a soft grunt, glances at me. Her lip curls. "Lawrence and I weren't blessed with any."

"Did you want them?"

"Well," she says, pauses for a moment. "Doesn't everyone?"

"I only know I do."

She presses her chin on a knee. "Can I be honest with you?"

"Are you not always?"

"Not about this."

"Then you need not answer."

Penny nods, but hesitates. Eventually, she straightens her legs and lays her hands on her lap. "Lawrence would've liked a son to carry his mantle. I talked him out of it."

I cock my head. Her neck is stiff, but her gaze darts my way before returning to the fire.

"He was my everything," she continues, "and I wanted to be his. If he'd had a son, I would've no longer been the most important person in his life."

I digest the answer, nod.

"Does that make me selfish?"

"Yes, but that doesn't make it wrong."

"Doesn't it? It was the one thing he asked of me, and I refused."

"If Father had made me a wife who told me I could not have a child, I would drive her away, as I did him. The preacher stayed, and so I think he wanted you to be his everything, too."

Penny presses her hand on mine and whispers, "Thank you."

When I'm dry and the storm calms, I make to leave. Penny remains sitting by the hearth, but appears behind me as I step outside and don my coat. Her arms are still folded, face pensive. "Jack," she says, leaning against the doorframe. "Otto wasn't a good man, but you are."

"I try to be."

"Mm." She bows her head. When she lifts it, there's no smile, but she seems somehow braver than so far. "I'm still afraid of you. I'm grateful for your friendship, but it's still difficult sometimes to see you as more than a metal monster." She grimaces at her choice of words. "No, not a monster—"

"Penny," I rumble, seeking a tone as patient as I can muster. "You needn't be so careful. My heartbeat is the pulse of ruin. To call me a monster is apt."

"But it's not something friends do."

"Friends are honest with one another. You admit to fearing me, and you should; I carry a cataclysm inside, and were Father to return and tell me to release it, I would not be able to resist him again. That, more than my body, makes me a monster."

She bunches her arms tighter to hide a shiver, but keeps her gaze on me. "Why did you resist him the first time? We've been nothing but vile to you."

"He gave me too big a heart, I suppose. I only wish he had filled it with something else."

She raises a brow, gaze sliding to my chest. "What if," she says with a lilt, "you gave some of that ruin to your kid?"

"That would make her a threat."

"I don't think it will. They say a soul is what makes one human. Lawrence thought God imbues a human shell with one, but I like to think it is a baser creation, one half from each parent as with any other piece of the human puzzle." She tilts her head. "I'm not devout enough to think God had anything to do with your, um, completion. I trust you take no offence at that notion."

"Your assumption is correct."

"Then, Otto gave you the entirety of whatever fuels you, whether you want to call it a soul or a cataclysm, yet you still became your own creature. Maybe that's what your child needs, too."

"I cannot do that. If she were like me, you would fear her. I want her to be loved by all."

Penny returns a slanted smile. "It's not as though a human soul is any less dangerous. We have an easier time tolerating one another because we look alike, but truthfully, there are people even in the parish I ought to fear more than you." She scoffs. "They've started saying the most awful things about me, too, because I like spending time with you."

"Then why do you?"

I follow her look behind me to find the crone across the street glaring at us. "You deserve it," Penny continues, louder. "You've been kind to me. There will come a day when I'll knock on your door without fear, without caring who sees me."

I rumble a hum. "I will consider your idea."

"And I wish you the best of luck. Bye, Jack."

Before Penny closes the door, the crone shouts, "Hey, giant! Did you kill the preacher so you could steal his wife?"

Penny shouts back, "Be quiet, Marcie. That's a horrible thing to say. You saw him slip off the roof with your own two eyes."

"That big bastard might've slathered the roof with oil during the night. Ain't nothing good gonna come out of consorting with the likes of it."

Penny groans, shakes her head at me, and goes inside. I walk off, ignoring the crone's distant interrogation.

The next morning, after I've fired up the furnace, I leave my hammer hanging on the wall. For now, I shape only thoughts, watching the skeleton and picturing a maelstrom like mine swirling within her frame. The gift of my father responds by swelling into an ache until I cannot bear it any longer. Here it may wander; Father built this room as a haven for himself, but it now protects those outside instead. I've ensured its integrity, for the very reason of having a place to unleash the cataclysm when the pressure builds up. It cannot escape the room any better than breach in.

I dig my fingers into the soft flesh of my belly, below the plate that binds my bones together, and pull. Skin tears with a ripping sound; bones come apart with a ring. My calamity flows out in billowing clouds, hissing and shrieking like a windstorm as it roils around the room, searching for living matter to corrupt. As it rots my skin, makes it fall onto the floor in shriveling clumps until my form is a simulacrum of the body on the table, I wonder if the townspeople would show me more respect if they knew some of their rumours and superstitions about me to be true.

I scoop up the rot and throw it in the fire. Skin will regrow, but for the coming days, I will not allow Penny to see me.

After it has wandered awhile and is angry with me for not letting it fulfill its purpose, I grasp the cataclysm and force it back in place. It screams horrid curses straight into my thoughts: how my child will bring ruin, corrupt the sole person I hold dear, and I will be there to watch Penny's eyes turn grey and wither as her skull grins at me under shedding skin.

It is not often I feel fear, but when I pick up my hammer, my arms tremble not from its weight. I pry loose a sliver of calamity and bring it to my anvil, hammering it from immateriality into solid form. It cries from being sunk into molten metal, entombed inside a nail-shaped coffin. That nail impales the silver heart of my child.

And it beats.

The nail melts, releasing the swirl to bounce inside its cage to the rhythm of her pulse. I may have made a terrible mistake, for it will grow there until it reaches the size of my own. For now, when I watch the skeleton rise and gaze at me, I cannot bring myself to care.

She pokes at her organs held in place with wires, flinches, seizes me in a lidless stare. For a while, we only look at each other, a teary father and my curious child.

She asks, "Who are you? Who am I? Where are we? What is this? What is that? Why are you big? Why am I small?"

A newborn human knows nothing, and gains the rudimentary knowledge required for asking questions only after it has mastered some basic abilities. My child comes equipped with the skills to think and talk and walk, and a hunger to know everything not imprinted in the spark of life I gave her. So she babbles an endless stream of questions, and I spend the rest of the day learning things about her through them as much as she does of me and the world.

Between asking why is it light on the street but dark inside and where does rain go when it's not raining, she wants to know why have I not killed everyone in the parish.

Penny has been silent since she sat at the table, clasping her cup of tea. Deirdre unleashes an inquisition upon her, but gives her no time to answer. Penny is yet unused to the idiosyncrasies of my daughter and does not know when to seize a moment to open her mouth. The girl is only quiet when she sips her drink or sleeps.

Deirdre's skin has grown, covering her frame in a veil that is soft, sweet, and innocent. I've cut her hair as best I can, and though the outcome is ragged, the short cut with her delicate features gives her a fairy-like appearance. If she could keep her mouth closed, Penny would adore her.

Alas, there is the matter of disturbing questions. Now that she understands basic concepts such as why she feels light-headed if she holds her breath and why juice tastes nice, Deirdre has moved on to moral dilemmas. "Why should I not release my cataclysm? Why should I not stab this knife into your chest? Why does your cup shake and mine does not? Why doesn't Daddy want me to hit you?"

When I fill her cup and she shuts up to suck on the straw, Deirdre smiles beatifically at the distressed Penny. A lucky accident, there; I hadn't expected her to spring to life the moment I plunged in the nail, but it appears the amalgam was soft enough—or the sliver of chaos small enough—for her to form likeable expressions. Even so, her sense of empathy has not developed enough. It makes the cherub's grin unnerving.

After another barrage of questions, Penny stands and says, "Jack, may I speak with you in the other room?"

Deirdre gets up to follow us, but I stop her with a gentle hand. "Wait here and drink your juice."

"Why?"

"She wishes to discuss private matters."

"Why?"

"Some things are not for you to hear."

"Why?"

I shut the door on her questions. Her muffled inquiries carry on through it.

Penny paces around the living room, arms bunched. "A talkative one, that."

"She troubles you."

Chewing her lip, Penny nods. "Did you wonder about the things she does when you were a child?"

"I still do."

"O-oh."

"She's cleverer than me. Maybe she'll come to teach me, one day."

"Hm." Penny turns for a look over her shoulder. Neighbours prowl in the yard, stalking Deirdre. They fear her more than Penny does, so much they would ogle openly instead of running away like they do with me. "I have to wonder again if it's a good idea for you to stay."

"This is my home."

"With your task complete, what do you have left here? There must be someplace else for you to live, where people leave you be."

"Once Deirdre understands why they are scared of her, she can dispel those fears. They will come to care for her."

"I used to call many of them friends," Penny says, a sourness in her tone. "They care less for me the more I come here."

"You don't have to."

She gives a half-smile. "Suppose I don't, now you've Deirdre for company. Maybe I should find some of my own."

"Have you considered leaving?"

Penny sits in the armchair, slumps over with her head resting on fists. "You know, I've been thinking about it. I'd hate to abandon the house, but it's too big for me to live in alone, and the ghost seems to be visiting more frequently. You'd think it would make me less lonely, but I only miss Lawrence that much more."

"Daddy," Deirdre says, hanging onto the door latch so that she swings back and forth against it. "I don't like how the people in the yard stare at me. Do people stare everywhere?"

"I don't think so."

"We should go someplace they don't."

"Wouldn't you rather stay here until they learn to like you?"

"I don't want people to like me if they don't like you too."

With a grunt, I turn to Penny. She returns Deirdre's smile before glancing at me. They begin to palaver on the justness of poking out someone's eye for looking at you while I think. "Then," I say, "perhaps we will leave. Together. You can stay with us until you find someone who is your everything, and to whom you are."

"I'd like that," Deirdre says.

Penny considers a moment and, looking at her hands, says, "So would I."

"Very well. Once Deirdre runs out of questions, we will leave the parish. I suspect it'll be another month or two."

"Why should I not ask questions? Do they bother you? Will I ever know as much as you? How much does Penny know? Why does the crone outside glower at me? Can I stab her? Not in the eye, mind."

Penny grins, though the last two queries make her wince. "That'll give me time to prepare. I will see you later. I should get to packing now."

A month after her completion, Deirdre knows enough to go an hour without blurting out questions. She looks about seven, with a braid Penny taught her how to tie. The townspeople have not warmed up to her, but others will; she is indistinguishable from a human child, with skin thicker and darker than mine hiding the metal beneath it. Deirdre is bright and bubbly and will make many friends, with the only detracting factor being her odd coot of a father who rarely leaves the house.

Penny has made a pact with the girl: until she finds herself a husband, they'll find something new to talk about every day. They've grown fond of one another, and this infuriates my calamity; when I watch them, I fill it with warmth that sends it recoiling as though smelted in a sun. Penny does not fear her anymore and often forgets about me altogether when they get caught up in conversation.

Rain hides our leaving as we walk toward Penny's house. Better this way, with the street deserted and us but two shadows in the downpour. The townspeople have broken our windows, yelled at Deirdre when she tries to play with other children. I've half a mind to stay only to spite them, but the girl deserves better.

Penny's house is dark, but I don't think much about it. She knows we're coming and must be ready to leave. When she doesn't answer my knocks, the darkness becomes ominous, and when I find the door is unlocked, the cataclysm answers by making my chest ache.

We find Penny in the living room. There are no signs of a break-in—she trusted whoever did this. The mud on the floor suggests they were many. On the wall, near the mantle, is a phrase smeared for us in red paint that makes me glad Deirdre can't read.

Deirdre asks, "Why is she hanging there? Why won't she say hello?"

I let her questions linger until she forgets about them and looks up at me, tilting her head, fingers locked behind her back. "Daddy?"

Gaze locked with Penny's everlasting stare, I say, "Deirdre, would you like me to tell you about your grandfather?"

She frowns, but nods.

Deirdre waits with uncommon patience while I cut Penny's noose and ease her down, carry her upstairs, and lay her on the bed. After I've pulled a cover over the body, I sit beside it and lift Deirdre onto my lap.

"When I was small," I begin, "I thought your grandfather was a bad man. He would always tell me how spiteful the people here were, but I tried my best to see the good in them. He was… difficult, and I thought it wrong of him to want to hurt people he didn't agree with.

"You see, he never found a wife, but decided he deserved a son, so he made me. But he made me too hard, too big, and people were afraid of me. He didn't have a choice—making me like this was the only way he could complete me at all. Only after I've toiled with you for so long do I understand how monumental such a task was.

"Now, the thing is, the people here are spiteful: they yell at their children, snap at their parents, are cruel to their neighbours. They liked your grandfather well enough, but the more they hated me, the more he hated them. Eventually, he wanted to release the disaster fueling me so that we'd have the town only for ourselves. I drove him away, and owe him an apology for it."

"Why?"

This is when I notice a lock of Penny's hair escaping the blanket's fold. Hiding it from sight, I say, "Never mind that. Now, Deirdre, would you like me to show you how to open your chest?"

When she doesn't answer, I turn from Penny to find the girl shying from me. "Deirdre?"

She folds one leg over the other and swings them back and forth, sucking her lip, making a hesitant sound.

"It's okay. It won't hurt," I say.

She looks at me with the same embarrassed eyes as when she broke a jar, shakes her head.

"No? Why not?"

"You'll think I'm stupid."

"I won't."

She leans against me. "I'm too scared."

"You don't have to be, ever again. We'll be the only ones left in the parish."

"I think we should run away instead. Right now."

"Deirdre, do you not understand what they've done? They've hurt her. Hurt her dearly. We can do the same to them."

She shakes her head, more vigorously.

"Deirdre—"

"Penny used to think monsters lived here, but then she learned they were kind and that's why I shouldn't judge people even if they're a little different." She looks up, eyes growing wet. I flinch with surprise—the girl has never wept before. Her speech quickens as sobs pervade it. "But she was wrong. They weren't kind at all. Grandaddy saw it and Penny must've too and that's why she wanted to run away with us and that's why... that's why..." She swallows hard, swings her gaze between Penny's body and me. "That's why they killed her, didn't they? Is that what's wrong with her? Is she dead?"

Stroking her hair, I say, "Yes, Deirdre."

She breaks, and it takes all my resolve not to rip open the bones trapping the roaring cataclysm. "Please, Daddy," she whispers, a chilling hardness beneath the sorrow. "Can't we go? They'll rot on their own without us, when we take away what little goodness they didn't."

My sigh rolls out with the sound of thunder, an echo of the vociferation within. I drop Deirdre off my lap to lift the body. "Very well."

"Are you bringing her with us?" Deirdre asks, rubbing her eyes and sniffling.

"We'll bury her away from here. I don't want her sleeping near this wretched place."

The rain ceases when we leave the parish outskirts. Penny's wrappings still drip after we've dug her a grave, far down the road where we can't see the houses anymore. I ask if Deirdre wants to say a few words and she ponders a while. "She should've lived with us," the girl mutters, bitterly. "You would've kept her safe from the monsters." We stand in silence for a minute, then she asks, "Do you really want to hurt the townspeople?"

This is the first lie I tell my daughter, and I suspect I will tell many more. "No. It's not right. Not even now."

"I will never hurt anyone," she says quietly, kneels down to finish Penny's marker. "No matter how much I want to. She made me promise."

"I'm glad for that."

Once she's satisfied with the marker, we carry on down the road, hand in hand. The girl says nothing, but maintains a pensive stare at the ground before her. Hours after we've left Penny, Deirdre starts asking about the new things we see. Days after, she starts to brighten up. Sometimes she tells me things I did not know, and I remember Penny's words about the formation of a soul.

I would've rather had two such creatures near me, but I choose to believe Penny rests easy, reunited with the preacher, and that a part of her will live on in Deirdre. My daughter may not be human, but within her dwells kindness I could not have created alone.

JACK was born for all the wrong reasons, and now seeks to set right the sin of his father by recommitting it for the right ones.

VILLE MERILÄINEN is a Finnish university student by day, writer of flippant tragedies by night. His short fiction has appeared or is forthcoming in *200 CCs* and *Stupefying Stories*, and long fiction is available on Amazon.

GRYPHONSHIFTER is a Seattle-area artist with a background in illustration. She graduated with a BFA in Digital Art and Animation from DigiPen Institute of Technology and now hones her skills with her own art projects. Though she has a wide variety of artistic inspirations, her art is most influenced by the challenging balance between wanting to draw really cute things and a fascination with creepy monsters.

SOMEONE'S CHECKING YOU OUT RIGHT NOW!

A profile by J. Chen,
AS PROVIDED BY S. QIOUYI LU

jiangshi888

29 • Columbus, OH

MY SELF-SUMMARY

Well, I guess I'll be upfront: I'm a jiangshi. It's kind of like a Chinese zombie, though that's not really accurate—trust me, I've tried hanging out with the zombie population here, and they thought I was nothing like them. But, look, we follow in the same traditions, right? They're undead, I'm undead; they get a bite or infection that turns them into a zombie, and I had an improper death that caused me to turn. They feed on flesh; I feed on qi. We're basically the same, really.

WHAT I'M DOING WITH MY LIFE

You know, "life" is a weird term for us undead. I mean, when I was alive, I was a grad student at OSU, but that didn't go so great, to put it lightly. With my death—my undeath?—I guess I'm mostly trying to get by. Homeostasis is all good, but I'd like to find some new friends, too. Plus I've been forced to become a night owl, so if you're looking for someone to explore Columbus night life with, I'd totally be up for that.

I'M REALLY GOOD AT

Linguistics? Well, I used to be. That was the Ph.D. program I was in at OSU; I was pretty good at completing the homework assignments, but research turned out to be something else entirely. I can still probably talk your ear off about syntax and semantics, though. But I should say right now, I *don't* judge the way you speak—in fact, linguists do exactly the opposite! We love to see all the diversity and difference in language in the world.

I'm also good at listening. Whether that's you talking about your hobbies, or talking about how rough your day was, I do all that active listening stuff and really pay attention to you. I love when people are enthusiastic and when they're being sincere. I'm always down for conversation, especially after trying to hang out with zombies—it's not that they're nonverbal or just grunt like what everyone thinks; they just have their own way of communicating, one that I ended up not being able to pick up. So it's been a while since I've sat down to have a chat in my own language.

FAVORITE BOOKS, MOVIES, SHOWS, MUSIC, AND FOOD

Oh man, I'm terrible at picking favorites. I'm weirdly obsessed with vampire media, though—I suppose jiangshi can be compared to vampires too, and it's interesting to see something that reflects my experience without being entirely the same. I don't tend to watch jiangshi films themselves—partly because of the language barrier (I don't actually speak Mandarin or Cantonese, even though I'm Chinese myself…) and partly because it feels weird seeing some of the depictions that veer from my own experience.

As for food? I've always been something of a foodie, but ever since I turned, I've had to tweak my diet. I can't be vegetarian anymore, so the most I can do is try to be ethical about my qi consumption. These days, the easiest food for me to get is live fish from Chinese supermarkets—once anything's been prepared, even raw sushi, the qi's already gone. I mean, I can still *eat* regular food; it just doesn't have the same nourishment. So I'd still be happy to go out to a restaurant with you. I'd just have to eat another meal by myself later.

THE SIX THINGS I COULD NEVER DO WITHOUT

Internet. Cliché answer, I know, but it's the truth.

Qi. Hey, a jiangshi's gotta eat too.

Front-facing cameras. Okay, hear me out. Mirrors are awkward because they repel me—that's just part of what being a jiangshi entails—so I have to use the front-facing camera as a mirror. Otherwise I'd look like a mess all the time.

Sleep. In this regard, I haven't changed at all since when I was alive.

Electric candles. I know, they look dorky, but they provide nice mood lighting for when I want to relax. I can't light regular candles because the flame is another thing that repels me. Makes candlelit dinners kind of awkward.

And, of course: CATS! Even undead people love our fuzzy companions.

I SPEND A LOT OF TIME THINKING ABOUT

Life, the universe, and everything.

Jokes aside, I've been thinking a lot about things like community and mental health advocacy recently. I never really thought about that kind of stuff when I was alive, but I probably should have. I was always your stereotypical Chinese grad student, working really hard and trying my best to be successful, but that… drove me over the edge, to put things lightly. Well, I won't let this section get dark. Let's just say that life doesn't end at death, and there's still a lot more for me to learn and work on. I'm slowly getting better and finding peace.

ON A TYPICAL FRIDAY NIGHT I AM
Waking up and figuring out what to do with the day/night.

YOU SHOULD MESSAGE ME IF
You're a jiangshi. It's not that I'm specifically looking for someone who matches my ethnic background, just that the shared experience makes it a bit easier, you know?

I'd love to make friends with people from different backgrounds as well. Are you a vampire? A ghost? I'm sure we can find common ground.

But honestly, if you're a living grad student, especially if you're feeling lonely, feel free to reach out to me too. I've been there before, and I just want you to know that you're not alone. If you're struggling with thoughts that are telling you to hurt yourself, to end your life, just know that you don't have to keep those thoughts to yourself and that you have someone out here who'll listen to you.

I know, it might be weird to be getting life advice from someone undead, but hey—that's the world we live in.

Message me, yeah?

J. CHEN grew up in Michigan but currently lives in central Ohio. A former graduate student, J. now focuses on advocating for mental health and self-care.

S. QIOUYI LU is a writer, artist, narrator, and translator; their fiction has appeared in *Strange Horizons* and is forthcoming from *Daily Science Fiction*. In their spare time, they enjoy destroying speculative fiction as a dread member of the queer Asian SFFH illuminati. You can visit their site at s.qiouyi.lu or follow them on Twitter as @sqiouyilu.

NOBODY WAS HERE

An account by nobody,
AS PROVIDED BY JORDAN DAVIES

Most passed as if I didn't even exist.

That was the simplest way—shamefully shameless in its execution.

For the ones that did notice me, the move was harder, less subtle. It usually involved averting their eyes as I looked at them, as if they could forget they saw me simply by focusing their attention elsewhere—on their watch, the traffic lights, the gum on the sidewalk. Anything but me would do. They liked to think that I didn't notice their apathy, but I always did. It was remarkable how much care people could take not to care.

By the time the sun was setting, I had four dollars and thirty-two cents in my cup. Not my greatest haul for an eight hour swing, but it would have to do. I stood on cramped legs, heaved my rucksack over my shoulder, and tucked my hard-won earnings into my good pocket.

The fiery light of twilight mixed with the desolate smog of the city to craft a rich cocktail of amber and copper. It was tantalizing to see something as inherently unappealing as smog shine so magnificently. Like all the beautiful things in this city, it was nothing but ugliness hiding behind a mask of pretty light.

I cracked the beer and took a long drink, the cool bubbles tickling my throat as they went down. It wasn't anything fancy, the cheapest brand, but after a day like today, it tasted sweeter than a woman and felt almost as good going down. Well, at least I told myself it did. It had been quite a while since my last, and memory didn't do sensation any favors. It's too bad too. If we all remembered pleasure as readily as pain, we might be a little kinder to one another.

Once finished, I put the empty can in my bag and stood into a dizzying head rush. I leaned against the wall to steady myself, relishing the numbing buzz. Possibly the only merit of an empty stomach was that there was nothing to keep the alcohol from wrapping you in its intoxicating embrace. It was almost like being under a warm fuzzy blanket. Okay, not really, but when your bed was a park bench, you took what you could get.

I had recently found the perfect bench too—sloped and curved in just the right way that you could lay on your side without your hip feeling like it was being ground into powder. Better yet, it was completely isolated by overgrown foliage and always vacant, as if forgotten by the world. At least, I hoped it was; there was something magical in remembering something everyone else forgot. It made it yours, in a way. I rather liked the idea of having my own secret place. It almost felt like having a home.

So you can imagine my surprise when I arrived at my little secret and found it already occupied. There, sitting on MY bench, was a girl, her bare dangling feet kicking absentmindedly at the grass. She looked about my age, but it was impossible to be sure; it was impossible to be sure of *anything* with her.

Every time I looked at her, it was as if for the first time. Her clothes gave the impression that she had been wearing something different a moment ago, but I could never remember what. A jean jacket? A black tee? A leather vest? Even looking directly at her, I could have never told you which. Her hair even seemed to change color with every turn of her head, as if the hues were dancing with the moonlight that shined down on her, illuminating her pale skin.

"Hey!" I said as I approached, doing my best to be undeterred by her strangeness. "What do you think you're doing?"

"What does it look like I'm doing?" she said without looking at me. "I'm sitting on my bench. You're welcome to join me if you must."

"YOUR bench?" I repeated incredulously. "You must be mistaken. This is MY bench. I've been sleeping here for the past few nights."

"Yes, I know you have," the girl replied, turning and giving me a stink eye. "It's been very annoying having you here, by the way. You don't leave me any room, and you snore rather loudly. Also, your feet smell when you take your boots off."

"My feet don't—" but then I cut myself off as I realized the implications of what she was saying. "Wait a minute, you've been watching me sleep?"

"Well, of course I have," she said. "Wouldn't you if you found some strange person sleeping on your bench?"

"Okay, that's the second time you've said this was YOUR bench."

"That's because it is," she said simply.

"I don't see your name on it," I retorted.

"Obviously not! Why would I do a stupid thing like that? Putting my name out there for anyone to see? What kind of girl do you take me for?"

"What's so stupid about putting your name on something?" I asked, caught off guard by the perfect seriousness of her answer.

"Everything," she said. "Names have power, you know. If you simply must have one, then you better make sure either *everyone* knows it, or *no one* does. I've worked hard for my obscurity, I'll have you know. I'm not going to ruin it by scrawling my name all over the place!"

"Why wouldn't you want anyone to know your name?" I asked, taking a seat beside the strange girl. She may have been sitting on my bench, but at least she was making an interesting case about it.

"Because when you give someone your name, you give them a little piece of yourself. You belong to them just as much as they belong to you. If *nobody* knows who you are, then you belong to nobody. You ARE Nobody. And *Nobody* is free in ways *somebody* can never be."

"Wait a minute, are you telling me that nobody knows your name? Not a single person?"

"Nope," she said with a proud smile. "I'm as nameless as a gust of wind, as unremarkable as a drop of rain in the ocean, and as easily forgotten as a passing face in a crowd."

"I don't think I'll be forgetting you quite so easily."

"Don't be so sure," she said. "Believe it or not, this is the third or fourth time we've met. You just don't remember because I'm not worth remembering."

"Why do I somehow doubt that?" I said, crossing my arms.

"You'd be surprised," she said mischievously. "Seems to me you're becoming pretty forgettable yourself, you know. I'd bet that over half the people who saw you today forgot about you completely after only a few minutes, if not a few seconds."

"Gee, thanks," I muttered.

"You're welcome," she said with a warm smile. "There's something terribly liberating in being forgotten, isn't there?"

I didn't respond.

After a time, she said, "It's like being a shadow. A shadow in the shade of an even bigger shadow, hidden from all except those who know how to look." She gave a gentle sigh, and observed me with moonlit eyes. "You know, as much as I would love to forget you the way you're about to forget me, something tells me it won't be that easy with you." She smiled at me and stood.

"Wait, where are you going?" I asked. "I thought this was your bench." She may have been peculiar, but I was beginning to enjoy her company. It had been a long time since I had such a long conversation with someone, let alone a girl.

"It still is," she said, ignoring my sarcasm. "But I have a feeling you're going to need it more than I will tonight."

"What makes you say that?" I asked suspiciously.

She answered with a quick wink before she turned and walked off, fading seamlessly into the darkness of the night.

I stared for a long time into the shadows of the trees before I finally lay down on my side across the empty park bench. For a moment, I could have sworn there was someone there, an echo of a voice ringing faintly in my memory, but when I raised my head, there was no one.

Normally, I would have welcomed my solitude, but now I almost longed for some company, even if just for a little while. I guess the problem with having a secret place was that it sure could be lonely sometimes. Eventually, I was finally able to put my head on my arm and fall into an uneasy asleep.

The next day, no one would even look at me.

I was in my usual spot, sitting next to the bus stop at the mall, my empty cup out and ready. I couldn't believe it, it had been over THREE HOURS, and I hadn't made a single cent! I didn't know what was going on, but it went well beyond the feigned apathy I had grown accustomed to; this was a sheer denial of my existence!

I wasn't even getting the usual sneers and disgusted grimaces from the stuck-up rich people. Normally they jumped at a chance to look down upon the less fortunate, but today they just marched on by without so much as a snarky upturned glance.

It was awful.

Being a beggar was bad enough, but being an ignored beggar was infinitely worse. I was degrading myself for nothing! And yes, it's always degrading. And no, you don't get used to it. The looks people could give you—like you were nothing but a roach they wish they could stomp out of existence, someone that the world would be a whole lot better without. It hurt every time.

You get taught a number of hard lessons on the streets, but that one in particular was beaten into you with every one of those looks—each its own cruel reminder that you weren't alone in the world because you wanted to be, but because everyone else wanted you to be.

Let me tell you, even though the result was the same, that made all the difference in the world.

"Having some troubles today, are we?"

I turned toward the voice. Surely they couldn't be talking to me, but when I looked, there was a girl sitting next to me, her legs crossed beneath her. She was looking right at me with a gentle smile that touched her eyes, which seemed familiar to me, but I couldn't place from where.

"… Are you talking to me?" I asked her tentatively.

"Of course! Who else would I be talking to?" she said.

"I don't know, anybody else! I seem to be the last person anyone wants to talk to today," I said bitterly.

"They're not ignoring you, you know," she said, but when I gave her a look she added, "Okay, well some of them are, but most have just forgotten about you. It's nothing personal, really."

"How can they forget about me? I'm sitting right here! I've been sitting here for weeks! Half of these people take the same buses every day. I see them every morning and every night, and whether they like it or not, I know they see me too."

"See, now that's exactly your problem," she said. "They don't like seeing your sorry butt sitting here every day, so they tune you out, forget about you, and move on with their simple little lives."

I grimaced as I looked up at the crowd passing us by without so much as a glance, my cup empty and ignored.

"Even if they have forgotten me, it doesn't mean they can't see me," I muttered.

"Doesn't it though?" she said, standing and straightening her... whatever she was wearing. "Anyway, I don't know about you, but I could sure use some breakfast. Care to join me? Or are you too busy being ignored?"

My empty stomach rumbled at the mention of breakfast. It had been over a day since I had last eaten anything, let alone a proper meal, and at this rate it looked like that wasn't likely to change any time soon. I looked up at the mysteriously familiar character standing before me and felt a gentle tug in my gut to go with her, as if she would somehow take me where I needed to go.

"I don't have any money," I said softly. I always got embarrassed admitting that, even to myself. Maybe I shouldn't have gotten that beer last night after all.

"I can see that," she said with a look at my empty cup. "Good thing we don't need money where we're going."

I followed the girl as she led us through a maze of crooked alleyways and back streets, the hidden arteries of the city where the bad blood flowed.

Even though I'd lived on the streets for over a year, I always tried to avoid places like this. I couldn't help but worry that if I ever fell into this hidden world, that I might never be able to escape it again, and any hope I had for a normal life would finally slip through my fingers forever. Life was too long and lonely a road to not hope for something better along the way.

We finally came to a stop beside an abandoned hotdog stand, left to rot next to a dumpster that smelt as though something had recently curled up and died in there.

"Two please." She said to the hotdog stand, holding up as many fingers to the empty air. I cast an uncertain glance through the deserted alleyways, just to make sure I wasn't missing something.

"Um... who are you talking to?" I asked her delicately, slowly beginning to not only question her sanity, but my own as well.

"The hotdog man," she answered. "I don't know his real name, of course. If people knew he existed, it would be very bad for business. Isn't that right, mister?" she asked the desolate stand.

"You do know nobody's there, right?" I asked her hesitantly.

"Of course I do! Who do you think I'm talking to? *Somebody?*" she said with some impatience. "And you know that too, silly, you just keep forgetting. You need stop thinking so much about where *somebody isn't*, and start remembering where Nobody *is*. Then, it'll all become clear to you."

"Isn't that the same—" I began to ask before something started to take form before me, like a forgotten memory rising to greet a familiar smell.

It was as if a veil of fog had been lifted from my eyes, revealing a destitute man behind the hotdog stand, turning two rats skewered on sticks over the sizzling grill. He cracked a toothless smile at me through his greasy beard. His right hand was missing at the wrist, replaced by a rusty spatula duct taped haphazardly around the stump, which he used to turn one of the rats. I rubbed my eyes and gawked at the man before me, unable to believe what I was seeing.

"Don't mind him," the girl said, gesturing toward me. "He still thinks he's somebody."

The man nodded and gave me a look with his one good eye, before pulling the rats off the grill with his good hand and handing them to us. The girl took hers without hesitation, and I gingerly followed suit.

"Thank you very much," she said, reaching into her pocket and pulling out a button and two rusted bottle caps, which she handed to the man's outstretched spatula.

"I threw in a little extra for last time," she said, and the man nodded kindly, placing the objects in the bottom half of a shattered mug. She said our goodbyes and we walked off together, the girl taking bites of her steaming rat with every other step.

"Go on, eat it before it gets cold!" she said between mouthfuls of seared fur and meat. "It's a lot easier to chew while it's hot."

My attention was on anything but the sizzling rodent in my hand. All around me, the barren alleyway had suddenly sprung to life, as if every forgotten shadow had leapt from its hiding place to dance in the sun.

There were tattered skateboarders airing over trashcans next to street musicians using the lids as drums. A bulbous old hag with wild fungi growing out of her humped back marched past, pushing a shopping cart filled to the brim with mushrooms, while a ragged clown on uneven stilts juggled a set of mismatched pins for a group of laughing children. A little girl in a gas mask sprayed graffiti on a wheel-less car, a vibrant piece that I'm sure wasn't there before.

"She doesn't consider herself an artist," the girl said, noticing me watching the painter. "It's just that the colors of loneliness can be quite beautiful sometimes, don't you think?"

"I don't understand," I said. "Who are these people? Where did they come from? Why couldn't I see them before?"

"We're who the world's forgotten. The ones who have slipped through the cracks. We're Nobody," she said proudly. "We live here, in the neglected places that no one else wants, hidden in the shadow of memory and lost identity."

"Why wasn't I able to see them before?" I asked, mesmerized by the overwhelming strangeness unfolding around me.

"Nobody here has a name that anybody can remember, and

there's great power in obscurity. As far as the world is concerned, we don't exist, and most people are so content going on believing that, that they can't do anything but. See that woman over there?" She pointed at a woman across the street carrying a grocery bag. I nodded. "Watch this."

So I did, following her with my eyes as she marched straight up to the woman across the street, tapped her on the shoulder with her skewered rat and then waved the half-eaten carcass in her face.

For a split second, a horrified look came over the woman's face, but as quickly as it came, it subsided, fading into mild confusion, before she gently shook her head and continued on as if nothing had happened. The girl walked back to me, taking another bite of her meal.

"Okay, how on earth did you do that?" I asked, amazed. "I thought that woman would lose her lunch."

"The power of obscurity," she answered. "Just like how fame gives a celebrity the power of influence and exposure, obscurity gives us the power of forgetfulness and invisibility. There's just as much power in nobody knowing your name as there is in everybody knowing it."

"Power? You mean like magic?"

"Sort of. Like a human magic," she said. "See, power resides where people believe it resides. Unlike magic, power has to be *given* to you, not made on your own. We're given the power of obscurity not by ourselves, but by everybody else. They choose to forget us, so they do. Like that woman there, she saw me, then forgot me a moment later, because as far as her mind's concerned, I don't exist. So to her, I don't. And neither do they." She gestured to the people around us.

"So why can I suddenly see you all then?"

"Nobody can see us. And it seems you're on the fast track to becoming Nobody yourself," she said with a smile. "I realized that once you started sleeping at my bench."

"YOUR bench?" I said, before she cut me off.

"Oh no, we're not starting that again," she said. "The point is, I knew you were one of us after you starting showing up there."

"How so?"

"Because that's exactly what I did when I first became Nobody too."

As she said it, a young boy in a tattered vest ran up and hugged the little girl, a smile beaming on his face. She hugged him back, and he smiled warmly at me. I hadn't been smiled at like that in months. I gave him my uneaten rat, and when he took it, he hugged me too, wrapping his little arms around my waist. I had almost forgotten what that felt like. It was nice.

As I watched him scamper away through the crowd, I began to notice others smiling at me as well, their eyes not just passing over me, but actually seeing me, acknowledging me, and internalizing my presence. When I smiled at them, they would smile back, even wave sometimes. The attention was overwhelming, like being freed from a cage that you didn't realize you've lived your entire life in.

"We stick together down here," she said. "When Nobody cares about you, then you learn to care for Nobody too. Now the question is, what are you going to be? Somebody or Nobody?

"It's not an easy choice," she continued when I hesitated to answer. "Becoming one of us means you give up any hope of a normal life. You'll never be seen by anybody ever again. You'll exist solely in the cracks of the world, perpetually on the edge of things. But you won't do it alone," she said, turning toward the crowd of misfits, outcasts, vagabonds, and drifters before us.

"When do I have to choose?" I asked her.

"Tonight. At the bench," she said. "If you want to be somebody still, tell me your name, and I'll never forget it, and neither will the world, and you can take another shot at having a normal life. Or don't, and no one will know your name ever again, and the world will forget you completely."

That night, I met the girl at the bench.

She sat with her legs dangling over the edge, her pale skin bathed in the moonlight. I sat down beside her. Then, I took a knife from my pocket and began carving something into the wood of the bench. She watched me all the while, a gentle smile on her face. Finally, once I was finished, she took my hand and together we faded into the night, like shadows in the wind, never to be seen or heard from by anybody again.

If you want proof that I ever existed at all, you'll have to find that secret bench, in that forgotten place, and look for a carving you won't remember you ever saw. A carving that reads: Nobody was here.

THE NARRATOR, whose name is known only by him, is a homeless youth slowly being forgotten by the world. His days are lonely and isolated despite him often being surrounded by people, from whom he begs for change. He has long since sacrificed his pride and dignity in the name of his survival; and suffers deeply from the pain of scraping a parasitic existence off a world that would rather forget him entirely. As he slowly slips deeper and deeper into obscurity, he learns the true power of being forgotten, and the freedom of being Nobody.

JORDAN DAVIES is 23-year-old writer from Canada's capital. When he's not typing away or with his head buried in a book, he can be found at the local skatepark, playing guitar, or walking his god Leeroy Jenkins through the woods. He's always felt like an outside observer of life more than a participant in it, like a reader to a book: one foot planted in this world and the other firmly in the realms of fantasy, but never belonging to either.

THE HIDDEN HISTORY OF SENECA LEE

An account by Seneca Lee,
AS PROVIDED BY ELISA A. BONNIN

Reality isn't a fabric, it's an ocean. It's eddies and swirls, it's ripples breaking away from the current. I was born in one of those ripples, in one of those small, self-contained worlds. I was never part of everyone else's reality, and once I found out the truth of that, once I broke away from my safe, sheltered cove and saw the wideness of the ocean, I could never see life the same way again.

My name is Seneca Lee. In my childhood, I grew up on Hilton Head Island, off the coast of South Carolina. Hilton Head is a small town in the winter, with a population of just about thirty thousand souls. In the summer, the population swells to as much as two hundred and seventy thousand. It always felt surreal growing up, like I lived in two different towns, or like the town I lived in went to sleep when the seasons changed and woke again in the summer.

I liked summers. I liked the warmth, the bevy of people who flooded the island's shores. I liked being able to get lost in the crowd, to exist in a space where no one knew if I was a local or not, no one knew my family, no one knew my name.

Winters were harder. In the winter, the town started to feel small, almost stifling. I was an odd child, even from the beginning. People talk in the South, especially in communities like mine, and though no one ever spoke about me where I could hear it, I knew that they talked. They blamed my strangeness on my mother—she was from the West Coast, and thus as bad as a foreigner, or they blamed it on me, for being born too smart, or they blamed it on my parents, for having me so late in their lives. Whatever the reason, I was different, and all of the other children knew it. I didn't *look* any different from them, didn't speak any differently, but children sense oddness like sharks sense blood, and my peers never let me forget it. I couldn't connect with them the same way they connected to each other, like they had all been born knowing a dance that I could never learn. And after a struggle-filled first two years in school, I stopped trying. I started throwing myself into other activities, started reading more and doing things where I could be alone. I started seeking out the company of adults, because at least they never excluded me from their circles. I started finding more reasons to be by myself, to be alone.

It was around this time that I discovered swimming. I was a natural at it, another oddity in a family with a father who wouldn't go out onto the water if he could help it and a mother who didn't much like the outside at all. Thankfully, my parents were supportive. It didn't take long for me to get on my school's swim team, and from there, I started getting involved in more aquatic events. Once I discovered how freeing it felt to swim, how *wonderful* it felt to have nothing but the water surrounding me, nothing but the waves and the light reflected off the water's surface to judge me, I started doing it more. I threw myself into my training. The water became an obsession for me. I needed to be in it, craved that freedom more than anything else. I would do anything to be allowed to swim. Since, as I mentioned, my parents were not much for the beach, I spent a lot of time with our next-door neighbor, an elderly retiree named Melissa Baker.

Miss Melissa lived alone and had the sort of accent that I had only ever heard on TV and in movies—according to my parents, she had been born somewhere in England. Most of the other children avoided her because if she ran into them, she bored them at length with her stories, but I liked Miss Melissa for one reason and one reason alone. Miss Melissa was like me—the water seemed to call to her. She took me to the beach or the pool multiple times as a child and was more instrumental than my coach in encouraging me to improve. With my parents both busy, I ended up spending most of my afternoons at Miss Melissa's house. She fed me cakes and told me stories, and for a while, I was content. For a little while, it didn't matter to me what the other children thought, what people said about me in the corridors, what people did to my locker if I happened to turn my back on it for a second. I had the water, I had my books, and I had Miss Melissa. I didn't want anything else.

Like so many things in childhood, that peace came to an end.

Growing up is hard for everyone, but for me, it was a special kind of torture, because along with the usual uncomfortable physical changes and mood swings that every twelve-year-old girl has to contend with, I started to change in other ways. To my horror, I became *even stranger*.

It started one summer morning, when I was in the shower. Like I mentioned before, my love of swimming was tied to an even deeper obsession with water, so my showers tended to be excessively long. I was standing underneath the stream of water, closing my eyes and imagining myself immersed in it, when something happened. The water around me *jumped*. At first, I thought it was just the splash of the shower stream against the water that had pooled in the bottom of the tub, but as I stretched out my hands and the water leapt into them, I realized that it wasn't anything that simple.

Heart pounding, I looked down at my hands, afraid of what

I would find. I stretched them out, studying them in the light, and promptly closed my eyes again.

My hands had changed, a thin webbing forming between my fingers like a frog's foot. My world shrank to a point as I slowly opened my eyes, flexing my fingers. And then, as if nothing had happened at all, my fingers spread apart, the webbing disappearing from sight. I raised my hand toward the water in the tub again, but nothing happened. There was no reaction, nothing to make me think that I hadn't imagined it.

Except that my heart was still pounding, going a million miles a minute, and I could feel my head spinning, my world darkening at the edges. I leaned back against the shower wall to catch my breath and then, when I no longer felt like I was going to faint, got out of the shower, dressed so quickly that my clothes turned damp from my skin, and ran outside.

It was a weekday in the summer, so my parents weren't home. Sometimes, I wonder if things might have turned out different if they had been, if they had been there to stop me and ask me what was wrong, but I'm not convinced that I would have told them the truth regardless. Either way, they were gone, so I ducked out of the house, locked up behind me, and ran to Miss Melissa's.

I didn't know what to say to Miss Melissa when she finally opened the door. I had come to her in a panic, but now that I was here, the words died in my throat. Thankfully, I didn't have to speak. Miss Melissa took one look at me, seeing my flushed face, trembling hands, and damp hair, and seemed to understand. She even smiled.

"Did something happen, Seneca?"

I didn't have a response. My mouth opened and closed helplessly. I must have looked like a fish out of water.

But Miss Melissa didn't seem surprised by that at all. She stepped aside, inviting me into the house as if it had been a normal day. "No need to say anything," she said. "I think I understand. Please sit down.

I've been expecting something like this to happen, to be honest. I think it's time I told you where you came from."

Miss Melissa brewed me a strong cup of tea, and I sat in one of her armchairs, my hands in my lap. My hair was still damp from the shower, and I vaguely remember my shirt clinging to my skin, but my eyes were on the older woman as she sat across from me, balancing a cup of tea in both hands. She seemed to gather herself with a breath before opening her mouth to speak.

"I'm not sure how to tell you this," she said, tapping her finger lightly against the side of her cup. "But you aren't human."

A lot of things go through your mind when you hear something like that. Anger. Disbelief. Fear. I stared at her, my mouth working as I tried to come up with the words to deny it, but something *had* happened to me, something strange, and my denial stuck in my throat.

"Ma'am?"

"You're not human, Seneca," Miss Melissa said. As if making a decision, she let out a long breath, setting her cup on the table in front of her and leaning back in her seat. "Do you know what a changeling is?"

I shook my head. I had never heard the word before.

"A changeling is a faerie child, exchanged for a human infant," said Miss Melissa. "Your mother was a selkie, child, a water faerie, and a good friend of mine. She left you in Mr. and Mrs. Lee's care."

I couldn't respond. It seemed so absurd, so impossible, that more than anything else, I felt anger. It didn't matter what else was strange about me. I was my parents' child. "That's not true!" I said. "That can't be true!"

"Haven't you ever felt different, Seneca? Felt like you didn't belong? Deep down inside, you always knew that you weren't like the others."

My face burned, and I looked away.

Her words sounded like an echo of myself, the very things I had been thinking my entire life. My hands started to shake around the cup of tea she gave me. I set it down on the table and hooked my fingers into the seat cushion below me, holding tight, as if I was trying to do something to anchor me to this world. My teeth clamped down on my lip so hard that they almost drew blood. My reality was spinning away from me, my world shifting on its axis, and trying to grab at it was like trying to hold water with a sieve.

"I can't be this—this selkie thing," I said. "My parents would have told me!"

Miss Melissa shook her head sadly. "Your parents don't know. They would have no way of knowing. I know this is hard to hear, Seneca, but you have to listen to me. Your parents' daughter was stillborn. That was why we chose her to exchange for you."

I shook my head, squeezing my eyes tightly. Tears welled up in them, and I almost managed to convince myself that this was some sort of cruel joke, that this was nothing more than a prank. "It's not true," I said. "It's not!"

"More things will begin to happen," Miss Melissa said, not unkindly. "You're at the age now where it's going to be difficult to keep pretending to be human, at least not without some assistance. You need to learn how to manage your abilities if you plan to continue living this life, Seneca. I understand that this is difficult to accept, but I'd like you to remember what I've told you, and *when* things start to get worse, I'm hoping you'll come to me."

I left Miss Melissa's house as soon as I could, and practically ran all the way to my bedroom. There, surrounded by my childhood things, by the pictures that showed me growing up, taking my first steps, sitting on my dad's shoulders and smiling at the camera, I started to calm down a little. The things that Miss Melissa had said, almost plausible in the gloom of her house, now seemed entirely absurd, as if I had only been dreaming.

There was no way Miss Melissa could have been telling the truth. I wiped my eyes and went on with my day.

Denial is the first stage of grief, and for the first few weeks after Miss Melissa destroyed my worldview and whatever claims I had to normality, I became an expert at it. I convinced myself that there was nothing strange about me, that everything was fine, that Miss Melissa was losing her mind in her dotage or even that that conversation between us had never happened. I threw all of my energy into becoming the most normal, most well-adjusted twelve-year-old girl that I could possibly be. Miss Melissa's story was always there with me in the back of my mind, but I managed to push it away for a time.

But despite my protests, Miss Melissa had been right about one thing. The strange events continued.

At first, it was small things. An almost pathological urge to be in the water, to take longer and longer showers, to swim more. At that time, it was summer on the island, and so I could tell myself that those urges were normal, that it was just who I was. But from that point on, things started getting a little stranger. I started dreaming about the ocean, started waking up to find webbing between my fingers and toes, webs that seemed to disappear when I calmed down. I developed a sudden craving for sushi, which I had never really liked before. When I was in the ocean, I started to feel like if I closed my eyes and drifted, I could swim away. From all of my cares. From everything. I could feel the currents getting faster around me as I slipped through the water, could feel the ocean molding itself to me, and I told myself it was all in my head.

But when things started happening that I couldn't deny anymore, denial turned to anger. One night, I looked at myself in the mirror and saw that my eyes, normally a pale blue, had turned an inhuman, amber gold, that my hair, normally blonde, had become black and coarse. I stood there, breathing in fear, my fists clenched against the glass of the mirror until the black and gold faded, until my normal appearance reasserted itself. Then the fear pooling in the pit of my stomach became rage, and I slammed my fists hard against the mirror.

It didn't break. It was made of stronger stuff than that. But now that denial was impossible, my mood took a turn for the worse. I started sulking, started spending more time than ever locked up in my room, away from the ocean, away from everything. When my parents weren't home, I threw things. I screamed and pounded my pillow. I hated everything. I hated my family for lying to me, I hated that I couldn't be their daughter. I hated Miss Melissa for ruining my life, and I especially hated myself.

Even with both of my parents working, my change in mood didn't escape their notice, but they declined from bringing it to my attention too many times, likely thinking my moodiness due to hormones, or other typical problems associated with growing up. Aside from a few worried conversations with my mother, they left me alone. So I sat up in my room for a week and sulked and stewed, all while the signs around me became worse.

Next was bargaining. I discovered, through some accident, that I could make my appearance return back to normal by remaining calm, by breathing deep and waiting until the strange features stopped breaking through. It was around this time that I started to feel the faintest glimmer of hope, that I *could* deal with this on my own, that I had somehow found the trick behind the transformations.

But of course, it couldn't possibly be that easy. As the summer wore on, the episodes became more and more frequent, their duration longer and longer. It was one summer night when my hair refused to change back, when a single stubborn streak of black remained among the blonde, that I finally broke down and cried. I spent the rest of the night in a sullen haze—depression—and the next morning when

I woke up, looked at myself in the mirror and saw that maddening amber gold interweaving with the blue of my irises, something inside me finally snapped.

Acceptance.

I still remember the look on Miss Melissa's face when I arrived at her door in the predawn light, having slipped out of the house while my parents were still asleep. She took one look at me, standing on her doorstep in an oversized sweatshirt with eyes red-rimmed from crying, and drew me into her house, sitting me down at the kitchen table while she made a pot of tea.

"You have to learn how to put up a glamor," she said when I started to calm down, holding my hands in hers. "We placed one on you when you were a child, but it's fading now. You have to be able to replace it on your own."

"How do I do that?" I asked weakly.

And so she taught me. For the next few hours, we sat cross-legged across from each other on her floor, and she showed me how to reach for the power inside myself, how to focus until I saw an image in my mind of what I was supposed to look like and let it take over me, changing my outward appearance. Now that she had taught me what to look for, I could feel the edges of the old glamor, feel the tears where my own power was starting to rip through. By afternoon, I was able to keep my appearance stable again. I learned that sometime while I was practicing, Miss Melissa had called my parents to let them know where I was. They were angry at me for leaving the house without telling anyone, but they didn't suspect a thing.

I practiced with my glamor until it felt easy, until donning it wasn't much different from putting on an extra layer of clothes. Little by little, I started to accept that Miss Melissa was telling the truth, that I really wasn't human. But that acceptance brought me a grief and heaviness that I felt whenever I looked at my parents. One day, at Miss Melissa's house, when she was teaching me how to drop the glamor as easily as I had learned to put it on, I brought it up.

"Should I tell my parents?"

"Well, that's up to you," Miss Melissa said, smoothing a coarse strand of black hair away from my face. "But keep in mind that they might not believe you."

I sat there for a while, staring at the ground, then asked the question that had been burning in the back of my mind, the question I had been afraid to ask, because I didn't want to know the answer.

"*Are* they still my parents?"

In answer to that, Miss Melissa drew me in close, enfolding me in her arms. She smelled like saltwater and the sea, and I didn't realize I was crying until I noticed that my face was wet. "They raised you, didn't they?" she asked. "They took care of you. They're as much your parents as anyone can be." I sniffed, and she drew me gently away from her, brushing her fingers across my face and tucking a lock of hair behind my ear. "There, now, don't cry. Here, have a look at you."

She handed me a mirror, and I looked at my true face for the first time.

All things considered, it wasn't an ugly face, but neither was it human. It was a sharp face, with a wildness inherent to it that was unfamiliar to me. My free hand brushed against my cheek, tracing the features slowly. I could feel my fingertips against my skin, could see my hand moving in the mirror, but a part of my mind still refused to see the girl I was looking at as myself.

My hair had gone fully black, falling down my shoulders and back in soft waves, and my eyes were sharp. They had become that same amber gold that I half-recognized from those glances into the mirror, but shining brightly now, with slit pupils like a cat's. A fine coating of hair covered my skin like soft fur, light gray with darker gray spots worked into it. My hands were webbed, a coating of dark skin spanning the gaps between my fingers. I stared at myself for a long time before I pulled back, letting Miss Melissa take the mirror away. She watched me, waiting for me to speak.

"I don't look like me."

"You do," Miss Melissa said, "and you don't. They're both you, Seneca, the girl that exists under the glamor, and the girl that doesn't."

The words made sense, but I wasn't sure that they made me feel better. I inclined my head in a solemn nod, looking down at my hands. Then, I drew in a breath and let my glamor fall back into place, as easily as if I were flexing a muscle. Fur and webbing retreated, my eyes shifted back into their normal shape and form, and my hair became blonde and straight again. I flexed my fingers, testing how I felt in this form that should have been familiar, probing at this new sense of disconnection like a tongue seeking out a gap where a tooth should have been. I should have felt like me again, but I didn't.

Part of me wondered if I would ever feel like I belonged in my own skin again. But I didn't have the words to explain what I felt to Miss Melissa, so I refrained. I thanked her for the lesson and went home.

Another time, when Miss Melissa was telling me stories about her own past, I finally worked up the nerve to broach the subject of her own humanity.

"You're not human, are you, ma'am?"

Miss Melissa gave me a wry smile. "Is it that easy to tell?" she asked. "I'm a melusine, dear, a sea sprite. I was one of your mother's closest friends."

"Do you—?" I gestured at my face, uncertain. "—Do you look like me?"

I had taken to slipping off my glamor when I was in Miss Melissa's house. I wanted to get used to the feeling, to feel more comfortable in my own skin, in both of my skins. Part of me didn't want to do it, but that made it all the more reason to do it anyway. She gave me a soft smile, looking at me over the cup of tea she was holding, and shook her head.

"No, dear," she said. "My kind look entirely different from yours. I'm afraid I had to do quite a bit more than a simple glamor to walk among you. But my face is the same as the face you see now."

"Oh," I said, stupidly. A part of me thought that it must have been nice, to have a face so *human*. Miss Melissa's face was lined with age, but I could tell that in her youth she must have been beautiful. Which I was envious about, to be honest. I had always thought, when I thought about it at all, that faeries were supposed to be beautiful, but I didn't feel beautiful, just strange and ungainly. I wondered if Miss Melissa had ever felt the same way.

"Can I see your real form?" I asked, looking up at her.

She smiled in response. "Someday, maybe," she said. "The next time we go swimming. My true form would be inconvenient right now."

I didn't bring it up again, but I had noticed that Miss Melissa had stopped taking me swimming with her, ever since telling me the truth about my history. I wondered about that, but every time I remembered to ask, I seemed to have lost my nerve.

It was late in November by the time I finally asked her about my mother.

I was sitting on her floor, doing my homework, and the question left my mouth before I had even realized I was forming it. Miss Melissa's smile was sad as she looked at me, and she put her knitting away. "Your mother—" she said, her eyes misting over with grief, "— now, that was a loss. She was the fastest swimmer in the old country, and easily the most beautiful. Titania herself was sad to hear about her death."

"She died?" I asked, feeling my throat get uncomfortably tight. It was odd, considering I had never known my real mother, but I still felt her loss.

"Yes, dear," said Miss Melissa. "Not long after you were born."

"What happened?"

"Well, there was a war. A power struggle, one of the stupid things that we fae constantly do to ourselves. But let's not talk about it, child. Go back to your schoolwork."

I went back to my assignment, but I couldn't focus. The words kept swimming on the page in front of me, and eventually I gave up. "Did my mother ever give me a name?" I asked.

Miss Melissa looked up sharply, her eyes fixing on me. I shifted, uncomfortable with the way she was looking at me. "Why do you ask?"

I shook my head, looking down at my hands. I had learned how to take off pieces of my glamor, so they were human for now. My selkie hands weren't the best at holding a pen. I couldn't explain the hole that had just opened up in my chest, a gaping void that I could never possibly fill. "I was just wondering," I said. "I mean I know I'm not... I'm not really Seneca Lee."

Miss Melissa almost sounded alarmed. "Why do you say that, child? You *are* Seneca Lee."

"The real Seneca died years ago, didn't she?"

"She was never alive, dear," Miss Melissa said. "She never had the chance to take your name, never had the chance to grow in it. *You* were the child your parents raised. You were the one they loved, the one they held, the one they rocked to sleep at night. Seneca is *your* name—as questionable of a name as it might be. It's who *you* are. Names are important to our kind, dear. They define us. Never forget your name. Never forget that it is yours."

I drew my knees up close to my chest, wrapped my arms around them and felt myself let out a little hiccupping sob. "I want to tell them," I said, tears blurring my eyes. "I want to tell them the truth."

"Okay, dear," Miss Melissa said. "Okay."

But I never did. I lost my nerve, and the next time I saw my mom, I couldn't speak. I hugged her, and she hugged me back. I think she assumed that it was something from school, because she kissed me on the top of the head and sent me to bed. I realized, looking at her and Dad, that I didn't *want* to tell them the truth. I didn't want them to know. They lived in a world where they had a daughter who was alive and who loved them, and they were happy there.

I didn't want to destroy that world by telling them that their daughter had died, and the girl they had raised was some kind of inhuman freak.

Instead, I curled up in bed, drew my pillow close to myself, and was miserable until I fell asleep.

On my thirteenth birthday, Miss Melissa surprised me by inviting me over to her house. There, she had a cake set out for me that was more than an equal to the one my parents had bought, and a wrapped bundle. Over some cake and tea, she passed the bundle to me.

"Here," she said. "It's time you had this."

I unwrapped it, feeling my hands trembling. Inside was a pelt, gray like the fur that covered my skin, with the same pattern of dark gray spots. It was soft in my hands, and I could feel power in it as I ran my hands over it, power that crackled and sent a tingle through my blood. It felt like it belonged to me.

I looked up at Miss Melissa, and she nodded.

"Your sealskin," she said, "Every selkie has one. It will let you take on your true form."

"This isn't my true form?" I asked, gesturing at my appearance.

"It is, but it's incomplete. Here. Let's go swimming."

I almost refused, because it was still early spring and the ocean was too cold to swim in, but curiosity overcame me and I followed her down to the coast. There, I wrapped the skin over my shoulders as she showed me, and stepped into the water.

I didn't feel cold at all. The pelt wrapped around me, molding to my skin, and when I looked down I realized that I was coated in thick fur, like a seal. My hands and feet had changed, becoming sleek gray flippers. Miss Melissa stepped in the water beside me and transformed, her legs turning into a slender golden tail, transforming her into something like a mermaid. She smiled at me, mischief in her eyes, and ducked her head beneath the water. She didn't come back up. I did the same, and the salt didn't sting my eyes. I chased after her, moving faster than I had ever moved before, until my lungs burned for air. She reached over, grabbed my arm, and looked back up at the surface, a long and terrifying way away.

Then she opened her mouth, and even underwater, I could hear her, understand her.

"Breathe."

I did. Air filled my lungs, and I looked around in wonder and realized that I *could* breathe. I breathed long and deep, and then laughed, swimming with her. For the first time in my life, I felt truly free. I felt like I belonged.

Later, when we got home, Miss Melissa gave me one last birthday present.

"A spell," she said. "One that you should learn, in case you ever need to use it. If you find yourself in danger, it will protect you. But Seneca, child, I want you to promise me something. You must never use this spell, except at great need. It's a terrible thing, to use this spell for nothing."

I nodded solemnly, grave with a sense of responsibility. "I won't," I said. "I promise."

"Swear it to me thrice," Miss Melissa said, unconvinced. "Your word given thrice is binding."

I did, repeating my oath two more times, and only when I had given my word to her satisfaction did she teach it to me. It was a terrible spell, and I swore to myself that I would never use it, except at great need. Never, ever.

At the time, I even meant it.

As the months wore on, I found myself settling into this strange sort of double life. It was the water, I think, that did it for me. The euphoria of being able to slip into my sealskin and disappear beneath the waves, as long as I wanted to, at any time of year. Before my thirteenth birthday, I was a scared human girl playing at having secret powers. With the advent of my sealskin, I was a selkie playing at humanity. I still went to school and put up the charade for my parents every day, but my heart wasn't in it. This had a downside in that that my grades started to fail, but the upside was that I no longer cared about my peers ignoring me. I had a secret that was more beautiful and grand than anything they could imagine, and it made me feel powerful, unique, special.

Of course, since teenage girls are the cruelest individuals known to man, my newfound indifference didn't make life better for me.

At some point, my peers started mocking me, but when I failed to respond, they began to ignore me entirely. I didn't mind that, even reveled in it, but when their indifference transitioned into hatred, I started to care. It was the little things at first, paper balls hitting the back of my head while I was trying to listen to the teacher, people going out of their way to sit away from me at lunch, girls gossiping in the corridors about me and sneering at me when I came too close. It nagged at me, fueling the fires of frustration. I told myself that I didn't care, and most days I even believed it, but as the months wore on and we started preparing to enter high school, even the swim team started alienating me, and I started to feel the strain.

With the strain came the pressure, and with pressure came anger.

The day of the swim meet, my last swim meet in middle school, I walked into the back room to get changed and found my swimsuit and gear stuffed into the trash, my swimsuit sliced to pieces and rude words scrawled on my bag in bright letters. That was the last straw. I stood over my ruined things, my fingers gripping them tightly, so tight that my hands trembled, and I could hear laughter in the distance. High, piping laughter. Cruel laughter.

They were laughing at me. A surge of rage like nothing I had ever felt ran through me, and I felt my glamor peeling away, felt a flash of bright and terrible power inside of me, that turned my eyes gold, that threatened to turn my hair black. Faeries are prone to caprice, to mood swings, to bouts of arrogance, but I didn't understand that then. All I knew was that I was mad, angry, and that the girls on my swim team truly had no idea who they were dealing with. I would make them aware.

I dropped my things back into the trash and walked over to the locker room's sink. I plugged the drain and turned on the water, letting the basin fill. When it was full, I plunged my hands into it and looked at myself in the mirror. My eyes were hard, almost unrecognizable. Although I was still wearing most of my glamor, there was nothing human in my face, just pure fey rage. My fingers brushed against the porcelain. I could hear their laughter behind me, knew where they were as easily as I knew where I was, and the blood rushed through my ears.

The syllables of Miss Melissa's spell moved smoothly from my lips.

Water congealed around my palms. I could feel it brush up against me, once, twice, hardening, sharpening. I was a blacksmith folding water into itself, over and over again, forging a sword that would bring death. And when I was done, when I had completed the weapon that would bring my vengeance, I would let it loose and it would seek blood. The laughter would stop, and they would know, those of them that survived, that I was not someone to be trifled with. I could almost taste it.

And then I could.

A bright, metallic taste filled my mouth, and I broke off the incantation mid-word. I looked up at the mirror and saw myself reflected there, saw that I had bit my lip hard enough to draw blood. My eyes, reflected back toward me in the glass, were wide and terrified and so, so blue. My face was a human's face again, the face of a girl who was terrified of what she had become.

I let out a ragged breath, the tension leaving my shoulders all at once, the weight of what I had been about to do pushing down on me and making me stagger, clutching the sides of the sink for support. The water became liquid again, trickling down the drain as I unplugged it. I stood there for a long time, eyes wide, listening to the giggles and the laughter, watching the water—my weapon, my arrow of vengeance, the last nail in the coffin of my own humanity—swirling down the drain.

Then I felt weak and dropped to my knees, clutching my arms close to myself and sobbing. I threw up.

At some point, after enduring more mockery from the girls who found me kneeling there in a puddle of my own sick, who didn't realize how close they had come to destruction, the coach found me. She got me cleaned up and scolded the other girls, even found me a spare swimsuit and tried to coax me into competing, but I had no stomach for it anymore. My parents came, bundled me up into the car, and took me home. I sat in my room for a good long while, staring at the walls, still tasting the blood in my mouth and remembering that moment, that awful, wonderful, terrifying, euphoric moment where I held life and death in my hands, where I stood at the top of the world and looked down and realized that I had *power*. My parents were sympathetic, but they didn't understand. They thought I was upset about being bullied. They didn't understand what had been going through my mind, what I was capable of.

They didn't understand that I hated myself.

Miss Melissa did. She knocked on my door under the pretext of coming over to give me some cookies she had baked, but when I told her everything that had happened, everything that I had thought of doing and had been about to do, she didn't judge. Her expression hardened, but she sat in front of me, taking my hands in her own.

"That's the price of power," she said. "You understand it now, and you will have to live with it every day that you live this life, Seneca. You will live every day with the knowledge, with the understanding, that humans are terribly fragile creatures, that you possess a power they could only dream of, that you could destroy them with a thought. And every day, you will have to look at yourself in the mirror and tell yourself that that is not the kind of person that you are, that that is not who you want to be. Every day, you will have to decide not to do it."

"I almost did," I said, feeling sick. "I wanted to."

"The only thing that matters, child, *the only thing*, is that you didn't."

She placed her hand on my face, giving me a sympathetic smile. Then, she got up, left the cookies on my desk, and turned to leave.

The next person to come into my room was my mother. She stood there for a long time, the door half-open behind her, and just looked at me. I didn't acknowledge her. I still felt sick and weak, angry at myself. I was afraid to look at her, afraid to touch her, in case the anger, the wildness came over me again.

When I did speak, the words that came out of my mouth were not the words that I had intended to say.

"I don't want to go to the high school."

Mom nodded, as if expecting that, then sat in front of me on the bed. "Okay," she said.

I blinked up at her. "Okay?" I repeated.

She nodded again. "Okay."

She explained that her mother, my grandmother, all the way in Washington State, had taken suddenly ill, and that she and my father had been seriously talking about packing up and moving closer to her. My dad had an opportunity to work in Seattle, but it wouldn't take effect until the middle of the school year. They had been talking about it, and decided that if it was alright with me, they were going to send me over there first at the end of the summer, to live with my aunt in the city and start attending school so that I wouldn't have to transfer out in the middle of my freshman year. My mother was seriously considering quitting her job to go with me, although she warned me that she might leave me in the city for a bit and decide to stay with Grandma, a couple of hours of driving away.

"If you're alright with that, Seneca," Mom said, cupping my face in her hands and looking down at me. "It will be different there. I don't want to leave you alone."

I stared at her, feeling numb. And suddenly, the entirety of what she was offering me washed over me. A new start. A high school in a place where no one knew my name. A city I could get lost in. As far away from this place and the people at my school as it was possible to go without leaving this continent and this country.

Away from the curse of my almost-sin.

My heart leaped with excitement, jumping into my throat. I barely heard that my mother was still talking, going on about how pretty it was out there, how there would be water even though it was going to be cold, as if I was someone fragile who cared about the cold. All I was aware of was that I was nodding at her, looking into her eyes.

"I'd like that," I said, and the hollowness in my chest started to fill, just a little. "I'd like that, Mom. Okay."

According to her birth certificate, **SENECA CATHERINE LEE** was born on Hilton Head Island in South Carolina, to parents Jasper and Samantha Lee. In reality, Seneca is a changeling, a selkie child exchanged at birth for a human infant. As a child, Seneca enjoyed swimming, Disney movies, and going to the beach. An outsider among her peers, Seneca preferred the company of adults to other children. After discovering the truth of her faerie heritage, Seneca moved to Seattle, where her adventure is likely to continue.

ELISA BONNIN was born in the Philippines, where she lived until the age of sixteen. Growing up, she enjoyed reading fantasy, writing, and going to the beach. Now, Elisa is a graduate student at the University of Washington in Seattle, WA, studying oceanography. She still enjoys reading and writing, and can be found working on pieces of creative fiction from time to time.

RIGHTEOUS ANGER

An account by Sarina Raubach,
AS PROVIDED BY LUCINDA GUNNIN

I'd be lying if I said that I never resented my parents. I have vivid memories of screaming, "You're not my real mom!" at my mother, mostly when I was 13, but I might have said something similar last week when she tried to talk me out of dyeing my hair.

The thing is, she was right when she said I had gorgeous hair. I have, better make that had, thick black hair that hangs straight down my back and gets almost blue highlights in the sunshine. But it's not the hair-color-of-the-month that everyone else in my school wears, and that makes me an outcast.

It's more than just the hair, I know, but I thought that if I changed my hair, made myself more like them, maybe high school would suck just a little bit less. Mom tried to warn me that it wouldn't work and said things like, "Someday people will appreciate you for who you are." I swear I think they teach you those platitudes in parenting school, or maybe the judge in my adoption told her to say things like that. She might even be right, but it doesn't feel that way when you're 16 and different from everyone else in your family, school, and hell, the whole town.

Martin and Linda Raubach adopted me when I was six days old. At least they tried to. Even though they were great foster parents, they had to fight through five social workers, two agencies, and three courts to be granted the right to call me their daughter. I was five before it was official. The Bureau of Angelic Affairs, Society for Shifters, and the Commonwealth of Pennsylvania all thought that the cultural differences between us would make it a bad match up.

By pretty much all accounts, it wasn't a big problem initially. I heard Linda crying to Martin one night that it was horrible how obnoxious his sister had been, telling them to wait until the right baby came along, one who was more like them, but for the most part they were able to protect me. I think they were told more than once how noble they were for adopting a savage like me, but they had no idea how bad it would get once Linda decided to go back to work.

The problem with her working was that it meant that I had to go to daycare with all the little cherubs of the neighbors. And I don't mean that their kids were angelic in any figurative way. Nope, these were blond-haired, blue-eyed, chubby-cheeked angel babies who, of course, could do no wrong.

I'd never bit anyone before I started daycare. Strange for a shifter, some might say, but Linda swears it's true.

On the second day there, they called her to come get me because I wasn't fit for civilized society and had bitten one of the other toddlers. They were going to lay all the blame on me until Linda showed them the marks where I had been bitten so hard it broke the skin. She told them, "Toddlers bite." I found out years later that she'd had to prove that I wasn't flexible enough to bite the back of my own leg to get them to concede that one of the cherubs might have been at fault. They still insisted I taught the other toddlers such uncivilized behavior.

And life went downhill from there.

After that, none of the other angels thought mom and dad were noble for adopting me. They thought they were crazy and that they would, of course, wake up dead one morning when I showed my true colors and went on a frenzied killing spree. In kindergarten, when one of the boys asked the teacher why we didn't have a classroom pet like the other classes did, Becky Jones laughed and said, "We already have one," pointing at me. And Miss Carter, who I thought liked me, said under her breath, "Because Sarina might eat it."

I heard that one a lot over the next few years. Like cats, I'm an obligate carnivore, but that didn't stop the school from trying to feed me that tofu mash the angels all like so well. When Mom, and my doctors, insisted that I had to have meat in my meals, the school decided I had to eat in an entirely different area so that my meat-eating didn't upset the vegan cherubs who insist they would never hurt a living thing. It wasn't until high school that they were deemed mature enough to see me eat a roast beef sandwich.

Of course, never hurting a living thing doesn't extend to me. That was just emotional abuse and never hurt anyone, right?

In gym, I was never allowed to play any of the games that required physical contact for fear that I might hurt one of the little angels. So I spent an entire childhood without being allowed to play on a soccer or softball team. I also never got invited to birthday parties, sleepovers, or dance classes. Apparently, shifters aren't very good at ballet or modern dance, or at least that's what my instructor told Linda.

And I'm not allowed to get angry about any of it. Sure, shifters generally have a rage issue, and as a wolverine shifter, mine might be bigger than most, but I can't even have a healthy level of anger. If I raise my voice, no matter how just or righteous my anger might be, it's always about race. I'm the angry shifter woman, clearly unable to control my "animalistic impulses." I'm an animal, just ask any of them.

Mom was probably right when she tried to talk me out of dyeing my hair. Even after spending all my birthday cash, the gift card I got for Christmas, and the little bit of money I could beg from Mom on it, my hair was never going to be like theirs. The color is pretty close, but theirs is baby fine and always lays right. Mine is thick and coarse and given to curling when the weather gets too humid. Still, I thought it looked nice. Apparently I was wrong. I wasn't prepared for the depth of their cruelty when I came to school this morning.

Becky Jones is still my nemesis after all these years. She's the head of the cheerleading squad, Homecoming queen, and likely to be the valedictorian, not because she's smarter than I am, but because I've been graded down for anything that deviates from the angelic norm. Didn't call a novel barbaric and simplistic? Graded down in English. Didn't participate in touch football in gym because I was forbidden to participate? Graded down in PE. Didn't acknowledge that angelic civilization is tops in the world? Graded down in world civ. Opted to add bacon to my quiche? Graded down in home ec.

I came into school today expecting some snark. I've lived with it my entire life, so why would today be any different? From "Wow, you really can put lipstick on a pig, or is it a wolverine?" to the comment that my manicure "hid my adamantine claws so well!" I handled it. They were, after all, just words, and not very creative ones at that. But when Becky decided to pour a bowl of beet juice over my head in the lunch room, I lost it. She ruined the pale yellow dress my grandmother bought me for my birthday and destroyed my hair color. I didn't use my claws, or my fangs, just punched the prissy little brat in her surgically-corrected perfect nose.

The lunch room monitor, who hasn't ever monitored anything, looked up from the book she was reading when Becky cried out. Then she suspended me. Yup, I got thrown out of school because a bully attacked me and I defended myself. Maybe I escalated it a little bit, but she deserved it.

I was so angry I was shaking as I went out to the parking lot to the car Martin and Linda got me for my birthday. I refused to let that little twit see me cry, so I left the school parking lot with tires throwing gravel, my years of frustration and repressed hatred bubbling over.

My first temptation was to go find Martin's sword. He's an angel of death, so his sword is much more effective than most of the weapons available locally. He's also unlikely to be using it today. He really only drags it out for formal occasions. But Dad doesn't deserve that. I can just see the headlines: "Adoptive Father Fails to Prevent Disturbed Shifter for Accessing Holy Weapon." I'm not disturbed, and Dad is always responsible with his sword. I'm just good at figuring out safe codes. Smiting a few of my classmates in anger might help me feel better, but it definitely wouldn't be fair to put Dad through that.

The second option would be to actually let my rage out. They're a bunch of simpering angels. One wolverine frenzy would end their perfect faces and honestly, there's a little part of me that would love to just scar Becky up a bit. You've wondered what prompts school shootings? I can absolutely testify. But Linda raised me better than that. I am not some crazy animal, slaughtering everyone who pisses me off. Besides, there's a small chance Mom can get the beet juice out and salvage the dress. Blood stains would never come out.

The third option, and one that seems to have worked for me thus far, is letting Mom handle it. I heard Principal Miller say once that Linda's like a rabid wolverine protecting me. She probably didn't mean it as a compliment, but Mom sure thought it was. She put it on our Christmas cards last year. Mom would definitely handle it, but I'm 16! I think I should fight my own battles.

My parents offered to enroll me in the private school in the next borough over, but I don't think that's the right answer either. I can't kill them all, I certainly can't let my mom handle it for me, and I won't run away. So here I sit, in the hard plastic chairs of Heaven's waiting room, a small slip of paper in my hand, denoting me as number 1,034. I didn't even check to see what number they were working on when I walked in. Rumor has it the Big Guy sees everyone who comes in, every day, no matter how long it takes. If it takes too long, I'll need to text Linda and let her know I'll be late for dinner. She worries.

I've still got beet juice dripping from my hair. I probably should have stopped at home to change before I came here, but who am I going to see that didn't already see it at school? It's a little uncomfortable, but if I had stopped to change or get cleaned up, I might have changed my mind about coming. Or I might have given in to the impulse to do something worse.

There's a shifter of some sort sitting a few seats over to my left, who looked up when I walked in, smiled, and shook her head. I'm pretty sure that even if she didn't go to the most angelic school in the state, she probably had some battles of her own. She went to the bathroom and came back with a tissue for my tears and a towel to catch the dripping beet juice.

"Thank you," I tell her, and she just smiles again, before walking back to her seat. Now that she's close, I can tell she's a bear shifter, but we don't say anything more. It's like we all know that we're supposed to just smile through our suffering. I'm fuming again and adding that to my list of grievances to take up with Management when it's my turn, but then I get distracted by the new guy coming through the door.

He is exactly the type of boy that Mom tells me to avoid. His look and his attitude scream shifter. His jacket is leather, and the tattoos I can see are peeking out from under his collar and his sleeves. I'm willing to bet he has more that I can't see. His ears are gauged, and his hair is dark purple. As he walks past me to get his number, I smell him. Not the musky pine scent I expect, but the floral sweetness of an angel teases my nose and makes me sneeze.

To my complete surprise, he grabs a number and comes back to the empty chair next to me. "Do you mind?" he asks, nodding toward the chair.

I stammer a bit as I say, "Not at all." I'm not used to anyone wanting to sit near me, especially no one angelic. He sits quietly for a few minutes, and I continue staring at my phone, pretending it's the most interesting thing in the world and wishing I had some game other than Candy Crush to play.

"First time here?"

I jump when he speaks, surprised again that he wants to strike up a conversation. Angels may not have the sense of smell we shifters have, but they have some sort of internal radar that lets them know where others of their kind are.

"Is it that obvious?"

"Yes, but only because first timers are the only ones who get nervous. Once you meet the Big Guy, you know there's absolutely nothing to be nervous about. He's like a weird cross between the Wizard of Oz and the best school counselor you ever met. He doesn't grant wishes, exactly, but he helps you see the things you need to see to be happier."

"So you've been here before?"

"I come here a lot. What's troubling you today, Sarina?"

"High school. Mom says it gets better. Heck, I've seen the celebrity-driven ad campaigns, but I'm not sure they're true. Mom and Dad still get a lot of shit from other people, usually because they adopted me, and don't conform to what everyone thinks angels should be."

If he has a problem with the language, I don't see a reaction that would have told me so.

He smiles, and somehow the entire day feels brighter.

"I think it gets better when you stop needing the approval of the Becky Joneses of the world. Do your parents mind the way other people treat them?"

"Not really. They only seem to care if what's being said hurts me."

He nods. "That's because your parents know that those other people make such comments out of fear, or ignorance, or even jealousy. They think they hate you, but they really hate themselves. And making you feel bad is the only way they feel better about themselves."

"You sound like Mom and the school counselor."

He looks kind of sheepish and shrugs. "I've been told that before."

"So how do I make it through high school when the deck is stacked against me, Becky Jones pours beet juice on my head, and no one has ever tried to be my friend?"

"Be their friend first."

I just stare at him and don't respond, so he continues.

"Not everyone in your school is like Becky, right? Find the ones who aren't. Invite them to get coffee or go shopping. Make the first move, Sarina."

"That's twice you've called me by name, and I'm positive I didn't tell it to you."

"I've known it since before your parents were sure they would choose it."

This guy was starting to seriously creep me out, but nothing bad could happen while I was in the waiting room of Heaven, could it?

"Nothing bad can happen to you here, Sarina."

Okay, that is seriously messed up. "Since when do angels read minds?" I bluster, hoping I can quickly attract the attention of the shifter who was friendly earlier. She'll help me out, I think.

"Surely you know I'm not exactly an angel," he says, and instantly I know.

"I don't really like the number system, so I walk through and see who needs me the most at that exact minute. You were oddly both the most distraught and the most logical person in the room."

"So you're the Big Guy?"

"I've been called that, and Buddha and God and a bunch of other things over the years. I don't understand the need for all the changing names, but whatever. I've got to say though, I really dislike the images of me that get passed around. Sometimes I'm fat, sometimes I have one eye, and sometimes I have this crazy beard. Don't repeat that though. I told Mohammad that a few years ago, and he went a little nutty in his interpretation."

"Do you always look like a tattooed wanna-be goth?"

"I look like what you need me to be. You weren't created in my image, I am created in yours."

Then I remember using profanity in front of him. There's a lump in my throat as I squeak out an apology.

And the jerk laughs. "I've heard far worse, I assure you. And you should never, ever apologize for being who you are."

By this time, I'm totally confused and out of sorts over the whole thing. "Fine. Let's just say I believe you. If you're in charge and made everything, why did you make people so cruel? Why did you make it so I didn't get to live with my birth parents? Why did Becky dump beet juice on my head?"

"Free will. It was all a matter of choices. You chose to get your hair dyed after your mother told you it was a bad idea. Becky chooses to be cruel. You chose to come here and think about positive change, rather than going all Columbine on her. It's about choices."

"Some of the choices suck."

"They do. And there's nothing fair or right about the way you've been treated and likely will be treated in the future. So I'm asking you to be the better person."

"About that, why do we always have to be the ones to shut up and take it? When do I get to be the oppressive dick?"

"Do you really want to be?"

"Yes. No. Well, yes, sometimes…"

"There's always someone who's got it worse than you do. Maybe not even the same person all the time, but every day there's someone."

"You know that's bullshit, right? I mean, if you're some omnipotent, omniscient being, shouldn't you have made it so that Becky and her ilk are the ones having to be the better person sometimes and have sucky choices?"

"I'm not omni-anything. I'm one guy who tries to help people make the right choices. And, no, if I were all-powerful and all-knowing, I wouldn't have people like Becky have the hard choices to make. They seem to be almost genetically incapable of making the right decision and being the better person."

"So you aren't going to fix this?"

"No, you are."

I start to ask him what the hell that even means, but by the time I've formulated the question in a less offensive manner, he's gone. It's not like he walked away. He's just gone. Poof, and the only sign he was ever here is the lingering sweet scent of roses in the chair next to me.

The bear shifter looks confused as I get up to leave. "Don't you need to talk to him?" she asks, as I stop in front of her chair.

"Not anymore. I figured it out on my own."

She smiles widely this time and wishes me good luck. I thank her and head for the parking lot, calling my mom. I've been treating her pretty poorly lately, calling her and Dad by their names instead of acknowledging them as my parents.

She answers on the first ring like she always does when I call her. No matter what she's doing, she drops everything for me. The thought brings a smile to my face, and I think that maybe the Big Guy didn't know what he was talking about. I'm not changing the world. She is.

"Sarina? Hi, honey, what's up?" Her voice is a little strained, like she's expecting trouble, which only makes sense since I'm calling her in the middle of the school day.

"Hi, Mom," I respond, hoping she can hear the smile in my voice. "I was hoping I could come see you and maybe get some advice about a problem I'm having."

It's the first time in years that I've asked for her help, and she sniffles a bit when she says, "Of course."

My plan is evolving as I make the short drive to her office, but I'm confident she'll agree. First, we'll go together to the school and protest my suspension. I'll do the talking; I'll stay calm, but express my anger at both Becky's actions and the school's way of dealing with it. If the principal doesn't see things my way, then maybe I will let Mom and Dad handle it. They've got a bit of experience.

Then I'm going to ask some new friends if they want to hang out tonight. There's a group of girls that Becky is always picking on, and each of them has always been nice to me. They might be angels, but they aren't all bad.

SARINA RAUBACH is a 16-year-old wolverine shifter desperately trying to survive high school. Her favorite things include coffee, hiking in Valley Forge National Park, and baseball. She blames her adoptive parents for her love of all Philly sports teams, even in the occasional winning year.

LUCINDA GUNNIN is a Midwesterner recently transplanted into the suburbs of the City of Brotherly Love, where she appreciates the milder weather, soft pretzels, and all-you-can-eat sushi. She still isn't sure she pronounces or spells Schuylkill right and hasn't gotten used to bridges that are two centuries old. She loves non-grape fruit wines, gaming of all types, and her very spoiled cat. She writes whatever catches her fancy this week, and has published poetry, science fiction and other short stories, and romance novellas.

A GOOD HEAD
ON HIS SHOULDERS

An account by Harry Arthur Cheshire,
AS PROVIDED BY STUART WEBB

It's not easy being a headless horseman. For starters, you've no idea how hard it is to type this one handed, especially as my detached head keeps rolling up under my armpit.

I must admit to not being much of an expert on the headless horseman myths. (I was never one for reading, even before my current circumstances. I did like the film, but mainly for Christina Ricci in a corset.) In fact, I wasn't much of a horseman. First ever attempt to ride the bloody thing, and now we're stuck together for all time. I was so smug about wearing the proper gear whilst my friends scoffed at me for playing it safe, but it turns out a helmet isn't much protection against decapitation via an overturning crane.

My name, by the by, was Harry Cheshire. I say "was" not because I'm (presumably; as I say, I didn't know much before, and you don't get a handbook) dead, but because even people who knew me don't tend to call me by name anymore. To my face, they usually scream loudly and run away. The local paper has imaginatively called me "The Headless Horseman," and occasionally, someone who thinks they're a literary type on Twitter will call me "Ichabod Crane." Which is just a whole Frankenstein's Monster situation.

To date though, no one has compared me to Johnny Depp. Not even in jest. But then it turns out no longer being able to eat isn't that great an aid to weight loss after all.

So at the age of 28, with my whole life in front of me and with many exciting career opportunities in retail work, I suddenly became an immortal instrument of vengeance. The problem being that it's really hard to carry out a vendetta against a crane (that's small "c" crane rather than Ichabod) that fell over because of a freak gust of wind. So my horse—who seems to have taken to the whole post-death lifestyle with considerably more ease than myself (give him a carrot and he's happy, even if he doesn't eat anymore)—and I are stuck roaming the country lanes with little clue as to what to do with ourselves. Though it has at least given me a chance to become almost competent as a rider. Practice makes perfect.

I don't actually know what the horse's name was before we died. We were only introduced once, and subsequent events kind of forced it out of my mind, but I call him Johnny Depp, and he doesn't seem to mind.

There is one real advantage to my current situation though—the one that's allowing me to communicate with you now—and that's that my phone no longer needs charging. Obviously whatever ghostly voodoo keeps me ticking also means batteries become immortal as well. I wasn't expecting that, but then most of the literature pre-dates the smart phone. They were probably still using call boxes in those days. (That's a little joke. As this will be read online, I think it's important to spell out which bits aren't supposed to be taken completely seriously to help the hard of thinking.) Though my family managed to end my contract within a mere five months of my death, as long as I loiter near the local country pub, I can use all the free Wi-Fi I like still. Sweet.

You might be wondering upon reading this how I can seem so detached (that's another little joke) about my horrible death and inexplicable headless continuation. But that's the thing: as much as I and people like me are portrayed as horrible scary monsters, it's really hard to manage to be more than wry after you've passed on.

I don't know if it's because death puts you on a higher plane or if it's simply because once you've woken up staring at the bloody stump of your own neck, it's really hard to maintain anger at lesser things. I'm not sure. But either way, I'm actually a lot more chill and relaxed these days than I ever was when I was alive. Customers taking half an hour to pay for items in exact small change used to inspire thoughts of murder in me. Now I have the irony of having the perfect temperament for supermarket work but a condition that means even Tesco wouldn't employ me.

This is why I'm sat squatting behind a beer garden, head under one arm and my phone awkwardly posed on a tree stump, trying to write this blog without knocking it off and cracking the screen even worse than it is already. Because the good (and bad, and generally indifferent) people out there need to know the truth: I'm not a monster.

This is important because, as I mentioned above, everyone I meet is terrified of me, and I seem to be stuck on these small windy country roads where people drive too fast, despite them being small and windy. They come damn close to killing any normal horse riders they see, so you can imagine how they react when they come across me whilst doing twenty miles over the speed limit just before a sharp corner. I've been headless for almost a year now, and I've been the cause of twenty accidents. That's despite getting drowsy if I try to go farther than ten miles away from where I died, and only feeling compelled to ride during the early hours. (Compelled by what, I don't know. I think it works like a pregnant woman's cravings. The rest of the time I lurk in fields feeling awkward as sheep stare at me.)

Not every accident has been lethal—hence all the "Headless Horseman" talk—but people have died, and died horribly. It's lucky for me that "Headless Car Driver" doesn't seem to be a thing, because otherwise I'd be knee deep in them by now, and that would result in some very awkward conversations.

And that might sound callous, but I remind you of the hard to be more than wry when in this state thing I mentioned earlier.

But seriously, I do care, despite my gallows humour. Horrible death isn't something that I'd wish on my worst enemy. Which previously would have been people that don't understand self-service checkouts but still insist on using them.

So let me implore those of you reading this who might be driving in the region of the Laughing Bat pub, if you see a horseman riding at night, just treat him as you would any other rider, regardless of whether he has a head or not.

Actually, on second thought, maybe treat him a little better than you would a normal rider, maybe like a human being. Slow down, give plenty of leeway (more so than usual—my peripheral vision isn't great), and be respectful of your fellow road user. Don't scream before shouting "IT'S A HEADLESS HORSEMAN!!!!" and swerving into a tree. It's not pretty, trust me. Brains and blood and guts just go everywhere. I usually wind up vomiting at the sight of it, and you can imagine what that's like. If you obey the Highway Code, I'll be more than happy to do the same.

Also, if you do see me, and aren't in a hurry, why not stop for a chat? It's a lonely life, there's only so much conversation you can have with a horse, and Johnny Depp and I have very little in common. I'm vaguely up to date with current events thanks to my phone, so let's have a debate about Donald Trump and how the Americans have gone crazy. Or we could watch videos of amusing cats. Anything really.

And of course, the important thing is, I am dead! I mean, you've got to be interested in talking to someone who can prove the existence of life after death right? Even if you can't look him in the eye easily. And even in my somewhat confused state, I think I can actually take a pretty good stab at which religion is actually right.

Yes, I thought that would grab your attention. Well, just between you and me, from the perspective of beyond the grave it's actually very obvious tha—

Editor's Note: The above text was found written on a smart phone with a smashed screen that was lost in the grass beside a tree stump outside the beer garden of the Laughing Bat public house. Though it did belong to the deceased Harry Cheshire, when passed on to the police, they considered it a hoax done in poor taste and place no credence in the "Headless Horseman" stories that have been run in the tabloid press.

There have been three more lethal car accidents in the area since this phone was discovered.

The horse's name was actually Spencer.

HARRY ARTHUR CHESHIRE (10th June 1987-15th April 2016), a much loved son and brother, was sadly killed in a tragic horse-riding accident this Friday. Harry had worked at Hoobrook Newsagents for five years and had achieved the role of shift manager. An active member of his local pub's darts team, he will be sorely missed by all who knew him. Spencer the Horse is to be buried with full honours by Yarwood Stables on the 24th of April. No flowers by request.

STUART WEBB has been an active member of *Transformers* fandom for over a decade, writing multiple comic reviews for tfarchive. com. Since 2012, he has been running the *Transformation* project at thesolarpool.weebly.com, where he looks at each issue of the British Transformers comic at a weekly rate. The first third of this titanic effort was collected in book form in 2015, with the second to follow by the end of 2016. Away from writing, he lives in Kidderminster, England, and is owned by a cat. The character of Harry Cheshire is named for his former high school.

SNAKE DANCE

An account by Epi,

AS PROVIDED BY JOHN A. MCCOLLEY

My name is Epi. I live in a jungle, but not the one you think, not the green one where I was born. Still, I can see why they call this crammed-together pile of concrete, metal, and sweat a jungle. The sounds are different, but still constant, the howls and hoots of beasts have a different timbre, but the beat, the rhythms... You humans haven't come as far as you pretend. We're all animals, predators and prey.

There's a lot of rot in the jungle, the dead pass and are consumed, destroyed, erased within days. Turnover, as you call it, is high. You treat each other the same way. If you come here looking for something, you may never leave. I haven't, but I am a hunter. The old prey is gone, but men are many. Your tenements shot up, flashed their colors, obliterating the homes nature arranged over eons. You humans are so certain of your right to take whatever you can lay your hands on, especially the males. In your arrogance, you become predictable.

A knock at the door. "Showtime." The single word impacts my body like the low rumble of thunder preceding the storm. We girls take last looks in the mirror, tilting feather headdresses into place, dabbing on makeup to complete our masks. The patrons here don't come for our faces, but the illusion must be unbroken.

We strut, one by one, then cram together onto the stage, spinning and undulating around metal poles, swaying to the music. Lights play over us, igniting flares of color on body glitter, the sheen of gaudy feathers, fans that are gradually discarded through the show, cast over salivating dullards in awe of skin.

The motion, the music carries me away, commanding my body while my mind slips back to the trees. I slither through the leaf litter, hunting, tasting the air for prey. A note of young mammal hangs in the air, a waft of capybara dances on my tongue, giving an edge to my appetite. The hunt begins in earnest.

"Epi!" A voice cuts through the fervor of the chase, shattering the memory-slash-daydream. I'm in a building, old, worn at the edges, filled with cigar smoke and sweat. The voice that called us to action rolls through me again. I turn. "Show's over, *gata*. You got a personal invitation. Room three."

Room three. I nod, only partly comprehending, as I'm still trying to pile my mind back into this tight skin, strange body of unnatural convolutions. Limbs. Ugh. So ungainly. By the time I make it off the empty stage, part the curtain and step into the narrow hallway leading to the private rooms, I'm mostly back. The majesty of the moment has fled, but not the hunger.

In a space that could be a closet, I try to grasp the moment again, but the tiny speakers in the corner sound tinny, empty. I can't smell my prey through the glass. I see him though, staring, eyes taking in my false skin, my curves, my hands sliding over all of it, reaching wide, inviting, undulating, hypnotizing. His hands slide over a much smaller area of his own body.

A mote, a whiff of hormones, sex is almost as good as fear for tracking. The hunger rises. I need more. My tongue flicks out, my true tongue, unfurled, forked, and free of the glamor that makes you see me as one of you. Something in the male's primitive brain, in full control now, catches the movement, and the chase is on. Panicked, he stands, zips, batters the door open from the inside, unable to understand the knob.

Like water, I pour through the cash slot. Sheets of colored paper fall like green, blue, red, and purple leaves to the floor. The door slams shut, but hangs a few inches open as I flick my tongue out over and over, relishing the tangle of scents. *Not here.* I have to remind myself. I turn to force my way back through the slot, though my blood churns to chase him now. A wallet. I nose it open. Rodolpho. I have a proper picture, a name, address. It wouldn't matter. I couldn't lose this trail if I wanted to. It's all I can do to go back to my side of the glass, a creature on exhibit. *Wait, Epi, wait. Tonight, then sleep for a week to digest. Just a few more hours.*

Forcing myself back into my less comfortable form, I let myself out of the booth into the cramped hallway behind and slip back to the dressing room. Or nearly. A wall of muscle and Aztec-styled tattoos barely covered by a white t-shirt blocks my way.

"*Dinheiro,*" he says simply, hand out. Our visitors pay as they go, part to go into the booth, the rest in one minute increments, or the show's over. The owner always gets his cut. He's a real animal. I reach deep for a disappointed expression to show the behemoth.

"What he left is on the floor of the booth. He was too excited to get it in the slot. Probably why he comes here instead of into a girl for real."

"Go get it."

I roll my eyes. No girl wants to go into that side of the booth. We all see what happens in there, and we know the cleaning crew, Carla, half-blind and arthritic. It doesn't bother me, but he can't know this. It might blow my cover, as they say on the television. "We're not allowed up there, you know. Too much danger of one of those horned-out weirdoes trying something. Get Carla to bring it to you."

"Carla's off tonight, sick. I'll walk you out there, so you don't get any trouble," Salazar rumbles like an oncoming storm. I slump my "shoulders" as though defeated, though I am so excited right now I have to keep thinking of my cover, my pass to this hunting ground. I could just hang outside and wait for these slobs to come out, follow them into the alley… but no, the old ways are too simple for this new world. I have to calm my blood and play the part. I can shed the mask in just another hour or two, find Rodolpho and then…

"*Esta noite*, Epi," Salazar says, pointing to the door to the front of the house. *Oops. Focus, girl, dinner is all but served. Let's not get tossed from the restaurant!* I walk toward the bright blue door hung with a sign telling the girls to stay away, "men only." Salazar reaches around, his bulging arm the size of most men's legs, and twists the knob, flinging the door open and catching it with thick fingers along the top edge just before it hits the pale yellow wall.

The hallway on the other side is covered in graffiti from years of operation, scratched, written with markers, pencils, even a crayon or two. They depict all kinds of sex acts, all in terribly childish drawing quality, and every curse word and bit of innuendo you can think of and more from thousands of hands.

We reach the door, still ajar, and Salazar tips his head to the side to indicate I should go in. I make a show of my disgust, contorting my features and turning away a bit, but he taps his foot, and I relent. The smell hits me right in the stomach. I flick my tongue out, just for a second, savoring, then struggle with all my will to focus.

Everything is as I'd left it two minutes ago, no surprise. I scoop up the bills from next to and atop the built-in bench seat and notice a thing that hadn't been there any of the last few hundred nights I've been doing this: a tiny black brick of plastic in the corner over the door.

"What the hell is that?" I ask aloud from reflex, too distracted by my hunger to rein in the question.

"Camera," Salazar said simply. "Boss gonna rake in some extra bills putting you girls' shows up on the Intertubes. One dance, one guy isn't bringing in enough, I guess."

Crap! Damn! This can't be happening! Hold it together, girl. "That show's not much to see. Guy didn't even last two minutes."

"Don't change nothin'. All you need is a couple minutes when you're not tryin' to impress anyone. It'll sell, I'm sure. You're a real eye-catcher."

"Uh, thanks. Here." I hand him the money and wait for him to turn around so we can vanish back into the better-kempt side of the wall, and I can start figuring out how to get into the office to erase the footage. *But what if he's already seen? When did those things go in? Are you crazy? You think you'd still be breathing if he'd seen what just happened in there? He'd have called someone, ratted you out for a few hundred real, and you'd be lying splayed out on a slab with half your organs in jars.*

Just calm down. Rodolpho can wait, but this can't. You've got to focus. Go to the office now. You haven't changed in the booths for a few months. There's no way he knows, unless he's watching right now. Head him off at the pass. I nod to myself and hang back as Salazar takes the cash to the office. *Maybe he'll open the door to give him the money, and I can talk my way in from there.*

The walking boulder of a man gets to the office and flips a little letterbox open, sliding the money in. *Damn. He is paranoid, cameras and a dead drop for the cash. I might be able to fit through, but that would defeat the purpose...* Salazar nods to me as he passes, going back to his post near the door to the front. *Of course!* I wait a minute, counting seconds until the bouncer is out of earshot. Unable to leave anything to chance now, I go to the corner and look down the hall. I see his foot sticking out past the next corner, where his stool stands.

Back at the office door, I close my eyes for a moment and summon a part of my magic I haven't used much since coming to the city. I think back over the last few minutes, locking on to the sound of Salazar's voice, the timbre, the resonant depth, the slightly nasal quality. I rap on the door. "Hey boss, we got an emergency out here. You'd better come." It takes a lot out of me, being tainted by this environment, all the concrete, the smoke. I relish the power of the living forest, miss it for a moment, before the boss steals focus back to the present.

"Told you," he grunts, "No disturbances. Handle it."

"Yeah, I know, boss, but they won't listen to me. It's uh…" *Damn, what was that tool's name? With the slicked back hair and that stupid cane? Ah!* "It's El General!" A crash from within, then the boss getting to his feet. I catch the sound of a zipper. Footsteps. I turn away, calling a smaller piece of magic, something based within myself, letting my color fade and twist to match the brown color of the floor tiles, then return to my natural form. Coiling as he fidgets with the door, I shoot past his feet when he exits and locks the door behind him. *I'll have to cross that bridge when I come to it.*

I shift to human form for ease of using the computer and searching. The room is dark. The computer's screen is blank. That seems like a good sign. I move the mouse, see what he'd been looking at before. Nothing happens. I hear the fan whirring. I know the thing is on. After a few seconds, I find the power button and push it. A tiny flare bursts into being at the center of the screen, then expands to show a beach scene peppered with rectangles with words beneath them.

I scan the desktop for a link or folder that looks like surveillance footage or a place for files to be sent to a website. I'm not very good with this technology. There's no call for it in the rainforest. Of course, the ants have their farming, and the tribes of humans hunt with darts and traps, but this, this is almost magic.

I click a few things here and there, finally realizing that one of the web browsers is open. I click on it and bring up a page that shows the front of this hole, at least what it looked like when it was opened, with no letters missing from the sign, no graffiti. It also has the name of the site. *I can use that.*

I hunt for the letters, sending them to the search bar one at a time. A whole list of folders and files roll up, including folders for each of the private rooms. I click on three. The dates run back to about a month ago. I breathe a sigh of relief. Today's was the only offense he could have caught. I go to the bottom file and click to open it just as a key slides into the office door lock.

I hit the monitor's power button, drop to the floor beneath the desk and resume my serpent form. I wait, watching the door open, light from the hallway cutting through the darkness. The light subsides quickly. Footsteps follow. "Idiot Salazar, 'I don't know what you mean, boss. I been sittin' out here waitin' for the girls' money, boss. Ain't seen El General in weeks, boss.' Was I imagining it?" He spits. "Ridiculous. It couldn't have been anyone else." He mutters to himself. The chair creaks as he sits back in it. The power button clicks and the tube charges again with an electric buzz.

"What the—" The boss stands again. I stiffen for a moment, then slide under the front of the desk. *There's nothing else I can do.* I resign to a risky course of action, an intrusive one that could come back to bite me later. On the far side of the desk, the boss leans forward, eyes wide as he watches the recording I was searching for. He holds his breath as he watches it again, clicking to stop it. He falls back into his chair, blowing out air as though deflating.

The low light cast by the screen is perfect for me to do what I must. I rise, hands together before me, sliding one way, then the other as my hips sway in the opposite direction. I hiss in the most ancient of languages, the primal energy of animals before thought, before reason. I dance, but there is more than seduction here, more than lust. That might have been enough, but I need him to be powerless. He is prey now.

I flow and swing, tapping more complicated rhythms than those we dance to on the stage. I can feel his attention, his mind blank, his fear turning to awe, openness into which I pour my own will.

"Stop the movie," I coo, sending the words to the deepest part of his psyche, where they will bubble back up. He hears them without voice, as his own thoughts. He leans forward, puts his hand on the mouse.

Click.

"Delete the file," I say as though asking him to hold me, to caress my skin.

Click.

"Is it gone?" He shivers. I can smell his excitement.

Head shake.

"Make it gone. You don't need that file for your website." *Why do you need pictures? I'm right here.*

Click... Click. Click.

"Is it gone?"

Nod.

I spin, once, twice, stopping facing away from him, swaying slowly, my flimsy skirt pulling tighter around my bottom, sliding down as I push up. "You will forget seeing me tonight. This dance was one of your fantasies."

Nod.

"You won't touch any of the girls anymore. I should be very jealous." Quick shake.

Moan.

"You'll paint the front hallway, fix the front, the sign. Respect your business. Cut the girls in on your website profits. I'll be going now. You won't ask where I've gone, and welcome me if I return." Slowly, slowly, I pull out from his mind, allow him to slide into a normal state of sleep. As he begins to snore, I let myself out. I've worked up quite an appetite tonight, and I've got to go find dinner.

EPI is a solitary survivor, a hunter adapting to a world changed around her by the machinations of greed. The jungle ebbs like a living tide leaving dead sand in its wake. She sees her prey as children building castles in the sand, unaware of the old world, her world. There is still magic here, and it is hers.

JOHN A. MCCOLLEY is a writer from New Hampshire turning out tales of steampunk, superheroes, paranormal, and science fiction while working on painting, found object, and recycled materials sculpture and raising his amazing son with his equally amazing wife and looks forward to doubly amazing twins this fall.

THE FACE ON THE WALL, AND THE CHAINSAW

An account by Green Man Project,
AS PROVIDED BY ERIN SNEATH

The Green Man project was a failure. The master alchemist said so, in front of his initiates, who visited him no longer after that. He broke his sacred circle, took his tools, and left me planted in the middle of the front garden. He plastered the stone Green Man face, the face that was meant for me, onto the side of the wall. He sold the house.

Homeowners came and went. Motorcars replaced carriages on the street out front. Men dug up the cobblestones and replaced them with asphalt. Most people ignored me. I didn't miss the attentions of the magically inclined. Watching was more entertaining, or so I believed, until Fay came into my life.

From her brief years as a tiny child digging around me for treasure, through her studying under the shade of my branches, she transformed into a beautiful human being. Unlike the others who lived at my house, she stayed for decades. She allowed me to keep a wild beehive. In return, I gave her lovers deep shadows to keep them from the neighbours' prying eyes. I kept the house cool in my shade in the summer, and in winter prevented the snow from piling up too high at her door.

Fay's accident happened beyond my line of sight. From that day, she stood no longer but moved with a whirring machine in the form of a chair. She never approached me again. Many of my roots poked up from the ground's surface, making the terrain too bumpy for her wheels. Still, it felt sometimes as though she were punishing me for something that a car did to her.

Her posture sloped forward over time. There was nothing I could do to help her. One day some people came in a van with flashing lights. They brought her outside in a bag and took her away.

Without Fay, I was only a tree, not a friend or protector to anyone. I would have preferred that I and the house and the whole garden rot rather than suffer new people to take her place. They came anyway.

The new people, a man and a woman, examined me when they moved in, just as they examined the front steps and the eavestroughs. They paid more attention to the stone face on the wall.

The woman, whose name was Scarlet, smiled. "When we have kids, we can make up all kinds of stories about that thing."

"You want to scare them?" said her mate.

"They'll love it."

My leaves warmed and fluttered.

Music rang from Scarlet's phone as she dug up surface rocks from the garden. She silenced the phone with the touch of a finger and went indoors. Her man, whose name was Clancy, picked up a long box and carried it over to me.

"Anything else you want from my parents' garage?" Scarlet said as she poked her head back out from the door. "Last chance before I throw stuff out."

He shook his head. "Tell them thanks for the chainsaw."

The word "chainsaw" made shivers run up my trunk. For the life of me, I couldn't remember why.

Scarlet said to Clancy, "Don't cut your hand off," after which her husband stuck out his tongue. She returned the gesture, and left in their car.

The object looked innocent enough. A metal slab, a silver chain, a boxy red motor on the other end. Clancy pulled a cord and the machine sprung to life with a buzzing, sputtering noise. He brought the slab, its chain dancing, to me.

Bark flew. Agony blinded me. I bled and wept sap. I screamed through vibrations in the ground. I struggled to break free, pulling my own roots out, feeling them tangle and snap against rocks. Which pain was worse, I could not tell, but before the chainsaw reached my core I launched myself forward, hitting Clancy on the head. We both fell. Night also fell as the sky filled with heavy rainclouds.

The stone face faded from the wall and became mine. Rage did to me what the alchemist community could not. I wore nothing save for wet leaves that stuck to my new human skin, which goose bumped in the chill of the air. I'd never had goose bumps before. I also had feet now. Toes. The glare from the streetlights stung. Damn Clancy and damn his chainsaw. I picked up one of the shovels he and Scarlet used for digging up rocks. The clouds opened and sent down a deluge.

By the time Clancy woke, I'd already buried his legs into the ground.

"Help!"

I watered the soil around him with a new cock, not that the ground needed more water than the downpour that hit us.

"Oh god! Who are you? What do you want?"

I watched as budding twigs grew from Clancy's arms. He pleaded with words that I could barely decipher under his sobs and the roar of the rain. I left him.

He had left the front door unlocked. I'd never been inside the house before. I explored rooms as leaves and twigs fell from my body onto the carpet. I could still hear Clancy's screams.

Good, I thought, now he knows how it feels.

Clancy's voice deepened and transformed into the creak of wood on wood. It was done. Maybe Clancy would enjoy the bees, and the morning sun on his leaves. If not, that would be his problem.

I caught my reflection through the glass. I looked human now, leaf-free except for a beard and the top of my head.

Scarlet returned in the morning. I didn't hear her from the upstairs bathroom, where I was figuring out shaving. Probably expecting me to be Clancy, she started speaking before she reached the bathroom door.

"Do you remember if we changed over our magazine subscriptions?"

I leapt for the shower to hide behind the curtain. Instead I slipped on a puddle of shower gel suds and razor-clipped flecks of green.

Scarlet recoiled when she saw me. Here I was, a great lumbering stranger in her home, naked save for the pink towel I'd found on the back of the door. She screamed. I tried to speak, to calm her down or apologize or both. No sounds came when I opened my mouth.

She grabbed an appliance, which I later learned was a hairdryer, out from the wall and hit me with it. The power switch flicked on. The machine roared, firing out a blast of painfully hot air. I'd seen wood burn, and though I was wood no longer, I panicked and fell into the far corner of the room, shaking. My heart raced, which was in itself a new and horrifying experience.

Scarlet's face softened. She switched the hairdryer off. I thought maybe she was done with me, but she flicked the screaming thing on again. I believe I may have whimpered. Scarlet turned it off again and unplugged it. Her cheeks flushed. Her breathing slowed. She tossed me a dressing gown. Clancy's, judging from the size.

"Who are you?"

If I could have spoken, I don't know how I would have replied.

My cheeks were wet. I was fairly certain I had already toweled them off after shaving.

Scarlet turned off the tap. "You're one of the Wet Bandits?"

The what?

"The Wet Bandits? Never mind. A break and enter thief who's never seen *Home Alone*. A break and enter thief who stops for a shave. Guessing you're a neighbour? A seriously weird neighbour who's afraid of hairdryers and needs to learn about boundaries? Joking. Not really."

She crouched down in front of me. "Did Clancy let you in?"

I pointed out the window, toward the tree that was once her husband.

"I don't know what kind of arrangement you had with the lady who used to live here," she said, "but you have to ask if you want to use our place for stuff. Where's your clothes?"

When I indicated that I had no answer to give, she grabbed the largest of Clancy's most well-worn tee-shirts and track pants. I put them on. They were small on me, comically so, judging by Scarlet's chuckle.

She walked me out. "If you see Clancy, tell him—"

I couldn't tell if she noticed that the tree in her yard was completely different. She may have done a double-take.

"Just point toward the house. Give him a stern look."

Scarlet made a joking frown. I was a city tree, used to watching and reading human faces. I cracked a smile without thinking.

I had no plan. I had no urge to replant myself, even if it meant giving the nice woman back her man. That could wait. I reveled in my new ability to stretch my legs and used them to explore.

The neighbourhood of antique brick and manicured hills rambled into a downtown of steel and glass that eventually flattened and spread out in long stretches of abandoned storefronts. Unlike the gardens of the hills where the house was, and the parks of downtown, there was nothing green there except the occasional clover and dandelion sprouting through potholes.

There were cars, of course. Cars changed the taste of the air from the time I first saw them, decades earlier. A car hurt my Fay. A tree remembers. I wandered into a parking lot and ran my fingers along their dirty metal surfaces. No, dirt was a good thing. This place was full of glass, the scorched ends of cigarettes, and used food containers.

I heard a man shout, "Think you can skip out on us now? Where's our money? Hey, I'm talking at you!"

The speaker, a wiry man, was not talking at me but at a young man, barely older than a boy, who tripped the wiry man's taller, brawnier friend and climbed into a boxy-looking vehicle. The brawny man thudded to the asphalt, landing awkwardly on his forearm.

The vehicle started rolling out of the lot. One more stupid car helping someone get away with some crime. I had to stop the thing, in memory of Fay.

I ran, building up speed, savouring my ability to run. I don't think the men saw me until it was too late. I leapt onto the hood of the car. It screeched to a halt. I made a fist from the hand on the arm that used to be my strongest branch and slammed it onto the windshield.

The boy scrambled out and pulled out his wallet, passing it with shaky hands to the wiry man and the brawny man. "Here. And my watch. I can get the rest tonight, I swear."

The wiry man took the watch and let the boy escape on foot, then he turned to me.

"That took some balls, son. What do you want?"

What did I want? To kill cars, maybe. Other than that, I didn't know.

The wiry one squeezed my arm and pulled out a shard of glass. I flinched.

He said, "You're a big one, aren't you? A regular giant. We could use someone like you."

The brawny man took him aside. "What are you doing? We don't know who this asshole's with. He could rip my arm off. My arm."

"Exactly," said the wiry one, smirking at his friend as he reached into his bag and fished out a package of what I learned later were pepperoni sticks. He handed one to me. "Have some. Good. Nom nom nom?"

I sniffed the thing. The experience was unlike anything I had known, like chewing the smoke from a neighbour's barbeque. I'd always hated the smell of barbeques. Now it made me salivate. I'd never salivated before. I devoured the whole stick in one bite. Meat and salt. I needed this.

"You're hungry? We've got more," said the wiry man.

I wasn't stupid. These were probably bad men. They'd taken from the boy, not the car, but they did give me meat. As they left the scene, the men whistled like one of the families across the street used to whistle to their dog. The wiry one waved another pepperoni stick at me. I followed, closely.

I heard the brawny man whisper, "You're mental," to which his friend replied, "You're bleeding."

I learned that the wiry man was called Sammy and the brawny one was Slip. They took me to a place that served fried breaded chicken in paper buckets, which we took to Slip's house. The basement felt soothing to my legs. My legs belonged underground.

Slip and Sammy's friends were there and they drank sweet drinks and liquors. I had never watched television before. It was mesmerizing. Sammy passed me every piece of chicken, one at a time, as I watched and ate. Soon there was nothing left but greasy breadcrumbs on the clothes that Scarlet had lent me.

To pay Sammy back, I had to hit someone else who owed him. We found the man. I hit him. He gave Sammy and Slip a stack of paper money. Sammy gave me a pepperoni stick and had me beat another person, and then another.

One night, they rewarded me with hamburger. I took the patty out first and stuffed it in my mouth. Sadly, it meant there was no more patty, but I consoled myself by eating the toppings next, and finally the bun.

This game went on for days, perhaps weeks. Counting small increments of time was new to me.

One afternoon, Sammy had me beat a heavily perfumed man in a suit, who proved to be in better shape than the others. The suit man bruised me and I scraped my knuckles when I swung and missed my target a couple of times. Ultimately, the suit man's clothing impeded his ability to defend himself. He fell. Sammy and Slip got their money. I got a whole pizza.

My knuckles bled dark sap through bandages while I ate. I wanted to quit this work and find another way to get meat. I wanted to see Scarlet. I had taken her man from her and given nothing in return. She wasn't the one with the chainsaw. Her Clancy might have even been ignorant rather than malicious, not that it made the result hurt any less.

I didn't finish my pizza. I gave the rest to Slip and left before Sammy could convince me otherwise.

I made the long walk back through the city to my garden at the house. It was easy to find. The soil called to me. The house was silent. I saw Scarlet through the kitchen window, sleeping with her head on the table.

She woke with a start when I knocked on the glass. She looked disappointed to see me. I wasn't Clancy.

She let me in, and brushed past me on the way to the living room. Contact with her skin gave me a chill down my lower back and my head became like warm, vapourous water. For a moment I forgot the pain on my scraped-up knuckles. She certainly didn't seem to notice them.

She paced the room. "People keep covering up my missing

THE FACE ON THE WALL, AND THE CHAINSAW 137

person posters. They're all rain damaged anyway. The police still can't find him. They asked me if he could have run away. Run away? He was excited about moving here! He had plans! We were going to—"

I don't know why, but I put a hand on her shoulder. She put her arms around me and sobbed. Nothing in over a century of life prepared me for such a human moment.

Once she had calmed, she examined my bandages. If she noticed the discoloured stickiness of my blood, she gave no indication.

After a time, I found myself hungry again and wandered back to Slip's house. He and Sammy brought me into the suburbs. They gave me leather gloves to protect me.

My target was a man with long hair and a tee-shirt with words printed on the front.

I couldn't read it, but Sammy did. "'Just Shy, Not Antisocial. You Can Talk To Me.' Really? Can I talk to you? About the money you fucking owe me? It's too late."

When I hit him, the tee-shirt man made a crunch noise. He gurgled.

Sammy cried, "Yeah!" I turned to see him water a pine sapling with a can of liquid that smelled like cars. Then he pulled a tiny stick out of his pocket and scratched it until there was a small, wobbly flame on the top.

Sammy said to teeshirt Man, "This is gonna be you."

He flicked the match onto the wet sapling. With a whoosh, it lit up brighter than the streetlamps, casting confusing shadows everywhere. It took a moment for the facts to sink into my head: Sammy was burning a baby tree alive, to make a point.

I should have known better. I should have refused that first pepperoni, however long ago that was, or at least the bucket of chicken.

The sapling couldn't fight back. I dropped to my knees and threw dirt onto the fire. If I could have screamed I would have. The horror of it all, and I had taken part.

Sammy said, "The hell's wrong with you?"

I rose and chased Sammy around the yard. I didn't mean to hit the tee-shirt man a second time. Sammy used him as a shield, and I didn't react in time to stop my arm. Tee-shirt man's neck came to rest at an impossible angle and stayed there.

Sammy dropped him and slapped the back of my hand. "That was stupid. You strong, me smart, remember? You act on your own and what does it get us? A dead body."

My eyes prickled and water blurred my vision. It was an accident. I didn't mean—

We both jumped when a moan escaped tee-shirt man's mouth.

His voice squeaked and cracked, barely human. "I can't. My hands. Where?"

"You stupid sack of shit," Sammy said to me. "Look what you did, asshole! Now he'll have to go to the hospital. They'll get the cops and he'll tell everything. It would be better if you did kill him."

Sammy grabbed a heavy stone from the garden and hit tee-shirt man's temple. The body was no longer a person. The sapling would never become a fully-grown tree.

I bolted.

Sammy called after me, "Did I say you could leave after what you made me do? We're gonna find you! Gonna break you 'til you're normal size, you fuck!"

Scarlet sounded annoyed when she opened the door. "It's late." Then she looked me over. "What happened? I know you can't answer. Sorry," she said. "Come in."

I hurried indoors, sunk to the floor, and hid my head between my knees. It was wrong, all wrong, and I had no voice to tell her any of it.

She said, "I'll make us some tea."

I shuffled into the kitchen, following the sound of bubbles. Scarlet poured steaming water into two cups, each holding a bag of herbs. I liked the smell of this tea. It reminded me of Fay, who sometimes drank from cups like these under the shade of my branches.

"Careful, it's hot." Scarlet handed me one of the cups. "Five months. The cops say I should get used to the idea that he's probably gone forever. Clancy, I mean. Sugar?"

I poured the white grains into my cup until Scarlet raised an eyebrow. Too much?

We stood for a while, silent, inhaling tea vapours and listening to the outside traffic. She helped me wash my hands, then spread some ointment on my wounds.

I'd gone back to the house to feel safe, failing to take her problems into consideration. Here she was, alone with no friends nearby, where her husband's things were probably a constant reminder that he was gone, that he was (to her knowledge) dead, and that there was nothing more she could do. Her loneliness might have been the only real reason she invited me in, the neighbourhood's weird giant mute. The thought hurt almost as much as the knowledge that it was all my fault.

"We could watch a movie," said Scarlet. "Take our minds off everything. I finally unpacked mine. My movies. Not my mind."

By the time we got to the couch, Scarlet's face was twisted up and red and wet. Picking up the remote, she said, "I think you'll like this one."

In a moment of impulse that I barely understood, I leaned over and wiped the tears from her face. She took my hand and held it.

Quietly, we did something I had seen Fay do with one of her men. The act somehow reminded me of the beehive I once kept high up on my trunk, whose occupants tickled the nectar from my blossoms. Unlike the randomness of bees, this was deliberate. We meant it. And unlike with Fay and her man, there were no smiles and giggles, only a shared aching desperation.

We heard a car pulling up outside. Probably a neighbour, I thought, until Sammy's voice shattered whatever fleeting comfort I had.

"Hey big guy! You didn't think I had people around here? That I wouldn't find you?"

We tumbled from the couch, wearing the same blanket and only that.

Scarlet whispered, "Who's that?"

I took her hand and ran around the room, opening every box and cupboard and drawer.

"What are you looking for?" she said.

I heard a window break. No time to lose. I ran to the front hall closet, searched through it, and pulled out the chainsaw.

"Whatever you're doing, stop," she said. "I've already called the cops."

She pointed to the screen on her phone, which was lit and covered with letters and shapes that meant nothing to me.

Sammy's voice called out, "It's either you or your girlfriend, big guy."

I kissed Scarlet and marched out the door, a giant naked man holding a chainsaw.

"No! Don't!" She raced out after me.

The moon was full and bright. I revved the chainsaw the way Clancy did, letting the sound trigger a cold sweat all over my body. I must have caught Sammy and Slip and the others off guard, because they backed away from the house.

Sammy said, "You don't want to do that, big guy. It's not the fastest way to kill, it's messy, and the whole neighbourhood can hear you."

I revved the chainsaw again. It sputtered.

Scarlet stepped out from the shadows. "Please. Please stop. For me?"

I had trouble breathing, needing air faster and faster. This machine had caused so much pain, not just to me but to her and Clancy and all of the poor souls who owed Sammy money, and their families, and the pine sapling. I had hurt everyone in my temporarily human existence.

Sammy and his people stepped farther back, some of them running away.

I nodded to Scarlet (I may never nod again), then I marched toward the remaining gang members. They scattered. Good. They were not my real target.

Police sirens interrupted me before I could do what needed to be done. The officers caught Slip, then Sammy and a few of the others while I hid in the house. I overheard Scarlet making her official statement. She didn't mention me.

I brought the chainsaw back outside at dawn. It grieved me to let her sleep when all I wanted was to tell her what I am, to apologize, to say goodbye. Without a voice, it was an impossible wish, though probably for the best. A goodbye might have choked in my throat and turned into kisses instead, if she still wanted them.

Scarlet ran outside while I felled the tree. It crashed down onto the grass, its branches blocking our view of one another.

"This couldn't have waited 'til breakfast or, I don't know, never?"

She walked around to where I had been standing but my human form was gone. The stone Green Man face reappeared on the wall. Did she notice? Did she wonder how it came back and why it now wore a smile?

Clancy climbed out of the wreckage, some bark and leaves still stuck to him. They held each other for a long time. I believe they cried.

The next summer was a busy one. While I never learned whether Clancy ever explained where he had been, he stayed by her side for good. Scarlet had a child, who was healthy, normal-looking, loud and full of laughter. Baby Vernon slept and played in his carrier while the new parents built their garden around me, incorporating the rocks and roots already present on the grounds, rather than digging them out.

I heard Scarlet tell stories to her little son. For what little he might have understood, he seemed to listen.

"... and then he made a great scary noise with the magic saw and the goblins ran off, never to be seen again. That's why it's on the house."

Vernon had another stray leaf on his head, an unseasonable springtime bud. Scarlet reached down and tried to brush it off, but the leaf was attached, as if growing on him. I couldn't tell, but hoped that Scarlet understood.

The Green Child laughed.

GREEN MAN PROJECT sprouted and grew up in front of a two hundred-year-old red brick house in the neighbourhood of Rosedale in Toronto. The alchemist known to us only as Hyacinthos, and his followers, all excommunicated from the Alchemy Guild in 1856, planted Green Man Project as part of an experiment, the details of which are lost to us. Mr. Project writes to us via symbols he grows onto his leaves, which the girls of the Weird Sisters Club at Scrimmage Finishing School collect every autumn.

ERIN SNEATH grew up on a lake in rural Ontario. She studied film at Ryerson University, and dabbled in animation before her love of screenwriting took over. She has been a freelance video editor, a barista, a luggage salesperson, and a nanny. She once sang on tour in northern Europe with her choir. Now she lives in Calgary, Alberta, where she still writes screenplays but also horror novels and short stories. You may find her in summer tent camping with her wonderfully supportive husband, friends, acquaintances, and musical instruments in the middle of a prairie ghost town.

TESTING THE WATER

An account by Shizuka Maki,
AS PROVIDED BY SEAN FROST

I ate at the tiny snack bar while scanning the bowling alley for large groups. The nachos were bland, but the oily cheese satisfied my craving. Balls thundered down lanes, sometimes ending in triumphant crashes, sometimes in embarrassing drops. Most of the customers were couples. A party of teens shouted and laughed across several lanes. They were too ordinary to be my quarry.

Over by the far left wall, a group of five took turns at the pins. They were an odd collection of players. One had a long black beard and wore vintage clothing. There was a massive man covered in denim and wild hair. A lanky guy who had poor motor control concealed his head with a hood, sunglasses, and allergy mask. A muscular blonde sat in a wheelchair, his legs wrapped in a blanket. Last was a jovial man in a track suit. This was the Campus Creature Crew, I was sure of it.

If I was going to approach them, I'd have to do so before I lost my nerve. I licked the cheese off of my fingers as I considered. They were all male, all European. Yet I had more in common with them than I'd had with the girls I'd grown up with. At least, I might.

I got up and threw the plastic tray into a recycling bin.

The ball smashed into pins, knocking down all but two. I turned back to retrieve the ball for my second throw and saw Jim grinning. A Bettie Page shirt peeked at me from under his open jacket.

"You've bowled before," he said.

I nodded and waited for my ball to return.

"I didn't know you could bowl in Japan."

I didn't know how to respond to that, so I just smiled and looked to the others. Mike had gone to the bathroom, and the others were talking to each other. Jim marked my score. The return thumped and my ball rolled out. I began to wish I'd just gone home. The crew had let me join them, but they hadn't been welcoming. I wondered if I should tell them what I was.

Humans have a particular scent, temperature, and vocal range, among other typical characteristics. While many other creatures may appear human, it's simple enough for us to tell the difference, particularly for those with enhanced senses. Jim—who, based on his own jokes, was likely a werewolf—had quickly verified that I was a monster. I hadn't always been one, though. Unless I was asleep, I could easily pass unnoticed. That might have been making them uneasy.

I'm not dead, like Barry clearly was by his stiffness and leathery skin. Mike's size and thick body hair marked him as some manner of ape man. With his air of superiority and the long white fangs visible under his well-groomed mustache, Ethan might have been a vampire. I'd seen people in wheelchairs cover their legs with blankets before, but Al's lower body was completely shrouded, concealing something that looked too solid and slender to be a pair of legs. Out of them all, only Jim appeared as "normal" as I did, and he still had that star on his palm. Not that he bothered to cover it.

Me, I had no visible sign of my difference. Not even stretch marks. Until I fell asleep, they'd be wondering if I was really one of them, and I wasn't going to be doing that in front of them. Telling them might not even help. How many Westerners knew about *rokurokubi*? Maybe one of these boys had watched enough *anime* to have seen one, but would he even remember? We don't tend to get a lot of screen time, and we're not exactly as memorable as *karakasa kozō*. I mean, once you see an umbrella with a big eye and a lolling tongue, it sticks in your mind. Apart from Jim's self-conscious dog jokes, no one was talking about their true natures, so I couldn't be sure if there was some rule against it.

Which left me no option but to bowl and pretend I didn't notice how much I stood apart from them. My second ball knocked down the two remaining pins, picking up the spare.

"Next time we bowl, you're on my team," Jim declared.

"If there is a next time," Ethan said.

I guessed that there wouldn't be a next time.

The cold reached through my tights and picked at my skin. I started jogging in place to keep my blood moving. Al looked up at me.

"Not used to the cold?"

"Not like this," I told him. "It's only November!"

"Welcome to Michigan."

It didn't help that it was night, or that Mike and Jim were taking so long with the lock. A few weeks after the bowling trip, the crew had made plans to go explore an abandoned hotel. Enough time had passed that my need for a social outlet outweighed my memories of how awkward the last event had been, and they didn't appear to be holding anything against me. So here I was, in a skirt and light jacket, already second-guessing my decision to come.

Ethan wandered over from his post overseeing the break-in. He grinned smugly.

"It won't be long now, Susie. I give it another minute before they give up and just pull the chain links apart. Then we can discover whether the premises are actually haunted."

Ethan didn't seem to care whether I was okay with his nickname for me. The others liked him, so I kept quiet about finding him unpleasant. In my head I called him *Iie-tan*, and I smiled. None of them would likely realize that it essentially meant "nope," but I felt better having a private pun for his name.

"Why didn't they just break it to start with?" I asked him. "A security guard could find us while they try to unlock the chain."

Al coughed purposefully, and Ethan assumed his lecture stance—feet planted firmly, hands clasped behind his back, standing straight, and looking somewhere above us all.

"When I made inquiries about this building to prepare for our tour, I learned that the bank stopped paying for security patrols six years ago. A guy comes around once a month in the summer, to mow and perform other light chores. Other than that, it's completely unmonitored."

Mike's grunt was almost loud enough to cover the sudden snap and rattle of the chain. Ethan grinned triumphantly and made a sweeping bow.

"Shall we?" he asked.

Wordlessly, I walked over to the gate.

Inside the hotel, it didn't feel as cold. Maybe I'd just gotten used to it, but it felt like the edge had been knocked down. Al and I had made our way to the manager's office, which was covered in graffiti, beer cans, and cigarette butts. The rest had gone upstairs to look for the ghost, but Al's wheelchair couldn't go up the stairs. With all of his advance preparation, Ethan had managed to overlook that obstacle. Mike had volunteered to carry him, but Al'd told him to go have fun stomping around.

I doubted that there was actually a ghost in the building. If there were one, I didn't want to meet it. Monsters are people, more or less. We can be good, or we can be bad, but we have personalities that are the same as those of humans. Spirits, though—they can be single-minded, often in their pursuit of causing misery. I avoided them, not believing myself to be exempt from their wrath. It hadn't been a difficult decision to stay down here with Al.

"Hey, Suzuka," Al said. I laughed at his pronunciation, and he shook his head. "I screwed that up again. Sorry."

"Shizuka," I said.

He repeated my name, coming closer but still with strange inflection. I considered, then nodded. I was becoming accustomed to hearing past the American accent.

"Anyway, Shizuka, I was going to say that you still look cold."

I stopped wandering around the office and studied him. Al sat contentedly in his chair, wearing a light jacket half-zipped over a t-shirt. His arms lay casually on the armrests. Yet he also looked uncomfortable, unable to meet my gaze and working his jaw behind twisting lips.

"It gets pretty cold in the Atlantic," he mumbled, by way of explanation. Then, more audibly but still without eye contact, he offered his blanket. "You need it more than I do."

He was embarrassed, I thought, because of whatever the blanket was hiding, but I couldn't pretend I wouldn't be grateful for it. I walked over to him.

"Thank you, Al."

He smiled briefly and lifted an edge of the blanket to hand it to me. I took it and kept my eyes on his face while I pulled, trying not to look at what he'd been hiding. I couldn't resist though. I had to know what he'd been covering.

"Fish!" I cried, immediately feeling bad for doing it. "You're a fish man!"

Al crossed his arms and frowned.

"We prefer merfolk," he said.

I quickly turned my head away from his scaled body and clutched the blanket to my chest.

"I'm sorry. I was surprised." It was a terrible excuse, but it was true. I had so many questions. I'd never met any merfolk before. They were rumored to be vicious. Yet I'd already been rude, so I kept quiet.

"Forget it," he said. "I've been called worse."

I wrapped the blanket around myself and sat beside him, leaning against a wheel. That way I wouldn't have to avoid staring. We sat silently for a few minutes, before he asked if I swam.

"I do, a little," I admitted. "I know how to float, so I don't drown at least."

"I was just thinking. It's my turn to choose what the club does next. A lot of our meetups involve tromping around places that my chair doesn't easily go, so I'm thinking of renting a pool."

I thought about that. Now that I'd stopped moving, I was feeling sleepy. Sleepy was bad. I didn't want it. I needed to keep Al talking so I could stay alert.

"What about Barry?" I asked. "He's a zombie, right? Should he get wet?"

"I don't know. I'm not even sure if he'd float or sink."

I smiled, although I wasn't sure if he was joking. My eyes closed, and I forced them open.

"Well, we need to find out," I mumbled.

"Yup," he agreed. If he said more I missed it, because I'd fallen asleep.

I awoke with my head drooping, which always happens when I fall asleep sitting up. My face was pressed into Al's blanket. It didn't smell fishy, as I'd expected it would. There was a certain dustiness to it—it hadn't been washed recently—but it had a good smell, a lived-in smell. A man smell.

"Albert," I said. I raised my head and kept raising it, my neck extending smoothly. I turned my head to face him. His eyes were closed, but he was awake. He made a questioning noise, a grunt really. I lifted my mouth to his ear, suppressing a laugh. "Do you like eels, Albert?"

He jolted and turned to my voice, his eyes filled with surprise. Then he frowned at my wide grin, but only for a moment. His eyes traced the long slope of my neck down to my body, still slumped on the ground beside him.

"How are you doing that?"

"It's just what happens when I sleep. It's kind of a curse."

"Who cursed you?"

I looked around the room. Albert was being dull. I needed to be amused.

"Nobody. Papa killed Mama, so now I'm a *rokurokubi*."

I could sense the others upstairs, a gift of my monster form. They appeared to be coming down. I doubted that it was because they felt guilty over leaving us behind. They could use some attitude readjustment.

"Shizuka, that's horrible! I had no—!"

"Forget it. There are people to scare."

I shot out of the room, leaving my body beside Al. I hadn't had room to really stretch my neck since coming to school, and it felt good to fly all out. The boys were coming down the south stairwell. I went up the east and raced across the second floor. Some of the doors had been broken open, but I wasn't here to explore.

The door to the south stairs was intact and closed. I hugged the ceiling and hung down beside the door, listening for the footsteps to come close enough. They came down, talking and laughing. I put my plan into action, swinging my head into the door to make a steady knock.

The voices grew stronger *thud* and the laughter louder *thud* as they approached *thud* then they were at the door *thud* and were about to pass *thud* when one of them stopped *thud* and asked the others *thud* if they'd heard something *thud*.

They listened, murmured, laughed at each other's nervousness. Then, because it had to be him, Ethan opened the door. My head swung out at them as I let out a long moan. For a few glorious moments, I saw them running in place and screaming, then Mike's giant hairy fist knocked me out. At least the last thing I heard was his surprised wail.

I came up for air, my eyes stinging from the chlorine. Barry remained sitting on the pool's bottom, where he seemed quite contented. I wished I'd taken Al's wager that he'd float. There was a splash as Jim did another cannonball from the diving board. I gave him a quick cheer when he surfaced, and he grinned as he swam for the edge to have another jump.

I headed for the ladder in the shallow end. Mike and Ethan were being good sports about sitting poolside, so I thought I should reward them with a social visit. Mike said his body hair reacted badly to chlorine, but I think he just felt foolish in a pair of swim trunks. Ethan hadn't even bothered with an excuse, but he wasn't complaining so I counted that as a victory for manners.

I climbed out and looked back into the pool. Al was happily doing flips in the deep end. It was nice to see him in his element.

I'd have to think of what to have us all do for my turn. I couldn't do anything themed to my curse—a slumber party with five guys was out of the question—but there had to be something we could all enjoy together. Maybe a night of ghost stories. Or board games. I'd figure something out. After all, we're all monsters in the Campus Creature Crew. We're more alike than not.

SHIZUKA MAKI is pursuing an undergraduate degree in microbiology at Wayne State University in Detroit, Michigan. Her current plan is to return to Japan for advanced studies. She is currently looking for a roommate who is not averse to suffering pranks in the middle of the night.

SEAN FROST is a software developer in Michigan, who writes comics and stories while watching horror and science fiction movies. He lives with four demanding cats and a very understanding wife. It is entirely likely that he has a few too many hobbies.

OLD COUNTRY WOLF

An account by Kico Farvak,
AS PROVIDED BY JENNIFER R. POVEY

Honestly, I might have cared about the view if I hadn't had only one thing on my mind at that point.

Solid ground under my paws.

Well, feet. There had been no privacy on the voyage, no way to sneak off and change, and it didn't look like it would be much better once we got ashore.

I tried to appreciate the view, I really did. A bronze statue of a woman holding a torch high, supposedly to welcome us. Or guard liberty. Or something. It was beautiful, but I wanted to see it from a platform that wasn't moving. And I wanted to find some place to run. The city beyond didn't look much like London. This city was reaching toward the sky, tall brick buildings, and the like.

They didn't let me off at the harbor. Or anyone else in steerage. But I got solid ground for a moment.

It moved.

I shook my head no. I'd been warned that after a long time at sea, the solid ground would appear to move for a bit, and that was why sailors walked oddly. The scents of unwashed humanity and sea salt were now mingled with city scents of horse and manure, and I thought I caught the distinct smell of a tanner.

No, they put us onto a ferry. To an island with an intimidating brick building on it.

Human bureaucracy. I needed my cousins, I needed pack around me. I needed fur around me.

But all I could do was, as so often now, pretend to be one of them. Let the sea of them carry me across the gangplanks, onto the ferry. Stuck in amongst them while we crossed the harbor, and then onto land again. For real, this time.

Lines of people snaked under a wooden canopy and then into a hall that smelled even more of unwashed humanity—a scent I'd grown so used to that I'd learned to ignore it, but now it seemed to wash over me more. Wait. Wait.

A man approached me. "Name?"

"Kico Farvak," I stated, studying him. He looked to be barely twenty. I managed to keep one hand in my pocket.

The other was visible, and I caught his sidelong glance, then the shake of his head as he dismissed old country superstition.

Old country reality.

"You need to come with me." His Slovak was good, fluent even. He rounded up some of the other Slovaks and hustled us into a room with a doctor.

A doctor. But he wasn't a Slovak doctor. He studied my hands, but made no comment about the unusual finger length. Our ring finger is longer than our middle. In the Old Country, this marked us. Let them discriminate against us. Except the Roma, who never minded us. Probably because the settled folk hated them too.

Then I was quizzed for all of two minutes by another man, before I was through. They didn't know what I was. Which was a good thing. Some people think we're a disease, we're contagious. They don't understand. It takes a lot to turn somebody into one of us. We only do it for people we really care about.

My journey wasn't over. But this part had been the most worrying.

I could handle more time on a train.

Twenty-four hours on a train. And my money had made a pitifully small pile when transformed into American dollars, so there was no way it was in a sleeper car. Taking time to run first? Not possible in New York, and I hadn't wanted to risk wandering outside it. Maybe Minneapolis would be better.

Polis. That was kind of pretentious for what was apparently a mill town. That was what cousin Stevek called it. A mill town. Cousin Stevek, though, was prone to understatement. I knew that, so I decided to reserve judgment on whether this mill town deserved the Greek word for city in its name until I got there.

I did manage to sleep on the train seat; it wasn't comfortable, but I managed it. And the train pulled into Minneapolis at about breakfast time.

Mill town? It was no London, and I shuddered at the thought of that city's seven million people, but I was sure it dwarfed Bratislava, which had always been my view of a city. Was this really Stevek's mill town? I strained my ears to understand the English spoken around me. I didn't realize then that Minneapolis was the largest flour milling town on the planet, or that it had reached its peak... well, none of us knew that.

I did know the place smelled of flour. I shouldered my luggage and looked around. And there he was.

We could always find each other. It went beyond scent, it was that sense of pack, of belonging, and I made a beeline for him. We hugged and slapped each other's back as one does when long separated.

"You finally made it."

"I did. I am not going back."

Stevek laughed. "Even if you change your mind?"

"I'm not getting on that ship again," I declared. It was a declaration I feared I would regret, though. His scent was not quite as I'd remembered it. No. There was female mixed with it. "Who is she?"

"Her name's Anna. You'll meet her." He grinned.

I relaxed. Of course his scent was different. He'd got married, and when you have a pairbond, your scent changes to be closer to your partner's over time. Humans don't notice it. We do.

He helped me take my luggage over to a cart drawn by a bored looking mule. Mules tend to be less bothered by our scent than horses, although horses can be trained to deal with us easily enough.

The animal flicked an ear toward me in comment that I was vaguely interesting, but not actually worth checking out. I hopped onto the bench next to Stevek.

The pack's home was on mud flats by the river and, Stevek mentioned, flooded like clockwork every spring. It was poor, this place, it was cheap clapboard housing.

We don't like money. Except when we wish we had it, but I suppose that's a lot of people. Point is, we didn't have money. That fact didn't bother me at all, that was normal for us.

What did bother me right off was that as I approached I heard English. Maybe they were practicing, and I certainly needed to.

Anna was a round woman with reddish hair. From her scent? From her scent she had only recently become one of us. As I said, we only give our gifts to those we really care about. That sometimes includes romantic partners. Often. Really, a marriage between one of us and a normal seldom works well unless we change them. We don't have enough in common.

She did not offer me a hug, but gave me an assessing look. My stomach was rumbling. Ship food followed by train food, and all of it human food. We need more protein and fewer carbohydrates than humans, to fuel the beast.

I smelled a very good meat stew, and I followed Anna inside. She ladled me a bowl, then one for herself, then sat down. "Welcome to America."

"Why are you speaking English?"

She shrugged. "I barely speak Slovak."

"So... You're second generation?"

"Of course."

But first generation in another way. And the stew, while good, did not taste like what my mother would have made.

"Stevek will help you find a job in the mills."

"I don't need a job at the mills. I need to run."

She smiled, and I saw the wolf behind it. "You'll need a job in the mills at some point. A run... I suppose." The wolf was there, but it was reluctant. Overly controlled. I wondered about her. Had she accepted the gift only out of love for her husband? A bad idea, that. You had to want it, had to love it.

But a run? I needed it. I had to find some place where I could run. I could not, would not, act like a human, working in the mill. I dared not go alone, though. Here, there were still wolves. Which meant some idiot might shoot at me, and although we don't take permanent damage from normal bullets, they still hurt. Yeah, the silver part's true. We aren't immortal or anything like that. We just heal. We just heal very well. Unless you use silver.

Sometimes boys annoy livestock. I learned fast not to do that. It just makes people hate us.

Or shoot our innocent beast-cousins.

Stevek got me a job at the mill. Six days a week. Six long days a week pretending to be human, speaking English. Never speaking Slovak, never speaking our own language.

They didn't even run. They didn't hunt. They barely changed. Every time I asked, so many times I got, "Oh, we don't do that any more."

They introduced me to something called a hamburger, which was good, but they didn't use the same herbs in the goulash.

I knew some of it was that they didn't grow here, but that wasn't why they didn't speak Slovak.

Because Anna refused to learn, and Anna refused to be anything but… who she was. The rest of the pack? They were American.

I realized that quickly. More than that, they were domesticated. They were mill workers and mill workers' wives. They sent the cubs to human school. The land was beautiful, a land of lakes and rivers. I discovered that Minne meant water in the language of the people who had been here before. Maybe those people had the connection to the land I felt I'd left behind in the Old Country.

That was it. No connection to the land. None of them felt it. They were turning into dogs, like the bitch I had met in London, who dressed like a high society lady and kept pets.

Dogs.

Domesticated. I couldn't stand it, I couldn't handle it. And it was bound to come to a head.

"Stevek. You've let Anna lead you into forgetting everything we are."

"This is who we are now. We're building a great city, a great country."

"Off the backs of people who have disappeared. Off the backs of people treated the same way those who remember treat us."

He laughed. "None of them recognize us. They don't know the signs. They don't wear silver jewelry because they think the scent of it will ward us off, will keep us away. They don't put it on their daughters... or even their sons... so we can't seduce them."

I opened my mouth, but he wasn't done.

"We can be treated as human beings here. We don't have to be—"

"We. Are. Not. Human." And I turned and stormed out. He was right. There was something seductive about passing. About people not suspecting me, about not having to worry that a mob with silver would come after me because they thought what we were was sexually transmitted and that I'd slept with somebody's daughter. Or somebody's son. I wasn't always too worried, if they were attractive and willing. It's not transmitted that easily.

I changed as soon as I was out of the city, ran along the river flats. We didn't need the city. We didn't need jobs in the mill, we didn't need to brush our fur and turn into lap dogs.

We certainly didn't need to pass as human.

No.

The only way I wanted to be treated as equal to a human was in recognition of what I was.

I'd lost my pack. I knew that in that moment. I'd come all the way here to find a new pack, and I'd lost them, but I still had fur around me.

With fur around me, I pointed my nose west, and I ran. In the wilderness, I might find wild men and wild women who would, if not accepting me—for nobody would—accept the wildness within me. Who would not turn me into a lap dog. Who would not accept the change only to tame others.

I ran. I ran for joy of running. I scented beast-cousins on the wind. One day this place would be tamed. I sensed that.

For now?

It would hold some place, some corner, for an old country wolf.

KICO FARVAK was a Slovak immigrant who passed through Ellis Island and joined the Slovak immigrant community in Bohemian Flats for a better life—or at least what he thought would be a better life. The fact that he also happened to be a werewolf very much in need of the support of a pack was unknown to the immigration authorities at the time.

JENNIFER R. POVEY is in her early forties, and lives in Northern Virginia with her husband. She writes a variety of speculative fiction, whilst following current affairs and occasionally indulging in horse riding and role playing games. She has sold fiction to a number of markets including *Analog*, and written RPG supplements for several companies. She is working on an ongoing urban fantasy serial that can be found at http://makingfate.jenniferrpovey.com/. Her most recent novel, *Falling Dusk*, was released in May 2016.

WHO'S A GIRL GOT TO DROWN TO GET A DRINK AROUND HERE?

An account by A,
AS PROVIDED BY ADAM PETRASH

I pour the man his piña colada. He's an older tourist. His fat, tanned belly hangs over his Speedo. He's obviously comfortable in his own skin.

"Cute costume," he says, through a thick Italian accent. Listening to him, I peg him as being from Capri. You get good at placing accents over the centuries, but hearing his voice irks me because it reminds me of my cousins—you know, the Sirens, those man-hungry bitches who are always singing.

"Right. Thanks." Tourists see the tail as a novelty. Don't even consider that it may be real.

I hand him his drink, and he smiles, as though he has a chance. I half-smile back to appear polite. He scuttles away, and I look to see if anyone is nearby before pouring myself a double shot of rum, pounding it back, the sweet nectar burning and numbing my head. I let out a heavy and satisfying sigh.

This world has gone to shit.

Gone are the days of Assyria. Thank the gods for that. You'd figure I'd be over him by now, considering all the lovers I've had since, but still... he was the first human: a handsome shepherd I accidentally killed, and haven't forgiven myself since. It's how I got into this whole mess in the first place. I didn't ask to be a mermaid when I threw myself into the ocean.

Now I'm stuck here—working at a wet bar in a hotel serving drinks to tourists because these greedy instant-gratification-demanding creatures have spent the last two centuries polluting my home.

And yet. I'm the sucker who keeps falling for them. The old man winks at me, from the other side of the pool.

Well, falling in love with some of them, anyway.

I pour myself another double shot, and it goes straight to my head. At this rate, I'll be drunk by noon. Perfect.

A couple swims up to the bar. Middle aged, the man turning grey, the woman hiding hers with blonde dye.

"I'll have a beer."

I pull a cerveza from the ice cooler.

"Lime?"

"No, a real beer, none of that skunk stuff."

"But this is beer."

"No, American."

"We don't serve American here."

He scoffs, looks at me in disgust.

The woman he's with is noticeably uncomfortable. "Honey, let's just go." The woman places her hand on his shoulder as if to show support, but also, it seems, to nudge him to turn and float away.

I hear him murmur, "Dirty Mexicans."

What an asshole. We aren't even in Mexico.

I had considered coming to the Caribbean centuries ago, but Columbus ruined that. Some explorer he was, mistaking manatees for me. Still, the hysteria it caused. Every fisherman was hoping to catch me in their nets. I still laugh at the thought of what they would have done if I had been caught. Gut me and eat me as a delicacy. Mount me to the front of a ship. Have me stuffed and hang me above their mantel as a conversation piece. Get real.

But.

I finally moved here in the aughts. Life in the Gulf of Mexico was good for a while. There were still some places that were remote and absent of tourists. But then the Deepwater Horizon oil spill happened and fucked all of that up. To think, one litre of oil contaminates a million litres of ocean water. It erodes the fins. Not to mention it can cause respiratory and cardiac malfunction. There was nowhere to go quickly enough that was safe, except to become a fish in a tank… serving drinks… to the same creatures who put you there in the first place.

I pour myself another drink. Double? Triple? Who cares? I tilt my head all the way back until the glass is empty.

"Hair of the dog?"

"What?"

I look to see a young man in front of me—handsome, dark hair, darker eyes that seem all too familiar, chiseled cheekbones hidden behind a beard. Tattoos of marine creatures in vibrant colours sleeve his arms.

"Yes," I said. "You could say that."

"Well, if you don't mind, I'll have what you're having." He smiles, and I find myself smiling back.

I pour him more than a few fingers of rum from the bottle I've been drinking out of and slide it toward him. He nods in thanks, and begins to chug. As he drinks, I watch how his Adam's apple raises and lowers until the glass is transparent.

"That's better. So. What's your name?"

"I've gone by a lot of names, and I don't like to give any of 'em out to strangers."

The first was Atargatis. The Greeks called me Derketo. I shortened it to A, but then that little fucking mermaid movie came out.

He looks at me with obvious curiosity.

"I'm Connor." He holds out a hand, and I take it. His grip is gentle, not firm, and his skin is surprisingly soft. We shake hands, but then he turns our hands so the top of my hand is facing up. He bows his head slightly. "Nice to meet you."

I feel a chill tickle from my torso up to my neck until my arms are covered in goose bumps.

"You too."

Connor doesn't leave, so I busy myself by cleaning already clean glasses with a towel. A few awkward moments pass.

"So. Where are you from?" he asks. "You don't look like you're from around here."

"Originally Syria. But I've lived everywhere I guess. Africa. Asia. Europe—"

"At last! Be still my heart! A fellow wandering soul!"

The statement makes me smirk, and I feel the slight sensation of warmth.

"You?"

"Originally Canada. Been to a few places, but I'm trying to see as much of the world as possible. Life's too short, y'know?"

"Yes. I suppose it can be."

I feel a fleeting moment of sadness come over me, forcing a frown. It kills my boozy buzz, because I've watched everyone I've ever loved grow old and die.

"Sorry. Did I say something wrong? I didn't mean to—"

"What? Oh. No. It's not you."

I take what's left of the bottle and pour it into his glass.

"There. Here's one for the road."

He looks at me, playing out future scenarios in his head before speaking, hesitating on all of them.

"Thanks, but I'm good."

I find myself wanting to speak, to say "stay," but nothing comes out, because I know how it will end. So I'm left to stare as he turns and swims away.

Is this how it felt to all the people I had to leave?

Me, a human planted on the shore. And him, the mermaid I once was.

A, short for Atargatis, is a mermaid originally from ancient Assyria, but after she accidentally killed her first human lover, she left in search of bluer waters. A drunk with poor coping skills, she has spent centuries swimming the oceans until there were no clean and safe places left to live. She now works as a bartender in the Caribbean at a swim-up wet bar.

ADAM PETRASH is a writer, poet, and journalist. He's the author of the novella, *The Ones to Make it Through* (Phantom Paper Press 2015), and his work has appeared in places such as *After the Pause, CHEAP POP, Devolution Z, Lemon Hound, Luna Luna Magazine, Spacecraft Press,* and *WhiskeyPaper.* He lives and writes in Winnipeg.

A TIME FOR QUIET

An account by Quiet Moss,
AS PROVIDED BY TIMOTHY NAKAYAMA

I was so on edge that I only realized the bird was there when it spoke up. "They are ready," it chirped.

"Thank you," I said.

The brown tree sparrow nodded solemnly before taking to the air again, heading straight for the place from which it had come: the top of the hill.

I took a slow, deep breath and began walking.

As I crested the hill, I saw the three of them, gathered together inside a ring of trees. I approached slowly, and they turned, almost in unison. The largest of the three natukkong nodded and gestured for me to come closer.

"You are the petitioner?" he asked, his voice pure, bell-like.

I nodded and bowed.

"We three are the Council of Raub," he said. "My name is Dawn-to-Dusk."

The one farthest away from me shimmered. "I am Sunlight-Through-Trees."

"And I am Raindrops-on-Leaves," said the other, a very faint, barely discernible echo trailing every word.

Our kind grows in size the more power we possess, a trait

common to other earth spirits as well. Dawn-to-Dusk was clearly the most powerful among the three. The other two natukkong were similar in both size and age.

"And you, petitioner?" Dawn-to-Dusk asked. "What is your name?"

"I am Quiet Moss."

"How old are you?" Sunlight-Through-Trees asked.

"Thirty-nine."

Dawn-to-Dusk smiled. "Very young." He paused for a moment, as if contemplating something. Then he nodded. "Tell us your story, Quiet Moss."

I was nervous, having to tell my tale in front of these three wise and powerful natukkong, but it was a tale I had to tell if my journey was to have any meaning.

I started off with my birthplace, Sungai Lembing. Before my time, the town had been a bustling hub of human activity. The humans had grown wealthy and fat from the mining of rich veins of tin deep under the ground, while the local natukkong grew big and powerful as more of the humans streamed into town, hungry for the riches made by those who came first.

Then I told them about the Sungai Lembing of today: a sleepy little town, the tin mines now silent and still, only a small number of its original population remaining, its glory years well and truly behind it. Many of the natukkong left too; only Baba, Mama, and a few old ones decided to stay put.

Finally, I told them about my decision to leave Sungai Lembing. The little town could barely sustain the natukkong that remained, and I had never been one of the town's natukkong to begin with, having lived in the forested hills outside the town for all my thirty-nine years.

I ended my story by asking that they consider my petition to make a new Home within the town of Raub.

A moment of silence passed.

Raindrops-on-Leaves was the first to speak. "You say your years were spent in the wilderness. No dealings with humans?"

"Some passed by," I said. "Explorers mostly, but their numbers are few. None settled within my Home."

"And you want a change now, is that it?"

It is one of the big distinctions among natukkong: how involved we choose to be with humans. There are two groups. The natukkong in the first group choose to have nothing to do with humanity, building their Homes in the wild places, in the jungles, swamps, mountains.

Natukkong in the second group live side by side with humans. This is a lot more challenging than living in the wilderness. Two different folks sharing the same space? Things are going to get a little complicated.

I used to be in the first group. Now I was in Raub to join the second group. Why would a natukkong *want* to make that change? Why go to all the trouble of sharing a Home with those humans, when there was far less hassle in just living in the forest, with the birds and mouse-deers and crocodiles.

The answer is power. It is what our kind must consume to stay alive. The land itself is a source of power, and since natukkong are earth spirits, we can tap into the land's power. So a natukkong can set up Home somewhere in the wilderness and gather the power emanating from that spot.

But another source of power is humans—specifically, their belief in us. The greater the number of humans who believe in a natukkong, the more power that natukkong draws from them.

Why the need for more power? Because natukkong believe that the more power we gather for ourselves now, the more we'll be able to enjoy the Great Beyond. Different natukkong prioritize this to different degrees.

For me, I was at that age where I wanted to explore, see more of the land, try new things. Baba and Mama had been making observations about the people of Sungai Lembing for years. I'd never gotten to know humans, but I wanted to know them. And I was honest enough to admit that the added power was a nice bonus. I could send some back to Baba and Mama and keep the extra to build up my supply for the Great Beyond.

So when Raindrops-on-Leaves asked whether I wanted to make a change, there was only ever going to be one answer.

"Yes."

"Are you ready for this change?" she pressed me.

"I do not know whether I'm ready," I admitted. "But I do know that I have not come all this way just to be afraid and not even try."

Sunlight-Through-Trees shimmered. "I like your attitude, Quiet Moss."

"You're saying yes to his petition, then?" Raindrops-on-Leaves asked of her fellow council member.

"Yes," Sunlight-Through-Trees replied.

"But where shall he set up Home?" Raindrops-on-Leaves asked.

"I think there are a few suitable spots," Dawn-to-Dusk chimed in. "Ones with not so many humans, so that he won't be overwhelmed. Secluded. Quiet. A good place to build a new Home. Hmmm. I know just the right spot!"

I'd made it! Baba and Mama would be so proud.

I didn't realize until much later that there was more to Dawn-to-Dusk's choice than the relatively smaller number of humans living there.

The first thing I did was to stretch my senses out, to see just what they'd given me.

The humans lived in two main areas, where old houses wound tightly around narrow roads. A row of even older shop-lots offered food and trade. More than a few abandoned buildings dotted the area, relics from an earlier time now fallen into disuse. There was a touch of greenery. That was about it.

By the time I reeled my senses in, I'd counted slightly more than five hundred humans living in the boundaries of my new Home. Very small, but very manageable.

The second thing I did—observe. Now I had plenty of time to observe humans up close and personal, and come to my own conclusions.

Not all humans believed in us. There were many beings and entities in this world fighting for the humans' beliefs, who fed on those beliefs, for sustenance and power, just like natukkong. I couldn't really begrudge them for acting in their own interests. Besides, there was enough to go around for anyone who put in the work. Belief was an eternal spring—it never ran dry.

Belief also came in varying degrees. Some thought of us only once in a long while. Then there were the devout. They placed red-painted shrines and altars inside the compound of their homes or outside the buildings where they worked. In these shrines sat an idol in the shape of a human, dressed in opulent raiment, surrounded by various offerings, such as betel nuts, betel leaves, lime, fresh flowers, raw coconut, or other fruits. A pair of white candles and three joss sticks stood before the offerings, to be used for prayers.

To be honest, though, all that red altar business, the idols and offerings—we natukkong don't need any of that. These things are just a means for the humans to wrap their heads around our existence. It was familiar to them, comfortable, a generations-old tradition.

I listened to their prayers. I was curious to hear what humans wished for.

Prosperity was by far the most popular. Good health and good fortune were pretty high up on the list, as was protection before the start of a journey.

The big question after all this was: how was I supposed to go about amassing power? The natural features of my new Home didn't lend themselves to obtaining much power from the land. In fact, my old place near Sungai Lembing gave off more power.

But I now lived with over five hundred humans. The gains were there, waiting for me—I just had to figure out a way to increase my standing among the humans.

I was pretty sure that the way lay in the humans' prayers. See, the way I figure it, natukkong gain power from humans believing in us. So there seemed to be two ways of strengthening the humans' belief. I could either get more of the humans to start believing in me, or strengthen the belief of those who already believed in me.

Out of the two, the first one seemed a lot harder; humans do not change their beliefs easily. The second seemed easier because the belief was already there. I just had to add to it.

But what could I actually do? We natukkong have an exhaustible supply of energy and can only do so much to manipulate the physical world. My energy was only a fraction of what an older, wiser, natukkong—like Dawn-to-Dusk—would have. I decided that I had to use it in the most efficient possible way. If I focused my efforts on those humans who had the potential to yield the most belief, I would get the most out of every drop of energy I expended.

With that in mind, I studied the humans, trying to figure out which of them would see the greatest surge in belief if I worked on their wishes.

I soon narrowed it down to three targets.

The first was a wealthy man. He was always wishing for more success and prosperity in his business. If I made things go right for him, I hoped that he would mention to his many acquaintances, friends, and family how I'd granted him good fortune.

That second was a meek young boy, who recited the prayers but whose heart was not in it. He dreamt of being popular at school. With him, I was hoping that being young and impressionable, he would be unable to keep his secret and end up spreading the word among the other children.

The third was a writer who was always pining for sweet love. My hope was that some newfound interest from the opposite sex would engage her inner muse, spurring her to work her belief into poetry and prose to inspire other humans.

The time came for me to work my natukkong ways.

The wealthy man I gave a dash of luck, just enough to tilt the opinion of anyone dealing with him from a neutral outlook to a favorable one.

For the boy, I wove gossamer threads of wit and clarity around his mind. He now had the right words to amuse, delight, and impress all his classmates.

I cast a minor glamor over the writer, bestowing a small boost to her presence and confidence.

My gifts were only temporary. Humans wanting permanent gifts would have to deal with very powerful entities, few of whom were benevolent or generous.

Exhausted from my efforts, I curled up and waited.

Things did not go as I'd hoped.

The wealthy man credited his smarts and charisma alone for the successful deals. The only thing he did with his newfound wealth was to splurge on more baubles.

The boy's popularity at school soared, but he had no confidence to do anything about it. He wondered when his classmates would find out that he was a fraud.

With several men showing signs of interest, the writer's focus was less sharp than it usually was, leading her to work less on her words and more on a possible relationship.

In short, nothing went as planned. I had failed miserably. When my energy returned, I gave it another shot, with different humans.

The results were exactly the same.

By then, nearly two months had passed. I was not doing well at all. The lack of power did not bode well for the coming months.

Frustrated by my utter lack of progress, I decided that I could do with a little help.

Dewy Cobweb only had a few years on me, but he'd been living in Raub for a while. I invited him to my Home.

"Hey, Quiet. How's it going? You settling in okay?"

"Hey, Dewy. Actually, I'm struggling. That's why I asked you here. For advice, if you have some to spare."

"I guessed as much," he said. "You're looking a little less substantial than when I first met you."

"It's been two months, Dewy. I can't seem to get more belief from the humans."

Dewy nodded in empathy. "If you've never worked with humans before, it can be a little frustrating."

"It's *very* frustrating, I expend all my energy, but get nothing in return."

"Hmmm. Tell me what you've been doing."

So I told him. He listened attentively throughout. After I was done, I asked, "What have I been doing wrong?"

"Well," he began hesitantly, "I think it's all in the approach. What you did? That's a pretty traditional way of viewing our living arrangement with humans. Maybe it could have worked a hundred years ago. But we live in different times now. The humans are more numerous now, and they go through their Ages much faster than we do. What works in one of their previous Ages might not work in this one."

"Are you saying I'm old school?"

"I'm saying your *approach* is old school, Quiet. There's a difference."

"Tell me then, Dewy, what I can do to earn their belief. What's the proper way of going about it?

Dewy drew closer. "I think there are different approaches to it, Quiet. If there was only one tried and proven way to go about earning the humans' belief, we would all be doing the exact same thing." He looked at me and grinned. "I know that's not what you want to hear. But as far as I've lived with humans, I think it holds true. Look, if you really want to get along with the humans, to find your place in the grand scheme of things, perhaps you might consider this: instead of trying to get the most out of your efforts, why not try understanding the humans. What drives them, their dreams, their friends, their loves. Things like that. To earn a human's belief, you'll have to understand them deeper than you do now. They're a varied bunch, humans, more so than spirits."

"Is that it?" I asked, sarcasm creeping into my voice.

"No, that's everything," he said.

Trying to understand humans may, on the surface, sound like something perfectly doable. But to me, it was a completely different way of thinking. Where did I even begin?

A full day went by before I groaned and gave up. So I set out to do the only thing I could think of: go among the humans, and *truly* observe. In the past two months, I had merely been seeing, drawing on my own preconceptions. This time, I vowed to go in with a blank slate.

I peered into the hearts of families and relationships. In the light of day, I watched them go about their livelihoods. In the darkness of the night, I watched as they dreamt of the future.

I learned that those who prayed out of concern or worry for others were more likely to pray than those who asked things for themselves. Their prayers rang out clearer than the rest. It seemed like shared experiences were important for the collective human consciousness, bringing them closer together, burning away the extraneous demands and wants.

I gave a man's dying mother memories of her past, freeing her from the pain and indignities of a slow death. I gave a new widow's two young sons clarity and insight into the life of their recently departed father. I wove a circlet of serenity for the mother who worried about her daughter's health; the daughter was in a far-away land, but at least I could help the mother.

I needed to rest for an entire week. By the time I was up and about, I felt a slow trickle of belief coming from the humans. The increase was only minuscule, but my elation and happiness were not. It was more challenging than the previous approach, but it *felt* good. Satisfying. Meaningful. Something that I'd never before associated with humans.

It was not long after this that I met Aunty Chew, the coffee shop lady.

She prayed twice a day, always at the same times, without fail. Her prayers were always the same—gratitude for what she had in her life, and the hope that she and the people around her would continue to live safe and blessed lives.

Aunty Chew was getting on in years, but her energy and passion for life were that of a woman half her age. Everyone loved Aunty Chew; she could not see it, but her soul shone with a glowing, shimmering radiance.

My new path of trying to understand humans dovetailed nicely into my curiosity about Aunty Chew's charmed life. I was intrigued. But there were limitations to observing her as a natukkong. She couldn't communicate with me, so I was a passive observer at best. But natukkong have a talent we share with other spirits—we can assume human form. We're weak in shapeshifting compared to other spirits, but it's a useful talent to have. The only drawback is that it drains a lot of power.

When the next morning came around, I walked into Aunty Chew's coffee shop, a man on the outside, a natukkong on the inside, nervous but excited. I walked slowly but steadily to a table, for I had chosen the guise of a man similar to Aunty Chew in age.

"What you want to order?" she asked. "We still got some egg-tart left. Some kaya puffs and *lobakgo* too."

"A cup of *kopi-o*, please."

"Har?" she said in utter disbelief. "Coffee only? Not hungry, ah?"

"No. Just coffee, thank you."

"Okay, okay," she said as she scurried off to relay the order to one of the kitchen staff. She came back moments later with a brown porcelain cup of hot black coffee.

"You've been working at this coffee shop for many years?" I asked.

Auntie Chew took this as an invitation to chat with me, which was just what I wanted. "You new around here? I been here for twenty plus years. I been here so long everyone seems to know me!"

"Really?"

Aunty Chew and I talked about the coffee shop, the shop-lots, the people who lived in this part of Raub.

When my energy began to flag, I bid Aunty Chew a warm farewell. I crumbled after that, thoroughly exhausted, but happy.

I paid further visits to Aunty Chew and her coffee shop over the next few weeks. She would intersperse bits and pieces of her own story into our discussion, like how she came from the slightly bigger town of Bentong but moved to Raub when her husband passed away. I enjoyed our chats, even though many human practices and traditions seemed so strange to me. But I listened with an open mind.

It was on my fourth visit that Aunty Chew told me about the abandoned theater.

The theater was popular in the late 70s, when men and women, boys and girls would dress in their finest to watch the matinee shows on the weekend, while at night, young men and women would hold hands and steal kisses in the darkness of the hall as their heroes performed deeds of derring-do on the screen.

She sighed nostalgically. "The last movie I watched there was *The Bride with White Hair*, back in the early 90s. Good memories. But they closed down for business ten years ago. Business was good, then suddenly not so good. I heard a rich man bought it. Wanted to turn it into a bird house. But in the end, nothing," she said. "You know the reason? Ghost!"

"Ghost?"

"Yah! That's why no bird house. Too many 'things' inside."

"Is it true?"

"I don't know whether true or not, lah," she admitted. "But you know, sometimes, when I have to pass that place to go to the marketplace, I see a face staring out at me from the windows. Like a small child's. I think maybe a child died there. Then it makes sense. If a ghost is inside, no birds will come! They can sense ghosts too!"

The thought of there being a ghost wandering somewhere in my Home was deeply disturbing. Natukkong are spirits; we're part of the cycle of life and death. Ghosts are aberrations because they exist outside the cycle. They're beings that should be somewhere else, but for whatever reason, are unable or unwilling to move on.

"This theater? Where is it?" I asked.

She told me, but then added, "Why you ask?"

"Sounds interesting. Might have a look."

"What?" she cried. "Go there for what? Nothing to see, lah! Only ghost!"

I hoped she was wrong.

The humans might have thronged its halls once, but those days were long over. The theater stood there, surrounded on all sides by abandoned shop-lots and flats. I couldn't sense a human soul anywhere nearby.

As I made my way toward the entrance, barred by a padlocked and chained foldable steel gate, I suddenly experienced the strange sensation that I was being watched by someone or something behind me. I spun around, but there was no one and nothing behind me.

I slipped through the doors, into a wide foyer. Narrow shafts of sunlight streamed in through the dust-caked windows. There was a short set of stairs leading to an upper floor, where double wooden doors stood on either side. The entire place was bare, except for dust and cobwebs everywhere.

There were footprints in the dust. Small ones, like those a human child would make. I extended my consciousness through every part of the building. It took a lot longer and used up more energy than I'd expected.

To my surprise, there was a human in the building, on the upper floor. Why hadn't I sensed them before, when I was on the outside? And what sort of human would live in an abandoned building? Was it a child?

And the air. There was an oppressive feeling to it. It weighed a little heavier, flowed a little more thickly inside this old relic of a building. I was disturbed by this. Something was definitely not right here.

I climbed the stairs. Once I'd reached the landing, I turned right. As I approached the double doors, I sang a few words in the ancient natukkong language, casting a ward of protection on myself.

I slipped through the doors into a large hall, with rows of dusty red seats, all facing a black stage. It was dark and dank. The air was musty and stale, stifling for any human.

Which I assumed was what that small shadowy form on the other side of the hall was, the one moving silently in and out of the spaces between the rows of seats.

Just as I was about to confront it, the small shadowy form stopped moving. It peered at me and said, "You're not my father."

The shock was in the fact that the little girl standing in front of me had spoken to me. As a rule, humans can't see us—that is why they communicate with us by praying at those red altars. It is why I had to assume human form to speak with Aunty Chew. A human with the Sight is extremely rare.

Her words were another mystery. *You're not my father.* A pure human child who had a spirit as her father?

"I am not your father," I replied.

"Do you know when he'll be back?"

Did her father live here with her? Was her father the wealthy man who bought the theater? But that man was a human.

"Your father is coming back?" I asked.

"He goes away a lot," she said. "But he always comes back. He brings me food."

The girl did look healthy, like one who had eaten well.

"Hey, do you want to play?" the little girl blurted.

"Play?"

"Yah!" she said. "My friends and I are attacking the castle!"

"Friends?"

"Yah! They're all here," she said, gesturing at the empty space behind her.

I'd been in her presence long enough to know that she wasn't the source of the oppressive feeling in the building. I was getting weaker. The enervating pall that hung heavy in the air had been leeching my energy; even the simplest of actions required more energy than usual.

"I can't stay to play, little one," I said.

"My name's Nadia. What's yours?"

"Quiet Moss."

"Well, Mister Quiet, I guess I'm playing alone." Then she let out a whoop of glee and dashed up the aisle, imaginary friends in tow.

I went back to the old theater three more times after that.

The second time, the girl was asleep in the same hall, a large threadbare blanket covering everything but her head.

I decided to search for the source of the unbearably heavy sensation in the air. The other hall was a mirror image of the one I'd found the girl in. On the lower floor were four rooms. Two were rooms where the humans had once performed their ablutions, while I couldn't guess the function of the other two smaller, bare rooms. On the other side of the building was a double door, chained and padlocked. I slipped through and found myself in a narrow back alley littered with green plastic garbage bins.

I couldn't locate the source of the enervating pall. Tired and defeated, I left the girl to her dreams.

The third time, I found Nadia on the lower floor, in one of the two empty rooms. She sat on the floor, eating a pile of human food.

"Hello, Quiet! You came back."

"Yes."

"Father left not too long ago."

"He brought you food?"

"Yes," she said. "I'd offer you some but I know you can't eat this food."

"How do you know?"

"Father can't eat it either."

Sensing that I was on the verge of discovering something new, I said, "Your father. Do I look like him?"

"No," she said, giggling, "but you both have a glow about you."

"Glow?"

"Yah," she said, chomping into a ripe banana. "Like light around your body."

That probably meant that her father was a spirit, just not a natukkong.

"Besides food, what else does he do when he comes back?"

"He teaches me things," she said. "Like the alphabet and numbers. Sometimes he plays with me. And he tells me stories too!"

It sounded like her "father" was a benevolent spirit.

"How often does he take you out?"

The girl gasped. "Out? No! Father says it's too dangerous out there!"

This was a sign in the opposite direction. Why was the spirit lying to keep her in this old theater? My very first thought was that he was feeding on her. But why go to all the trouble of bringing her food and teaching her new things?

"I told Father about you," she said, then giggled. "He thinks I have a new imaginary friend."

"Oh. So you do have imaginary friends," I said.

"Doh," she said, sticking her tongue out. "I know they're imaginary, lah. I'm the one who created them!"

A new thought struck me. Could this "father" of hers be the source behind the oppressive air saturating the inside of this theater?

There was only one course of action left for me.

"When does your father usually come back?"

"Don't know," Nadia said. "Maybe once a day. Sometimes every other day." She eyed me shrewdly. "You want to meet him, huh?"

"Your father sounds interesting."

"He is! Really!"

"Hopefully I'll meet him next time," I said, a plan already forming in my mind. But I had to leave now—once again, my energies were flagging. "Farewell, Nadia."

"Come back soon!"

I was convinced that the "father" was the key to unraveling this mystery. All I had to do was lie in wait for him among the abandoned flats.

I settled down and waited.

It was noon the next day before I felt his presence. I felt him enter the cinema, whereupon his presence then became muted and weak. I hurried out from my stakeout spot and slipped through the theater's front doors.

Now that I was inside, I could feel the full force of his presence again. Once I reached the landing, I quietly uttered the words for a protection ward. I glided toward the hall's opened doors.

"Oh, thank you, Father!" That was Nadia.

"Eat up," said another voice. Expressive and energetic best described it.

From my vantage point by the doors, I could make out their forms, sitting against the wall on the other side of the hall. I focused on the "father"—a slim man, bespectacled and sporting neatly combed-back hair, dressed in a tattered black suit. I had to admit, his shapeshifting talent was much better than mine.

I stood up and glided toward them.

Nadia was the first to look up. "Quiet!"

The spirit-in-human-form's jaw dropped and his eyes widened in shock as he caught sight of me.

"What?" he yelped. "You're actually real?"

"What are you?" I asked. "Why are you keeping this child here?"

"What is a natukkong doing here?" he shot back.

"I don't want trouble," I said calmly.

"Did *he* send you?" he spat, his eyes burning with fury.

"Father?" Nadia said, her voice trembling. "What's going on?"

"Get behind me, *sayang*," said the spirit-in-human-form. Nadia's face scrunched up in confusion, but she obeyed him.

"Look, I think there's been some kind of mis—" I began, but just then a huge ball of force slammed into my chest, and I was thrown backward.

Urgh. I was not hurt; what I had been hit with was made for pushing objects away, not for wounding. I reached out to grab him. He leapt nimbly up onto the back of a chair. I followed up with another swipe; a blur of motion later and he was up in the air, leaping over my blow with ease.

Which worked just fine for me. I whispered a stream of words in the ancient natukkong language, and a hundred tiny white glyphs materialized in the air beside me. With one flick, I sent them spiraling up into the air toward him. The glyphs slapped onto every part of his body; he fell to the floor with a dull thud.

"Father!"

"It's okay, Nadia," I said as I approached.

"What have you done to him?"

"Just revealing his true form."

There was a crackle of energy as the glyphs lit up, did what they were supposed to do, then faded from sight.

Where before there had been a human male lying on the floor, now there was a small, curled up cat-like creature. It was a civet, a creature that resembled a cat, but with a longer body, shorter legs, and a much longer tail; there was a black band of fur across its eyes, and a combination of black bands and spots along its body and tail.

I know civets. They make their homes in the forest. Spirits whose main body came in civet form however…

"Bajang!" I hissed.

Humans who have been corrupted by the Sight are known as *dukuns*. They hate spirits, seeing us as nothing more than potential minions who can be dominated to serve at their beck and call. Their studies into black magic grants them the power to cast various malicious cantrips and spells, chief among them spells of servile enthrallment that can bring a spirit under their control. Spirits give *dukuns* a wide berth, even those powerful enough to resist their spells.

A *dukun* often has familiars. A bajang is one such familiar. It is brought forth into existence through an arcane ceremony that involves the body of a stillborn child. Stealthy and nimble, bajang are often used by the *dukun* for spying or scouting.

The bajang's favorite food is human children.

"Have you been fattening this girl up all this while, bajang?" I growled.

The bajang got up, tottering uncertainly on his short legs; the glyphs of revelation also drained a small amount of the target's energy.

He placed a paw on the back of a chair to steady himself. Nadia stood up to help, but he gestured for her to remain as she was, on the floor. He then glared at me. "Who are you to judge me, natukkong? If you intend to harm her, I'll char your ass."

Something was amiss. Why did the bajang appear to be genuinely protective of the girl?

"I'm not here to harm anyone," I said. "I just want to know why this girl, Nadia, is in this theater, and why you're keeping her here."

He scrunched up his cat-like face, about to shoot off another fiery retort, but then seemed to think better of it and said stiffly, "So you're not sent here by *him*?"

"I don't know who you're referring to," I said. "My name is Quiet Moss. This theater became part of my Home months ago. I came in and discovered the girl. I was surprised when I discovered she had the Sight. But I was more surprised to learn that she has a spirit for a father."

"Your Home, you say," the bajang said. "But why did you check out this theater in the first place?"

"One of the humans told me about this building. She thought that a ghost walked its halls. I came over to discover the truth."

"And you found Nadia."

"Yes."

"Tell me," he said, "did you feel her before you entered?"

"No. I only sensed her presence once I entered."

"Did you find that strange?" he asked, giving me a pointed look.

"Yes," I said, "but I didn't know how to explain it. I experienced the same with you. When you entered the theater, I felt your presence weaken considerably. But when I came in, I could sense you as I did outside."

He nodded. "One last thing. Do you find anything strange about this theater?"

I knew he was leading me somewhere, I just couldn't see where. "The air. There is something—" I trailed off as I searched for the right word. "—wrong about it. It drains me."

The bajang smiled satisfactorily, as if he had given me all the clues I needed to solve the puzzle.

"You know why the air in here is like this, don't you?" I said.

He nodded. "It's the reason why Nadia can't leave."

"She said you told her it was dangerous."

"She can't leave this theater because there's a curse on it."

A curse. That would explain the enervating pall in the cinema. But curses are not something I, or most natukkong, are familiar with. Curses involve the dark arts, or black magic. Natukkong were earth spirits, our power came from the land. The two are diametrical opposites.

The bajang on the other hand, being a creature created by such dark arts, had to be far more knowledgeable about curses. So I asked him to tell me the whole story.

"This theater was doing very well in the past," he began, "but fifteen years ago, a man got envious of the theater owner's success. He paid a *dukun* to cast a curse on the theater. Five years later, the curse had taken its toll and business slowed to a trickle. Eventually, the humans stopped coming. The owner sold the theater to another human. This second owner tried to turn this place into a birdhouse.

But the swiftlets would have none of this foul curse! They locked the building down and no one has done anything to this place since then."

I nodded, taking it all in.

"About five years ago," he continued, "before the curse spread and seeped into the surrounding buildings, someone dumped a baby girl at the back entrance. I don't know how she got in, but by the time I noticed, she was already inside and sound asleep."

"Wait. Where do you come into this?"

"Aiyoh," he lamented, "I was just going to get to that part, lah. You see, the *dukun* who brought the curse down upon this theater? He was once my master."

"You say that like it's in the past," I said, trying to keep my tone neutral. "Is that the way of things?"

The bajang sighed. "He *was* my master. He made me. Used me. Made sure I came here every few weeks to check that the curse was in place, that no other had come to dispel it. Not that they would have succeeded if they tried. The curse is very powerful."

"Wait," I said, "You keep on saying that this *dukun was* your master. When and why did you leave him?"

He fell to all fours, his eyes downcast, his expression pained. "I worked for him for more than twenty years. Then he learned how to create toyols. You know, those dead babies? Once he had those dumb bricks working for him, I was surplus to requirements. Said the toyols made better housekeepers and messengers than I ever could. Said he even considered unmaking me."

"Not a hard task for a *dukun*," I said.

The bajang scowled. "Yeah, well, fortunately for me, the request for the curse on the theater came along, and the master saw the perfect way to be rid of me. He sent me to babysit the curse. Back and forth, over and over. After a while, his attention shifted to other matters, and I was quickly forgotten. I still had to do the whole back and forth thing though, because he never lifted that task off of me. Soon, I grew weak, as he'd stopped feeding me milk and eggs regularly. But just as I grew weak, so did the link between me and the master. He didn't even care. So what if he lost me? He had his toyols."

"You were free," I said.

"Yeah. By then, I'd already been checking up on Nadia every visit. She couldn't leave the theater. She'd been born just outside the back entrance, left there to fend for herself, and somehow made her way inside. But because her birthplace was on the theater's doorsteps, her Fate and the curse were intertwined. It didn't want her to leave. It could continue feeding on her life force, bit by bit, keeping itself strong, as long as she lived. I tried every trick I could think of. But I couldn't take Nadia out of this place. I was no match for this wretched curse. So I did the best I could. I brought her food, taught her things a human child would learn from their parents. I just couldn't give her what she needed the most. To be free from this place."

Nadia, who had hitherto been listening with rapt fascination to the bajang's words, got up on her feet, her face wet with tears. She went up to the chair, gathered the bajang in her arms and pressed her wet face to his body.

"I have to admit," I began, my voice quiet, "when you told me what you'd done at first, I found it hard to believe. After all, you're a bajang, and all spirits know that *dukuns* are fallen into Evil."

He looked up at me, the tears running down his face his own. "I cannot change the circumstances of my birth," he said. "But I can change the circumstances of my life."

I sighed. I had gotten everything so completely wrong.

I was thinking on ways to help Nadia when I heard a strange whooshing coming from the center of the hall. There was a green mote of light there, dancing about in the air. It grew bigger and bigger into a pulsating green disc of light that merely bobbled in the air. There was a sickly smell upon the air as well.

"It's the curse! It's the curse!" the bajang wailed.

"The curse?" I said. "But why's it appearing now? Don't curses just... exist?"

"I told you this is a powerful curse!" he moaned. "It trapped Nadia in here. Now it's coming for us!"

"That doesn't make sense," I said. "You've been coming here for years. And I've been coming here for the past few weeks. Why would it come for us now?"

"You're dense!" he yelled shrilly. "Can't you see what's going on? It saw that we expended our energy in that little battle, and it's been biding its time ever since, waiting for our energy to ebb. Now it's shown itself, and come for us. We're nothing but food for it!"

The green disc of light bobbled in the air a few more times then cut through the air, throbbing with malevolent energy.

Before I could react, Nadia threw herself in front of us, into the green disc's path.

"Don't you dare harm Father and Quiet!"

"Stand back, Nadia!" the bajang cried as he leapt straight toward her back, intending to topple her to avoid a collision with the curse.

The bajang might be quick and nimble. But us natukkong aren't so bad ourselves.

I stretched out my body and shoved bajang and human aside, sending them stumbling into a row of seats.

"Leave them alone," I said softly, staring right into the green disc's light. "And get the hell out of my Home."

I reached out and enveloped the curse, anchoring myself firmly to the floor, summoning every measure of power I could from the land beneath me. I felt the curse writhing and squirming beneath my grip before numerous tendrils shot out and wrapped around me, draining my energy. But I wasn't about to let go. The curse was powerful, but it got greedy. It had materialized to feed on us, to destroy us—but that also meant that *we* could now destroy *it*.

Baba and Mama's faces flashed before my eyes. Sungai Lembing.

Aunty Chew's face too, her will to soldier on even when Fate had been cruel and Death had taken her loved ones. Dozens of other faces as well, of the humans who shared my Home; faces and numbers to me when I first came, but now I *knew* them. Dewy Cobweb's words came back to me. So too did those of Dawn-to-Dusk's, Sunlight's, Raindrops', and all the other natukkong who had wished me well even though I was the new guy, even though I was a foolish young natukkong who knew nothing.

This was my Home. This was my Place. This was where I was meant to Be.

I dredged up every last bit, until I was on the verge of being merely a vessel and conduit for whatever energy came from the land. The Great Beyond was beckoning, but I hung on, determined that my one last act upon this world would be to make Baba and Mama proud that their little boy had done what was right.

There was a light touch on my body.

I felt the bajang's energy—bitter but surprisingly warm—flowing into me, lending me strength. It surged wildly, a thing of entropy, but I brought it under my control and joined it to my own.

"The name's Gombak," said the bajang.

I could feel the curse giving way. But it had been here a very long time. I could feel its power coursing through me, lashing me with a fury born of hate, envy, and black magic. Its presence corrupted, blighted, destroyed.

Another light touch—a small but strong hand.

Despite the white-hot pain racking my insides, I smiled to myself. The curse had dark and ancient power. But I had something better.

I had hope.

I shouldn't have been surprised though—she was perfectly healthy despite being in this accursed building for years. Her energy was even more chaotic than the bajang's. It was raw and without direction. But it was also warm, sweet, and invigorating. I reined in its wild flow and channeled it into the conflux of energies pouring from me.

There was a scream that threatened to tear at the fabric of my very being. I couldn't tell whether it was mine or the curse's. I didn't care.

I could see nothing, but I heard the walls crumble, the windows shatter, the beams snap. Instinctively, I wrapped my body around the girl and bajang. I held them close as the world unraveled and collapsed around me.

"Hey, Quiet, you hurt?"

I could feel someone poking and prodding my body. I guess I had to be grateful I could feel anything.

"Very," I said. "Now stop doing that."

A high-pitched squeal of delight came from my side. "You're all right!"

I pushed myself up. The theater was no more. The entire upper floor of the theater had collapsed, leaving only huge chunks of concrete, steel cables, wood, and bricks behind inside the foyer and out on the streets. Nadia was dancing excitedly among the rubble, joy and happiness radiating from her face.

"It's so *light* out here," she said. "Everything's so beautiful."

Gombak leaned against my body and gave me a pointed look. "I'm guessing we'll have to get her used to living in the outside world, huh?"

"We?"

"You and I."

"Oh."

I tried to get up, but I couldn't. It was going to take a while before I could.

As I lay there, feeling the gentle wind go straight through me and soaking in the warmth of the sun, I thought I saw something to my right, beyond the ruins of the theater.

A large figure stood atop one of the shop-lots, a tree sparrow perched on its wide shoulders, silhouetted against a clear and blue sky and the glorious blaze of an afternoon sun. The figure nodded. It was a proud nod that said *well done*. Then it faded from sight, and there was only sky and sun.

"Hey, Quiet. Any ideas where Nadia and I could shack up for the time being?"

"Give me a moment… Gombak."

Well done. Hah. I guess that was all right. Better than what I was expecting. But that was the old Quiet Moss. A naïve Quiet Moss. Hah. I wondered whether it was time for me to change my name.

But that was neither here nor there.

Right then, Quiet Moss suited me fine.

There was no need to worry. With friends by my side, I can do anything.

Baba and Mama would ask me about my work.

I would tell them about my life.

Things got a lot more interesting from then on.

QUIET MOSS is a young natukkong who enjoys spending most of his days and nights observing, studying, and getting to know the humans he shares his Home with. Sometimes, he even talks to them. The natukkong of Raub have noticed that young Quiet Moss seems to be smiling and laughing a lot more nowadays.

TIMOTHY NAKAYAMA was born and raised in Malaysia and currently resides in Cambridge, Massachusetts. His short stories have been featured in various anthologies such as *Fish, Lost in Putrajaya, KL Noir: Yellow, PJ Confidential*, and *Little Basket 2016: New Malaysian Writing*. He has also written short stories in comic form, many of them featured in anthologies published by GrayHaven Comics.

THE OUTSIDER

An account by Bonnie Wolf,
AS PROVIDED BY VALJEANNE JEFFERS

*I*slipped off my jeans... my panties... racing through the snow, becoming one with the night, the trees luminescent in the glow of a pregnant moon. I unbuttoned my blouse and dropped it to the ground. My change began—even before my bra joined the trail of clothing I left behind. As I reached the clearing, I became wolf. I stopped, lifted my nose and howled, a cry at once sorrowful and beauteous. In the distance, my brethren answered the call...

The thumping on the wall behind me woke me up. "Shut the hell up, you *freak!*" a voice bellowed. I pushed my comforter back and slid out of bed. I found my way through the dark easily—one of the perks of being a werewolf—to the bathroom. I opened the cabinet and pulled out my pill bottle.

Empty! How did I let this happen?

There was a pounding at the door, and I quirked my mouth. *Justin.* I'd been expecting him. I walked to the door in my nightshirt, cracked it to the safety latch, and peered out. Sure enough, it was Justin, the building manager, his purple and hazel eyes gleaming with agitation. Like all Ghouls, he needed ten hours of sleep, and I'd just cut into two of them. The Nadir was a potpourri of Fae races: vamps, werewolves, fairies (usually immigrants from an impoverished dimension), and

Ghouls. Ghouls were the ruling class. They controlled the economy, and so controlled the Realms. Fuchsia, where I lived, was the most prosperous.

"I know, I'm sorry. I uh… I forgot to refill my prescription. It won't happen again."

"Yeah Bonnie, that's what you said last time. And the time before that. Ya know, I cut you a break letting you move in here—most folks don't rent to your kind." He lifted a pointed finger, and picked a red morsel of flesh from between his pointed teeth.

"Come on, Justin!"

He shook his head, tossing his dreds about. "No can do, Bonnie. Not this time. I been getting complaints. Consider this your two weeks' notice."

I slammed the door and stood there, trying not to burst into tears.

Going back to sleep was now out of the question. I turned and flicked the light switch on. The sight of the studio I called home, with my futon, potted plants, and bay windows was almost more than I could bear. I'd fallen in love with the little apartment. It was walking distance from work, and in an upscale neighborhood too.

Where am I gonna find somewhere else to stay in two weeks with my record?

I made my way through the living area to the kitchen, and started coffee brewing.

I stepped outside into the early dawn. Fuchsia this time of day was a crystal, dew droplets sparkling in the windows, and the two suns dancing about the scrapers above. I glanced up and to my right at the *Belle de jour* clock tower, visible from any point in the Realm. I'd come to think of it as *my clock*. I nodded good morning, as was my habit, turning my collar up to the nippy breeze. I walked a block to the newsstand where I worked.

The owner, Pedro, a short balding Fae, had already set up, and was having his breakfast of flesh, scallions, and eggs. It smelled disgusting. He would too, once he was finished.

Pedro smiled his pointed-tooth greeting, his yellow and blue eyes crinkling up at the corners. "Hey kiddo, what you doing here so early?"

I made my way behind the counter. "Can I borrow your tablet when you're finished?"

"Here," he slid the hard scroll toward me, "I'm done." He sensed my agitation. "You wanna talk about it?"

"I got kicked out of my place this morning."

"Aw, that's a shame! Why?"

I shrugged. "Same reason as before. Changing in my sleep." Pedro was a mixed race Fae: the child of a Ghoul and a fairy. Because of his heritage, he thumbed his nose at the caste system, calling it *basura*, which was why he was willing to hire me. But Pedro could afford to live like he wanted to. He looked like a Ghoul and smelled the part.

"How long you got before you have to move?"

"Two weeks." Saying it made it real. I felt the tears about to fall, and dropped my head. I started scanning the scroll for vacant studios. Pedro was good people, but I didn't want to cry in front of him. I tapped the vacancies that looked promising. The raised print lit up. They'd stay illuminated until I touched them again.

Pedro had a makeshift coffee pot he kept behind the counter. His diet might be disgusting, but he made some of the best java I'd ever tasted. "Here, kid." He handed me a cup. "This'll boost your spirits."

"Thanks." I put the tablet under the counter, and started formatting the scrolls for the customers. Most of them were Ghouls. I steadied myself, like I did every day for what I called "the once over." A smile as the customers took in my deep brown skin, the smile dying as they spotted my pointed ears, pierced at the tip, just below my close-cropped hair. Other customers ignored my ears, or pretended to, and flashed tolerant grins. This reaction wasn't any improvement. It felt like a watered-down racism. Still, these politically correct ghouls would be less likely to attack me. Most of the other races had surgery to pass; fairies would clip their wings, vamps have their teeth filed down, and werewolves, their ears rounded. The procedures were painful and left scars. I refused to hide what I was.

At 4PM, I asked, "Is it okay if I take off early? I need to follow up on some of these leads."

"Yeah sure, Bonnie. I can take it from here. I'm about to close up anyway. It's slow today. Listen, kid, don't worry about that apartment business. It'll work out. Anyway you got people right—people like you—you can stay with?"

I smiled tiredly. "Sure, Pedro." *Yeah sure. Way over on the rough side of town.* I picked up the tablet and started down the street to find a hot spot. I needed a refill on my meds.

Hot spots, portals to the different apexes of the Realm, weren't hard to find. Not if you were gifted with the Sight. *There.* I spotted a tiny circular rainbow across the street. I approached it slowly. Hot spots were temperamental. If I ran toward it, it might bounce away—or worse, vanish.

When I got close, I whispered, "Orchid, please." I grasped the circle and stretched it until it was large enough for me to step inside.

Mama Pepper's realm was tropical and surreal, shifting and changing colors with my every step. It gave me a headache. *How does she deal with it?*

After a few minutes, the Realm settled into place, and I saw her little cottage, framed by high grass and wild herbs of pink, purple, and orange. I made my way to her door. Before I could knock she called, in a voice like the smooth rhythm of a drum, "Come, come, child. What you stand out there for, huh?"

She knew I was coming. I opened the door and stepped into her low ceiling kitchen, the walls lined with shelves of exotic jars. Mama Pepper, a fairy with mahogany skin and sharp features, was stirring a pot. Whatever it was, it smelled delicious. A pan of fresh rolls sat atop the stove. As usual, she wore a dress with the back cut out. Her gossamer wings were retracted, but an open-backed garment gave them space to breathe.

She put the spoon down and waved me over. "Come, give me hug. What you look so sad for? You hungry?" Mama Pepper liked to cook, and to feed me. She always said I was too thin.

I suddenly remembered I hadn't eaten since noon, aided by the wonderful smells coming from the stove. "Yes, ma'am."

"Well, get a plate, you know where they are. Wash your hands first."

I pumped water onto my hands from the sink. *Why doesn't she get a new faucet?* I know she can afford it. I pulled a plate and a fork from the shelf behind me, went to the pot, and lifted the lid. She'd made red beans and rice, my favorite. I spooned some onto my plate and took a roll from the pan.

I sat down at her tiny table and started to eat. After a few moments, she put glasses of tea on the table and joined me.

"Mama," I said around bites, "I need more pills, and stronger this time. I had to take too many of the other ones."

Mama Pepper chewed serenely. "I knew that would happen."

I cocked my head and frowned. "Why didn't you tell me—better yet, why didn't you give me a stronger dose to begin with?"

"If I told you, would you have listened? I'll try to make one stronger this time. But it won't matter. You can't oppress what you are. Sooner or later, your true nature will break free. And you be right back at the beginning. Why you don't just stay with your kind, huh?"

I tore my eyes away from her dark gaze and dropped them to my plate. "I can't... Where I live now it's clean. It's safe. Close to my job too. I can make more money. I like it—I love it."

Mama scowled. "Oh yes, safe. You love it. It's clean, close to your job. Where you can't keep a place to stay. Where they stare at you like you're a freak, *n'est pas*?"

I felt the tears threatening to fall again. I wasn't about to tell her I'd gotten kicked out again. *She probably already knows.* "Maybe I am," I mumbled.

Mama Pepper eyed me sternly. She held up a finger. "No. Don't do that. Different don't mean freak. It means *different, n'est pas*? You don't let them Ghouls rent space in your head." Her face softened. "Why not come stay with me awhile, huh?"

I shook my head. "I can't, Mama. It's too strange here. It makes me dizzy."

Her small mouth turned up in a smile. "That's you, child."

"What you mean?"

"You're confused, conflicted. So Orchid mirrors it."

I felt my jaw tensing up, like it did whenever I stubbornly held my ground. *Just like Daddy. I miss him so much. He would know just what to say to ease my mind.*

Mama Pepper saw that I'd made up my mind. She reached across the table and patted my hand. "I get your pills." She rose from the table and walked over to the shelf to her left. Murmuring in a singsong whisper, she plucked a brown bottle from the shelf and placed it on the counter. She waved her hand across the top of the bottle. When she lifted her hand, it was full.

I got up and pulled the cash from my pocket. She shook her head. "Go on with you, *Cherie*. You keep your money. The pills won't last. I don't feel right charging you."

I spent the rest of the afternoon with the tablet clutched to my chest, hunting for studios, talking to landlords. I encountered the tolerant smiles I'd come to hate, along with firm *Nos*, as well as outright hostility. Then there were the signs that said, "We only rent to GHOULS!"

Before I knew it, dusk had fallen. I was too tired to keep going. *To hell with it. I'm gonna visit Charlie.* I started looking for a hot spot. Charlie's realm was in a rundown side of town, dangerous too. I'd get home late, if at all. *It'll be worth it.*

I smelled them before I heard them... the heavy reek of carnage that Ghouls carried with them. I could smell their hatred too, their rage that anyone different would dare exist in their world. They were coming for me, three of them, their footsteps heavy and purposeful. They meant to kill me.

Fear and anger fueled my *change*. Snarling, I whirled just as they came abreast of me, hair covering my body. Claws drawn, with my free hand, I slashed across the chest of the one closest to me—a big Ghoul with gray and green eyes. I drew blood, and he fell back. Cursing, I clutched the tablet with both hands and battered the one to my left across the head. As I struck the other one, the tablet shattered.

Dropping to all fours, I loped down the street, searching desperately for the hot spot. *There! Right there! Straight ahead!*

I was hysterical. The hot spot sensed it. It bounced away. I chased it.

"Please—!"

Just as I reached it, the closest Ghoul grabbed my jacket. It ripped. The second one snatched my purse away. I heard my pills fall to the street. Cursing and sobbing, I turned and hit him *hard*, throwing all my preternatural strength behind the punch. He toppled backward. I stood and grasped the hot spot with both hands. "Please don't vanish! *Onyx!*" I pulled it open and jumped through to the other side. They wouldn't follow me into the Wolf Realm.

I stumbled down the street. Brambles, trash, and high grass lined the avenue. The tall duplex was a welcome sight. I knocked on the door, crying still with anger and loss. My pills, the tablet, my purse… all gone.

Red-haired, freckled Charlie, his pointed ears pierced like mine, opened the door. He grinned. "Bonnie—!" he broke off and frowned. "Baby! What happened?"

"They came after me—three of them!"

"Come on over and sit down." He led me to a threadbare armchair. A couple sat on the couch adjacent to it. They looked on sympathetically. Charlie left the room and came back with a beer. "Here." He sighed. "Bonnie, I don't know why you insist on living among them. You gonna get yourself killed."

I couldn't answer. I had no answer.

"Stay with us tonight… Stay with me," he said softly.

I held his gaze a moment. I nodded.

The tall dark man on the couch got to his feet. He smiled at me, showing his fangs. *Vampire.* This house was open to all races. He walked over to the Victrola, put a record on, and sat back down beside his girl. I heard sudden gunfire outside. The shots faded into the backdrop of my mind as I listened to the music, a jazzy fusion of instruments. I sipped my beer, feeling my angst float away. I was with friends.

I'm gonna figure things out.

BONNIE WOLF is a twentysix-year-old werewolf, living in the Fae Dimension. This Dimension, and all of its Realms, is ruled by flesh-eating Ghouls. Jobs are plentiful in the Fuchsia Realm, where Bonnie lives; housing conditions are also superior. But Fuchsia is populated by mostly Ghouls, who despise other races: werewolves, fairies, and vampires. Woe to any Outsider who dares live in Fuchsia! They must face a day to day ordeal of being treated like an outcast, a freak, and risk even death, if caught alone on the streets after dark by the master race.

VALJEANNE JEFFERS is a graduate of Spelman College, and the author of *The Immortal* series; *The Switch II: Clockwork*; *Mona Livelong: Paranormal Detective*; and *Colony: Ascension*.

Valjeanne was featured in *60 Black Women in Horror Fiction*. Her stories have been published in *Steamfunk!*, *Genesis Science Fiction Magazine*, *Griots II: Sisters of the Spear*, and *The City*. *The Switch II: Clockwork* was nominated best ebook novella of 2013 (eFestival of Words). Her short story "Awakening" was published as a podcast by *Far Fetched Fables*. She is also one of the screenwriters for *7Magpies*, a film anthology. Purchase Valjeanne's novels at: www.vjeffersandqveal. com

PLAYING THE GOOD GIRL

An account by Tommy,
AS PROVIDED BY DARIN M. BUSH

I had a vodka rocks sitting in front of her seat at my bar as soon as the clomp clomp of boots preceded her arrival.

For some reason, this attractive, slim woman walked around in clunky army boots. They were black and always immaculate. They matched her typical outfits: dark or black jeans, subtle but elegant tops or classy t-shirts, and a leather jacket. The boots just didn't suit her somehow.

She came over to the bar and sat down on a stool with her usual simple movements. Actually, she sat down on *her* stool. I mean, she wasn't the only one that sat there, but nobody who came in after sundown or on a Saturday used that stool. The regulars knew who she was and, for the most part, they left her alone.

Like I said, she was beautiful: dark hair, olive skin, black eyes. I don't mean brown eyes; I mean black. As far as I could tell, her irises, or whatever they're called, were so dark brown it looked as if they and the pupils made two big black circles. She had this dramatic stare she would level at anyone who tried to engage her socially.

Now I got the stare. "What's this, Tommy?"

"What's what, Raib?"

She shook her head. "Rayb." She pronounced it down in her throat.

"Raib."

She looked at me as if I was about to be assigned summer school. Then she seemed to pick which fight to fight, and held up her tumbler and glared at it.

"What?" I said. "Come on, Raib, don't you recognize vodka on the rocks? Just like you always get. By some miracle did you change your preference?"

She pulled her long black hair away from her face. She held the tumbler in her hand as if it was a science experiment. "I see vodka. I just don't see ice. Is this a ball in my glass?"

"No," I said, "it's an ice sphere. It's all the rage now, so I kind of had to buy one of those machines."

"Oh, yes," she sneered. "It's very classy. What's the point of this, Tommy?"

"The idea is the sphere melts more slowly. It cools your vodka but doesn't water it down as quickly or at all. At the rate you usually drink, you'll get all the vodka out and still have that big old sphere of ice ready for a refresh."

"Please tell me this bar isn't going to become trendy." Her black eyes rolled and glared at me in challenge.

"No, I promise, no trendiness here in this bar. Not as long as I'm the owner."

She smirked; she didn't smile. I think I said before that she was beautiful. Her face was elegant, eastern European, or something like that. Her mouth and jawline were strong and shapely. I wouldn't normally care, or mention it, but it was always in my mind that if she would smile, Rayb would knock people over.

Yeah, I admit it, something about her intrigued me. She'd been sitting at my bar, drinking vodka, most nights for at least a year. She never ordered food, she never talked to anyone, and every word out of her mouth was bullshit. I was positive she wasn't crazy, but my gut said she was hiding something.

I thought maybe I'd finally break down and confront her about that. Someone got in my way.

Another of my regulars, Ashleigh, Ashley, whatever, poured herself into the stool next to Rayb. The men in my bar were all after Ashley, but they had no chance. I enjoyed watching them flail, though.

"It sure is hot in here tonight," Ashley said to no one, and everyone.

Rayb's eyes twitched, but otherwise she ignored the intruder.

"I mean," Ashley continued, "How can you wear all that black and leather?" She tilted toward Rayb, who gave a non-committal grunt with a small jerk of her head. Ashley's eyes assaulted Rayb's entire length. It was softcore porn. "Honey, those combat boots are very hip, but they aren't very flattering. I bet you have pretty feet."

At the word "feet," Rayb's face stiffened, she set down her tumbler, and looked at me. "Tommy?"

"Raib?"

"More vodka. Less Barbie."

Luckily, the vodka was behind me, so I could turn away and hide my smile from the eager lesbian and her reluctant prey. I heard Ashley make a "humph" noise as she retreated. When I turned to pour the vodka, I saw Rayb's face was a little red and pinched.

"I'm glad that question is answered," I said.

Rayb glared at me. "Question?"

"Yeah. After blowing off every guy in the bar, there was this lingering question. Ashley might have helped us answer it."

"I'm not a lesbian, you asshole."

She called me "asshole" about twice every visit. It was her way of saying I had tried—and failed—to amuse her.

"So, you're picky then?"

"No, that's not it."

"We're not good enough for you?"

"We?"

Oops. "The royal 'we,' Raib."

"Rayb."

"Raib."

"Oh, forget it. You'll never get it right."

"I'm sorry, I can't quite get the 'y' to come out. Besides, you're changing the subject. We're just not good enough for you. You drink my alcohol, but you barely speak to anyone here, and sometimes only to me when I make you."

"It's complicated. I've told you."

"Bullshit." I crossed my arms at her, as they taught us in pub owner training. Okay, maybe I am an asshole.

The glass came down hard and loud that time. "What did you say?" Some part of me thought she had just growled at me. Like, animal growl. I made myself stay put. I knew she respected strength of character. I can fake that.

"Bullshit. Crap. Horseshit. Every answer you've ever given me has been veiled, avoiding, or an outright lie. You're working hard to hide something from—well—everyone, as far as I can tell."

Rayb looked around. The crowd was thin. It was early yet. She had plenty of empty space around her. She had them trained. "You don't know anything, Tommy. Let it go. You don't want to know me."

"Why not?"

Her head sank. She looked defeated. Sad, not angry, which was her usual stance.

"Come on, Raib, tell me you're about to hit me with, 'You can't handle the truth!'"

"Asshole."

"It's my job title."

She actually laughed. "Tommy, come on, why do you even care?

I pay my tab. I've never hurt any of your patrons." She said "patrons" the same way I would say "alley cats."

"I don't know." I didn't know. I thought about it, but couldn't find it. I think I might have reddened a little.

Rayb rolled her eyes. "Please, please, save me."

"Hey, no, be cool," I stammered. "It's just, I'm a bartender. I've been one for a long time. Longer than you'd believe. I'm not used to having so much trouble reading someone. I know you're hiding something, but I have no idea what."

"So, when I tell you to drop it," she said with a cold voice, "and that you can't handle it, and that you're better off minding your own damn business, do you think I'm joking?"

"But, Raib, do you have anyone to help you mind your business?"

"What are you babbling about?"

"Who takes care of you?"

She mumbled.

"Huh?"

"No one!" she yelled, and the empty tumbler cracked in her clenched hand. How the Hell? Maybe she had cracked it on the bar before.

The other customers all stiffened at her outburst. Some stared; some looked away. I thought I heard Ashley chuckle.

I reached for Rayb's hand, full of broken glass, and she recoiled. "Don't touch me!"

"You're bleeding." Or something. The sticky liquid dripping from her hand was not red. It was brown. What? I needed to get her out of sight, and get her some first aid. "Let's get you a bandage," I said, a little too loudly.

I waved at Charlie to take charge of the bar, jumped over it—no, seriously, don't judge—and took Rayb by the elbow. "I've got a first aid kit in the office."

Rayb looked down at her bleeding hand, and her eyes went wide.

Maybe she had just realized she was bleeding coffee. In any case, she let me lead her into the back.

I opened my office door, waving her in. I had a private little half bath in my office. I kept the medicine cabinet stocked with first aid stuff and all the weird items a bar owner might suddenly need. I closed the office door behind me and headed to the little sink. I was an old hand (no pun) at the minor injuries that come with serving alcohol and bar food.

Rayb clomped over to the sink, holding her injured hand. I warmed up the water and unpacked some ointment and a couple of bandages. As she rinsed, gritting her teeth, she said, "Get that goo away from me. I don't need it."

"You don't need antibiotic? For a bleeder like that?"

She pulled a hunk of glass out of her palm, and turned her eyes to mine. She looked tired, beaten. "Please, Tommy, just trust me on this."

"So that's what it looks like."

"What what looks like?"

I handed her a bandage. "The no-bullshit version of Raib."

"Rayb." She twitched her head. "Sorry, never mind."

"So?"

She ignored me, making a show out of wrapping her hand. I leaned down enough to glare into her eyes. "So what?" she said.

"So, so."

She shook her head.

I felt the veil dropping again. I wasn't having that. "Now that I've seen the Kahlua and platelet chaser," I said, "maybe you can tell me what's going on?"

"Platelet chaser?" She tried to deny a smile. My kung-fu is strong.

"I've seen the blood, Raib. Don't deny it. Tell me why it's brown."

"No."

"Yes."

"No!"

"I'm not going to drop it, Raib."

"Then I'm never coming back here to your stupid bar!"

"And the number of friends you have minus one, me, leaves you how many, exactly?"

"You fucking bastard." She didn't yell; she didn't scream. She just said it. Coldly. She sat in my office chair and seemed to collapse under the pressure of her isolation. I started to worry I had gone too far when she said, "None." Again, so coldly. My heart almost broke in that moment.

"I'm sorry, Raib," I said, as gently as I could. "I wish you could trust me."

"I do, Tommy, I do. But, but, this goes beyond trust."

"So, you trust me, but—"

"My situation is," she searched for a word, "unique."

"Unique?" Eyebrow. "Or, dare I say, very unique?"

"Asshole." A smile. Aha.

"You know you can flee after you tell me? That's still an option."

"You think you're up for this? You seriously believe you can handle anything?" The last few words came out like the voiceover from a horror movie trailer.

"Yup."

"So, this is that point where we do or say things, but we don't know why? Right?"

That threw me. "You mean, like, in a movie or something, where the characters know they're being stupid?"

"Of course not, you moron." She smiled. "You and your damn movies. I mean that I want to be honest. I want to tell you. I just can't."

"Then show me."

"What?"

"I've seen the blood, Raib. Can you show me more, without words?"

Her beautiful, harsh mouth opened. It closed. She shut her eyes.

She reached down to one of her combat boots and started unlacing it. She looked as if she was going to cry. She slid the boot off, and it clunked to my floor.

It took me a second to register her foot. She was not wearing socks. She had no toes. The skin was black. Not dark brown: black. And it wasn't skin. It was horn or hair or bone or whatever hoof is made of.

It was a hoof.

"It's a hoof."

She pinched her eyes closed. "You're a genius."

"You have a hoof?" I shook my head. "Do you have two?"

Her booted foot clomped down on my concrete floor. Yeah, she has two.

"Are you a faun or satyr or something like that? You're not a Greek goddess or a Gorgon?"

"I'm almost impressed," she said, "and completely insulted."

The sight of the hoof had sabotaged my intuition. I had no idea how to read her at that moment. How much of that was sarcasm? I didn't have to play stupid; I embraced it. "Impressed?"

She rolled her eyes again. "Yes, you almost named a list of things that have hooves."

I was happy to get "almost." Now for the other shoe to drop, so to speak. Big, cheesy smile. "Insulted?"

"I'm. Not. Greek."

"Oh, that. Sorry." I looked back at her hoof. She grabbed for her boot. "Then, you are—"

"Arabian. Persian. Mesopotamian."

"Mesopotamian?"

"The family goes way back."

"So, the family. Yeah. Tell me more about that."

"I'm a ghūl."

"Right, I know. A very nice-looking one, too." I really wish that hadn't come out of my mouth just then.

The boot came up in her hand, as if she meant to hit me with it. "Are you mocking me?"

My hands went up. "No, no, I think you're an attractive girl. Woman! Woman." Oh, Hell.

Her empty hand did a perfect facepalm. "You total and complete idiot. I said 'ghūl' not girl." Then her face went red, and she tried to hide behind her one hand. "Attractive? You think I'm attractive?"

Shit. "Yes, always have."

The flush disappeared. She pointed to her hoof again, challenge all over her face.

"Yes," I said, "even now, even with hor—"

"Don't you dare say the word 'horse'!" I felt white hair start to grow out of my head. Holy Hell, she could angry face like a Disney villain.

"Then, waha? Uh?" I'm a genius.

"Ass."

"Right. I'm an ass. Yes."

This time she did throw the boot at me, but not very hard. It hit my thigh and fell to the floor between us. "No." She knocked her forehead with her fist. "Ass. Donkey, mule. Ass. Hooves of an ass." She pointed at her foot.

"Ohhhhh… those are the hooves of an ass. Okay."

"Get it now?"

"No."

"I have the hooves of an ass."

"But you said you were a—"

"Ghūl."

"Ghoola."

She cursed, I'm sure, but it wasn't English. Then she said, "Ghūl. You idiots who speak Anglo-Saxon changed it to ghoul." She looked as if she might spit at the word.

"Oh, ghoul. Right." I blinked. "Wait, one of those creatures that—
" I stopped as another angry glare was loaded into the chamber, ready to fire. "Um, you know how we depict ghouls, right?"

"Wrong. You depict ghouls wrong."

"Well, apparently, if you are one."

"I am one."

"Then let's start over with the whole gahuul thing and—"

"Tommy, give it up."

"Okay, Raib, okay. Ghoul thing."

"Rayb."

"Don't deflect. What is a ghoul?"

"A ghūl is a nigh-immortal spirit, a jinn, with a body that extends into your existence."

"Jinn?"

"Genie."

"Oh! Those. Okay, got it. Explain 'extends.'"

"Some people, especially in the so-called New World, would lump us in with daemons, demons. It's not the same."

"Okay, demons I understand."

"You and those damn movies again."

I smiled at her. "Sure, movies."

"You goofball nerd."

"Nerds don't usually own bars. Moving on. Extend?"

"My essence is from another, let's call it 'plane.' This body is only an interpretation of that spirit. I have some ability to alter it."

"Like a glamour?"

She halted mid-flow and raised an eyebrow at me. "Yes—"

"So this version of you that I see is part of you, inspired by you, but not what you really look like?"

She smiled a wicked smile, and I noticed her teeth distend slightly into sharp points. Nosferatu would have been jealous. She looked disappointed when I didn't faint dead away or piss myself.

"Impressive. Makes flossing easy."

"Asshole. Anyway, yes, you're right. I can change shape, sort of, but I look as I'm supposed to look, whatever form I pursue."

"You mean you didn't choose to look like a model for Harley Davidson?"

That got a blush, but she fought it off. "A runway model with hooves?" She made it sound cliché.

"Good point. Why would you pick those, if you're trying to appear human?"

Rayb had spent most of our time together over the last months looking at me as if I was an idiot. Now she made a face that clearly said, "There are service dogs for people like you." "Pick? Pick!"

"Sorry, sorry! Then why?"

"It's the ghūl's mark. No matter what we look like, we have ass's hooves. It's always been true, far as I know. We have stories about mixed parentage or a curse, but those stories came from outside my family. The truth is lost."

"Maybe Set?"

"Set?"

"You know, god of storms and disorder?"

She glared at me yet again. This was going well. "Egyptian. The Egyptian god of those things."

"Well," I shrugged, "maybe one of your ancestors pissed him off. Head of a donkey, right?"

"Sometimes. But actually no one is sure what kind of animal—"

This time I cut her off. "It makes sense to me. Head of a donkey, ass's hooves. Your family was cursed with the Mark of Set."

Rayb closed her eyes, shook her head, and looked back at me as if I was a child with an electric outlet and a fork. "The Mark," she said, "of Set. Fabulous."

"So, just the hooves?"

She rolled her eyes and crossed her legs. She pulled her tight, black jeans up enough so I could see the olive skin of her ankle. "Right?" she said, as if asking if the peek-a-boo machine was finally out of quarters.

"Summer at the beach must be complicated." I pictured her in a bikini and those massive boots.

"Stop that!" she growled. So much for my poker face.

"Sorry, sorry."

"Besides, if I'm going swimming, I just go as a whale."

"Okay, now who's being funny?"

"No, seriously," she said with a proud, almost goofy smirk.

"A whale? With hooves?"

"The hooves are inside the tail, like a normal whale's feet."

I whistled in appreciation. "Beauty and brains."

"Stop flirting with me, Tommy."

"Why?"

"Look," she sighed, "you're very cute, and charming and all that, and obviously you're not running screaming, but it would never, never work."

"What? You don't like movies?"

"Again with the damn movies!"

"Look, I'm not asking to meet your grand-ghoul-parents next Ramadan."

"You racist—"

I waved that away. "Whatever. You know better than that. I'm saying that I just want you to consider hanging out with me at a place that serves real food, with forks and such."

She sighed and deflated again. "Yeah, real food," she said.

"Wait. You don't actually eat—" I searched the room for a thesaurus or an English teacher. "—what the movies say you guys eat, do you?" Whew.

"Corpses? No, that's old propaganda. What I actually eat is worse in some ways, according to some cultures." She saw me making the "go on" face. "No, no. No way."

"Way. We've come this far."

Rayb scowled at me. "Yes, we've come this far. Too far." She pulled her jeans down and made to put her boot back on.

"So, let me get this right," I said, trying to sound thoughtful. "You don't want me to know what you eat, which is not corpses. What could be worse? The only thing worse I can imagine is live bodies."

"Of course I don't eat live bodies," she said. "Ewwww."

"Then you don't eat... any... excretions?"

"Ugh. No! I'm not a catfish."

"Then tell me."

Her face tightened again. "No."

"Okay, I'll keep guessing."

"Stop!"

"Not until you tell me what the big stupid deal is. I've seen the hooves; I've seen the teeth. You don't eat dead people or live people. What could be so horrible, then?"

"Placenta!"

She burst out so suddenly I wondered if I'd heard her correctly. Maybe it was a ghūl curse word and my brain tried to understand and failed. "What?"

She got quiet again. Her head sank. "Placenta."

"That sounds familiar. Something with hospitals or nurses."

"Placenta. The organ that connects a fetus to its mother."

That word I knew. Don't react. Don't overreact. Don't weird out. "Oh, placenta. Of course." I dove for incredulity and skepticism. "Really? That's your food?"

She lifted her head, her challenged face glaring up at me. "'Really?' 'Really?' That's the best you can do?"

"Well, it seems improbable and impractical."

"Improbable? Do you even know what that word means?"

"It's unlikely." A laugh burst out of me, despite trying to keep a serious face.

Rayb tapped her fingers on her forehead and ground her lips together. "You truly are the biggest douchebag I have talked to in a very, very long time."

That got my serious face back. "Don't be rude. It's simple. How is that your only way to get sustenance?"

"It's simple in that my people aren't people. We're ghūls. Our nutritional needs are just very specific. Our metabolisms require the most efficient food source. We can starve to death trying to digest wimpy food."

"Wimpy?"

"You should feel lucky. If human flesh was good for us—" She smirked at her own joke, but I saw something else behind her eyes.

"I appreciate the humor, but you're still not telling me the whole story."

"Because I don't quite get it myself. It's a bit weird, even for me."

"Don't get it? Don't get your food?"

She scowled afresh. "Do you know why you eat protein?"

"It's good for me."

She shook her head. "You're a genius." Somehow, that one hurt more than all the times she had said "asshole." "Do you know exactly why you need to eat protein, what your body does with it?"

"I'm a bartender, not a doctor."

"I'll take that to mean, 'No, Rayb, I'm a normal person who eats without understanding the process.' I'm the same."

"Okay, fair enough. But I can see you've got a hypothesis."

"Well, yeah. Okay. Remember I said I'm from... somewhere else?"

I nodded.

"When a new life is formed, some energy is drawn from my home plane into yours by the human fetus as it begins to grow."

"Human only?"

She waved a dismissive hand. "Animals draw from a different plane. When I consume the placenta, I also get some residue from that energy transfer."

"You eat soul leftovers?"

"No. Don't be so naïve. The misconception of a soul is ridiculously oversimplified. I'm no soul eater."

"You just eat afterbirth and after-transfer?"

"After-transfer?"

"Pla-soul-ta?"

"Asshole." She tried not to smile. I won again, but who's keeping track?

"So," I continued, "what's all this grave-robbing and child-eating crap that goes with the modern ghoul myth?"

"Well, over the centuries we've had to work hard to get proper food supplies. For thousands of years we could just pose as shamans or witch doctors, but it's much easier for us to appear female to you, so we've mostly been witches or midwives. As your society has gotten more squeamish, we've had to be more subtle."

"Squeamish?"

"Is 'sophisticated' less painful?"

"Sure. Yeah. That." Yes, she's right about "squeamish." I just couldn't let it slide for some stupid reason.

"Moving on. In order to get our food, we had to stay near pregnant women. For a long time, you lost a lot of mothers in childbirth. It wasn't that complicated for us to dig up the dead mother and put her back, without anyone noticing usually."

"Usually? When one of you got caught—"

"Yes, it was assumed we were going to eat the corpse. No one ever bothered to ask for details, assuming they caught us, which they usually didn't. We can move very fast when we have to."

"And the child eating? I suppose you would dig up babies that died in birth."

"Of course. But also, a women who had one baby—"

I rapped myself on the temple. "Of course. Hanging around families, digging up babies, they assumed you ate children."

"It didn't help that ghūls became a favorite way to scare children into behaving."

"You make this all sound as if it's behind you."

"Thankfully, it is." She smiled with sad eyes. "I thought I told you what I do for a living."

"You're a doctor of some kind, but I always thought, because of how you say it, that you had a PhD in something like archaeology or literature—" My mouth fell open. "Wait. You're not... are you..."

"An OB/GYN and midwife, yes. I also run an abortion clinic."

"You have a medical degree?"

She actually blushed. "Um. Well. I have seven."

"Seven?"

"I have to go back every once in a while, to make sure my credentials are contemporary."

"Contemporary? Seven? Then you must be—"

Her eyes squeezed down on my words. "I'm in no mood to tell you how old I am."

Therefore, I shut up, groped about, and changed directions. "Well, Raib, it's a brilliant solution."

She smiled. "I thought so. As long as I maintain a high turnover in my staff, no one has a chance to figure out why I'm so hands-on."

I admit it: that sentence required some effort to ignore. I struggled not to imagine what she implied. "High turnover? You mean you're always firing people?"

"No, nothing like that. For a few decades, I just treated them roughly and gave them no reason to feel comfortable."

"What a great boss you must have been."

"Yeah, I'm not proud of that. It felt terrible. But I had to hide in plain sight. It took a while for me to find a better system. I started training the crap out of them, sending them to get certifications, giving great recommendations, but not paying very well. They pursued their careers and quickly got better jobs, often with promotions."

"That sounds better. No one stayed out of loyalty?"

She sighed. "I kept them at arm's length. I was cold. Not mean or anything. I just never gave them anything to connect to."

"That sounds horribly lonely, Raib."

It looked as if she was fighting back tears. "Rayb," she said, as if merely out of habit.

"You know, you don't have to be so alone."

"Who would—" she began.

"Like you? Date you? Want you?"

She blinked wet eyes at me, waiting. Hoping?

"Look, how about you and I go out once, just once, and we'll see how it goes? We'll skip dinner. I've got lots of good ideas."

She raised her eyebrows.

"No, none of them are movies. Calm down." I took a deep breath. "What do you say?"

"I still don't know."

"Do you have an actual objection?"

"No."

"Not interested anymore?"

"Anymore?" She rolled her eyes. "Cocky bastard. No, that's not it."

"Then it's settled. We'll go out Saturday. Don't dress up; be casual. Wear those boots. Meet me here at your usual time."

She looked down at her boots, smiled, and then frowned back up at me. "So you can show off to your pub full of admirers?"

"No. Stop that. We can sneak out the back. Or we can meet at the coffee shop on the corner."

"No, here's fine, I guess. But if I even suspect—"

"Yes, yes, you'll rip my arms off, got it. If that's that, then we're agreed."

"I still don't see why a human being like you would try to date a ghūl."

"I'll pass over the speciesism and say I was going to ask you what a ghoul like you was doing in a jinn joint like this, but I'll save it for another day."

Rayb shook her head and tried to bite back a groan.

"Besides, who said I was human?"

She glared at me. "What the Hell?"

"Interesting choice of words. Maybe this will earn me some of your trust." I quickly loosened my belt and untucked the back of my t-shirt. Before she even realized what I was doing, I pulled three feet of red, fleshy tail out of my pants leg. Rayb stared, open-mouthed, at the sharp nub of barbed, blood-red bone at the tip.

I smiled down at her. "You're not the only one around here struggling to fit in."

TOMMY (*DMB: last name withheld on threat of dismemberment*) would rather remain anonymous. He owns a bar; don't ask where. He has a tail, yes, but that's none of anyone's concern. After three dates with Rayb, neither has consumed or murdered the other, thank you very much, mind your own damn business.

DARIN M. BUSH is an author, speaker, educator, and victim of excessive personality from Atlanta, Georgia. He also uses the word "panel" as a verb, due to his recently acquired addiction to sitting on panels at conventions, discussing science fiction and fantasy. This is his second story published by *Mad Scientist Journal*. His ego is accessible through his Amazon author's page, and his id is on display at Facebook.com/DarinMBush.

AN ABSOLUTE AMOUNT OF SADNESS

An account by Hassan,
AS PROVIDED BY ALI ABBAS

It was raining stair rods. The rain fell in straight, hard spears that turned perpendicular in the sudden gusts of wind. Drops splashed up from the ground like the spreading skirts of old women. London rain, different in its taste and texture from showers, drizzle, and mizzle. London rain, and I was going to walk through it under a small black umbrella.

Walking is my thing. "My brains are in my behind," I joke frequently. "I can't think sitting down." But the truth is I struggle to control my temper. My passions are sudden and incandescent, frequently destructive. So I stride through town. No ambling, nor idling. Even when there is no direction or deadline, I move with purpose and energy. I grind whatever is on my mind beneath my feet until it is so disassembled and thoroughly examined, I find either a solution or suspension. Walking is a protection that leaves me safely exhausted and grounded. No longer a monster, but a man again.

Superstition runs deep in my people. They say I carry a Djinn, a being of fire I must either tame or tire. It is, of course, a tale for children to explain a foul and uncertain temper, a lessening of the blame by assigning it to an external agency. That day of rain I felt something of the truth in their belief. Meeting after soul-sapping meeting at work had left me seething. Nothing was done, no progress was made, and we simply traipsed back and forth over the same old ground. I'd snapped a biro under the desk during the last meeting, trying to contain the urge to speak my mind and wreck my career.

By the time I came down the stairs, I was desperate for the measured solidity of my walk home. I gave Carole at reception a wave and turned up my collar, readying myself to step outside. I reached into the side pocket of my satchel and found nothing.

Carole tapped on my shoulder. "Looking for this?" She held the compact form of my umbrella. "Young lass dropped it in earlier, I didn't know whose it was, but now I know." She gave me a grin and walked back.

I took a half step toward her to ask more questions. I hadn't used my umbrella in the morning, and the rain had started in the afternoon. There was no way I could have dropped it, but it was undoubtedly mine. The Djinn was pressing. I let the mystery go.

There is a pavement etiquette that is doubly important in the rain. One does not launch out of a doorway into a stream of pedestrian traffic. Those already on the move have the right of way. You sidle out, carefully, find a space in the flow, and keep pace for a few steps. In a mass of umbrellas at varying heights, it is essential to tilt and lift in case you take someone's eye out. Only then can you set your own pace, weaving through the other walkers.

It was in that moment of decision that I felt a stutter of unease. I jostled a man with a dripping fedora and leather briefcase. In the chorus of "I'm sorry," I saw her. Space opened between the crowds of overcoats and hunched shoulders. She was different. Eye catching.

Our encounter was inevitable. The weight and gravity of every person on that busy thoroughfare drew the universe in, ensuring its occurrence, spinning other meaningless events off as ephemeral chaff.

Something willed me to cross the street in just that break in the traffic. Our paths touched at the corner.

In another time, in any other place, we would have passed one another without a thought. Londoners are atomistic; we move in a way that diminishes the existence of anyone else except as an obstacle or an annoyance. We weave through the crowds of indifference to different speeds and destinations. All of that changed.

She was drenched. Her dark blue sweater had become a cloud, holding so much water that it hung off her in an amorphous mass. What struck me most was her face. It might have been unremarkable in the dry, yet somehow the wet made it compelling. Framed in ragged strands of ash blonde hair, it was pinched and pale. There were dark smudges around her eyes, and she was washed through with a sense of enormous sadness. All the sorrow in the world was captured and cast in the turn of her lips, the angle of her head.

She stopped when I stopped. The rhythm of the pavement was broken, the Brownian motion of human particles disrupted.

"Here," I said, holding out the umbrella. "It looks like you could use it." The impulse was sudden and irresistible, a white hot instinct that briefly burned out the Djinn.

She looked at her sweater in wonder as it gave off a whisper of steam. We both took a half step forward like courtly dancers into the limited shelter of the umbrella.

We were alone, curtained from the rest of the world by the rain sheeting off the umbrella all around us. The crowds bent their paths as if we were streetlights or bollards. In the thundercloud darkness around her eyes, her irises were glacial. She could have been a Nixie, far from her Nordic home under a curse, carrying with her all the colours of frigid mountains and ice rimmed lakes. She could have been just another Londoner, caught out by the rain. Either way, she did not seem out of place on that dismal corner.

It was under her silver grey regard that I felt a stab of doubt. I could feel the movement of all those homeward bound bodies. Their momentum tugged at me, they wanted me to go home too. She seemed to waver, my uncertainty threatening her existence.

Then her eyes shone back into focus. I was flooded by the enormity of her melancholy. I could not discern if she carried her sorrow, or was sorrow made flesh and water. If I stayed there, the sorrow would reach out and envelop me. Was she a cloud that I would pass through breathing, moistened as if in fog? Was she a lake, its depths dark and unknowable, in which I would drown?

The doubt spread like a stain. Londoners never stop, never talk. It is not fear of interaction that makes us so, but preservation of sanity. We are so many, and so closely packed together, that to let in one is to let in all. We could lose ourselves entirely. What had this girl, woman, cloud, creature done to me to break that sense of self-preservation? The moment was elastic, spreading and stretching. It lasted as the doubt seeped further and further until I was the avatar of uncertainty as much as I perceived she might be the bearer of all the world's dismay.

She put up a hand but stopped short of placing it on my chest. The entreaty to stop was clear, and I had had no answer to the offer I had made. She dropped her hand and looked down, almost demure. Raindrops tipped from her hair and teetered on her eyelashes, indistinguishable from tears. She looked up again, first from beneath those lashes, and then pinning me on twin spears of ice.

I knew then this was not fate or physics. The encounter had been orchestrated. This was my regular journey home from work. I searched for her features in the shadows of memory. Had she watched me from the arched entrance of the library? Had she trailed me as I struggled around tourists, the Djinn simmering and snarling in my steps? She had read my weakness: tears and those eyes. This encounter was planned and to a purpose all its own. My first impression clattered against the other attempts at recollection. Nixie. Was she suffering under a geas, seeking to quench or cure it with a supernatural assault on my person?

There was no one else. We stood in a cocoon of water. I was pinned by those frigid eyes, trapped in a moment that sucked time until the rain was an ocean falling solid and entire around our bubble.

The doubt mutated even as it dissolved me, making room for something else. I felt the chill fingers of fear claw inside. Had I only walked on by, the seconds pouring past me would be mine. Instead, I had given way to the thoughtless impulse, to be trapped in her gaze of steel and ice.

"You'll get soaked, and I'm already wet," she said. Her accent was particular, the distinctive stress and cadence of a Swede, but here it meant nothing. She could yet be a sprite, or just another Londoner in this heaving melting pot. She made no move to step around me, to leave our little bubble of time and space.

The stillness re-kindled my fire. The Djinn that had almost extinguished itself in the impetuous joy of giving roared back with all the pent up frustrations of the day. In the madness of that stellar passion, I shrugged.

Nonchalance is the London way, in the face of terror or kindness. "Kings Cross is just over the road. I'll be out of the rain soon enough. If you're heading down Judd Street you're going to be walking a while yet." I lied casually with a veneer of inconsequence. The station had not been my destination. I had planned on walking several miles yet; up York Way and onto Brecknock Road. I held out the handle.

My own eyes are black rum, fire and warmth. I don't know in that moment of forever, when the rain fell like the ocean, what she saw reflected in them. How deeply did she pierce me, drawing out the knowing of my unwelcome accomplice, and what did she leave behind?

Rock ice fell in the liquid amber furnace. Then she smiled. Her melancholy lifted as she perceived my gift was not some hollow altruism, but meant something, would cost me something. Time returned to its normal passage. The rain fell once again as drops: hard, fast, and separate. I almost lurched into her as I felt the surge of the crowds.

She steadied me with her smile as her smudged, knife sharp eyes tried to drag me back in. She could have been at war with herself. Were we similar? Did she too carry a maddened passenger that made wild demands, urging her to draw me into the well of her sorrow? Was she trying to tame it with the ancient magic of receiving a gift, while it slavered over the scent of my desiccated desert blood? I saw the darkness deep behind her eyes, the secret beds of snowmelt rivers. Her smile was winning, like sunlight reflected off new snow.

"How will I give it back to you?"

The flames leapt white hot from my clenched fists, one in my pocket, one around the umbrella handle. Just as I had thought we had reached an equilibrium, she had poured the evanescent vapour of insult on me. Now I could not hold back the Djinn. I had offered the gift without let or hindrance. There are rules written deep in my bones. A gift once offered can never be taken back.

She felt the heat hammering off me, steaming her wet clothes, pushing away the insistent passers-by. Her hand closed over mine. A cool flask of water under the blistering desert sun. She held him at bay for me.

Ice melted. Her eyes warmed from frigid grey to the pale blue of a clear midwinter sky. Perhaps my gift had lifted her geas, or she had scalded her faerie spirit with the incitement of my own. Perhaps it was just that someone, in the cold air and hunched shoulders of a London street, had lifted their eyes to meet hers and noticed another being in need.

My grip loosened on the handle. My other hand emerged, pliant, uncertain of its role now that the Djinn was doused and cowed by a girl in a sodden sweater. I wanted to touch her, but she could have been as fleeting as a snowflake, and I dropped my hand. My heart hammered catching up the beats it had missed when the world blurred by. Or perhaps it remembered what it felt like to fall in love.

I shook my head. "Keep it, or pass it on to someone else who needs it." I gave her a smile in return. Just for us, the clouds lifted and the sun shone through the London rain into the little universe under our umbrella. It broke the spell, or the moment, or just that fragile mood that could only exist in a moist gloom.

I could sense her stillness, and hear the rain hammering on the umbrella as I strode away. I pinched the lapels of my jacket closed over my tie. By the time I had crossed the road and stood just in front of the station entrance, she had gone, lost in the crowd or poured into the rain.

I felt it then, the weight of the water on my shoulders, dripping through my hair, ruining the cut and fall of my suit. I felt disembowelled by loss, weightless and dizzy, clumsy and disoriented. The umbrella was nothing, easily replaced. I could not condense the loss into something tangible, only a sudden appreciation of absence.

It was as if the girl in the sodden blue sweater carried an absolute burden of sadness, and by relieving it, if only for a moment, I now carried some of it myself. She had dampened the hot, sand-laced scouring wind of my passing with the sodden gust of her own stormy passage. The water and the sorrow were now a part of me. Had I in turn cast a handful of sand into her arctic maelstrom?

I realised then that she and I were more similar than I could ever have imagined. We were both Londoners, and bearers of heritages that were bound by the million tons of concrete and steel around us. I was born not two miles from where I now stood, who knows how many years or generations stood between her and the black ice pools of her origins. And yet our difference was written in our eyes, and she carried all the sorrow of her migrant ancestors with her.

I remembered then that I had learned how to describe the rain from other migrants. "Stair rods" was a term I got from an Ulsterman who was also a Londoner. "Old ladies skirts" was from the Baltics, and another Londoner.

Her sorrow was born out of a sense of longing. It said "I love this place that has taken me into its embrace, borne me and bred me. But my bones know of another home that I have now forsaken, and to which I can't return except to marvel at its difference, and leave diminished."

The station was tempting. I would be well on my way by the time the rain stopped, and I would get home dry. And there was no remnant of the friction of that day in me. The Djinn, if such a thing even existed, had been trapped in a cool slumber.

But I had to walk. I carried the spin of sorrow, the weary weight of understanding I had unwittingly accepted. I abandoned the station and slipped by those hurrying for the shelter it provided. The world was now invisible behind the raindrops on my glasses. I could not see the pitying glances of the people at the bus stop, or the antagonism of the wealthy hailing taxis and seeing me as competition. I didn't need to see it.

My feet knew the route; London is my town after all. I turned up York Way and settled into the steady stride that would see me home. In those first steps, I could feel the sorrow seeping through me, from top to toe as the rain found a way behind my collar and down my back. The sorrow would reach my feet before I got to Tufnell Park, and I would push it through the soles of my shoes into the grey immensity of London's pavements. We would not meet again, but she and I were not alone, atomistic, unconnected. And I would leave her sorrow ground into the miles of concrete to be washed away by the rain.

HASSAN is a second generation immigrant who lives and works in London. He is a marketing executive in a multinational firm, a job which involves a large number of meetings and very little actual work. He is a divorcee in his late thirties and spends his evenings trying not to be set up by his parents with "good girls from good families" back home.

ALI ABBAS is a writer, carpenter, and photographer born and bred in London. He is the author of *Image and Other Stories,* a collection of seven short stories that examine themes of love, loss, and the haunting nature of bad decisions; and *Hajj—My Pilgrimage,* a light-hearted and secular look at the pilgrimage to Mecca that is at the heart of the Islamic faith. Ali maintains a blog at www.aliabbasali.com

ART BY **Shannon Legler**

SHANNON's professional title is "illustrator," but that's just a nice word for "monster-maker," in this case. More information about them can be found at http://shannonlegler.carbonmade.com/.

ELIZABETH FRANK'S DECAYING ORBIT

An account by Elizabeth Frank,
AS PROVIDED BY GARRETT CROKER

The townspeople came to cut off my head tonight, which is why I didn't finish my 250-word report about "the perfectly choreographed cosmic dance of the solar system," as Mr. Stevenson liked to refer to planetary orbits, that was due in the morning.

It's not that my head didn't come off for them. It did. That wasn't the problem.

"It isn't dead!" they cried before they scattered, the shame as bright as the fear in their eyes. Oh, they had no problem calling me Elizabeth (or, in Mr. Stevenson's case, "Miss Frank") during the day, but as soon as the mob got together after dark I became "it." Tonight was yet another failure for them. They still hadn't figured out how to kill me. It would help if any of us knew what the hell kind of monster I was in the first place, but at least we could all cross any of the varieties that died by decapitation off the list, which wasn't nothing. I'll go ahead and call that a silver lining. I want to know what I am as badly as they do.

Still. Ugh. First period is going to suck tomorrow.

"This," Mr. Stevenson said, holding a banana high in the air so the whole class could see, "is a penis."

I have to sit in the front row because I'm technically nocturnal and even with glasses I don't have very good day vision. It hurt to crane my neck (which was still healing) to stare up at the blurry yellow phallic symbol. I rolled my eyes in two sweeping, exasperated arcs, one after the other. I may not have a penis, but like everyone else in the class I know perfectly well what a human one looks like.

This impromptu and obviously improvised sex-ed lesson had been inspired by what I took to be a frantic e-mail from the principal, whose panic at this year's accreditation process had already led him to discover a half-dozen such lessons that were supposed to be mandatory, much to the exasperation of the faculty. The good news was that it gave me an extra night to finish my science report. The bad news was that the banana had obviously come straight from the faculty lounge and was badly browned.

"And this," he said, holding up half a cantaloupe, flesh side out, in his other hand, "is a vagina."

He hadn't even bothered to scoop the seeds out.

It was just as obvious, unfortunately, where the cantaloupe had come from. Its other half was scattered across Mr. Stevenson's desk, tooth marks still visible in the remains of what had obviously been his breakfast before it turned into the class vagina.

Was that a juicy shine lingering on Mr. Stevenson's otherwise perpetually chapped lips, or was I only imagining it? I thought of the cantaloupe in my own bag, which Mom had packed for my lunch, and began to feel sick. Melon was one of the few non-meats I could regularly keep down, and since I preferred to eat my meat (very) fresh, melon was all I usually ate when people might actually see me.

I didn't think I would be able to stomach my lunch after this.

Something collided with the back of my shoulder and fell to the floor with a small clattering sound, and something else bounced off the scab on my neck before dropping down the back of my shirt. Somebody snorted, only barely trying to hide the laugh. I tried not to think too much about the logic behind being afraid enough of a thing to want to cut its head off, but also comfortable enough with it to instigate and laugh at. Mr. Stevenson didn't do anything when this happened, like usual. I just kept my eyes forward.

"And this... Miss Frank, please pay attention," the lumpy authority figure said, holding up a condom that, distressingly, he had not needed to improvise, "is a condom."

I didn't hear much of the rest of the lesson, as I was busy trying to ignore all of the sick feeling that had settled in my gut, the lingering pain in my neck, and the rising tide of emotions that every soft collision against my back brought.

Aymberlynn bounced alongside me at lunch, gorging herself on my melon, which I had not been able to eat after all. Her parents *really* liked the letter Y. She preferred to go by Amber. My stomach made a noise like a jaguar (the animal and the car), and I did my best to ignore it.

Her hand that wasn't cradling a cantaloupe slice was swiping energetically up and down the screen of her phone. I didn't need to look to know that she had it open to Wikipedia's exhaustive list of monsters. She was frowning.

"I can't believe they actually tried to decapitate you," she said. "God, what is wrong with people?"

"They didn't try to," I said. "Technically, they succeeded."

"Yeah, well, *technically* they're all a bunch of sweaty ballsacks," she said.

I remembered the shame shining in her father's eyes from the night before as he tried to make himself just another face in the vanishing crowd, but didn't mention it. Amber was well aware of her father's torch-carrying hobby and didn't need me to reinforce her convictions about just what kind of a ballsack he was. Amber was better with colorful adjectives than I was, anyway.

"Still," she said while chewing, scrolling rapidly down the page with another flick of her thumb, "that does narrow it down."

At that moment a football spiraled hard into the back of my head. I felt the scab at the base of my neck tear as my head lurched forward and gagged on the milk-of-magnesia taste of what passed for blood in my body as I bit deep into the flesh of my tongue.

Amber spun and was halfway down the hallway backing the boy who'd thrown the ball, a senior jock slash honor student slash walking acne scar, into the lockers. If I wasn't still smarting from the impact, I would have smiled at the sight of the six-foot-some-odd meatbag cowering before Amber's (admittedly muscular) five-feet-if-she-stands-on-her-tiptoes frame.

"What exactly is your problem, dickshit?" she started, bits of melon flying from her mouth. It only got better from there.

Amber can make it not suck to be me sometimes.

By the time the sun set and I could get out to hunt, I was keep-your-pets-indoors levels of starving. That was actually one of the reasons the townspeople were so afraid of me. There was a time once when they only treated me like a regular old complete and total outcast. But then one night I got really, really hungry and our resident cat lady, old Mrs. Meriwether, forgot to count heads properly when she called in her brood for dinner. I came upon the fat white tabby crying outside her door to be let in a few hours after sunset. Mrs. Meriwether opened the door a few minutes after that to a sight she'd rather forget.

I'm a carnivore, alright? I mean, aside from the occasional melon. And a girl's gotta eat.

Anyway, word got around, and before a day had passed, the rumor was that Mrs. Meriwether had caught me hunched over the still moving body of a half-eaten four-year-old human child. They came with actual torches not long after that, and we all found out for certain that I wasn't the kind of monster that would burn to death.

I was really beginning to regret giving that cantaloupe to Amber when I spotted an owl with one eye at the exact moment I noticed a raccoon with the other. I had to make a decision quickly: the owl would taste better, but the raccoon, backed into a narrow dead-end alleyway, would be easier to catch and have more meat on it.

I was stalking the raccoon before I even realized I'd chosen, hunting instincts kicked into high gear. Every one of my muscles was tight with the anticipation of my upcoming attack. All eight claws extended involuntarily from my fingers.

The dirty trash burglar never stood a chance.

It tasted even worse than it looked, but for the first few minutes I barely cared. All that mattered was the heavy weight of meat in my gut and the deep relief of warm blood coating my parched throat.

Soon, I came back to myself a little, chewing the chunks of flesh I ripped away from the dead animal more and more deliberately as I went. Though the kill was fresh, the meat had a slightly rancid quality to it, as though all the refuse the animal had managed somehow to keep fat on had been absorbed directly into its cells.

I gagged, but kept chewing, hunched over in the alley as small as I could make myself in the hopes that nobody walking by would notice. I at least had to finish.

I killed the thing, after all. The least I could do was finish.

Nearly done, I cracked open a leg bone and let the marrow drip into my mouth. Unlike the meat, the raccoon's marrow was delicious, salty and buttery and just a little bit sweet, completely incongruous with the flavors surrounding it. I thought of this as dessert. I had earned it.

By then, I had almost returned to my senses. My stomachs were stretched tight, and I basked in the serotonin rush that accompanied the sudden bloat of my organs. I heard the familiar sounds of the night in my hometown, the steady crush of pebbles under passing tires, the distant chattering of aimless teens out later than their parents would like but not so late as they wanted, and the odd but pleasant silence of a small town settling in for the night behind it all. My anxieties calmed a little. Now that I was actually able to pay attention, I could tell nobody was around to find me.

I rolled the marrow on my tongue, savoring it.

The smell snuck up on me at first. If I had still been hungry, my head would have spun, but on such full stomachs it actually made my belly clench a little. It smelled delicious.

I couldn't help it. I couldn't eat another bite, but I had to see what it was, *had* to know what delicacy these alleys had been hiding from me for so many years, what delights I had been missing out on when I hunted.

It wasn't any of the common fare, not the gamey scent of birds like the owl, nor the sweet fat (but otherwise plain) scent of domesticated animals. This was different. This smelled like something that had been made for me, just for me and nobody else.

I followed the smell to the back of the alley, the very deadest corners of the dead end, but there was nothing. I looked wildly in as many directions as I could, eyes moving independently of each other so I could see more at once. But there was nothing.

I felt panic rising in me. Here was this thing, a thing I *needed*. And it wasn't just food. This, whatever it was, was part of my identity. The craving was so pure I thought that if I could just find it, if I could just satisfy it, it would at last help me understand what I was.

My left eye settled suddenly on the corner of the alley. It wasn't a dead end after all, not in the true sense. The wall at the end of the alley didn't quite connect the two buildings; there was a space between them. It was far too small for me to squeeze into, but it could fit an animal. I got close to the wall and shoved my arm in the crack as far as it would go.

The thing was there, soft and fleshy and wet. I drew my hand out and tasted the wetness, the blood, on my fingers.

It was so very sweet my knees almost went out beneath me.

I reached back in and sunk my claws into the flesh to grab hold and pulled. It resisted. Whatever it was, it was a little too big for the crack, had been forced roughly inside. I pulled again, hard, and it moved.

It slid out with a slightly sickening sound and thudded to the ground, and then I saw what it was.

"No," I said. "No, no, no."

The child might have been five or six years old. Its abdomen was torn open, ribs broken outward so they looked like fingers reaching for the sky, organs gone.

"No," I said again, and ran.

I closed the door behind me as softly as I could with shaking hands. I wasn't trying to hide the fact that I'd been out late like Amber sometimes had to do. My parents understand why I need to go out so much after dark, and it's even saved us some trouble on those nights when a mob stopped by and I wasn't in. No, I just didn't know what else to do. I wanted to tell somebody about the child's body, about how the smell and the taste made me feel, revulsion all mixed up with desire. Even the aftertaste, by then sour in my mouth, made some part of my brain think very seriously about going back.

I needed to tell somebody.

I didn't know how.

I stood facing the door trying to breathe evenly, to control my shaking before trying to walk up the stairs to my bedroom. I must have stood there like that for a minute—two minutes? Three?— before it occurred to me that the light was on, even though it was past midnight and my parents never stayed up past 9.

I turned, not sure what to expect. Mom was sitting at the head of the dining table, her hands cupped around a mug of coffee that wasn't steaming anymore. Dad sat straight across from her at the other end, one hand resting on top of the other. Even though neither one was looking at me (they both had a tired, lost look in their eyes), there was no question they both knew I was there.

Mom only turned to look at me once I sat down. The lost look on her face disappeared as soon as she did, like marker being wiped from a dry erase board, as if her own misery could not exist in the face of my own. Dad's gaze didn't change. He sat there like a statue.

"Oh my God, honey, look at you," Mom said, putting her hand on mine the way mothers do. "Your fur is completely on end. And you're freezing! Elizabeth, what's wrong?"

I almost told her. It almost all came pouring out. I was so close. But when I looked in her eyes, I saw how red they were. She had done a poor job of cleaning up her makeup, and little black splotches rimmed her eyes. Now that I was paying attention, I realized she even smelled like the salt her tears had left on her face.

And when I looked across at Dad, I could see how carefully he was avoiding my eyes, how little he allowed himself to move, as though any shift in his position would cause his whole body to fall apart.

"It's... nothing," I said. "Nothing I'm not used to, anyway. Some jock hit me with a football earlier."

"Oh, honey," Mom whispered, and that was all she said for a long time.

I wanted to stand and go up to my room and fall asleep and

wake up to find that none of this had happened, and that I've been a normal 15-year-old girl this whole time, with normal eyes so I could disappear into the back of the class and a normal appetite so I could buy a school lunch and cheat on the salad diets I was failing to be on with my friends, plural, and normal limbs so that I didn't have to lope around everywhere like some kind of prehistoric bird and clutch pencils awkwardly in my four-fingered hands, and a normal fragile body so that if anybody ever cut my head off again I would just die already.

But Mom's hand stayed on mine, just firm enough to keep me from pulling away. Her shoulders heaved once, and a single sob as deep as the ocean on the darkest night escaped.

"When your father and I found you, we never thought it would be like this," she said. I stiffened. Mom and Dad rarely ever talked about finding me, or about taking me in. As far as any of us liked to acknowledge, I had always been theirs. "I can't stop them. I try. I do. I try *everything*, and nothing ever works. When they came last night, I didn't know what to do. I didn't…"

I shifted the positions of our hands so that mine was on top of hers. "Mom."

"I didn't do anything!" she cried out, making even Dad flinch. "I just stood there."

Then her heaves came in like the tide, steady and unrelenting.

A part of me knew that this scene, my mom crying and me consoling her, should be played the other way around, and that part of me was screaming in my head as loudly as it could. It wasn't Mom whose head had been cut off. It wasn't Mom who had to live with a barrage of insults and objects every day of her life. It wasn't Mom who had just found a little kid's body, torn open. And it wasn't Mom who was trying desperately not to wonder how it would have tasted fresh.

It wasn't Mom who should be allowed to cry.

But it was Mom who was crying.

I sometimes thought that if I just died for real one of these times, it would make things so much easier for Mom and Dad. I don't want to die, but I'm not a fool either. I knew that if I did, things would be a lot simpler for a lot of people. I suddenly understood that, at some point, maybe all the time, Mom must have thought the same thing, that some small part of her knew how much easier it would be if I were gone, and that this same small part of her actually wanted it.

How guilty must she feel for that one small part?

"I'm so sorry," she said. "We never thought it would be like this."

"Mom." I squeezed her hand. "Dad. It's okay. I'm okay. It's just another stupid boy, like all the rest. *Nothing* they can do will ever hurt me."

Her heaves stopped, and she looked at me with wide eyes, loving eyes, guilty eyes. Dad's eyes were closed.

"I love you so much," she said.

"I have school in the morning," I replied. I took my hand away from hers. "I'd better get to sleep."

"You like the taste of human blood?" Amber whispered, so loudly it sufficiently defeated the purpose of a whisper. At least nobody passing us in the hall seemed to notice. "Oh my God, that's amazing!"

"Jesus Christ, Amber. It is *not* amazing," I said. "What is the opposite of amazing? Because this is that."

"No, seriously," she said. And then, "Wait. I have an idea."

Amber loosed an arm from her backpack and spun it around to the front of her body in one quick, practiced motion. She unzipped the front pocket just enough to shove her hand inside and made faces while she searched for whatever it was she was trying to find. When she didn't find it, she pulled her hand out, grabbed the Sanrio charm she'd attached to the backpack's main zipper, and tugged upward.

Again, she dug around the guts of her bag until this time her eyes lit up.

Triumphantly, she pulled out a pair of scissors, small enough not to count as a weapon in the eyes of the school, but still sharp enough to actually be one if the opportunity presented itself.

I didn't know what the point of this was until she started pressing one of the blades into her left thumbpad.

"Amber, no!" I yelped. A few of the students around us actually turned to look, but quickly looked back away when they saw it was me.

I grabbed at the hand Amber was holding the scissors in, but it was too late. A thin line of blood crossed her thumb. She shoved the thumb in my face. Any closer and she would have painted my upper lip a bright, disturbing red.

I closed my lips tight and turned my head away as much as possible. I tried to grab the hand and push it away, but Amber's reflexes were insane. No matter how fast I tried to grab her hand and no matter how much I squirmed to move my head out of the way, she somehow managed to dodge every attempt and keep her stupid thumb square under my retreating nose.

Finally, she pulled her hand back.

"Nothing?" she asked.

"Nothing what?" I said, barely even trying to keep the annoyance out of my voice.

"You don't want to eat me?" She sounded disappointed.

"No!"

Then I realized that she actually *was* disappointed. She was actually pouting. I swear to God, any other person in this hellmouth of a town would have been thrilled to learn that, no, I didn't actually want to eat them. But not Amber.

It would have made me smile if it weren't so twisted.

After a moment, her face became thoughtful. "That means it's not human blood, then," she said. "It must just be children. That's actually really good to know."

"How?!" This was just too much.

"No, seriously. Hear me out. I've been thinking lately we've been trying to identify you all wrong. I keep going over and over this list of monsters, and a lot of the information we have on them is pretty unreliable. We just had this unit in psych about how bad eyewitness accounts are, and that's all we have for most of these. For some of them, we have even less than that. So I've been going back through the list and identifying only essential characteristics. Like, werewolves: we don't *really* know what they look like, but the transformation bit is non-negotiable. Vampires: do they burn in the sun? Do they glitter? Different accounts say different stuff, but they definitely drink human blood. Furry trout? Maybe they grant wishes and maybe they poison water supplies, but they definitely have fur. Otherwise, they'd just be trout."

"Okay, Jesus. I get it, Amber."

"So, what I'm saying is now we have a little more essential information on you. Maybe we threw out a possibility before because we made some assumption we didn't need to. But eating children, that's solid gold for us!"

"I don't eat children!" I yelled, and that definitely got a few looks I wish it hadn't.

"Whoa, okay," she said, actually quiet enough this time that only I could hear her. "Having a taste for children, I mean. I know you don't like it, and I get it. I do understand. Nobody in their right mind would like what you're going through. But this actually does get us closer to knowing what you are."

Maybe, I thought for the very first time in my entire life, *I don't actually want to know.*

"By the way," Amber said, curiosity clear on her face. "What did the cops do when you called in that body?"

"I," I said, the words dying on my lips. Somehow, between the shock of finding the body, of tasting it, and being so tired, and comforting Mom and Dad, and trying to just make it through another day at school, I hadn't realized how bad it would look for me when somebody eventually found that body, ribs cracked open like a crab, claw marks all over it, organs missing. My voice came out very small. "I didn't tell anyone."

Amber's eyes got very big.

And then the bell to go to class rang.

The torches were out before the sun even went down that night, only a few at first. They moved slowly, from house to house, gradually adding to their number. I put my textbook down and watched them gathering from my window, little orange blurs in the failing sunlight.

There was something strange about how they were coming together this time, and the more houses they stopped at the more obvious it became why they started pulling the mob together so early. Normally, one person would run ahead of the group, only knocking on the doors of reliable torch-carrying citizens. But this time, they were stopping at every house along the way, the whole group together, and it looked like *everyone* was joining in.

When the last of the light fell behind the horizon and I could see clearly again, I understood why. Right there in the center of the expanding torchlight, hoisted high into the air by a pair of strong arms, was the body of the child.

They were using it to rally the biggest mob the town had ever seen against me.

"Leave," Dad said, his hand on my shoulder startling me. Mom stood behind him, the silent one now, and I wondered how they decided which one of them spoke up when and which got to be the statue. "Go hunting. At least make it hard for them to find you. On foot outside at night, you have the advantage. Your mother and I will stall them."

It was so strange how little he resembled the silent figure at the table a night ago, how much strength he had gathered since then. Where did it come from?

I looked out the window again at the now massive crowd. I could run, and I did need to hunt. On a normal night, they'd never find me if I didn't want them to, but with this many people searching, all with torches to burn away the shadows? It would be tough to stay hidden.

I scanned the mob. There was Mr. Stevenson, and there was Amber's dad, both right up front. Everywhere I looked, I either saw somebody who I knew or the parents of somebody I knew. And they all hated me so much for being whatever the hell I was that they would try to kill me again tonight, and if they failed they hated me enough to try again another night. They would keep trying until it worked, and all I had ever wanted to do was stay out of their stupid way.

Maybe Dad was right. I *could* run.

Maybe somewhere else, it wouldn't be this way. Maybe. And it's not like this awful town deserved my loyalty, anyway. When it came down to it, except for my parents, the only person here who had ever been nice to me on purpose was Amber.

"No," I said.

Dad's firm grip faltered on my shoulder. Mom made no move, and no sound.

"I'm sorry, Dad," I said. "But screw that."

A few minutes before the head of the mob got to the house, I jumped up to the roof. As long as nobody came with a ladder, that would slow them down enough for me to do what I had planned.

Looking down, I saw my parents waiting outside the front door, my vanguard. It must have been freezing, because they were both shivering, but it's hard to sympathize when you're literally cold-blooded. I tried, anyway.

"You guys should go inside," I said down to them. "You don't have to do this."

They looked up at me, resolved to their course, eyes shining in the night like tiny moons in decaying orbits, firm in the knowledge that the only thing left to do was fall, and wait.

For the love of God, I had to stop doing my science homework before people tried to kill me.

The crowd was beginning to arrive. They had kept the child's body toward the front of the mob, like a battalion flag, Mr. Stevenson always by its side, Amber's dad always by his. This was it, then. There was only one thing left to do.

I had never really tried to find out how loud I could be, so I didn't know what to expect. When my voice came out, it actually shook the air.

"LISTEN UP, DICKSHITS," I said.

Saying the words, I felt suddenly calm.

"THAT"—I pointed a long claw at the body—"IS NOT MINE."

Nobody moved. I don't think they knew what to do. I had struggled against them in the past (they wanted to *kill me*; how could I not have?), but I had never actually stood up to them, never talked back. Even I was surprised by how much of a voice I had.

Their inaction gave me some confidence.

"AND YOU KNOW WHAT? HOW DARE YOU—*HOW DARE YOU*—EVEN PRETEND TO THINK THAT IT IS. I HAVE GONE OUT OF MY WAY AGAIN AND AGAIN TO PROVE THAT I AM NOT DANGEROUS, AND YOU ASSHOLES JUST DON'T CARE, AND I DON'T KNOW WHY."

Still, nobody moved. Just cowards after all, all of them. The very first second I actually challenged their shit, it fell apart. It pissed me off. How could they be so weak? How could I have let them do what they did to me for so long when they were so stupid and weak the whole time?

"TELL ME WHY!" I bellowed, my voice somehow even louder.

It was Amber's dad who finally stepped forward, and behind my anger and my pain, I actually kind of respected him. Of all the invertebrates here, his model came with a backbone. Of all the people here, only he had raised a kind person.

"We have the body!" he yelled back, pointing at the child. "It's right here! You can't deny it anymore. You can't deny the evidence."

"THAT. IS. NOT. MINE." I growled.

"Then who did it?" he yelled, and the crowd roared behind him, life coming back into it.

I didn't have an answer for him.

"And it's not the first time you've done it, either," he yelled, facing the crowd instead of me, feeling their support rallying behind them, hoping to nurture it. "We all know about Mrs. Meriwether's grandson."

The mob exploded in agreement.

"No," I yelled back, the power in my voice lost. "That was a cat. Mrs. Meriwether never even had children. That's why she keeps so many cats. How could she have a grandchild?"

But nobody heard me.

Everything happened fast after that. Amber's dad moved toward the house. Dad got in his way, but Amber's dad hit him, hard. The sound his fist made against Dad's skull was not that of flesh and bone on flesh and bone, and as Dad crumpled to the ground, I realized Amber's dad was wearing a pair of brass knuckles.

"No!" I cried. Mom ran to where Dad had fallen.

The torches pressed together and moved forward. The crowd grew so dense that the light dazzling my eyes looked like a single blaze. I could hear Amber's dad pounding on the front door, and then the sound of fists joining his.

Somebody started to drag Dad away from the house, and when Mom tried to fight them, another person grabbed her from behind and pulled her away too. Amber's dad stopped pounding on the door and took a few steps away. Turning to the crowd again, he yelled.

"Burn it down!"

Mom kicked and bit at the man who had her, but his grip was strong. As a handful of torchbearers moved to place their flames against the house, to set *my home* aflame, her kicks grew more and more desperate, and another man stepped in to help the first. She couldn't do anything against them.

And in the middle of all of this was the body, the poor, dead child, who had probably only ever wanted to grow up and live a normal life and have friends and learn to love, but whose guts had been ripped out instead, who had been made a victim against his will, a rallying cry for violence without his consent.

Mr. Stevenson had never left the child's side, had kept one hand on the body the whole time, holding it aloft.

For just one small second, he pulled that hand away. He moved a finger, thick with the corpse's coagulated blood, to his mouth. And he sucked, a look of pure pleasure crossing his face. Nobody but me saw this.

His eyes met mine, one at a time, and he smiled.

"YOU!" I yelled, pointing directly at him, my voice strong again.

The torchbearers moving to set the house on fire stopped in place, as did almost everyone else. Slowly, their heads turned in the direction of my finger.

I leapt high into the air, claws extended, fur raised, and just before I came crashing down on Mr. Stevenson's shoulders I saw him transform, and he looked like me.

His cartilaginous frame bent against my impact but didn't break, and he rolled gracefully with the hit, throwing me into the crowd.

Somebody caught me, staggering back into another group of people, but kept me upright.

"Are you alright?" they asked.

My head spun so fast to face them I almost tore the scabs on my neck again. I grimaced.

"You came here to kill me," I snapped. "And you're really asking that question?"

I wanted a response. I wanted to stare down their fear and their shame and force them to stare back, but I didn't get the chance. Mr. Stevenson barreled into me, and the moment was gone.

We rolled in the street, fighting each other on instinct. My body did things I had never known it could do, claws extending an extra inch at least, jaw unhinging, spikes lifting menacingly out from my spine. And every predatory change in my body was met by an identical one in Mr. Stevenson's.

I dug my claws into him, tearing out chunks of flesh, trying to get at his organs, trying to rip them out of him, and his likewise sunk into me.

I snapped my unhinged jaws in the direction of his neck. They closed with a sickening sound, but on air only. He bit back, and I recoiled as he had, avoiding his bite by mere millimeters, his breath a stale mix of melon and blood in my nose.

I ripped my hand out of him and felt something come free with my claws. He yowled in pain and grew more desperate. Somehow, his panic made him stronger. Faster. And all of my anger, all of my hatred couldn't keep up.

I thought of Mom being held by those bullies and Dad lying prone in the front yard from the blow to his skull, and I fought harder. I still couldn't keep up.

We rolled and somehow he was on top of me, pinning me down. I couldn't move.

"Do it, then," I spat. "Just do it."

He laughed then, a choked and terrible sound. "Do you think if I actually knew how to die we would have tried so many different things on you?" Then he lowered his head to my ear and whispered, "I don't know what I am, either."

The world disappeared in a blaze of light, and I heard Mr. Stevenson's cries. Then his hands were off of me, and I closed my eyes tight and turned away. My jaw settled back into its hinge. The spikes along my spine retracted. And the wounds I had suffered began to hurt.

It only dawned on me slowly that the townspeople had come to my aid finally, dislodging him from his place atop me with their torches.

"You can transform to look like a human?" Amber whispered excitedly while doing something on her phone. Then her tone shifted. "Crap, I had eliminated species that can transform. I'm going to have to start over all over again."

"It *is* kind of amazing," I said. "I really don't know how to do it yet, though. I can't wait to look normal."

Amber looked up from her phone long enough for the screen to go dark. The look on her face was strange for a moment, anger warring with confusion (and was that betrayal?), and then she got it back under control.

"I like you this way," she said, matter of factly.

"Amber," I started, but didn't finish.

Then she was back to her phone, scrolling quickly with her thumb. "So does this mean that Mr. Stevenson is your real dad?"

"First of all," I said, "yuck. Second of all, he's gone now and we'll hopefully never see him again. Which is great because I never finished that stupid report and also because I hate him. Third of all, if you're still counting, I live with my real dad already." (Dad was home getting a week's paid vacation by way of apology for the disgusting bruise covering half his face.)

The whole time I spoke, she never looked up from her phone. A small smile bloomed on her face.

"Hey, I've got something to show you," she said, tapping something on the screen and holding it out to me.

It was a Wikipedia page, cross-linked from their list of monsters, with the header "Elizabeth Frank." Just below that was my 8th-grade photo, which Amber knew was the only class photo of me I actually liked. I scrolled a little bit, and found a page full of subheadings which included things like "Physical Characteristics," "Local Misrepresentations," and "Known Weaknesses."

"It took me *forever* to get this approved," she said. "Total pain in my ass. You have no idea. And now I guess I'm going to have to edit the whole thing again."

Not holding the phone, she swung her arms awkwardly at her sides, crossing them briefly in front of her before dropping them again.

"I mean, listen," she said. "I'm still trying to figure out what you actually are. I'm not going to stop. I just thought in the meantime this would be good enough. Now you exist. Officially."

Like I said before. Sometimes Amber makes it not suck to be me.

I tapped on the heading for "Known Weaknesses" to expand the section. There was only one word there:

None.

ELIZABETH FRANK is a monster of indeterminate origins residing in the American northwest *[1]*. Cold-blooded, covered in fur, and largely invulnerable, she possesses a unique combination of reptilian, mammalian, and legendary traits. Though many fear her for her differences, she is not hostile to humans and her hunting actually keeps local vermin populations down *[2]*. She will finish her stupid science report if it kills her, which it won't *[citation needed]*.

GARRETT CROKER studied writing at UC Berkeley and received his MFA in creative writing from Mills College. He is a monster of the genus *Homo Scriptorus*, a much feared species known for subsisting on caffeine-based nutrients and possessing a particularly thick epidermal layer. Find him online at garrettcroker.com and on Twitter at @garrettcroker.

THE WOMAN FROM KISTHENE

An account by Sheriff John Beaumont,
PROVIDED BY J. C. STEARNS

If I'd known who it was before I got to the diner, I'd have been more excited to go. I wouldn't have moved any faster, mind, but I'd have been taking my time to build the tension rather than just wanting to spend more time driving through the leaves. All the same, I knew it wasn't a routine call. Maybe I've just been waiting for so long I was starting to imagine things, but even before I knew who it was, I knew that something was up.

Madison's didn't look any different when I pulled up. Same neon sign with the same broken letters desperately begging travelers to "E-t at Ma-ison's." Same regulars parked in their normal spots. Same smattering of traveling folk who'd taken pity on the sign. The damage from the storm was still evident, even though it had been repaired. You could tell which of the light poles in the parking lot were new, standing out from the others by their lack of weathering. The windows that Maddy'd had to replace had been in long enough to be as dirty as all the others, but you could still see the scars around them where the plywood had been nailed on.

My deputy, Mike Scoggins, was waiting outside. He had his hat in his hands, nervously rotating it around and around. He looked like he was hoping the hat would act as a shield from my wrath. Honestly, I wasn't angry. I came into these situations as severe as I could, but if I'm laying all my cards on the table, I do that to put the scare into the punks from the city.

People think it must be a hard job to be a sheriff in such a small community, but it really isn't. It's true I know most everyone's dirty laundry, but as long as they don't bother anyone, I don't see a need to bother them. The city's like a merry-go-round on a school playground. Everyone already got it going, so all I have to do to keep it spinning around is to give a little push now and then. It's peaceful, really.

Mike probably could have handled a disorderly call on his own, but I think he prefers to take the cat up a tree calls and leave the harder ones for me. Not that I blame him. He's got that baby face and the "aw, shucks" manner that people think of when they talk about small town law enforcement in a good way. I tend to take the mirrored sunglasses, "back the way you came, boy" kind of calls. It's not out of a preference for that kind of work, you understand, but my scarred face makes me a better fit for "bad cop."

"Maddy asked them both to leave," Mike started as I got out of my cruiser, "but they told her to piss off. When she said she was going to call the cops, they just laughed at her."

I sighed. I put on my mirrored shades, and took a moment to set my face into as grim a look as I could.

As soon as I stepped in to Maddy's, I recognized him. To be honest, I always thought he'd look older. I mean, he wasn't going to be gracing the cover of GQ anytime soon, but he definitely didn't look anywhere near as old as I knew he had to be. He had black hair, thick black hair. It framed his head, flowing from hair to sideburns and down into beard seamlessly. There wasn't even an attempt to control it, or shape it, but it found its own shape nonetheless. The gleaming black ringlets swirled around in lazy curls, all drifting in the same direction. It shone in the light, looking almost oily. Somehow I knew it wouldn't be. It had that swirly, lazy grace and supernatural darkness that is usually associated with the King of rock 'n roll, although Elvis had never let his hair get this long and unruly. He even had the one curl across his forehead like the King.

I hadn't realized I was approaching him, hadn't even been aware of moving, until I was at his table. I'd thought about this moment before. I think every man has thought about this moment, or one like it. Somehow, I was unprepared for the reality. He didn't even see me, not even when I stopped next to their table. His gaze was fixed, unblinking, at the window, although whether he was staring at the sea or off at some point beyond the horizon I couldn't say.

"I smell bacon," snorted the other one. I hadn't paid attention to the other man sitting at the table. When he talked, I didn't see how I could have missed him. He was huge. Easily over six feet, and probably knocking on the door of seven, this ogre had to have outweighed both me and Mike combined. He put his hand up, and I thought for a second he was going to grab for me, but then his fingers flickered over the table in the nimble dance of those used to feeling around for things. I realized he was blind a second before I saw the thick shades on his face, burn scars creeping up from the left side. I wondered if the right side was blind, too, or just smooth flesh.

"Well that's funny son," I said, "I was just about to say that I smelled something burning."

His mouth fell open, and I think he might have brought the situation to a head right then and there if the King hadn't put his hand on the giant's shoulder. He tore his eyes away from the window, finally looking at me.

"Easy, Paulie," he said. "Go away," he said to me, and I heard a saga in those two words. His voice was rich and deep, powerful. A voice people loved to listen to, to obey.

Behind my glasses, my eyes started to drop to the table. Doubt started to creep into my throat.

And then I saw his chest. His Hawaiian flowery shirt was open at the top, and a few wiry chest hairs crept out. They were no longer the powerful obsidian color of his hair. Instead, they were the slate grey of an old man. It was like a spell breaking, as I saw him all over again. The lines around his face told me the many miles that separated him from his heyday. I took a deep breath.

"I was just about to tell you the same," I said.

The King leaned forward, and I'm not sure if the saltiness of his breath was due to the half a plate of fries he'd eaten or not. I suspect he always had a lingering aroma of salt.

"It's funny," he said, "you trying to poke fun at my son over his scars. What's that expression you rednecks have about pots and kettles?"

"Oh these?" I asked, holding up my hand. Two lines of scars trailed around my index finger, like melted wax poured onto the skin. I fingered my collar, where the veins of sunken, knotted flesh peeking out hinted at a much uglier memory hidden beneath my shirt. "Or did you mean these?"

"Was someone playing with matches?"

"Of course not," I said, not moving my head. Only my mouth moved on my face, the rest of me locked in the practiced stillness of a predator. The mirrors over my eyes betrayed nothing. I could see him starting to get agitated. He was used to getting fear, and I was giving him none. "Worked animal control for years. We've got some nasty snakes in the area."

"Good thing they moved you to a desk there, Barney. Any longer and you might have wound up hurt." He sat back. He could have been a neo-classic oil painting, "Tough guy waiting for reaction." I gave him none.

I smiled. For someone that I'd always heard prided himself on his creativity, he'd opened up pretty weak. I'd heard every insult the winos and punks and vacationers could think of, and it's been a long time since some aging drunk with a potbelly has been able to rattle me, no matter how scary the stories I've heard about him.

"Andy."

"What?" he asked. This was clearly not the reaction he'd expected.

"I'm a sheriff, asshole. Barney was a dispatcher." I stood up, signaling for Tom, Maddy's busboy. "There's Griffith reruns on TV Land every afternoon. You should go check them out. At your hotel." I turned to Tom, who'd just arrived. "Clear this out. These folks are done."

He didn't believe me, or maybe he thought we were still playing. Either way, he reached out his hand for a French fry.

With as much economy of motion as I could manage, I tipped his plate over, not even watching as it crashed to the floor.

Finally, my disrespect got the better of him. I'm sure he'd learned to cope with a great deal of insolence over the years, but there was only so much he could stand. With a bellow, he lurched to his feet. His son followed suit, the chair he'd been sitting in flying into his hands like magic. I dodged back as it whistled past my head.

I ducked under the King's wild haymaker, and punched him in the face. If it had been a normal drunk, I'd have taken him down textbook, all neat and nonviolent. But this was a special drunk. That black hair flapped as he crashed to the ground. I turned in time to see blind Paul lunging at me. Behind him, I could see Mike jumping forward, fumbling in his pocket for something. Paul's hands grabbed at my chest, fingers flickering upward until they snaked around my throat. I felt them start to close down and wondered if he'd kill me before Mike wised up enough to shoot him. I lashed out at him with my fists, but I couldn't get any decent leverage, and even the shots to his face didn't seem to faze him.

As suddenly as they'd latched on, the fingers went slack. Paul slumped forward with a kind of tidal slowness. He didn't catch himself, just fell face first onto Maddy's floor. Behind him, Mike looked from me to the laid-out giant, eyes wide and fearful. He clutched his blackjack in a white-knuckled hand. Not standard issue, but once you've had to wrestle a two-hundred-pound felon who was flying on meth, you learn to carry a little non-standard come-along for just such an occasion.

The King was trying to stand, and I stepped up behind him. His hands groped ahead of him, seeking a chair or table to help him up. Tom took a step away from the grasping hands. Just to make sure the bystanders all stayed on my side, I pushed Tom out of the way.

"You leave him be," I said, and the King looked around in confusion, although later everyone would swear he'd been coming at Tom with murder in his eyes. I grabbed him by the shoulder, my left hand grip a little weaker than my right. I hauled him to his feet and gave him just enough of a push to piss him off more. He hollered and swung at me for the last time. Without the distraction of his behemoth son, I could concentrate fully on my target. I sidestepped his wild swing and grabbed him by the back of the head with my good hand. Pushing him forward along his own momentum, I planted one foot in front of him and sent him to his knees, his head crashing down onto the neighboring table. Suddenly struck by my own rage, or maybe just by how cruelly symmetrical it would be, I wrapped my fingers in that black hair, dry and silky, and smashed his face into the table. He slumped to the floor with a groan, blood pouring from his nose.

We couldn't get Paul into a sitting position in the back of Mike's cruiser, and so he wound up sprawled across the whole back seat, which was fine with me. That only meant that I could drive his father to the station by myself.

On the ride back, out of the sight of witnesses, I expected him to be scarier, but whatever power he'd had, the King was just a busted old man now. He glared at me from the back seat, dried blood staining his beard like flotsam on the surf.

"If you knew who I was," he said, "you'd have never touched me."

I let the threat hang there for a second. I waited for his eyes to break away from mine in the rearview, to glance out the window. Was he thinking about home? Could he even go home anymore?

"I do know who you are."

His eyes snapped back to the mirror, narrowed in suspicion. Slowly they widened into disbelief. I only smiled. He slumped back into the seat, clearly not sure if he should believe me or not. The station was another ten minutes away. He began muttering under his breath, eyes closed. I could see sweat beading on his forehead.

I grinned. I'd expected this. Where was it going to come from? In his heyday, he'd had a dizzying array of tricks to waylay travelers who displeased him, so it might be anything.

We were nearly to the station when I saw it coming. A horse, brown and muscular, lurched out of the bushes and lunged across the road. If I hadn't been looking for it, I would have smashed it. I swerved around the animal, resisting the urge to laugh. I recognized it as Frank Jericho's horse—a formidable race horse in its day, but far past its prime. I doubt the King was aware of the symmetry.

Once we were clear of the animal, I drove for another minute or so. Then I slammed on the brakes. The King flew forward, crashing into the grate that separated the seats. He gave an undignified squawk, blood flowing down his face again.

"Try that shit again, and I'm going to do a whole lot worse to your boy than putting out his fucking eye."

He gaped at me. As impossible as it seemed that I could know, he finally believed me. The threat wasn't necessary, though. Sweat poured off of his brow, mixing with the blood. He panted, his whole face nearly as red as the blood staining his beard. He didn't have any juice left, and we both knew it. I saw him try to puzzle out how I knew, and finally give up. He stared back out the window. Some might call him broken, but I knew better. His type took a lot to break.

"How'd you know?" he asked.

"I knew you'd come eventually," I said. "Ever since the storm."

He nodded. "They said it was like it appeared out of nowhere," he said. He wasn't even paying attention to me, not really. He was looking at the trees out the window. All over the place, you could see the stumps of the ones that had been torn down when the wind came through. The forestry service had been working non-stop to clear out the bulkiest of the timber, but the entire department could work at it for years and never cut up half the trees the storm had destroyed.

"It did appear out of nowhere," I said. "It was like magic."

"Like an act of god," he said. We both went quiet for a little bit.

"Just a storm," I said.

"They used to think all storms were from the gods," he said. "Things change."

I looked back at him, the blood drying in his inky hair, and he was the same as every other drunk old man in the back of my cruiser, suddenly looking back at all the wrong turns life had taken. I let him think about it for a minute. I wonder if he was blaming himself or everyone else, but before I could ask we pulled into the station.

I hauled him out of the cruiser and threw him into a cell, then helped Mike bring Paul in. It took me about an hour to process them, and to falsify the necessary paperwork in the computer. Fortunately, we have an older system, although Mike wouldn't have questioned me even if I had told him what I was doing.

"Well, mister," I said, standing outside the King's cell. "Looks like you won't be going back to that hotel after all."

"What do you mean?" he growled. "You going to lock me up for brawling, that it?"

"Oh no," I laughed. "Taking a swing at a sheriff is the least of your troubles now. Seems like your fingerprints were already in our system." His eyes narrowed. "You're wanted in connection with an open rape case in our jurisdiction."

He gaped, unbelieving. "What the hell is this?" he bellowed.

I left him to rage in his cell, and went out to show Mike what I had "found" on the computer. I told him where I was going, and made sure he was okay until I got back, suggesting he might want to call Mr. Jericho and tell him his horse had gotten loose.

When I got to the house, my wife was just finishing her breakfast, the news droning on in the background. Our house isn't the biggest or most expensive one in town, but we get by just fine. We've got a porch with an ocean view, but she always eats in front of the TV. So do I. I don't think we've eaten on that porch one single time since we bought the place. She looked at me quizzically when I came in. We've been married long enough to know when something's up. I kissed her hand, wondering if I'd done the right thing. Wondering how she'd react.

"We arrested him."

Her eyebrows arched in confusion, soft eyes widening as she mentally answered her own questions.

"You arrested—?"

"Yes," I said. "He was here with one of his sons. Paulie."

Her lip started trembling, and I desperately wished I could put an arm around her shoulder. I couldn't, of course, and I suddenly wished I could shed the tears she was refusing to. I just stood there as she sat down. The light of the rising sun was coming through the window from our porch, the porch we never sat out on, filling the living room with a golden radiance, reflecting off her hair like a bronze mirror.

My wife has gorgeous hair. Everyone knows that she used to have gorgeous hair, but I don't think most people realize she still does. It flows. That brownish blondish red of a carpet of fallen autumn leaves, it looks like something that could only be described rather than actually witnessed. It looks warm and inviting, begging to be touched, to be stroked. I know better, of course I know better, but it looks so enticing that even I forgot myself once. But only once. I thought familiarity might eventually give me a free pass, but that wasn't the case, and I've never tried again.

"I need to go see him," she said. Not want, she'd said, but need. Of course she did.

She was silent as we drove in. I can't really blame her. Around us, the last autumn trees clung to life, the skeletal prognosticators of their inevitable futures lording over the melancholy rainbow on the ground.

Sometimes, when she was driving us into town during the fall, I would squint and her hair would seem like a part of the trees, like the entire forest was pouring off her scalp. Never for very long. If she caught me staring, she'd be very cross. Nine years ago, I'd bought a convertible for us just so I could put the top down in the summer and enjoy the way her hair whipped around in the wind.

"Vacationers gone?" she asked.

"A few still around, but they've mostly left," I said. If she didn't want to talk about it, that was fine with me. I'm a man, and I understand all too well the idea behind burying your pain until the right time. "Fall's almost over."

"I hear it's supposed to be a cold winter," she said.

"I hope so."

My wife and I love winter more than most. We'd dated for a few months when I found out about her past. She'd told me the whole story shortly after we'd started sleeping together, even though I already knew most of it from school. I think she'd been surprised when I still wanted to see her. I knew it wasn't her fault, none of it, and it certainly didn't change the way I felt about her.

I rolled over against her in my sleep and wound up in the hospital that November. Even though I told her it wasn't her fault, I think she still blamed herself. When winter came, I knew I had to come up with something to show her how I felt, to show her that we could make it work, or she was going to leave. She'd never been ice skating, and to be honest, neither had I, but I pretended that I was an old hand at it, even practicing in private. Finally, I managed to convince her to go out with me when Pindar Lake froze solid.

I made up some cock and bull story about how you weren't supposed to wear a hat and scarf when you were ice skating. I wanted it to be a surprise. Every time she complained about the cold and told me she wanted to go home, I would grab her by the hands, laugh, and spin her back onto the ice, and say "Just a little more." Again and again we dashed back and forth, until finally, as the sunset painted the sky a deep purple, she pushed past me, declaring that she couldn't feel her ears, her nose, or her fingers.

I didn't grab her arm this time, but instead, put one hand on the back of her neck. I felt the movement under that flowing curtain, but it was slow, limp. She jerked away out of instinct, and then looked at me. I smiled, holding up my undamaged hand, and in her eyes the pieces finally came together.

She lunged at me, and she kissed me for the first time, decades of passion unleashed in a moment. We made love right there on the frozen bank of Pindar Lake. Some day, I know, I'm going to get frostbite, but she and I still love winter. Between ice skating, caroling, shoveling walks for the elderly, and every other excuse we can think of, we spend more time outside during the winter than during the rest of the year combined.

"I hope so," I said. "Snow waist high." She smiled and squeezed my hand, but she didn't look at me.

She fell quiet for the rest of the ride. I know her better than to ask if she was alright. She had her own demons to deal with, and if a little bit of quiet time helped her, then I could suffer a little bit of silence. When we got to the station, I didn't say anything. Mike stood up when we came in, but I silenced him with a wave of my hand. He knew my wife—hell, everyone in town did—and if there'd been another deputy around, I think he might have taken the opportunity to step in with the prisoner and tune him up a bit.

We stopped outside the door to the holding area. My wife reached out a hand to stroke the side of my face, to trace the scars with a light finger.

"I'm sorry," she said.

I took her hand and kissed it. "Don't be," I said. "It's always been worth it."

He was staring out the window of his cell when we came in. The police station hadn't always been a police station, so we'd needed to add bars to the inside of the windows, but I don't think he was looking for an escape. Just staring out at the bay with that nostalgic look. She didn't say anything to him, just stood in front of the bars and waited.

Eventually, he turned his head to look at me, and his brow furrowed when he saw her. Confusion turned to recognition, and a moment later, to realization.

"You?" he asked, although I'm not sure who he was addressing, or if he was asking about her identity, our relationship, or something else entirely.

"Yes," she said. They stared at one another for a time. He stood and stepped forward, his shoulders squared. She didn't blink, nor back down. She was beyond fearing him now. Maybe it was the blood on his beard. Maybe it was the bars. Maybe the years. Hell, for all I know, the chest hairs did the same for her that they did for me.

"You think this is going to change anything?" he said, defiant.

"Probably not," she said. I was proud of her. If it was me, I don't think I'd have been able to put as much venom into two words. "But what's the average sentence for a rape?"

"Oh, the report says he has a previous out-of-state sexual assault conviction," I said, "so the court can give any sentence it likes. And you know how these backwoods judges are. What's the word?" I snapped my fingers. "Draconian, that's it."

She'd proven all she needed to, and I couldn't stand by any

longer. I stepped up to stand next to her, not intimidating, but at ease, hands on my belt. Whether or not she needed my support, I needed to support her. He broke then. Well and truly broke. His shoulders sagged, and that aura of power just left him, like water rushing out of a burst barrel.

He may have been broken, but he still had enough spite left to sneer at me, and point at my left hand, where the scarred index finger refused to close over my belt. "Was it worth it?" he asked.

I slid the hand around her waist, and smiled at him through my shades. The mirrors over my eyes reflected nothing back to him but his own defeat, doubled in the lenses.

Finally, then, he looked away from us.

She ran her fingers through her hair and brushed one hand along my arm.

I lifted her hand to my lips in our kiss. Her fingers tasted like her hair smelled.

She nodded to me and turned to leave.

I don't know what possessed him to do it. Maybe he thought her curse was hers to bear and wouldn't affect him. Maybe he wanted to prove he could still touch her, no matter how much had changed. Maybe there's just something about being worshipped that makes you think you're entitled to things that aren't yours. His hand surged out between the bars, faster than I could react, and grabbed her shoulder in a grip as strong as a riptide.

There was no hiss, no rattle, no warning. There never is; I know from experience. The asp at the nape of her neck got him first, roiling through her hair to sink his fangs into the hairy wrist. The adder that sprouted from just below the crown of her head struck a split second later, followed by the fat viper behind her left ear. Each of the serpents vanished back beneath her hair as suddenly as they'd shot out, each one drawn tight against her scalp, patiently waiting for another fool to lay hands on what wasn't theirs. He recoiled, screaming, but she didn't break stride. I wondered, and still wonder, if that moment was worth the two thousand years that preceded it. I doubt she considered it a fair trade.

I stared at him for a minute. He'd sat down on the bench in the cell and wouldn't look at me. He cradled his arm. The venom would scar horribly, I knew. Still, he'd taken three sustained bites and wasn't showing any signs of dizziness.

"You'll be fine," I said. "Although you might not want to try that again." I turned to leave.

"It was accepted back then." He sounded sullen and pitiful. I looked back. Another withered old drunk, just like every other aging bad boy. I could even see a gray hair or two on his head, now that I looked closely. A slight thinning in the hair on his crown. Liver spots on his hands. "Expected, even."

"Things change," I said. Then I left him there, alone in the cell, with iron bars between him and the sea.

My wife was waiting for me in the car.

"You want to go have lunch?" she asked.

"Are you going to cook?" I started up the cruiser and pulled out of the parking lot. She fell in love with me because I treated her like every other woman. And of course, that's what she was. A woman, like every other. Her history didn't change that.

"I thought we might eat out on the porch," she said, running her fingers through her hair. "I hear there's going to be a storm this afternoon." She reached over and squeezed my hand.

"I thought you didn't like the ocean," I said, kissing her fingers.

A look passed over her eyes, like a dark sea storm that blows in and then out again just as quickly. Then she smiled and shrugged. "Things change," she said.

SHERIFF JOHN BEAUMONT is a career law enforcement administrator, amateur historian, and winter sports enthusiast. He enjoys clam chowder, hard root beer, and Bob Seger music. He lives in an undisclosed location in New England with the love of his life, an art historian who spends her free time researching home renovation and wondering if she could sue Versace.

After a long and failed career in alchemy yielded nothing but a time consuming and expensive formula for turning gold into lead, **J. C. STEARNS** was forced into freelance writing to make ends meet. Currently he dwells with his wife, child, and menagerie of animals in the swamps of Southern Illinois, where he seethes with resentment against the world that has denied him the fame and glory he feels is rightfully his, and gleefully plots his revenge. His work has previously been published in *Under the Bed* and *Selfies from the End of the World*, and he is a regular contributor to *Quoth the Raven*.

WHEN THE TIDE TURNS

An account by Sophie Melencamp,
AS PROVIDED BY MAUREEN BOWDEN

"Here am I, thy babe's father, although I be not comely.
I am a man upon the land, I am a Silkie on the sea."
("Silkie," traditional folk ballad)

I was seven years old when I first met my dad. My mother had flitted off to the Glastonbury music festival with her current boyfriend, leaving me with my grandmother, Nanna Verity, a mad old hippy.

Nanna never missed her after-dinner walk along the beach. She said, "Come with me this evening, Sophie. There's someone who wants to meet you." I expected it to be some geriatric rock star from the olden days. She knew a lot of those.

We sat on the sand. The sun was setting, staining the clouds pink, and sending silver ripples across the incoming sea. A great seal rose from the waves, its black satin coat shimmering in the evening light. Its flippers began to elongate into arms and legs, and its body contracted and slimmed to human form. The seal was gone. A naked man stepped from the breakers and walked toward us.

"Nanna," I said, "that seal's changed into a man, and he's got no pants on."

She reached inside her Donkey Sanctuary tote bag, pulled out a Greenpeace bath-towel, and threw it to him. "To spare the child's blushes," she said.

He wrapped the towel around his waist and sat, facing us. "Thank you for bringing her to me, Verity. May I speak with her alone?"

"As you wish, but she stays here, and she's too young for you to tell her otherwise." She stood, and moved away from us, calling back to him, "I'll be watching you."

"What's your name, girl?" he said.

"Sophie Melencamp. Are you a rock star?"

He laughed. "No, Sophie, but I've met a few. I'm your dad."

This was an interesting turn of events. "I didn't know I had one."

"Everyone has a dad. Maybe some of them aren't worth having, but I will be. I promise."

"Why? What will you do?"

"I'll take you to swim with me in the sea."

"You can't. Mother says I'm allergic to sea water."

"Is that what she told you? Ah, well. I expect you'll grow out of it." He stood up, as Nanna walked back to us. "I must leave now."

"Will you come again?"

"Yes, when you need me. I'll come when the tide turns."

Dusk was falling and the night air was cold. I shivered. Nanna picked up the discarded towel and took my hand. "Time to go home," she said, tugging me away. When I looked back, the man was gone, and a black satin shape dived beneath the waves.

"Don't tell your mother about this, Sophie," Nanna said. "It will only upset her." She needn't have worried. Mother had as little to do with me as possible, and I'd stopped trying to talk to her about anything. Instead, I told my best friends, Laura Logan and Tegwyn ap Owen (known as Welsh Teg).

Teg laughed. "Crackin' story, Sophe, but we has a fibbin' situation, isn't it?"

Laura said, "Sophie's not fibbing, Teg." She turned to me. "I believe you, even if he doesn't."

Teg said, "Nah, it's like vampires and werewolves. They is just in daft stories, look you."

Laura shook her head. "The stories about them might be daft, but that doesn't mean they don't exist."

"Well, leastwise they doesn't live by yur."

Teg changed his mind three years later, when we had a school trip to the seaside. My mother said, "Remember, Sophie, you mustn't go in the sea. It'll bring you out in a rash." She gave me a letter for our teacher, Miss Barber, warning her about my allergy.

I sat on a rock, watching the rest of the class splashing around in the breakers, and I felt the pull of the sea. It was so strong that I decided to risk the rash, and if it upset my mother, that was tough. She'd upset me often enough. I ran to the water's edge. Miss Barber shouted, "Sophie Melencamp, come back here." Ignoring her, I pulled off my clothes and waded in.

The sea welcomed me. I dived, laughing, beneath the waves. My sleek, black body glided, twisted, and turned. Breaking the surface, I looked back at the shore. My classmates stood watching. Some ran, screaming, back across the sand. Their terror alerted me to my transformation. The shock returned me to human form. Laura met me, with no sign of fear, as I waded ashore. She wrapped me in her beach towel. Teg stood at the water's edge with my clothes folded over his arm. She took them from him and led me to the ladies' toilet block.

"It's alright, Sophie," she said, as I dried and dressed myself. "Nobody's sure what happened. We'll just say you swam out too far and you were frightened."

Miss Barber was waiting for me when we emerged. I don't know what she saw, but adults are good at not seeing what doesn't make sense. She said, "I hope your mother doesn't blame me for this. How's your allergy?"

I said, "I think I've outgrown it, Miss."

Laura and Teg told our classmates that the seal they thought they saw must have been a trick of the light, but the school bully, Seth Warner, wasn't passing up the chance to be a pain in the backside. Next day, in the school yard, he flapped his arms as if they were flippers, and jeered at me, "Oink, oink. Here comes Fishface."

Teg called to him, "You needs a good kickin', boyo."

Seth goaded him, "Come on then, Ivor the Engine. Let's see ya try, look you, isn't it?"

Teg hurled himself at Seth, and they were rolling around knocking seven kinds of thingy out of each other when Miss Barber turned up and dragged them apart.

They were suspended from school for a week, and I swore that one day I'd have my revenge on Seth Warner.

I was scared and confused by what had happened to me, but I knew it must have something to do with the great seal that had turned into my dad. I tried to get some sense out of my mother. "Mother, tell me about my dad," I said.

"I've told you before," she said. "You don't have one, and you needn't call me Mother any longer. You're nearly grown up now. Call me Willow."

I screamed at her, "So, I don't have a father, and now I don't have a mother, either. Not that you were ever much use, anyway."

She backed away from me, turned, and fled out of the room. I heard her crying as she ran upstairs.

Nanna found me trembling with rage. "Why does she hate me?" I said.

"She doesn't, Sophie. She hates your father, and every time she looks at you, she remembers what he did to her."

"Tell me about him, Nanna."

She sat next to me on the couch, and held my hands. "He's a creature called a Silkie. You've seen him in his true form."

"The seal."

"Yes. He takes human form to come ashore and breed, then he goes back to the sea, but he didn't tell Willow. When they became lovers, she believed they'd spend their lives together."

"When did she find out?"

"He disappeared before you were born, and he turned up again when you were two days old, gave her a bag of gold to pay for your upbringing, and told her he'd be back to take you when you were ready to go with him." She took out her handkerchief, wiped a tear from her cheek, and blew her nose. "He broke her heart, Sophie, and love and hate can be hard to disentangle. When you're older, you'll understand that."

"Didn't she want me to go?"

"No. She told you to keep out of the sea so you wouldn't find out that you're not fully human."

"But she doesn't love me."

"She's afraid to love you because she believes that one day you'll go with your father. She's the way she is because he made her like that."

Although I felt more understanding toward her, my mother's problems mattered less to me than my own. "I don't want to be a Silkie, Nanna." I said. "I want to be an ordinary girl."

"That's what you are, as long as you stay out of the sea."

By the time we reached our teens, my classmates had forgotten what they saw at the seaside, and accepted Teg and Laura's story. But Seth continued to taunt me, calling me Fishface, giving me no peace.

One day, he left a rotting piece of salmon in my desk. I faced him. "I won't forget this," I said, "and I'll make you suffer for it." For a moment I saw fear in his eyes, then he made an obscene gesture and turned away.

Teg and Laura supported and protected me. Outside school, I spent more time with them than I did at home. I liked Laura's house. She said it was more than two hundred years old. Our other friends called it creepy, but I felt safe there. It had high ceilings and solid, wooden doors. Laura said they were English oak. The heavy window shutters in her room were gouged and scratched. "That's called provenance," she said. "It means the enhancement of age." They kept out the night, Seth Warner, and the pull of the sea.

One summer evening, Teg and I called at her house for her. "Laura's having an early night," her dad said. "She's not feeling good." That happened regularly. She didn't talk about it, so neither did we.

The two of us walked along the beach as a full moon was rising. "Fancy a swim, Sophe?" he said.

"I can't, Teg. I'll change into a seal."

"I won't lie to you. It's a bit weird, like, but you is what you is, see? I reckon I takes you as I finds you."

The sea pulled me stronger than ever. I said, "Right. Let's do it."

"Tidy."

We swam side by side, a human boy and a Silkie girl. Later, we walked hand in hand along the shore. We didn't mate. He was Laura's, that was understood, but we basked in our companionship. I didn't want to lose it, but the sea called to me.

Laura was the only one who seemed to understand my conflict.

"Sometimes I think I should go with my dad," I told her. "Do you think that's stupid, Loz?"

"No, it's not stupid, but you belong here. You can't go." She twisted her fingers around strands of her hair, and her voice shook. "Unless," she hesitated, "if you were brave enough—"

"Then you think I should?"

"I don't know, Sophie." She shook her head. "But I don't think your mother or your father should decide for you. It's up to you."

Near the end of the school summer holidays, Teg booked a trip along the North Wales coast, for himself, Laura, and me, on the Llandudno ferry. "It'll be a good day out, I reckon," he said. "You'll enjoy it Sophe, and you'll be on the sea, but not in it, like."

"Tidy," I said.

With a warm, late summer breeze in our faces, we leaned on the ferry rails. The gulls screeched and swooped from the top of the Great Orme, and the Snowdonia peaks straddled the horizon.

From the Menai Straits, the fast flowing currents between the island of Anglesey and the mainland, we could see the turrets of Beaumaris Castle and the island's shoreline. Children played and chased the waves, while their parents sunbathed on the sand.

A slurred voice shattered the tranquillity, "Well, if it isn't Fishface, Ivor the Engine, and the freak from the House of Usher."

Seth was waving a half-empty bottle. I recognised it as the cheap wine that Willow snaps up from Asda's sin bin. He staggered toward us. Laura, usually so placid, sprang at him, tearing at his face with her nails. He stepped back, reached for the rail to steady himself, missed, and tumbled over the side of the ferry.

Teg shouted to me, "Sophie, you has to save him. The twonk never learned to swim, see?"

"Why should I? He's tormented me for years."

"Fair point. I grants you that, but I knows a lot about that boyo. When he was a kid his mam ran off with a plumber. His dad got drunk and never sobered up. He's the way he is because life made him like that. Isn't it?"

Nanna had said much the same about Willow, without the "isn't it."

I pointed to the Beaumaris sands. "I'll take him there. Phone for an ambulance."

I became the seal as soon as I hit the water. Seth was thrashing his arms about and screaming. He screamed even louder when he saw me. I was enjoying this. I wouldn't let him drown, but I wouldn't be gentle with him, either. I head-butted him, breaking his nose and knocking him unconscious. Keeping him afloat with my flippers, I swam to the shore, dumped him, and stayed nearby until I saw the paramedics running toward him, then I turned to the open sea.

I was at peace, in my element, with no more conflict. The tide had turned, but I wouldn't leave the people I loved without saying goodbye.

Nanna deserved to be the first to know. "You still meet my dad on the beach, don't you?" I said to her.

"Yes, to talk about you."

"Tell him the tide's turned." She nodded, and I knew she understood. "And tell Willow that soon she won't have to look at me anymore."

"She'll miss you, Sophie."

I shrugged. "I can't forgive her for not being a proper mother, but I don't want to cause her any more pain. When I'm gone, will she be able to stop hating my dad?"

"Maybe. I hope she can become the person she was meant to be."

Nanna, Teg, and Laura came with me to the beach. My dad stood waiting at the water's edge.

Nanna kissed me. "I'll be here every evening," she said. "I hope you'll come to meet me sometimes."

"I will, I promise. You'll always be my nanna."

Teg hugged me. "And I'll always be your friend, see? I'll be waitin' when you comes by yur."

"Tidy," I said.

I knew he didn't understand why I had to go, but Laura did. I'd guessed her secret. She threw her arms around me and held me close. I pictured her in her room, behind the solid oak doors, clawing at the shutters, and howling, as the full moon rose. I whispered, "When you're ready, be brave enough, and let the wolf run free."

SOPHIE MELENCAMP lived with her mother and grandmother, and attended Emrys ap Ewan Comprehensive School, Abergele, North Wales, until she was sixteen years old. She left home in mysterious circumstances, and rumour has it that she now lives with her father in the Orkney Islands, off the northeast coast of Scotland.

MAUREEN BOWDEN is a Liverpudlian living with her musician husband in North Wales. She has had seventy-two stories and poems accepted for publication by paying markets. Silver Pen publishers nominated one of her stories for the 2015 international Pushcart Prize. She also writes song lyrics, mostly comic political satire, set to traditional melodies. Her husband has performed these in Folk clubs throughout England and Wales. She loves her family and friends, Rock 'n' Roll, Shakespeare, and cats.

HOME BY HALLOWEEN

An account by Willow MacKenzie,
AS PROVIDED BY MICHAEL M. JONES

The queasiness came upon me in English. As Ms. Troutman unpacked symbolism in *A Separate Peace*, I got the all-too-familiar rumbling in my stomach that said I was going to hurl. I didn't try to get her attention; I grabbed my backpack and raced for the door. Troutman didn't even bother pausing her lecture, instead just sighing as I left. I could feel the classroom staring at my back. Once again, I'd shown weakness in front of the herd. There'd be gossip in the cafeteria at lunchtime for sure.

Ten minutes later, I was a miserable mess in a restroom stall. After the puking came the shivers and sweats, leaving me wrung-out as a used dishrag. I dug my Thermos out of my backpack and gulped down some of its contents, face puckering in disgust. If you threw willow bark, leaves, and sap into a blender with secret herbs and spices, and turned it into a noxious smoothie, you'd have what I called "green sludge," the only thing that helped me recover from these episodes. An all-natural remedy guaranteed to restore vital nutrients, perk me up, and strengthen me against the oppressive taint of the mortal world.

The doctors thought I suffered from a weird form of iron deficiency-based anemia mixed with ill-defined allergies; we'd gone through years of tests and treatments with increasingly niche specialists before my parents, fed up with the lack of success and no answers, turned toward less orthodox treatments. Acupuncture, holistic medicine, homeopathy, naturopathy—you name it. They tried everything until they found a solution. That's how I'd ended up in a restroom stall, drinking green sludge and loathing my life.

At Alabaster Court, the private school I attended, everyone knew me as the pale girl with the weird condition, and they all speculated on just what my deal was. I had a doctor's note that said I could leave class anytime I felt sick, and that my "medicine," while highly unusual, was perfectly acceptable and didn't contain anything illegal or hinky. The nurse's office was always open to me, and I was permanently excused from sports. Because my parents had donated a new computer lab, everyone was just fine with it.

Everyone except me.

My name is Willow MacKenzie and I want to go home. I've been trapped on Earth, in the body of a human girl, for sixteen years, seven months, and three days. Your iron, your holy symbols, even the salt you put into everything—it's all slowly poisoning me. With the attacks coming on a more frequent basis as the green sludge loses its effectiveness, I'm not sure how much longer I'll last.

Of course, I was never expected to survive this long to begin with. Changelings rarely are. My human parents just had the resources and tenacity to do the impossible. I should have withered away and died in a matter of months, but they'd fought tooth and nail to keep their daughter alive. And they didn't even know the truth about me. No one did. I can't even imagine telling them that their true child had been kidnapped by Faerie, an imperfect duplicate left in its place. I didn't want to know how they'd react. Would they still consider me theirs? Would they feel cheated?

"Willow? You okay?" That was Savannah, my best friend, checking on me. I put away my Thermos and exited the stall.

"Yeah," I said. "I'll live." I went to the sink to splash cold water on my face and try to make myself presentable again. I made a face at the mirror, which reflected back bright blue eyes, almost translucent skin, and coppery-red hair that fell limply past my shoulders. There were dark circles under my eyes, and a thinness to my features I hated. I looked as wretched as I felt. I gathered my hair back in a loose ponytail and took a deep breath, trying to perk up. "What'd I miss?"

"Not much," Savannah said. "I took notes and got tonight's assignment. Another essay. Pick a color in *A Separate Peace* and relate it to a character." She joined me at the sink, her reflection appearing over my shoulder. She was tall and elegant, with smooth dark skin and bouncy curls, and a knack for dominating volleyball and basketball courts with enthusiasm and presence if not skill. My condition made me shorter and scrawnier than other girls my age; I looked like a misplaced freshman. The contrast between us was almost painfully funny.

We both sighed. Troutman loved essays. There was a theory that she suffered from insomnia and assigned them either to have something to do all night, or because they bored her to sleep. "Thanks."

"No problem." I was just to the door when Savannah caught my arm and gave me a long, worried look. "Are you okay?" she asked me again. "I mean, like really okay?"

I forced a weak smile. Years ago, my mother had officially deputized Savannah to keep an eye on me; even though we were a long way from the playground buddy system, she still took the duty seriously. "Like I said, I'll live. It's always worst in October. I swear I'm allergic to Halloween."

She let me go. "Fine," she said, still sounding dubious. I couldn't blame her. She'd known me for most of my life, ever since we fought over crayons back in kindergarten, which meant she had better insight into me than just about anyone else. And yet...

I'd never told her that I was really one of the Fae, an elfin spirit swapped for a human child, and that ever since I turned thirteen, I'd been having increasing vivid dreams of an otherworldly realm filled with miracles and wonders. I felt this indescribable longing, this deep yearning for somewhere I'd never been but knew as well as my own neighborhood. I dreamed of ethereal beauties with pointed ears and sharp features, and felt a strange kinship. The dreams, which lingered even after I woke up, had led me to myth and fairy tales, and to the indisputable conclusion that I wasn't human. Everything finally made sense. The more I dreamed of that other world, the less connected I felt to this life. I looked at people and was startled at their round ears and soft faces, I grew twitchy around electrical appliances and moving vehicles, and even my parents sometimes felt like strangers. Caught between dreams and reality, it was getting harder to remember which was which.

You're supposed to tell a best friend everything, but Savannah was rooted quite firmly in the real world; she thought fantasy books were silly and demanded plausible science in her science fiction. This was nowhere near her sphere of comprehension. She could understand "Willow's health is messed up," not "Willow's not from this plane of existence."

I got through the rest of the day without any more problems. After school, Savannah and I walked home. Despite what I'd told her earlier about my condition being worst in the fall, I still loved the crispness of the air and the smell of leaves and smoke that always seemed to grow strongest as October moved toward November. There was something familiar and subtly reassuring about the change of seasons. Savannah chattered about the Halloween party she was throwing and reminded me that I'd agreed to help decorate. I nodded in all the right places and promised to drop by early. "Though knowing me, I'll be tossing my cookies before the evening's over," I grumbled. "You'll be bobbing for apples, I'll be praying to the porcelain god."

She patted my shoulder. "Come as a zombie and no one will know anything's wrong," she teased. "You're certainly pale enough."

I jabbed her with a sharp elbow in response.

We reached my house first, and she went on her merry way while I headed inside. Mom was prepping a meatloaf for dinner, and Dad was still downtown at the office, practicing the arcane arts of intellectual copyright law. I hung around the kitchen long enough to get a hug and to reassure Mom all was well, since the school had an annoying tendency to phone her whenever I had an episode. I waved the Thermos at her. "Magic sludge," I said with forced cheer. "Cures all. Now if only we could work on the flavor. Is there any way we can add coffee? Or chocolate? Or even a sprig of mint?"

She laughed, shaking her head. "Considering how delicate the balance of ingredients supposedly is, I don't think we can add anything else, even for taste. Though we can ask Dr. Amara about it at next month's appointment."

I shrugged. "Just a thought." It was an old, familiar exchange, as we both tried to make the best of an otherwise shitty situation. I swiped a box of low-sodium wheat crackers from the cabinet and mild cheddar slices from the fridge, kissed Mom on the cheek, and headed upstairs to my room. Keeping up appearances was hard, but necessary. If things went according to plan, though, I wouldn't be here for next month's appointment. Or, for that matter, Savannah's party.

I'd finally figured out how to go home. And on Halloween— on Samhain, rather, the older and more appropriate name for the holiday—I was going to make it happen.

For the past few years, I'd claimed to be sick on October 31st. With my history, no one doubted me. I'd actually been trying to open a way back to Faerie. I'd cobbled together folklore and other stuff I'd found to create plausible rituals, but no luck either time. I guess if it was easy, it wouldn't be the stuff of myth and legend. I'd spent most of my free time prowling through used bookstores, searching online forums, and weeding out a ton of false leads. Finally, just last week, I'd gotten my hands on a digital copy of a book that supposedly had all the answers.

Alderman's Rituals, Secrets, & Cunning Lore was full of folk remedies, anecdotes, charms, and spells. A lot of it sounded pretty dubious—wash your face in a mixture of pickle juice and mint to remove unsightly blemishes—but some of its contents had a weird ring of truth. They spoke to long-buried instincts and memories, and I knew, just knew, that something within its pages could help me. I was right: there were several rituals that could supposedly allow one access to other places. The land of dreams. Realms of the dead. The Hall of the Mountain King. The Dark Forest of the Fae. It was that last one that interested me.

At dinner, Dad asked me about school, forcing me to drag my thoughts back to the mundane world. Like Mom, he was concerned about my earlier episode, but I settled his worries before distracting them with complaints about Ms. Troutman's obsession with essays. I'd grown good at deflection over the past few years, determined to keep them from realizing how bad things seemed to be getting, or finding out what I was really doing.

I felt kind of bad for them. They'd spent so much time, energy, and money over the years keeping me happy and relatively healthy. They'd never even flinched at the costs. Though I knew I wasn't really their daughter, I'd never felt otherwise. They loved me, and I loved them, and the thought of leaving them—leaving all of this—behind tore at me. For three years, I'd wondered if I could do it, if I could step away without looking back, if I could walk away from comfort and security, the familiar and the safe.

But I didn't belong on Earth, and it was killing me. I had to go home.

I helped with dishes afterward, as always the obedient child, before escaping to my room to do homework, including Troutman's damned essay. I know—what's the point when I had other things to worry about? It just felt right to keep up with the routine until the last moment. Like if I pretended everything was normal, it would make it easier in the end.

The days leading up to Samhain both flew and crept by. I agonized over every minute and yet the days passed in a blur, as I maintained my usual façade while making sure I had everything I needed. I went to classes, turned in homework, even caught a movie with Savannah and some of her friends from the volleyball team, and generally played the role of ordinary girl. I had two more episodes; each time the green sludge did its job, restoring me even as it redoubled my determination to see this through.

The hardest part of my preparations was deciding what to take with me. I spent hours debating over what would fit in my backpack, and what to leave behind. What would I need? What represented the life I was about to leave behind for good? In the end, the meager contents of my jewelry box, and a small photo album containing pictures of my parents and Savannah joined spare clothes and toiletries, and tools for the ritual. It wasn't much, but I'd never been one for accumulating stuff. I'd always figured I'd be dead or gone in a few years; what was the point of collecting things or thinking about the future?

I tried to explain things to my parents in a letter. I started it a hundred times, but couldn't find the right words. I didn't want them to worry. I didn't want them to waste time looking for me. Finally, I just wrote, "I'm sorry. This is for the best. I love you." I planned to leave it, and the Thermos of green sludge, on my desk. That, at least, was one thing I wouldn't miss.

This year, Samhain fell on a Friday. I spent the time after school helping Savannah decorate her house, turning it into a spooky celebration of cobwebs, skeletons, spiders, ghosts and creepy music. As twilight approached, before her guests arrived, I made my excuses, claiming I just didn't feel well and should get home before anything happened. Savannah, sweetly trusting best friend that she was, accepted this, and told me to text her later.

I paused. I hugged her fiercely. "I love you," I said, surprising myself. We were best friends, but we weren't all that touchy-feely. But I was going to miss her more than almost anyone else.

She hugged me back reflexively, but her body language told me she was just as startled. We let go of each other. She eyed me funny. "I'm flattered," she said dryly, "but I'm pretty sure I don't swing that way. I was waiting until college to figure it out, though." She seemed on the verge of saying more, but paused, as if trying to read my expression.

My cheeks burned with embarrassment, and I muttered something about not meaning it that way, and I clearly had to go home and lie down, and fled. Stupid sentimentality. I was about to leave all of this behind. I had to let go. This is why I'd avoided any such things with my parents this morning; I was too afraid I'd say something, give myself away. Or worse, have second thoughts.

An hour later, I was in a nearby forest, where I'd discovered a fairy ring in a meadow just a few days ago. The ring was a good 20 feet in diameter, ominous in the dying light and elongated shadows of the nearby trees. I'd set up candles at the cardinal points of the circle—north, south, east and west—and bowls of water at the opposite corners, forming an eight-pointed star intermingled with the fairy ring itself.

Earth, air, fire and water, all represented.

A fairy ring on Samhain under a full moon.

There couldn't have been more magical symbolism involved if I'd brought in a leprechaun riding a unicorn. (Not that I knew where to find either of those…)

It would have to do.

My heart pounding like a jackhammer, I settled down in the middle of the circle, cross-legged. My mouth was suddenly dry; I took a sip from the water bottle I'd brought for just this instance, and tried to calm down. Now that I was actually about to do this, I was shaking with nervous anticipation. I breathed deeply to center myself, before reading aloud the ancient words as described in *Alderman's Rituals*, my e-reader in front of me to keep me on track. I'd spent hours practicing, the unfamiliar vowels and syntax sounding like angry cats fighting in a sack to my modern ears, sounding like home to my Fae spirit. They tripped off my tongue like liquid silver, forming a glowing circle of alien words on the ground around me.

The wind picked up. The candles flickered and flared, their fire reaching like hungry fingers toward the sky, and the bowls of water chimed like so many bells. Part of me hadn't expected any results; I almost lost my place out of surprise. After all, my other attempts had failed. But I kept going.

Magic slithered through me, coming from somewhere deep within, pouring forth from my skin, leaving me shaking and weak. Something creaked—or cracked—in the world, and a door appeared before me. It was oak and silver, it was water and fire, it was a hole in space. Through it, I smelled green things and fresh water and strange spices.

It smelled like home.

I stood up, and reached to the door. I touched it. It opened. Or maybe it simply ceased to be in the way, because I could feel something—an oddly-chilly lack of something—and my fingers went through...

I yanked them back quickly. I retreated a few steps. This was it. I grabbed my backpack. I paused for a second. I thought of friends and family, modern conveniences and fast food, and everything that had made up my sixteen-and-change years on Earth.

I thought of throwing up, of being weak and anxious and allergic to everything around me. I thought of that certainty I'd die before I got old. Life or death. Known or unknown. Home.

My skin tingling and heart thumping, I stepped through the portal. For a single eternal second, I turned inside-out, stretching away to infinity and shrinking into nothingness, before I was on the other side.

I was alone in a dark forest. The trees loomed hundreds of feet above me, unspeakably old, a primeval landscape untouched by human civilization. It was night, with only the faintest hint of moonlight breaking through the canopy. A thin, well-worn path stretched before and behind me, winding into the forbidding distance in either direction.

I was standing in the place I'd dreamed of for so long. With a gasp, I looked around for signs of life, of familiarity, of welcome. I took several steps, first one way then the other. Nothing. But there was a presence, and then "Got you!" Something fell on me from above, knocking me to the ground and pinning me before I could escape. I screamed, but the sound was cut off by a hand over my mouth. I tried to bite, and was slapped for my efforts. "Stop that!" A second later, something very cold and sharp rested against my throat. "Move, and you die. Make a sound, and you die. Blink twice if you understand me." The voice was girlish, and musical, and uncomfortably familiar. All I could make out was a vague outline. I had the impression that she was my age, but it was all happening so fast.

I blinked twice. I was frozen, both by the body now straddling me, and the knife that held me in a state of terror. I tried not to breathe.

"I'm going to get up, now. Don't try anything stupid." Again, I blinked twice in acknowledgement. That seemed to satisfy her, for she climbed off me. I struggled to draw in a deep breath. "Get up," she ordered. I did.

And finally, I could get a good look at her.

It was... it was me?

Red hair, pale skin, blue eyes. But her features were subtly alien. They were sharper, fiercer, stronger than my own. Pointed ears swept back through the long red curls. Her expression was impatient yet faintly amused. I looked at this version of me, and knew without asking that this was how I could have looked if I'd grown up on this side of the portal, if I'd never been sick. Where I was wearing jeans and a sweatshirt—sensible enough for traipsing around the forest—her outfit consisted of a tunic and pants in shades of green and brown that blended in with her surroundings. They were functional and pretty, each item a work of art in its own right. Her leather boots were sturdy, but with delicate stitches, and the sash tied around her waist glinted with silver inlaid threads. A silver crest in the shape of a full moon pierced by a thorny rose was evident on her left shoulder. I wondered what it signified. Her knife looked like it had been grown from wood and stone, wickedly sharp and beautifully dangerous.

She caught me staring, and arched an elegant eyebrow. "And who in the name of Oberon are you?" she demanded.

"W-Willow MacKenzie," I replied haltingly.

Her lips pursed. "Isn't that interesting. My name is also Willow. Of the House of the Midnight Moon, sworn to Queen Mab of the Unseelie Court."

For a long moment, we stared at one another, two sides of a coin. We'd never been meant to meet, but here we were. "I've come from Earth," I volunteered.

"I can smell it on you," she said, nose wrinkling in disgust. "Iron and fossil fuels and chemicals, seeped into your pores." She looked me up and down. "Hasn't done you much good, growing up there. You look like a bedraggled pixie."

"I know. Earth was killing me slowly. That's why I had to come home to Faerie."

A laugh escaped her, quick and scornful. "You? Come home to Faerie? This isn't your home, Willow MacKenzie. It never was. I can tell. You're a changeling." She stared at me, eyes glittering. "You're *my* changeling. No wonder I was drawn to this spot. Something told me I had to be here, and now I know why."

I nodded, though her demeanor was making me uneasy. "That's right. I… am a changeling. We were switched at birth. I was supposed to die, but I didn't. And here I am."

The other Willow shook her head. "That just proves it. You don't know what you're getting yourself into. If you'd any sense, you'd never have come at all." She sighed, her expression relaxing a little. "Faerie is complicated where changelings are concerned. They're not fond of humans either, but we fulfill a number of roles. Servants. Slaves. Pets. Entertainment. There's a persistent rumor that without humans, the Fae would be unable to dream or create anything new, that we keep the stagnant spark of their imagination from going out completely." She held up a finger in warning. "Never say that in front of the full-blooded Fae, they consider it heresy. The nicer ones will just take away your voice so you don't blaspheme anymore. Some will actually make you vanish permanently." She jabbed the finger in my direction. "You, though—you're just a magical construct that didn't even have the good sense to wither properly. You've been tainted by humanity without any of the useful side-effects. The full-blooded Fae will eat you alive… literally. And that's if you're lucky. No, you shouldn't be here. There's nothing for you in Faerie."

There was anger in her words and pain in her eyes. She all but spat out the last words, causing me to step back, taken aback by the ferocity. For a second, it was like she'd let a mask slip to reveal the wounded animal beneath. "So what am I supposed to do?" I blurted.

She shrugged. "Go back to Earth and die like you were supposed to." I gaped at her callousness. "Or stay here and sooner or later something bad will happen to you and that'll be that."

"That's not very helpful," I snapped.

"I'm not very helpful," said the other Willow, glowering at me. "You know why they took me? Because some Fae noblewoman wanted a baby for a pet. But that only lasted as long as I was cute and cuddly.

Once the novelty wore off, she traded me for a clockwork nightingale, and I became the playmate for a spoiled young Sidhe who beat me at the slightest provocation. When I finally fought back, they sold me as a kitchen drudge, and so on. I went through a dozen owners in as many years. I learned to fight and hunt and kill, solely to prove my worth, because you do *not* want to know what happens when the Fae no longer have a use for you." And her expression conjured up a thousand potential fates, each worse than the one before it. "I've finally achieved a measure of status that lasts as long as I don't fuck up. If I return with a changeling—*my* changeling, of all things—in tow, it'll ruin everything. Go *home*, Willow MacKenzie, while you still can. That portal closes at dawn."

"Why… why did you never try going home?" I asked.

"Because by the time I was old enough to think of such a thing, I'd already been transformed by Faerie food and magic. I'd fare even worse than you have. That's one thing the legends got right. Once Faerie has its hooks in you, there's no turning back." She shook her head. "This is where I belong. But not you."

It seemed like the argument was going in circles. "If I go back, I'll die."

She shrugged. "You're pretty much human. All humans eventually die. You'd just be getting it over with early."

"I don't want to die *yet*!" I exclaimed. I'd spent years wondering if I'd die before I made it to college, before I found romance, before I had a chance to live. I'd abandoned my life on Earth for a chance at survival here.

The other Willow shot me a scathing look, before turning away. "Get used to it."

Something I'd read in *Alderman's Rituals* teased at the back of my mind. I frowned, trying to recall it. Something about transferring essence. "Wait. Before you go. You were drawn here. Why?"

"Because we share a connection. When they created you to

replace me, they linked you to me, drawing from my humanity so you'd be convincing enough for the short time you were supposed to exist. Only that link never broke. So when you opened the portal, it brought us together. I think we're the sort of problem Faerie doesn't like to have around."

I nodded. It all made sense. "So my problem is that... I'm too human for Faerie, but have too much Fae spirit for Earth, right?"

"That sounds about right."

"And you possess too much humanity to be respected here, but can't survive on Earth?"

Other Willow eyed me suspiciously. "Get to the point."

"What if we swapped the bits we don't need? I give you my Faerie spirit, you give me your humanity?"

She blinked. "I... huh. That is some strange human logic of yours, Willow MacKenzie. I'm no sorcerer, but it sounds sensible enough. But how do we do this?"

I quickly retrieved my e-reader from my backpack and called up *Alderman's Rituals*. I was mildly surprised to realize that the device worked here; I wasn't even sure why I'd brought it, since I doubted there was a way to recharge it once it ran out of juice. Habit, perhaps. An accidental, fortuitous link to my past. I used the search function to find something appropriate. There it was, a spell designed to transfer essence, restore balance, and call like to like. It involved blood. Naturally. There are certain things which remain true in any magical tradition. We each cut our palms open, using the deadly hunter's knife she'd threatened me with originally. It was so sharp, I barely even felt the pain as it sliced through my skin. We reached out to each other, clasping hands so our blood would mingle.

"Earth to Earth," I chanted, focusing on everything I knew of being human. I thought of my parents. I thought of Savannah. I thought of school, and routine, and of pizza and bad comedies and everything else that had formed my daily existence.

"Faerie to Faerie," chanted the other Willow.

Magic flared, electricity arcing between us, and my essence ripped out of me in a soul-searing pain that threatened to overwhelm me. I saw the agony in the other Willow's eyes, and determined to hold out as long as she did. As my spirit left me, I became aware of a deep, painful hollow, a gaping wound in my core. But just as quickly, I was filled by something rich and warm, refreshing and cleansing. It felt like the Earth itself, reaching inside to claim me. I was renewed. I felt strong and whole at last.

We broke apart with identical gasps, stepping away from each other to survey the results. The other Willow looked much less human, her sharp features more exaggerated. She was taller, thinner, more… Fae. She flexed her fingers, the cut on her palm already healing with shocking speed. "Yes…" she murmured. "It worked." Her grin was feral and a little wicked. "You have my gratitude, Willow MacKenzie. Go, enjoy your human life."

The magic had also healed my hand, leaving behind a faded pink scar, a reminder of what we'd done. "I plan on it," I replied. I could feel my new connection to the mortal world. I knew I'd be healthy, I'd no longer need the green sludge, no longer suffer from episodes. I was human through and through, and would take whatever came of it. "Good-bye, Willow of the House of the Midnight Moon. I hope you're happy and successful." I turned, suddenly eager to be rid of my frightening mirror self. The woods no longer seemed like home; I was a trespasser, and my presence would no longer be tolerated.

"Perhaps one day, I'll come for your first-born," she said with a throaty chuckle. "If I'm ever in the mood for a pet."

I looked back with a fierce glare. "I know your tricks. I'll be waiting." I stepped through the portal, and it closed on the sound of her darkly rich laughter, making me shiver. But determined to put this behind me, I packed up my stuff, and began the journey home.

WILLOW MACKENZIE is sixteen years and seven months old, and attends Alabaster Court Preparatory School in Puxhill. She's amazed to have lived this long, and has made no plans for the future. Her hobbies include sarcasm, worshiping the porcelain god, and esoteric research.

MICHAEL M. JONES lives in southwest Virginia with too many books, just enough cats, and a wife who keeps a light in the window for when he wanders strange paths. His fiction has appeared in anthologies such as *Clockwork Phoenix 3*, *A Chimerical World*, and *C is for Chimera*, as well as at *Inscription Magazine*. He is the editor of *Scheherazade's Facade* and *Schoolbooks & Sorcery*. For more information, visit him at www.michaelmjones.com.

ANIMALE,
PIECE BY PIECE

An account by Alec Guzman,
AS PROVIDED BY MATHEW ALLAN GARCIA

On the day Terra found her *Animale*, construction of Talbot's Hall of Wonderment and the Fantastical had begun at the base of Culder's Canyon. They erected a steel beam that you could see off the freeway, a yellow "Coming Soon" banner waving from its tip. When they put up the gold and red tent in August, you could see it poke up over a canopy of lush green and brown, wood and forest, and it'd remind me of Terra. How we'd sat there on the cliff, paw in paw on that June afternoon, two small shocks of brown hair and sets of honey-colored eyes.

I suggested baboons. I liked their exoticness. It's why I liked that some skinchanger in New York found his *Animale* in a Bengal tiger in Central Park, another in a rhinoceros on Catalina Island traveling in a herd of buffalo, a poison dart frog in a shopping mall planter in Downtown Los Angeles.

Like them, I envisioned something out of the ordinary. And, for that summer at least, I pictured a pair of baboon sun-tanning among the runners and hikers of Griffith Park.

"Maybe it'll be a rocket, Alec?" Terra said to me, of the

construction, her voice coming out a gibbering, baboonish squawk. Several hikers looked up from their trails, pointed up at us. Children laughed. I heard hushed, out of breath whispers of "skinchanger" and I smiled. Things were good.

Terra knew what it would be of course, said so on the sign, but it was her daydreaming ways to ignore the facts, to speculate for the sheer fun of it.

A crew of fifty or so workers built for the following three months, laying the foundation, erecting the stadium seating in a circle around the beam, a large shed tucked off into the cliffside where I assumed the animals would be kept. We'd meet up after we each got out of work—me from my desk job, Terra from teaching piano at the Music Institute—and we'd shed our human forms and sit there, like it was a thing. Our thing.

I couldn't stay a baboon for long, usually. I changed back several times as we sat there, but Terra always said she felt more comfortable that way—"fuller" was the word she used. I'd heard that when a skinchanger finds their *Animale*, it's like realizing you've been wearing size 8 shoes when you've been a 10 all along. Her eyes were brighter when she was a baboon, and my heart raced to meet her enthusiasm, but fluttered just out of reach.

When we got back to the car, on that last day, when she changed forever, I opened the car door for her, and when I turned I saw Terra, still a baboon, skulking low to the earth, grunting up at me in disapproval, her eyes glazed in tired recognition.

"So this is it, yeah?" I said, my voice soft, weak, and low. I ran a hand through my sweaty hair.

I knew I shouldn't have been surprised. That it'd happen eventually. My stomach sank, and my body felt weak, like I didn't even have the energy to fight it, to argue with her.

I wanted to tell her to stay with me, to wait until we found our *Animale* together. That I was afraid of the gaping hole she'd leave in my life.

But she just stood there, silent, watching me for a moment before she ran into the woods, her brown-gold coat glittering in the sun.

In front of the mirror, I watched as my arm bloomed a shade of deep red. A puddle of blood, almost black, covered my skin as scales formed on my arm. Claws, jagged and sharp, erupted from my fingernails, and somewhere in my stomach, fire.

I miss you.

The form didn't hold. It never did for long. Terra's face flooded me, and my skin returned to its usual shade, my claws back to fingernails, and the fire grew cold.

I banged my fist on her piano and the keys thrummed under the lid, the wood cracking.

"Shit…"

It'd been three weeks since Terra left. Her things still littered our apartment, though. On her piano bench, music notes were laid out by song title. She'd had a music recital for her class coming up, and she'd been deciding on the songs. Mail addressed to her was piling up in her spot by the microwave, and two tickets to opening day at Talbot's Hall of Wonderment were tacked on to our calendar.

On the date, written in Terra's loopy handwriting, it said: THE BABOONS RETURN TO THE CIRCUS, AND ALL IS WELL WITH THE WORLD. She wrote it across three dates because she didn't have room, starting on September 5th.

It was the calls I hated the most, though. Her clients. Students. Faculty.

I'm sorry, she's not here, is all I said. All she'd want me to say.

Terra kept the fact that she was a skinchanger a secret from just about everyone she knew. Even our friends didn't know, because she said she didn't want anyone to look at her strange, like they looked at me sometimes. She didn't want clients she grew fond of dropping her because of what she was.

I told her not to worry about it. That when someone belongs to *any* group of people, there's always some other group who hates them, for no better reason than to hate. Because they're different.

On the kitchen table, her Transformation Registration Card (TRC) sat inside a plain white envelope, ready to be mailed. It's how they track us once we've changed for the final time. On the news, there's talk of tighter restrictions, a chip or something, because some people were afraid. They're afraid of *us*, like being a skinchanger made us any more likely to kill someone.

I filled out Terra's TRC the day I came home without her. It has to be filled out and sent within a year of transformation, and an official copy was supposed to be sent back to the filer within three weeks of receipt.

I knew I had time to sit on it, but I wanted to get it out of the way, before it grew weight. Before it'd be impossible to pick up. The thought of mailing it, though… I hadn't been able to do that. Doing that would mean it was over. Would give the whole thing a sense of finality I wasn't ready for.

I looked at my arm, and tried again for the change. Closed my eyes to see the beast.

You just have to give yourself to it, Alec.

Terra must've told me that a hundred times. Mostly when I tried to change into something new. See, I always changed in steps. A piece at a time. She told me that was wrong.

Just give yourself to it, she said. *Stop being afraid. Stop trying to get everything perfect. To be* right *all the time.*

It was easy for her to say, easy for her to *do.* She gave herself to her music every day, surrendering to whatever she was feeling on the tips of her fingers. Surrendering was easy, getting it right was hard.

I got the idea from the cover of a videogame a friend lent me. No one's ever tried it before. On it, a beet-colored dragon flew over a medieval city, tearing down towers, setting barn houses ablaze.

I lifted my arms to my face and tried again.

Just give yourself to it.

Talbot's Hall of Wonderment and the Fantastical was bigger up close. You walked a short two-mile trail up the mountainside, running up beside a river that chuckled upstream instead of down. Frogs croaked and plopped into the chuckling stream as I passed.

I decided it'd be a good way to say goodbye. My things were packed, our rent paid through the end of the month, giving me just enough time to find another place that didn't remind me of her, that didn't *smell* like her. Part of me hoped maybe I'd see her somewhere in the crowd. That'd she'd smile at me, and things would be good again.

There was a healthy flow of people coming on opening day. Lots of children. They watched the trailside attractions and laughed. Clowns acted out classic circus fair antics on the water's surface, and underwater lights blew up the sky. Across the little stream, fog hugged the ground, and acrobatic shadows flipped through the air. Fireflies danced through the night.

When I came up to the tent, the smells hit me. It smelled of all the midway carnivals I'd ever been to when I was a kid—of salted peanuts, greasy cinnamon crusted churros, and funnel cakes, mixed in with the sharp aroma of elephant shit and hay. They were smells of my childhood, of growing up.

Entering the dimly lit tent, I took my seat.

It was pretty typical for a circus show. Acrobats dangled off the ceiling, doing somersaults and flips midair as the audience beneath gasped at their split-second saves. Contortionists contorted themselves into incomprehensibly small containers. Clowns with too-big red shoes bumbled across the stage wetting the audience, getting a laugh.

It wasn't until the fifth act that the show started. When the real wonderment began.

The lights went out, and a couple of people in the audience screamed.

There was the palpable silence, like everyone was holding their breaths, when a voice boomed from the top of the tent.

"Talbot's Hall is proud to present, The Wonderment of the Seven Continents. Animals from around the world like you've never seen them before."

The lights came on.

Terra stood in the spotlight.

The seating lights that signaled the end of the show had barely come on when I walked down the benches into the ring, walking straight for the Ringmaster. He was a short man, a large hat held to his chest, balding head glistening under the spotlights. He smiled at me as I came near, an eyebrow curled up.

"There's been a mistake," I said.

"Huh?" His smile looked crooked.

When the last of the audience stepped out, his smile dropped off his face, like it was never there. His voice dropped two octaves. "What do you want, kid? You're not one of those animal activists are you? God knows I've been through enough of them already."

"No," I said. "But my girlfriend's in your act."

"Oh yeah?" He smiled again, but it was of the shit-eating variety. He ripped his fake mustache off as he turned and stalked back through the curtains, leaving me behind. I followed. "Which one is she? Listen,

I don't care about your relationship problems. Tell me which one she is, and I'll fire her. I don't have time for this."

"The baboon," I said. "The piano player. Her name is Terra."

The man looked at me, not as surprised as he should be. He broke into laughter.

"Any problems here, Mick?" It was a clown, Bumbo I think his name was. He still had his red rubber nose on and a smear of white paint was streaked off his face. I could smell the sweat and gin on him. Poofs of red hair jutted out from the sides of his head.

"No. No problems, Dino," Mick said, patting Bumbo on the shoulder. "Get your boys cleaned up so we can celebrate a successful opening day. This kid and I have business to discuss in my office."

Mick's office doubled as the animal shed. An overturned bucket was his chair, and a coffee table piled with papers, bills, and newspapers made up his desk. He walked over to the elephant cage, picked up their only water bucket, and tossed the contents out. He offered it to me to sit down. I kept standing.

"You got proof, kid? Show me her TRC."

"I…" I trailed off. I never mailed it.

"See, cuz I have forms for *all* these animals saying I got them fair and square."

Fakes. They had to be. Every one of these animals was a skinchanger. The things they did, no animal could be taught to do them. No way.

"Let her go," I said, my fists shaking. For a moment, my flesh bloomed beet red. Mick stood up, watching me, a hand gripping a metal-tipped stick by his side. I wondered how many of the animals he'd used it on, how many times he'd used it on Terra to get her to play for him. "You know what she is. You know what I am now, too. If you don't let her go—"

"You'll what? You'll *what*, kid? Kill me? Turn into a grizzly bear, eat me, then run off with your little monkey girlfriend and screw to your little heart's content? Shit, son. Do you really want that? What'll the papers say 'bout this, huh? They'll string the both of you up. Make an example for the rest of you freaks."

I opened my mouth to talk, but I felt the fire burn up my throat, melting my insides.

"That's right. Cuz these are all my animals. *Mine.* You skins are *all* just a bunch of fucking animals. I don't care what some goddamn piece of paper says."

Before I could move, two heavy hands gripped my shoulders, and I was pulled back through the curtain.

From the open shed door, I heard Mick say: "Now get the hell out."

I rubbed the bruises on my cheeks, flinching as the throb reverberated through my jaw where the men kicked me. They threw me into the stream when they were done, laughing as they headed back into the tent.

My eyes hurt from the glare of the sun as I walked up the sidewalk, making my way to the mailbox, holding two TRC forms in my hand. On Terra's, on the field marked *Species Transformed/Location* I wrote down that she'd changed into a firefly in the Mojave Desert. Something they'd never find if they went to look for her.

The other TRC had my name on it. It said the same thing.

Tucking it into the mail slot, I let it fall.

We'd found our *Animales* together after all, even if it only was on paper.

I watched Terra play the piano, her fingers dizzyingly fast as they maneuvered Alkan's *Scherzo Diabolico.* A thread of string was tied around her neck, the skin puckering as her handler tightened his hold. Her eyes were honey-colored, brown-gold coat muddied, losing its color, patches of fur gone. When she stopped, the audience cheered, children laughed, clapping.

Part of me wondered how they didn't know, the other part knew they did. That they knew it was Terra playing that piano. Terra with the noose around her neck, splitting her skin as her fingers danced on the piano keys. Terra bleeding, her chest heaving and falling, mouth opening up in a frightened baboonish sneer as the audience thundered on, demanding more.

The flames licked up in the pit of my stomach, and I stood.

My arms, legs burned as scales covered them, as wings beat themselves free from my shell. My vision bled red with murder. The children screamed. Heads turned, and Mick's jaw gaped. I could see myself in his eyes, my wings extended, my face a horribly contorted vision of rage, my forked tongue tasting his briny sweat in the air.

Give yourself to it.

Terra pulled against the noose, stepping toward me. She wasn't afraid.

And as I gave myself to it, completely this time, I saw us both sitting on the ledge of a cliff, paw in paw—*Animales*, together forever—right before I flew down the stands.

Dragon.

Beast.

Animale.

ALEC GUZMAN resided in Los Angeles, California, but his whereabouts are currently unknown. Up on the hills of Griffith Park, if you look closely, you can still see two small shocks of brown hair and honey-colored eyes.

MATHEW ALLAN GARCIA is the fiction editor of *Pantheon Magazine*. His fiction has appeared or is forthcoming in *Mad Scientist Journal*, *Kasma SF*, *NewMyths.com*, and the *Suspended In Dusk* anthology from Books of the Dead Press. You can find his complete bibliography on www.mathewallangarcia.wordpress.com

GETTING LOST IN MILAN

An account by a young girl,
AS PROVIDED BY MARINA BELLI

I can feel the trains, like bugs scuttling up and down my arms. It's not just the trains. I can feel the trams, too, and the buses and the water flowing through the plumbing, each like a different undertow in my limbs. Words whisper in the air, never silent for even the briefest of seconds, even if nobody around me is uttering a sound. I scratch my arm under my parka, where a traffic jam itches like hell.

"Are you okay, young lady?" a male voice asks.

I nod and slowly turn to look at the man sitting by my side on the stone bench. His hands clasped on the head of his walking stick, the old man is perusing me under bushy, white eyebrows.

"I'm fine, thanks."

The man nods, but he doesn't look a bit persuaded. The lights flooding the underground platform make the wrinkles on his face look even deeper than they are.

"Bad day?"

I can't even muster the strength to smirk when I say, "More like a streak of horrible days."

The man nods again, this time like he believes me. Like "streak of horrible days" is more his thing than "girl lying about how she feels."

"Things suck, sometimes. Then, they either worsen or get better."

"Epicurus."

The man smiles and his eyes twinkle. He pats me on the back, and in the moment his hand touches my shoulder, I can see through him like he was another part of me. He's seventy-six, last year they replaced his hipbone and now he enjoys walking again. He loves reading, wandering through the Braidense National Library, sitting under a tree in Parco Sempione, and watching the dogs run around. He lives in an old *casa di ringhiera*, third floor, brown tiles, cream-coloured walls, a floral pattern on the sofa. He's alone, after twenty-seven years with his companion. They were bachelors together and now he's a bachelor alone, and he longs for company, for somebody to speak to at the end of the day and first in the morning.

The train scuttles down my left shin, approaching the ankle.

"Your train'll be here in a minute, sir," I say.

His eyes glazed, the man looks around, having forgotten my whole presence. I swipe my hand in front of his face; the old man doesn't even notice it. A moment later, the whooshing of the air signals I was right. The man turns and stands up as the train appears, dashing along the platform.

I always found subway trains so noisy they were hateful. It has changed. I still hear the noise, so shrill and earsplitting that everybody on the platform smirks and reacts to it, in one way or another. Yet it soothes my nerves. Like it wasn't a metallic shriek, but the gurgling sound of one of those relaxing fountains.

I shake my head and close my eyes, try to get a hold on myself.

It's been days, now. These perceptions I shouldn't have. These unsolicited glimpses into the past and lives of other people.

A long *beep* precedes the closing of the doors of the train. It's gonna leave in a moment. On a whim, I stand up and walk toward the train. Instead of leaving the station, it remains still, as if waiting for me to give it my permission. All its doors open as I approach.

Inside, the car is almost empty, just a man in his thirties to my right, near the junction to the next car, and a woman in her sixties, two seats to my left. I sit in front of the woman; she doesn't seem to notice me. When the train moves, she lifts her head from the book she's reading. Dark eyes, dark red lipstick. Her gaze passes right through me, something not so strange in Milan. The woman scans the walls sliding behind me, then clears her throat and returns to her book.

I close my eyes and lean back. My head rests against the window, its vibrations propagate through my bones and sinews and muscles, fusing me with the train. I can count twenty-nine passengers plus the conductor, I can feel each and every one of them, like needles pricking my skin.

My body... it is just one of the many I can feel seated on a train that is a bug running along my body, that is on a train that is... God, I could get lost in this fuckin' riddle trying to short-circuit my brain!

The needles—the people—come and go. The train fills up and empties and fills up again and empties one more time. I don't want people to come near me, to touch me, and people abide. The seats to my right and left are always empty. Even when the train's packed full, nobody is able to notice those two empty seats.

Nobody sees me. Nobody bothers me. Nobody looks at me. But I can feel them nonetheless, thrashing around, keeping a rhythm on a plastic seat with colorful nails, thumping a foot against a pole painted a bright yellow, trying to squeeze through the doors when they're closing.

I leave the train on another whim. The station is Duomo. I stagger on the platform and follow the crowd upstairs, one staircase after the other. I choose the passages that will expel me from the bowels of the city just to the right of the statue of the King.

Dusk is turning into night, but Piazza Duomo is still bustling with people. Tourists and citizens looking for an *aperitivo* crowd the bars, somebody dares the chilly air and sits at the outdoor tables, chatting and drinking. The daylight's all gone, so most of the guys who make a living by selling pigeon food and taking photos for the tourists are gone too.

I reach the equestrian monument to King Vittorio Emanuele II, with its bronze king that has been green for who knows how long and the two stone lions lazily resting on the base. I look up to the right lion, the one whose paw rests on the shield with the word *Milano* etched on. A pigeon is perched on its muzzle, but it takes flight as soon as the lion lowers its head to peruse me.

In another life—one that in these days seems a million years away—the lion and I spoke about something very, very important. I can't remember what it was, no matter how much I try. The lion blinks and nods a courteous nod. It yawns with the rumble of a crumbling mountain, a rumble nobody seems to hear, and then gets back to being just a statue.

"Hey! You can't ignore me like... like..."

The lion gives me a disdainful look, then its voice rumbles, "It doesn't work like this, sorry. You have to know and possess the rules."

I shake my head, uncomprehending. The lion doesn't care. It doesn't look at me or speak to me for the whole time I spend sitting under the monument. It has got a century of experience feigning lifelessness. I can be as stubborn as I want; I have no chance of winning.

So I sit and look at the people and try to ignore the unnatural perceptions filling my brain. I sit and stare for so long, I find myself envying the people around me. They go about like they know who they are, what they want, where the heck they're running to. Like their past, present, and future belong to them. Like they possess the rules of their lives, to use the lion's words.

I, on the other hand... I'm forgetting things and losing myself a bit more every time I discover I can sense something new, and this whole thing's so frustrating I'd like to howl. Maybe that's why the noise of the underground soothes me: because when the underground bellows and screams, it's doing it for me too.

Gotta avoid these thoughts. Don't lean in. Resist them. Leaning in is unhealthy. Resisting is fuckin' healthy. Resist with all your strength.

My legs suddenly feel restless; I can't stand the idea of sitting here one more second.

I leave the statue and head toward Via Torino. A boy riding a red bicycle barely avoids me. He's singing an obnoxious song by one talent show star or the other; the tune sticks to my thoughts like chewing gum under the sole of a shoe.

Even though most of the shops are already closed for the evening, Via Torino is still a mess of people. A couple of teenagers are having a heck of an argument near a bus stop. She's calling him a liar and a cheater and the scum of the city, while he keeps on pledging true love and complete faithfulness.

Another whim: I touch his shoulder and her cheek, their lives and hopes and dreams lay open in front of me. She's scared, better make him run with false accusations than be left behind when he'll fall in love with somebody else. He doesn't want to be left, better a girlfriend he doesn't really love than no girlfriend at all.

Idiots.

They make room for me to pass between them without stopping their fight. I shake my head and go on, leaving them to their useless quarrel. A tram passes by, cars honk, a motorcycle zigzags to avoid a bunch of crazy pedestrians that cross the street at odd angles while they whistle and shout cheerful nonsense.

In a storefront window, a shop assistant is straightening a blue dress on a mannequin. The plastic white head turns to look me in the eye with dead, plastic pupils, and mouths a silent, "Kill me, please!"

I avert my eyes and walk faster. *Merda*, it was way better when nobody and nothing could see me!

Churches. That's another thing I sense on my body. Churches

and chapels, synagogues and mosques. Places of worship. When I'm far from them, they feel like a cross between a knot and a pulsing scab, like they wanted to gently remind me there exist places where people gather to pour faith toward their gods. Then, when I actually pass in front of one, it's like a stab of light exploded for a split second in the center of my brain while a chorus of voices tried to deafen me with their clamor. With the Duomo, the brain punch was so strong I faltered when I just reached the underground platform. With all the other churches, it's easier.

So I just stagger and stumble when I walk in front of Saint Satyrus, to my left, and, later on, in front of the Temple of Saint Sebastian, to my right, and the church of Saint George, again to my right, and a nondescript office building to my left, and I don't even want to know what they worship in there.

I reach Largo Carrobbio and pause for a moment. The street splits up in three directions and I have no idea where should I go. Or where I wanted to go, if this walk ever had a purpose.

How long have I been walking? Can't remember, and the fact the city seems to slide around me, like it was smaller than it should be, doesn't help the figuring out.

My feet choose for me, they lead me to the middle road. Corso di Porta Ticinese. I walk slowly and stop when I reach the Columns of Saint Lorenzo. This time, the flare of light and voices in my head has nothing to do with the stop. There's a single, distinct voice, screaming in the distance. It's not pain, not fear. Just a voice, neither male nor female, screaming for the sake of it. I follow it, leaving behind the Roman columns and the whiff of ancient wine that permeates their white stone. I follow the north side of the Basilica until I meet the gate for the park that surrounds it to the east. The gate is closed for the evening, but as soon as I approach it, its iron bars bend and open for me, like the curtain on a stage. They silently close behind my shoulders as soon as I'm inside the park.

I leave the paved road behind, and my heels sink into the wet ground. I kick the shoes away, feel them tumble and hit the wooden fence that encloses the area meant for kids to play in. Orange lights illuminate the edge of the park, where the paved path is flanked by stingy bushes and wooden benches. The grass is wet and ticklish, it makes me wanna smile.

Why should I smile? Can't think of a single reason why.

Who cares? I smile and walk faster, hugging the eastern walls of the church and in pursuit of the screaming voice. When I reach the main apse of Saint Lorenzo, I slowly back from the wall and look up.

There's a figure, perched on the church's dome. It should be too dark and the figure too far to make it out, and yet I can clearly see it. As I walk back, the figure turns to watch me and launches a high-pitched shriek.

"Da fuck do you want?" it then asks, standing up from its crouching position and giving me the middle finger.

Which, all in all, is quite a feat, considering it's an angel made just of big squares and triangles of stained glass.

"Da fuck do *you* want, screaming asshole! I'm just passing by! I could hear you from the damn Columns!"

"I'm practicing, bitch. Gonna smash those pious churchwomen's ears, next time they come to pray and weep! It's gonna be great!"

"Do you *really* think they're gonna hear you?"

"They will! See, that's what I'm practicing for! If I sing loud enough, they'll finally hear me! It'll be majestic! Mark my words, majestic! Ha!"

I shake my head and keep backing away from the church. The angel screams one more time. It jumps down from the roof, glides on shimmering glass wings and lands in front of me, graceful like a prima ballerina and colorful like a stroboscopic peacock. The black, delicate painting that creates its features pouts as it studies me, from head to toes and back.

"So, anyway, who da fuck are you, uh?"

I can't remember my name. A part of me knows that this hole in my memory should plunge me into an abyss of panic. Instead, I feel like I don't have the time for that, not right now. So… it wants to know who am I? I shrug and say: "Just me."

"Well, just me, fuck off."

I flip it the bird. I turn and walk away and, strangely, the angel has nothing to say. It just screams again, this time more like the singer of some metal band.

I meander through the lawn surrounding the church and wonder who had the gall to call this a park. An inexplicable sadness grips my guts when the ghost of a memory—fire and death and a cheering mob—flickers into existence twenty feet to my right, and then disappears back to oblivion. I shake the memory's charred taste away, and reach the fence that closes the south side of the park. Again, the bars silently open up and close for me, giving me free access to the sidewalk on the other side.

The asphalt is warmer than I thought; the air smells of exhaust and dust. Left or right?

Right, one foot after the other. I'm thirty feet away from a stop when an orange bus arrives. It idles there with its doors ajar. A strange rattling sound comes from the vehicle. I have to know what's its source.

I jump on the bus from its rear door, and as soon as my feet touch it, I can feel it and its contents burning in my mind. Waves of magic roll toward me, they crash and part a couple of feet before me, bathing the empty seats to my sides in a foam of spent energies. The bus closes its doors and leaves the stop.

It's me, and the driver, and a guy dozing on the first seat up front, and a babysitter hushing a little girl sobbing in her arms, and a man who looks like he lived his life too fast and rough, and a woman with bright blue hair. And the source of the rattling sound: a trio of figures standing at the center of the vehicle, who look like three haystacks.

Three walking haystacks who decided to wear colorful, round masks with jutting "hats" sculpted like human figures, and come to Milan to spend a winter vacation dancing and shaking on a bus.

I can't see a single inch of the limbs of the people hidden under the costumes, just rows of dried palm fronds shaking left and right and up and down. Without stopping their rustling dance, the haystacks turn toward me and offer me a good view of their masks. One is green and topped by a black man spearing a white pig. Another one is cobalt blue, white dots line its eyes, and the figurine on top is a coral woman cradling a green sprout in her hands. The third mask is painted the pinkest of pink. Golden earrings dangle from its oversized lobes and its hat is shaped like a couple of men riding a stylized golden lion, arms and legs flailing as kids would do while on a bike.

There's power in the haystacks. It's not inherent in the human figures wearing the masks; on the contrary, it's something bestowed on them. Something bound to their costumes that's filling them for the time being.

The pink one takes the lead and steps forward, shaking and jumping while the bus travels at a slow pace through Milan. The other two masks follow it, forming a V shape. I can't see their limbs, but I've no doubt their movements mean aggression. As if to confirm it, they pretend to leap forward, and magic pours from their fringed forms. Another wavefront runs toward me, just as the little girl's cries grow louder and the masked figures start chanting in an unknown language.

Again, the wave crashes and parts before me. This time my ears are full of the sound of a storm raging and beating against the wharfs.

A third and then a fourth wave of magic crash around me without even stirring my hair, but the little girl's wailing like a banshee. The three masked figures' chant is growing frantic, spiteful even, and it's grating on my nerves.

Time to put an end to this silliness.

I grab the nearest seat and will the bus to stop. It abides, none of the passengers mind it. The doors open with a hiss, and I step toward the trio. I indicate them and, with a flick of my wrist, the open door to their left.

"Off the bus! Now!"

"You have no power over us," the trio says in unison. Definitely not Italian, nor English. A hint of French, round vowels, a whiff of sub-Saharan Africa.

"Guess what? I do. Now get off my bus, you're upsetting the child."

The masked figures stop their dance and back off. One strained step after the other, they reach the open door without turning away from me. They hesitate on the edge of the door, they even shake as if they were fighting my order.

"Off. Now."

They leave the bus and I let the door close. My hand hurts from the strength I was clasping the seat with. The vehicle moves again. I sink to the floor and bend forward, my forehead pressed against my knees. The little girl's still crying, but in a more subdued way. It still grates on my nerves, and again I have that short-circuiting feeling of being a passenger on a vehicle and the vehicle itself and of having the vehicle running on my body.

'Fanculo. Can't stand it anymore. Not with this feeling... like something's calling me.

I stand up. The next stop is so near I can see it, but there's a damn traffic jam, this one pulsing and scraping between my shoulder blades, and the bus won't move. The babysitter is telling comforting nonsense to the kid. The little girl's eyes are fixed on me, except they're glazed over, like she's seeing through me. Like the eyes of the man in the subway, or those of anybody else who happens to look in my direction.

"You're welcome, anyway," I say. The girl can't even hear me, I'd bet on it.

I ask the doors to open again, then I jump off the bus. I walk

between a stuck car and the other, avoid being run over by a black
motor scooter.

I reach the nearest entrance to the metro and stop in my tracks.
A woman wearing a burgundy coat and matching wide-brimmed hat
and high heels stands at the top of the stairs. I know I can't move past
her, unless she gives me her permission. As if sensing me, she turns to
look at me. Grey feathers, not skin, cover her fat neck, and her head
is that of a giant pigeon. The skin around her beak is the same color
of her coat, smaller emerald and purple feathers form a double collar
around her throat.

"What… Who are you?" I ask.

"A queen," she says in a twittering, soft voice, then she adds, "A
beggar. A mother. A cannibal. Abundance and starvation. Nobody
worth remembering."

I shake my head for what seems the millionth time today.

"And who are you?" she asks.

"Just me." I repeat.

She nods, pauses. Her head jerks to and fro, like that of a pigeon
studying me, then she asks, "How many of us have you already met?"

"Three?" my voice asks on its own accord. It doesn't sound very
certain, but I feel even less so. No idea what the pigeon lady and I are
talking about.

The pigeon lady smooths the left lapel of her coat with a gloved
hand and nods. "You'll have time to meet the others. It was a good
idea on your part to come see me this soon." She curtsies, and there's
a look of mischief in her golden eyes when she straightens and backs
away.

"I'm not sure—"

"Shush, it's okay, m'lady, it's okay, you'll understand in no time."

A sound like dozens of wings fluttering, the smell of stale bread and
stagnant water, a cold shiver down my spine. The pigeon lady is nowhere
to be seen, no matter how much I turn around and peer through the

shadows cast by the trees and cars. Speechless, I descend the stairs.

The inside of the station is well lit and smells of popcorn. The turnstile opens on its own accord, no need for a ticket. I slip past it, my naked feet slap the floor as I walk through the tunnels and reach one of the platforms.

My head hurts. I need to sit down and rest. I lower myself on one of the steel benches shaped like strings of round, red seats. The man or woman who had this idea must have been a hell of an idiot.

There's something I should think about, something important, but I can't muster the energies to do it. My head hanging low, I sit and stare at my feet, my elbows firmly planted on my knees. Tired, that's how I feel. Like I haven't been sleeping for the last sixty hours and now I'm being stretched in too many directions at the same time.

The platform's empty, loudspeakers murmur a commercial, the buzzing of voices is still with me. Fuck this.

It's a jolt of ice down my veins. The loudspeakers shut their traps, the lights dim to a penumbra and then get brighter, sunset-style. I can sense the Wi-Fi repeaters sizzle and die, somewhere in the station. Silence, blessed silence.

I sigh and sit straighter. If only the calling I was feeling had vanished too... Unfortunately, it's still there, only... Can a call be qualified as "tamed"? Who cares, this is. It has become gentler, it feels like a cat purring against my shins, a light drizzle on a summer day.

Cautious footsteps approach the platform from the tunnel to my right. I turn in that direction in time to see a couple leave the brightly lit tunnel. A short woman in her twenties, plump lips and hair dyed black, and a tall guy in his thirties, his head shaven like a billiard ball and fresh scars on his left cheek. Claw marks left by an enormous, six-fingered cat.

The moment the couple sees me, their expressions change from caution to excited fear. The hands of the both of them leave the pockets of their respective jackets, almost in unison. They run toward me, she smiles and calls a name. It echoes around the empty space along with the thumping of their running footsteps, gets lost over the rails.

I spring to my feet and back away, not daring to lose sight of these people.

They slow down, exchange a befuddled look. He stops and grabs her arm, obliging her to halt too. The woman looks at him, confusion warping her features, then at me. She says that name again, bites her lower lip while watching me with pleading eyes.

There's a part of me that thinks she remembers that name. She's sure that name means something important. It could even be my name, she suggests.

But that part of me is too dizzy, too lost in the gaping holes of my memory to be sure of anything. Too eager to find any sort of lifeline and never let it go.

What am I sure of, then? I'm sure I'm scared. It's ice in my brain and fire in my feet. Scared even though that dizzy part of me says that I can trust these strangers. Even though it says that the three of us know each other well, that there's comfort to be found in them, no matter if I'd swear I never saw their faces.

"It's us," the young woman says, gesticulating to indicate the guy and herself.

They take a couple of cautious steps toward me, I take four more away. I can't trust my forgetful part.

"She doesn't recognize us," the man says to his companion, who shakes her head. "We're scaring her."

I take another step away.

The young woman pleads, "No, no, it's okay, I swear, it's okay! Stay, please! It's me," and she says a female name that sublimates in the air the moment it leaves her lips.

"Sorry, I don't know you," I say, and a part of me screams the word *lie*. I hastily add, "You confuse me with someone else."

Goodness! My voice sounds scared shitless, a tiny thing made of fear and strings wound too tight. The icy grip engulfing my brain is turning into panic. I can't stay with these people. I can't trust them, or my memory, or this unnatural pull I feel toward them. Not my place. Not what I should do. Not...

"Please," the woman calls again. "We've been looking for you for the whole day! Come back home. Everything will be okay, I promise, together we'll figure it out! We'll find a way to solve everything."

I shake my head, retreat a bit more.

There's a train incoming. It will be here in forty seconds, I can feel it running along my left pinky. I just need to stall these two long enough...

The man takes a step back and lifts his hands, palms toward me, in a placating gesture. That's the moment I notice it.

His companion is scared and worried *for* me; he, on the other hand, is scared *by* me.

"Why are you afraid?" I ask him.

His words are cautious, as if he thought I'm the Queen of Hearts, ready to behead him for a wrong syllable. "Because you are scared, honey, and I'm not sure you'd be able to control yourself if you felt any more scared than this."

How can he be so right?

He lowers the zipper of his anorak and slowly pulls something from the inside pocket.

"For you," he says, and throws the thing in front of me.

It skids on the floor until it stops against my naked toes. It's a small pouch of red fabric with geometric symbols stitched in black and white thread. The pull I felt now calls me toward it. I take the pouch, gently squeeze it before stuffing it into a pocket of my parka. The train enters the lit area just as my hand leaves the pocket.

"Honey, please."

The train stops, its doors open with a *beep*. People leave the train, they brush past me and the couple without noticing us. As if these two people were now part of my bubble of irrelevance.

Two steps back, that's all it would take me to flee.

"It's ok," the guy says, the tone of acceptance and sadness unmistakable.

"No, it's not—"

He cuts her out, his eyes not leaving mine. "It is. It really is ok. Go, if you must."

The train awaits.

One step back.

"No!" the woman calls, as a tear rolls down her cheek. It tastes of salt and heartbreak; I can feel it on my tongue.

The guy restrains his companion, resists her screaming struggles. Jaw set. Steel eyes not daring to leave mine.

The train and its warmth seem to call me, a new pull I don't know if I want to resist.

I close the distance in a heartbeat. The young woman's eyes go wide as a new tear falls from her eyelashes to my arm. I grip his bicep and her shoulder, and it's a flood.

Her life was painted red and blue, now it's a stark grey; there's the smell of raw meat and cooking food and the murmur of house music, the comfort of order and the heady taste of the fight. His life is made of stereos blaring rock 'n' roll, cigarettes chain-smoked while working on some magic trick or another, flashes of joy and rage, postcards from a not-so-distant country. And all through their memories, there are gaping holes, like angular shapes cut away from one's family photos to obliterate the sheer existence of that nasty relative never to be mentioned again.

And I'm the nasty relative, ain't I?

I lean in and kiss the man's cheek, bow down and kiss the woman's lips.

They both tremble with something that is not fear, but tastes very much like it. Like people on a safari looking at a family of elephants strolling by, not so sure the car would withstand their might if something angered them.

And yet, despite the fear-like feeling coursing through her, the woman responds to my kiss and tries to catch me, to hug me. She, too, wants to grab a lifeline and never let it go. But I'm no lifeline. Her hand passes through my arm, like it was made of mist.

"You know where to find us," the guy says.

I nod. I have no clue why should I feel the need to look for them, but he's right, I know where to find the two of them.

In another heartbeat, I'm standing just inside the train's doors.

"I love you!" the woman screams, and I smile and feel childishly happy, even though I can see she's trying so hard not to bawl in front of me.

Her companion waves his hand, looking dejected and lost, a joyless smile plastered on his lips.

I let the doors close. The train gets in motion and carries me away.

She loves me. I have no idea who I am or who she is, but she loves me.

I close my eyes and lean forward, my forehead pressed against the glass pane in the door. This time, the short-circuiting feeling is dimmer. This time, being the train and the whole underground system and just another person traveling through Milan is not that bad.

This time, I have the feeling I could lose myself in all this, and maybe that's how this whole life is meant to be. I already forgot my name and past, and who those people were to me.

With time, I will lose myself in the city, and those two will forget me too, and that day I will stop feeling like I'm slowly being unraveled by cruel hands.

I collapse to the floor, hug my knees and cry. Lulled by the train that rocks along the tracks and zigzags on my skin, I cry and cry until the train stops for the night.

THE NARRATOR is a young woman, suffering from progressive memory losses and feeling things she should not feel. She roams the street of Milan, Italy, but she can't remember if she's on an errand or simply lost.

It was love at first sight between **MARINA BELLI** and books. Then, when she was eleven, she used to skip catechism classes to go to the local library, read great stories, and try her hand with this "writing" thing. She's been a librarian, an English teacher for entry level students, an editor, a roleplayer, and a clerk for the Town Hall. She lives in a small town in northern Italy and mainly writes and self-publishes in Italian, her mother tongue, but she's forcing herself to write in English too. You can find her at https://spaceofentropy.wordpress.com/.

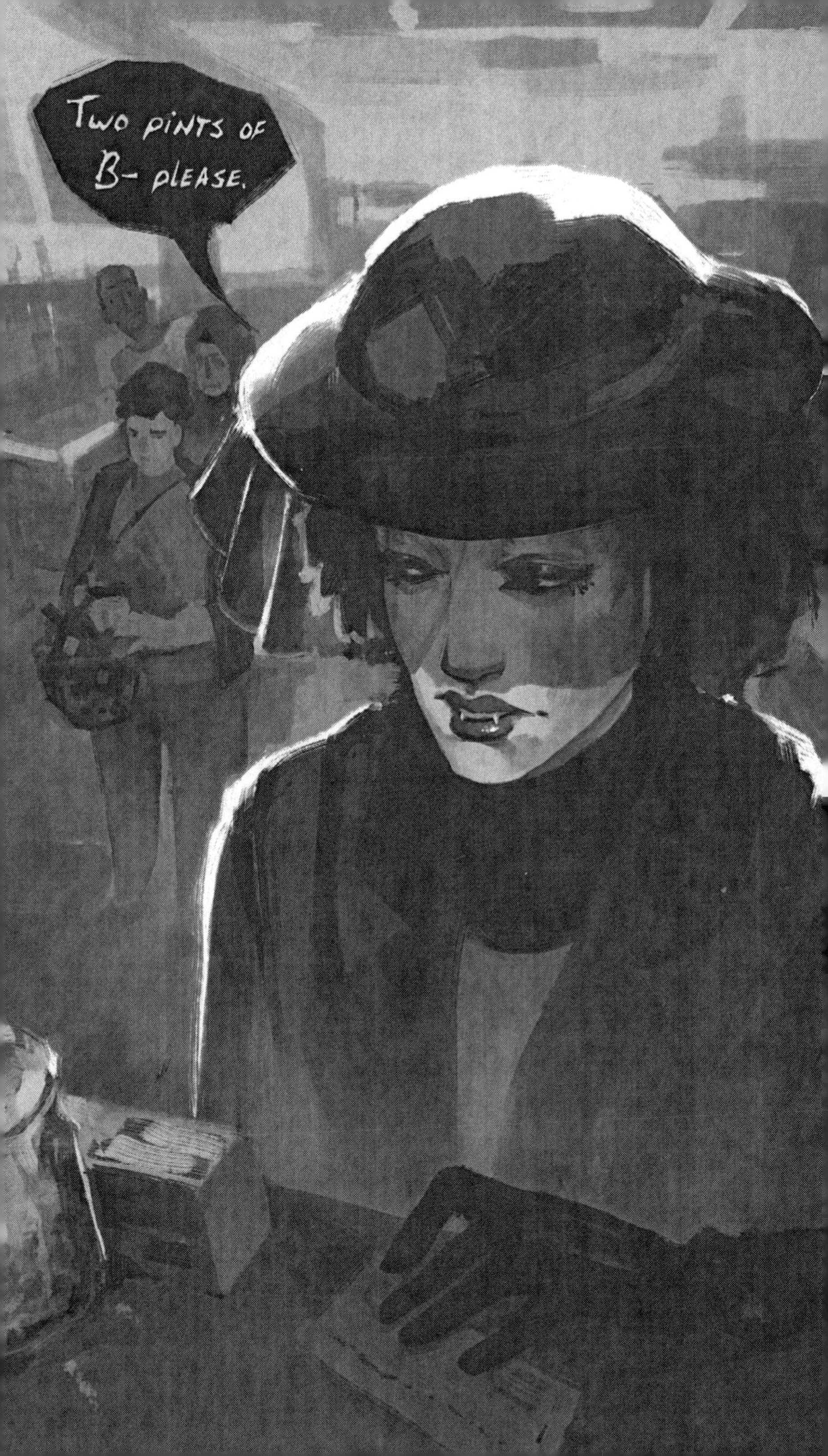
Two pints of B- please.

HELLSPAWN
SEEKING FEMALE

An account by Peter,
AS PROVIDED BY DARREN RIDGLEY

"**P**eter, we're going to need you out for confession in three."
The floor director's voice carries through the closed door to my bedroom.

"Yeah. Right away, Jeremy." My voice is more sigh than speech.

"You all good?"

"I'm fine. It's been a crazy day."

"I know, buddy. Almost over."

I look at myself in the bathroom mirror, considering everything—the straightness of my collar, the length and pattern of my stubble. Makeup took care of the bags under my eyes before they cleared out of here, at least. I run my hands through my black hair, feeling the thickness of it. Suzanne in hairstyling is going to be pissed off at me for ruining the work she just did on my coiffure, but whatever. They want authenticity? Let 'em see me a little disheveled.

It ain't easy looking for love. Not in general. Definitely not on reality TV. But there's really nowhere else for the son of the Devil to find a bride these days.

I step out of my room and follow Jeremy down the spiral staircase of the mansion, out of the foyer, and into the warmly lit living room, a fire burning in the hearth. Jeremy positions me on a stool, the fireplace in the background to my right, so that the viewers can equate the image with the passion supposedly burning in my heart. If only they knew what else was burning inside me.

I hope there's passion soon, anyway—right now, it's still mostly fear, anxiety. I want one of these girls to be the One, but it's still too early.

The set lighting makes the room even hotter than the fireplace. I wonder if I'm sweating through my shirt, but nobody says anything. Jeremy holds up his clipboard, full of leading questions.

"So what's going through your mind, Peter?"

Peter. A fake name I chose for myself when I was released upon the world. A dig at my counterpart. The name of His most devoted disciple, who was also somehow the one who never seemed to grasp any of his master's rules. I lied about my job for the show—"financial planning" is pretty much all they get around here, so it flew under the radar easily. Hell took away all of my more interesting powers when I refused to fulfill my purpose, but I've still got a knack for faking credentials, setting up dummy companies, all of it. Being the son of the Father of Lies has its benefits.

Jeremy looks at me expectantly, motioning for me to speak. Got to stay focused. Don't blow it.

"Well, it was really, uh—" *Remember to use a lot of cliché words.* "—Intense. Very intense. The girls were all great, and there was a lot to do at the ranch. I mean, where else do you get to go on romantic horseback rides with eight beautiful women, right?"

I force a dumb, open-mouthed chuckle for the camera. Everyone in Hell is pissed at me for this. *Run for office,* they said. *Then, take your black throne in Jerusalem,* they said. But Hell's no better than any other isolated, crazy-pants hermit kingdom: they can never hold on to sleeper agents because they all realize how good it is on the outside. Why would I want to end the world? The world has sushi and amusement parks and women. That last one is a tough nut for me to crack, though. I thought it would be easy for me to find a mate, but as it turns out, my gifts for deception don't extend to pick-up lines—most women actually feel uneasy around me. A gut instinct. My fellow monsters are no better. Tried it with a succubus, but she was too intimidated, dating the boss's son. Lady vamps and harpies were no better—they know that if I do what I'm supposed to, it's the end of their world too. To them, I'm the enemy.

When *Medusa* doesn't want to look you in the face, that's when you know you've hit rock bottom. I spent three days watching Nicholas Sparks movies and drinking red wine to get through that funk.

But here, I have a chance. Here, in the manufactured constraints of the show, all my prospects are either fame-hungry or unhinged enough to suppress their gut instinct and transform me into Prince Charming in their own minds. While they do that, it gives me a chance to actually get to know them, let them get to know me. Show them there's something more to me beyond being a harbinger for a dragon, rising from the sea. I make great cannelloni. I'll do just that for the episode where they visit "my parents," which I'm putting off until I can hire a fake mom and dad and buy property in rural Idaho.

"So you have eight women out there, Peter, and seven roses. Who are the favourites going in?"

I let out a deep sigh, showing my stress. I'm both putting on a show for the camera, and I'm not. I want this to work. This is my last chance at ending the loneliness that's defined my whole life. But to say that my emotions don't show on my face is an understatement. I was made to be a sociopath, after all. Some parts of that stuck, others didn't.

"It is tough, I have to say. They're all a lot of fun to be around. Tanya is great, she's such a blast." Tanya, the one who claims to be a psychic. *Bullshit.* Tanya's fun, kind of kooky, but she's no mind reader.

"But Alex... I dunno. Alex didn't seem to have a lot to say. I'm not really feeling anything with Alex? You know?"

I say it like it's a question. Alex, unlike Tanya, actually *is* a psychic... or a sensitive, anyway. She's been weird around me since our one-on-one last week. She's barely come out of her room since then, and sat on a hay bale for the whole group date, refusing to get on a horse with me because of a "stomach ache." Right now, she's probably vomiting up iron nails in her room and doesn't know why. I'll be eliminating her tonight. If she stays on, it'll cause a world of trouble. Other girls might leave. The show might get cancelled. Then, back to solitude and Armageddon. I can't do that.

I fantasize about it all the time. Visiting wine country. Sharing a milkshake. And yes, even a long walk on the beach at sunset. When I asked him to go on a trip to Cuba with me, Azmodiel laughed so hard for suggesting it he spat a razor blade into my shoulder. I had to get a tattoo over the scar.

"Anyway." I continue talking to the camera. "I'm not going to kill myself too much over this decision tonight. I know it'll be hard on the girl who gets eliminated. That's going to be tough. But right now I don't know if we're at 'soulmate' territory with any of them yet."

Jeremy has me repeat the last couple sentences a few more times. They'll pick the best answer in editing. The camera guy clears out, and Ben from wardrobe arrives with a fresh tux for me to wear to the elimination ceremony. As I get changed, I lift up my undershirt to inspect my abs. It's not like they're going to be seen during this next shoot, but it makes me feel better to know I'm not looking bloated. Things are looking pretty good. Thank... thank *somebody* this place mostly has red wine in the cupboards, and no bread.

While I get dressed, Neal, the show's host, approaches me, and I already know what it's about.

"Peter," he whispers, even though he doesn't have to. "You know I'm supposed to go through that with you, on camera. Not Jeremy."

"Look, I've been very clear about this. No host interviews from now on."

Ever since I started the show, Hell has been trying to intimidate me out of it. They think I'm soft. Maybe they're right. They marked Neal for death after the first episode, and after that, all of the dailies where he was in the same shot as me showed distortions that looked an awful lot like someone had drawn a scythe coming at his head. They thought it was just a glitch in the digital camera. I know it's not. Anyway, we can't send that to air, and all they know is that it doesn't seem to happen when I'm not in the shot. I can't let Neal's death mess this up for me, either.

Upstairs, I can hear a chorus of the same high-inflection voice, coming out of seven different mouths, to seven different cameramen. I don't know if it's the effect of knowing they're being recorded or what, but every single contestant sounds the same. Hell has not spawned a hydra with a voice as annoying as their collective talk-moaning. It's the one thing I truly hate about all this. One voice is silent, however. There are probably a lot of interns getting her ready for this shoot.

I go out into the courtyard, which is flooded with light even though it's 9:45 at night. I stand on the top of the little staircase at the door and wait for the girls to filter in. They come in one or two at a time, taking their positions in a two-row choir formation according to Jeremy's exacting instructions. A sea of bleach-blonde tops in black dresses, with one redhead, Julianne, thrown in for... what? Diversity? Sometimes I wonder if there's a dead Confederate general casting this show.

Alex comes in last, practically led by the hand by a producer, trembling in her black dress. Her mascara isn't going to hold out for long.

I look at the group, and my stomach ties into knots. I think about spending the rest of my life with any one of them. I think about whether or not any of them can save me. If this bombs, that black throne might start looking better, and then goodbye, sushi.

We start recording. The whole thing is very efficient, very professional. The showrunners have done this enough times that it ought to be. I hand out roses to gleeful would-be TV stars, or girls hoping to become beloved enough by the audience that by the time I cut them, they get their own spinoff. A couple of them, namely Julianne, actually made an impression. I make eye contact with her, and she smiles. I run my hands through my hair, all nerves, and try to suppress a blush.

Seven roses get handed out and by around the fifth, everyone's figured out the result. Neal begins making the big announcement.

"Alex, I'm sorry, but you did not receive a rose tonight. Is there anything you would like to say to Peter before you go?"

Alex vigorously shakes her head no. It reminds me of how Mussolini looks right before they shove hot coals up his ass to start the day. She mumbles "no" over and over again.

"Cut!"

Jeremy stomps up to Alex, but slows his roll when he gets to her and begins whispering sweetly. Honestly, the way they browbeat the girls into acting the way they need is so predatory. Jeremy has no reason to fear Hell—when he gets there, they'll likely hire him.

"C'mon, sweetie. I know it's upsetting. You've all put a lot of yourselves into this," Jeremy coos. Alex keeps shaking her head. "We're going to do that one more time, just walk up to the stage, take Peter by the hand and have a few words. We're not going home until we get that. Okay? Okay."

Alex tries, very hard, to maintain her composure when Jeremy calls "Action!"

"Alex, I'm sorry, but you did not receive a rose tonight." Neal's delivery gets a little more crisp on the repetition. "Is there anything you would like to say to Peter before you go?"

Alex takes half-steps toward me. They'll cut it together in editing to make her seem to be walking faster. Nobody calls cut on this one. She makes it up to me, and I hold out my hands to grab hers. I'm not trying to scare her. Her reaction is beyond my control. Honestly, I feel bad for her.

Our fingers touch, and I feel the warmth of her flesh. She responds to my grip as if I've stuck sewing needles into her fingertips. She winces, wails, and begins roaring.

"You speak lies black as night. You are no saint. The saints weep at your image." Alex's voice cracks and spittle flies onto my tux while she speaks, her voice escalating with every sentence. Her hand flies up and she tries to claw me, but I catch the strike, shocked as anyone.

Two teamsters rush the set and grab her, dragging her away. She wails over and over again. It reminds me of home.

"He will unmake all that is. Do you hear them? The children cry. The babies cry. All across the land. My sisters, a serpent slithers amongst you." She gets dragged, kicking and screaming, to a limo waiting in the driveway, around the corner and out of view.

Jeremy gives a sarcastic golf clap as the limo doors slam shut and the vehicle peels away.

"That's a *great* blooper for the end-of-season special. That is gold." He retakes his position and tells the crew to get ready to begin recording again.

The girls all stand gobsmacked until Julianne, the redhead, leans over to Tanya, the fake psychic.

"I've been waiting four weeks for his serpent to slither amongst me, ya heard?" They fist bump.

I motion to Jeremy until he looks at me. I discreetly point at Julianne.

"One-on-one date," I mouth.

Jeremy nods.

PETER (an assumed name standing in for one which must not be spoken) was sent to Earth from Hell in the mid-2000s by his father Satan, for the purposes of ushering in the apocalypse of Revelation. However, he came to love and assimilate into human society, and has rejected his supposed destiny in order to pursue love. After being rejected by his fellow monsters and striking out on the human dating scene, he hopes reality television will provide the stage on which he can find his one-and-only. He enjoys red wine, movies, and carbs.

DARREN RIDGLEY is a journalist and speculative fiction writer living in Winnipeg, Manitoba, Canada.

TO COME AND GO

An account by Jack,
AS PROVIDED BY JIMMY BERNARD

The day the dead started coming back to life, a lot of people thought it was the end of the world. Army stations got set up, people flocked to churches and mosques, homes were boarded up, and everyone was downright scared. The president made a speech from some underground bunker, advising everyone to stay in their homes as long as this crisis was going on. I honestly don't remember much from it, except that my mom was constantly watching the news, and my dad was loading up his shotgun. I remember him shooting one of the dead persons in the head. It was our old neighbor, Herb Fillin, who had died earlier that year. It was gory and traumatized me pretty bad. I swear, I couldn't look at a plate of spaghetti for months without thinking back to that poor dead guy.

It wasn't long until everyone realized that the dead weren't attacking the living. In fact, they weren't acting like the Hollywood zombies at all. Nobody bit anybody, there were no moans for brains, and not a single soul got dismembered. The dead who came back to life were no more than that. It turned out that some kind of exotic bacteria was the cause of it all. It revitalized the body and brought the host back to life, in a way. The Returned—as people started calling them—weren't really alive. Their heart didn't pump blood, they didn't need oxygen, and any food they ate came right back out. They could speak, move, and think though, so they weren't that different from the rest of us.

After that, it didn't take long until the protests began. The Returned wanted jobs and their old homes back, which had often been sold to new people during their absence. The living people didn't like that at all. They took to the streets with signs and songs and all kinds of angry shouting. I remember my dad taking me to one of those rallies once when I was eight years old. We drove down to city hall, where a group of about a hundred people had gathered. My dad had a big smile on his face, which looked weird, because he wasn't the smiling kind of man.

"Look, Jacky, sane people, just like us," he said. I looked at the crowd and didn't see any sane people. All I saw were angry men with red faces and beer in their hands. The people of Milton, my town, had changed from soft and understanding to enraged and bloodthirsty. It wasn't until later that I realized they were scared. They feared for their jobs, their homes, and the unknown threat that came with the Returned. I guess it's a normal way to feel, but at that time I didn't understand it. Perhaps I never will.

My dad lifted me on his shoulders and joined the crowd. Some guy took a picture of us with a big camera, which made a loud clicking noise every time he snapped a shot. That picture made the front page of the *Milton Daily* the very next day, with a headline reading: LOCALS JOIN PROTEST AGAINST THE RETURNED. My dad was mighty proud. He cut out that article and hung it in his office for everyone to see. He worked for the city, digging holes and paving streets, but he liked to sit in his office from time to time to pretend he was someone else. Someone bigger.

When I turned twelve, the social unrest had increased. The protests were still going on, but now small gangs went out at night to attack any Returned they could find. I had a friend at that time named Peter. We used to walk home from school together. One day, we walked by the old Miller barn, which was nothing but rotting wood, an abandoned tractor, and empty fields. We had this game where we threw rocks or bottles to see who could throw the farthest. I was smaller than Peter but had a better arm than he did. That day, I had just set a new record by throwing a rock all the way to the rust-covered tractor. It made a metallic sound when it landed, and both of our mouths fell open.

"No way," Peter said.

"Guess you might as well quit," I told him.

"You got lucky, the wind carried it," he said. I laughed and sat down on the ground while Peter got in position to throw his bottle. He had this focused look on his face, as if he was in the Major Leagues, getting ready to throw the winning pitch. He took a step back and hurled his entire body forward, making a deep grunting sound as the bottle went flying. We followed it with our eyes, me hoping it wouldn't reach the tractor, and Peter hoping the opposite. The bottle twirled toward the ground and disappeared in the grass with a dull thud. We looked at each other, wondering why it hadn't made that sweet shattering noise. We walked through the grass toward the point where the bottle had landed. Peter was the first to see it. He stopped and turned around, holding his hand to his mouth while gesturing me to not go farther. I remember asking him what it was, while I eagerly ran forward. By the time I saw it, he was already throwing up his lunch. The Returned, or what was left of him, had been burned. The black skin had red patches and cuts on it where the attackers had beat it. Its jaws were open in a silent scream for help. I remember seeing broken teeth and a big gaping hole in its abdomen, the point where the knife had gone through him.

I fainted.

I woke up on the couch at home. My mom put a wet cloth on my forehead while my dad talked to the sheriff. As soon as he left, my dad gave me a look filled with contempt and disappointment. I'll never forget that look. It was as if he was ashamed to even be in the same room as me. His coward of a son who couldn't stand seeing a dead Returned. His weak boy who hadn't been filled with joy when he saw the result of a lynch mob. I guess it was at that moment I knew me and my dad would never get along.

When I was fourteen, I got into a fist fight at school with a few older kids during lunch. It was spring, but warm enough to wear shorts. I was eating my lunch with Erin and Brad (Peter and I had split a few years before that, no reason other than life). We were talking about whatever it is fourteen year olds talk about, when we heard cries coming from the Corner. See, every school has a Corner. It's the spot where the fights happen, because the teachers can't get to you right away. With us, it was next to a bicycle stand.

We got up and instinctively ran toward the noise. A group of teenagers had already formed a circle around the fighters, keeping the teachers out as best they could. Erin and Brad got held back, but I managed to slip through and end up in the front row. I was surrounded by roaring sounds of primitive pleasure and encouragement, and it was with little surprise that I found myself cheering along with the group.

The fighters were Jeremy Strip and Nick Cluster Junior, two kids who looked like they belonged in juvie instead of high school. Jeremy was holding someone, while Nick was beating them with everything he had. I saw a small leg kick up and hit Nick in the chest, causing him to stumble back a bit. Jeremy struggled to hold on and, in doing so, turned toward me, giving me my first good look at their Returned victim. I think it was her eyes. They weren't filled with pain or anger, just sadness. She looked at me for a second and seemed to ask me to look away, as if she wanted nothing more than to be dead, as she had once been. It's easy to recognize a Returned. Their skin gets a grayish shade, their eyes turn light blue (almost silver), and their hair slowly turns white. When I saw her, I immediately knew she had once been dead and had come back to life, only to be beaten up by Jeremy Strip and Nick Cluster Junior.

"That bitch! Hold her still, I'll kill her all over again," Nick shouted, as he got in position to start his beating once more. I don't know why, but I ran forward and hit him in the back of his head. Pain flashed through my hand. It felt as if I had hit a brick wall and a thousand needles had exploded under my skin. Nick fell forward, grasping his head, and tripped against one of the bicycles. I turned toward Jeremy just in time to see a massive fist come at me. The pain in my hand went away, as a fresh stab of pain filled my nose, causing my eyes to blur and me to fall down.

By the time the teacher got to me, I had bruises all over my back from Jeremy's boots. My hand wasn't broken, but the doctor told me I was real lucky. He didn't know that my dad would be waiting for me at home. The school had called him up to tell him I had stopped a fight between two boys and a Returned girl. By the time I got home, he was drunk and swinging his belt. That was the second beating I got that day, and it didn't feel any better than the first. After that day, Jeremy and Nick were always gunning for me, hoping to catch me alone to continue their assault. They'd both gotten detention and a beating from their dads—for beating me up, not the Returned girl, obviously. I'd like to tell you they never got me again, but that's not how high school goes.

I didn't see the girl for a week after that. I was walking through the hallway on a Friday when I saw her standing at her locker. Someone had taped pictures of zombies and corpses all over it and she was cleaning it up. Whenever kids passed her, they giggled and muttered insults. She didn't respond to any of it though. She just kept on cleaning the mess from her locker. Part of me wanted to walk away, to avoid this girl who had gotten me into trouble already. Another part of me, the fourteen-year-old part, saw a girl and wanted to talk to her. I summoned up all my courage and went up to her, trying to think about what those cool guys in the movies would say.

"Hi," I managed to mutter. She glanced at me and gave me a slight smile, before turning back to her locker.

"Want some help with that?" I said. She looked at me. I felt my cheeks turning red, so I started pulling down the junk from her locker before she could say anything. Everyone who passed us was dumbfounded. First I'd saved her from a beating, and now I was helping her clean her locker. It didn't take long for the word to spread, and by the end of the day, I was the guy dating the dead chick.

"Thank you," she said, after I'd pulled the last piece of tape off. Her voice was soft and slightly muttered, like an animal afraid to draw attention to itself.

"You're welcome. Glad to help," I said.

She gave me a small smile and opened her locker.

"I'm Jack, by the way," I said.

She took out her books and looked at me, wondering why I was still talking to her. "Hello, Jack," she said.

I laughed. "Can I know your name?" I said.

She hesitated for a moment. "Emily. My name is Emily Overleed," she said, closing her locker.

"Nice to meet you, Emily Overleed."

She smiled one last time and walked away.

That weekend was terrible. Anybody who's ever been a love-struck teenager knows how it feels to be separated from your crush. I couldn't eat, sleep, or even think straight. The only thing that was on my mind was her. I doodled her name all over my textbooks. I listened to cheesy love songs and pictured the two of us together. I even sat down and wrote a love letter, which I immediately tore to pieces, for fear of my dad finding it. For the first time in my school life, I wished for the weekend to pass and Monday to arrive. When it finally did, I must have been the only kid with a smile on his face while entering school.

I practically ran to her locker, nervous and unsure of what I was going to say. During the weekend, I had pictured us in a romantic relationship. The only thing I had forgotten to picture was how we got to be in that relationship. When I turned the corner and saw she wasn't there, I felt my heart break. An entire weekend of waiting, only to not see her now. I walked up to her locker and started looking around, hoping to see her coming around the corner. But she didn't. I lingered as long as I could, until the bell rang and I had to run to class.

It was during recess that I saw her again. She was sitting in the shade with a book in her hands and earmuffs on, even though it was warm outside. I had been walking toward Erin and Brad, but changed my mind immediately, not that they minded. Ever since I had stood up for Emily, they were a bit afraid to be seen with me. I crossed the playground and stopped in front of her.

"Hi, it's me again," I said.

She looked up at me and closed her book. "Hi?" she said.

"Mind if I sit with you?" I said. I sat down without waiting for an answer and smiled at her. "Why do you wear earmuffs? Aren't you way too hot right now?"

She lowered her head. "They help with the noise," she said.

"What noise?"

"The insults."

I opened my mouth but couldn't get anything out. I turned my head and saw every eye on the playground turned toward us. It was quieter than usual, as if everyone was mesmerized watching the dead chick talk to the weird kid. When I looked back at her, she was frowning.

"You should leave, before you get in trouble," she said.

I laughed, a sound that echoed across the still school yard. "What, because of them?" I said, while pointing at the kids. "Fuck them!"

A collective gasp went over the playground, one which Emily shared. She opened her mouth to say something, but I cut her off.

"I don't care what they think. I want to talk to you, so that's what I am going to do," I said.

She smiled, and that was the first of many times I saw her cry. I think that was the moment she started liking me. It was also the moment I lost all respect and friendship, from peers and teachers. Not that it matters, because it was the moment I met the best person I've ever met in my entire life.

We started hanging out a lot after that awkward first meeting. We shared lunch breaks together, talked about books, and every day I walked her home. She lived a few blocks away from me with her dad and sister. They were all Returned, and all of them stared at me when I walked in there for the first time. Emily introduced me, and her dad gave her a worried look. I didn't blame him; I knew they didn't have it easy.

"Hello, sir, I'm Jack Rosen," I said, trying my best to look trustworthy. Her dad didn't open up to me right away, but eventually he did. After a few weeks, I was a regular guest at the Overleed house, which was nice. Emily's dad and sister were very friendly and wonderful to talk with. Mr. Overleed wasn't like my dad at all. He was calm, open to new ideas, and always available for a good talk. He made me wish my dad was different and not so angry all the time.

I took Emily over to my place once. As soon as she entered, my dad started shouting insults at us and threatened to call the police. I was so angry, I could've hit him. That night we had one of the biggest fights we ever had. He slapped me with his belt, I threw bottles and anything I could find at him, Mom cried, and it was all out chaos.

I ran away eventually, to the only place I could go. She was awake and took me up to her room. I remember being nervous and forgetting all about the fight. It was the first time I had been in a girl's room, and I didn't know what to do.

"Sit down," she said, patting the bed. The lights were out, but the drapes were open, filling the room with the pale light of the moon falling through the window. Her face looked white, as if she was a part of that universal shine coming down upon us. I remember looking at her and trembling. My body felt cold, even though it was midsummer.

"Relax," Emily said. She came closer and told me to close my eyes, which I did. The kiss was short and sweet and filled with teenage awkwardness. When it was over, I remember wanting a second one. I leaned forward and kissed her again. I'll never forget that first kiss. It was the best first kiss I could've wished for, even if I had no clue I was wishing for it.

I got a car when I turned seventeen years old, the result of working at a gas station every weekend for two years straight. We took drives to the beach a lot. Emily liked the sea. She loved taking her shoes off and walking through the salt waves as they slowly advanced upon the sand. Those times were the best of my life. Just me and her, looking at the ocean, and dreaming of a future together. We talked about "later" a lot. Emily's body aged, but she couldn't have children. We considered adoption, but she ultimately decided not to. When I asked her why not, she said she didn't want to have a baby whose mom was a Returned.

I asked her how she had died once. It was a tough thing to ask and an even tougher thing for her to answer.

"I don't like talking about it," she said.

I frowned and felt blood rush to my face. "I'm sorry. You don't have to say it if you don't want to. I understand," I said.

She sighed and held her hand to her forehead. "It's just I remember how I died, Jack. I remember the sensation of life leaving my body. It's not a pleasant thing to remember, I can assure you of that."

I told her I bet it wasn't.

After a few moments of us staring at the ocean in silence, she started talking. "We, my dad and sister, were in the city to watch some zombie movie, irony right?" she said with a grin. "Anyway, when we left the theatre, we found some guy standing by our car. At first we thought he was drunk, except he wasn't. He shot my dad in the heart and my sister twice in the stomach. He did me last." She lifted her shirt, showing me her belly with three silver-dollar-sized holes in it.

"I'm sorry," I said, not knowing what else to say.

She gave me a sympathetic smile. "Don't be. I'm in a better place now."

That night I dropped her off at her apartment and was invited inside. She took me to her room and locked the door.

"Kiss me," she said, while taking off her top. It was the first time for both of us. There was no romantic music, no passionate Hollywood-style love making, only two kids who didn't know what to do and had high hopes for life. When it was over, we fell asleep together. The next morning, her dad woke us up. He frowned at me for a few seconds, but eventually smiled and nodded, as if he was glad that it was me.

My dad was less happy.

"Been banging your dead chick?" he said as soon as I entered the house. Mom was sitting in the chair, staring at the blue curtains.

"Who cares," I said as I headed for my room.

He stood up and blocked the doorway, his big red face right in front of mine. "I care," he said.

I smelled the beer on him and felt my stomach turn. "Leave me alone." I tried to pass him, but he wouldn't move.

"Did you like it?" he hissed, bringing his face closer to mine. "Did you like that cold pussy?"

I didn't think about it. My hand flew at his face and connected underneath his eyeball. He stumbled backward and fell with a mighty crash. I flew at him but got kicked in the knee before I got there. For an old man, he was surprisingly fast and agile. By the time I had recovered from his kick, he was already punching me wherever he could.

That was the second time I took a major beating after throwing the first punch. Somehow, that time hurt more than the first.

The police were called in, and my dad got taken away for the night while I spilled blood all over my room. I was done there. His last comment had been the infamous drop. I grabbed my bag, filled it up with clothes, gathered what little money I had, and left.

On my way out, I passed my mom in the living room. She looked at me with tears in her eyes. I felt bad for leaving her, but I couldn't stay anymore and she knew that. I kissed her on the cheek and left. That was the last time I ever saw my mom alive.

I took the car to Emily, where else? She listened to my story and comforted me as best she could. Eventually I went and got a motel room for the night. I'm still amazed I managed to survive back then, being the dumb teenager I was. If it wasn't for the job at the gas station, I don't think I would have ever been able to stay alive that long on my own. But I did. I got a one room apartment and a job at a college bookstore, which was very nice. I never went to college, but being surrounded by books and smart people made me feel right at home.

Emily did go to college. She was one of the first Returned to get a bachelor's degree. Her picture made the paper, and it had me in the background, smiling like an idiot. That was the second time I was in the news, seventh page this time. Don't think my dad hung that article on the wall of his office.

Emily started working, and we managed to buy a small house in a quiet part of the city. I upgraded to junior manager at the bookstore, and life was good.

I got a postcard every Christmas, New Years, and birthday from my mom. At first it was her signature, with "Dad" added to it in her own handwriting. Over the years, the "Dad" changed into the writing of my father. I started calling home, but still not as much as I should've. My dad and I never spoke. Whenever I called, he was out in the yard or working in the attic or doing whatever he could to get away from me. Mom told me he had quit drinking and was actually doing well.

Guess I knocked some sense into him.

Mom died of liver cancer seven years after I had left home. I was heartbroken and looked everywhere for help. I even went to some college friends I had made, asking them if she would be able to come back as a Returned. Turns out the government had eliminated the R-bacteria (as they called it) a few years before. The only Returned alive were those who had come back during the initial uprising.

Emily did what she could. I asked her about the afterlife once, and she told me it was nice. She stared out the window and seemed to be drifting off as she talked about it.

"There's a pure blue ocean where the water is always warm, and the beach is clean and nice," she said.

The thought of my mom there made me happy, even if it was just for a little while.

We went to the funeral together. There weren't a lot of people there. Turns out I wasn't the only one my dad had driven away with his anti-Returned attitude. When we got there, I was surprised to find him in a wheelchair. The long years of digging holes had finally caught up with him. He had lost about fifty pounds and looked more like a weak old man than the monster of my childhood. We shook hands, and he gave me and Emily a smile.

"I'm glad you came, both of you," he said.

I didn't believe him, but it was a nice thing to hear, especially for Emily.

I'd like to say my dad and I got close again, but this is no movie. Some wounds are just too deep to be healed. He died three years ago, from a heart attack while he was sitting in the park. He's buried next to my mom. I cried when I heard the news.

A few years passed, and everything went well. The Returned got accepted more, which was nice for all of us. Eventually Emily and I didn't even have to worry anymore when we went out late at night. The fear of a raiding group attacking her was as good as gone. People changed. It didn't happen overnight, but that doesn't matter. Life was good, even if it was never meant to last. Like all good things, it had to end sometime.

I woke up on a Saturday morning to find Emily sitting upright in bed. When I asked her what was wrong, she didn't respond. I touched her shoulder, but couldn't get a response from her. My heart started pumping like a jackhammer as I got up.

"Honey, what's going on?" I shouted, while shaking her shoulders. I was about to call the ambulance when she came back.

"Oh," she said, as if she was woken up from a dream. "What's going on?"

I told her about what happened and she just stared at me, as if I was making up stories. We eventually passed it off as a brain fart, stress, and need of a vacation, nothing more.

It was more.

These episodes started repeating themselves and getting longer as well. One day I came home to find Emily under the shower, where I had left her that morning. Her skin was all wrinkled, and she remained catatonic for an hour after I had gotten home. After that, we both agreed that it was time to see a doctor.

Doctor Feldman was a forty-year-old doctor who specialized in Returned cases. He listened without saying anything as we told him about her episodes. When we were done, he took a few scans of her brain and asked her to perform some simple tasks like touching her forehead with her pinky and pinching her nose. I knew something was wrong as soon as I saw Emily grab her ear instead of her nose.

The doctor knew as well.

"It seems, for some unknown reason, the R-bacteria is slowly dying, causing the host to fail as well," he said.

I felt as if I was underwater. Everything he said sounded muted and far away. I looked at Emily and saw she had her lips pressed together so tight they formed thin white lines.

"What do you mean?" I heard my voice say.

The doctor gave me a defeated look. "It means that your wife is going to die. I'm sorry," he said.

The words didn't register with me. Emily was young, she wasn't supposed to be dying. She was supposed to be healthy and grow old and be with me for the rest of my life.

"How long?" I heard her say.

The doctor shook his head. "Seeing as the episodes are increasing in length, I'd say not long."

"How. Long," said Emily.

I grabbed her hand and squeezed it. My eyes started tearing up and my breathing came in shocks. Nothing made sense anymore.

"A month, at most," Doctor Feldman said. "We don't know enough about the R-bacteria to cure this condition. I'm afraid there is nothing we can do."

We talked some more, but nothing mattered after that. Emily, the woman I loved, would die all over again. I cried all the way home, but she didn't drop a tear. She just stared out the window. When we entered our house, she collapsed at the doorway, letting everything out. Her cry was filled with fear and anger. I sat down and held her tight, cherishing the touch of her skin, the smell of her hair, and the taste of her lips. Death has a way of adding perspective to things.

I took a vacation from work to be with her in her last days. She started becoming weaker, sometimes not even able to stand up. I kept her in bed most days, reading to her or talking about the old days. The episodes started happening more and more, each time lasting longer. Two weeks after the visit to the doctor, Emily went into an episode she didn't get out of for two days. When she finally woke up, she gasped and looked at me with fear in her eyes.

"Jack," she said, tears rolling down her cheeks. "Jack, oh God, I thought I was gone. I thought I wouldn't come back this time. Oh Jack, I can't. I can't, please, Jack, I can't." Emily cried for an hour before falling asleep.

I sat next to her, softly brushing her white hair and pulling the blanket up so she wouldn't be cold.

A few days before the end, she asked me to take her to the ocean.

"Just like old times. I want to see the ocean with you, one last time," she said.

I packed some things, loaded up the car, and carried her downstairs. She'd lost weight and felt like a child in my arms. Her hands grasped my shirt, and I could feel her faint breathing on my neck. She was exhausted once we got to the car and fell asleep.

The drive to the ocean was long and hard. Memories of our life together came flooding back to me, and I knew I was not ready for what lay ahead. Every time I passed a corner, I thought back about us, about her. I passed the gas station and thought about her laughing that time I had spilled gas all over myself. I passed the library, where we'd spent so many hours searching for books. Whatever I passed, I thought of her, and I realized that she was everything. She was my whole life.

We got to the beach and it was quiet, which was perfect. It was a gray day, and not a lot of people were out. I woke her up and carried her over the sand, to the edge of the ocean.

"I want to feel the water on my feet," she said.

"I can't put you down, you won't be able to sit upright," I told her.

She frowned, and I saw sadness come over her.

My heart wasn't able to see her like that at the end of her life. I carried her to the point where the waves hit the beach and kept going until I was waist deep in the water.

"What are you doing?" she said. "You'll get a cold."

"No I won't," I said, while lowering her feet so they could feel the water.

Emily closed her eyes and smiled. For a long time, we just stood there, like we had always done. Just me and my girl and nothing but that big ocean in front of us.

"Soon you'll be here, honey. You'll go to sleep, and you'll wake up here. A blue ocean, a nice beach, and nothing but good things," I said. I looked at her and saw her big eyes staring back at me. Her mouth was open and her lips were trembling.

"Jack," she said. "I lied."

"What do you mean?"

"You felt so bad, about your mom and all, I just wanted to make you feel good. There is no beach. I made it up," she said.

I looked at her and shook my head, not understanding what she was trying to tell me. "I don't get it. What is the afterlife like then?"

Her eyes grew big and she started breathing frantically. "There is nothing, Jack. Just an immense black void with not a single spot of light or touch or sound. That's it. That is all there is waiting for me," she said.

I tried to say something, but Emily shook and went off into one of her last episodes. I took her home and prayed for her to come back. Her words never left me. All this time, I thought it wouldn't be so bad for her. She would go to that wonderful afterlife, but now I knew different. Now I knew she was going to something far worse than this.

Emily woke up one last time. I was in bed next to her, and we held hands. She smiled at me and kissed my lips.

"I'm sorry I lied, honey," she said.

I shook my head and told her it was alright. We said we loved each other, not that it needed to be said.

"I can feel the end coming, Jack," she said. A tear ran down her cheek as I kissed her. I never wanted to stop kissing her. I wanted to be with her forever, without ever having to say goodbye.

"I know there is nothing but darkness waiting for you, but I promise I will look for you. And maybe, just maybe, we'll be together in the dark and we could shine some light around us," I said.

She smiled. "That sounds lovely. So lovely."

Those were the last words she ever said.

I buried her in a nice coffin with a view of the ocean. Her dad and sister were at the funeral, but they weren't doing much better than Emily. Turns out her dad had been getting episodes as well, and her sister was feeling a bit strange lately. They didn't have to tell me, I knew all about it.

Coming home after the funeral was the worst of it. It's all manageable when you're surrounded by people and arranging things, but once you're alone? That's when the misery begins. I closed the door and shouted out to her that I was home, never getting a response. I went to the bedroom and saw an empty bed, there where my girl used to be. I smelled her pillow and cherished her fleeting scent.

I don't know if she is in a good place, or if she is back in that darkness she talked about. All I know is that I'm going to her. I've lived my entire life loving a dead girl. No point in living without her, I guess.

JACK is an average guy working in a college bookstore. He doesn't have a lot of close relatives, but he is married to a wonderful woman named Emily. They're perfect for each other, even though Emily died a couple of years ago and came back to life as one of the many Returned.

JIMMY BERNARD is a twenty-six-year-old writer from Belgium with a degree in Applied Psychology. He works as an HR analyst and spends his free time reading, playing guitar and piano, and writing stories. He started writing seriously when he was twenty-five and has published a handful of short stories so far.

THE CHILDREN OF ECHIDNA

An account by an unknown gorgon,
AS PROVIDED BY AMELIA FISHER

That morning, I put on the blinders for the first time.

There are more straps than I can make sense of. They are durable, leather and metal, ugly things built to be strong, not comfortable. My mother helps me secure them, and afterward, when she looks at my new face, she takes too long to smile. There are no mirrors in our house. I cannot know what she sees. What I see is a world grown much darker than before, the tilted glass pressed tight to my skull.

"God keep us safe in this place," she says. It's not one of the prayers I recognize, but she speaks it like one. I do not entirely know what she means, but it scares me in a way I do not understand.

Kaitep says that all cities are the same. She is full of that kind of wisdom lately, and though I remind her that she is only a handful of years older than me, I feel the heavy weight of her words. Maybe she is right. Maybe there are cities just like this one, in the land we've left behind. If so, I've never seen them, and maybe I never will. Maybe, maybe, maybe. There aren't many things I know for sure these days. Only that home has become a far-away place, where once it was all I knew.

Our parents react in different ways. Mother has turned wholly practical. I cannot glimpse the thoughts that go on behind her frenzy of activity. She works hard to grow into the house where we live now, which is larger than our old home, but colder and uglier too. She fills it with the smells of familiar cooking, made different and strange because the spices are different. She begins a new drawing on the wall, but there is little time, and it stays incomplete.

Father says we came here for a better life. He repeats this, whenever any of his family looks unhappy. It has become his mantra. The more he says it, the less I believe. We've come here, he seems to say, and therefore life must be better. If it isn't, then it was all for nothing.

"He's a fool," Kaitep says when we're alone in our room. "He's dragged us halfway across the world for no reason." Her words strike me in the stomach. She was never disrespectful to our father before. Maybe she never had a reason.

"Maybe we'll go back home, then," I say. I hate the way my voice sounds so much smaller than hers, the way she swallows it up when she laughs.

"We never will," she says savagely. "He'll never admit we've made a mistake."

I do not want to be like my sister. I want to believe that here, in this strange city, I can find happiness. But my head still aches where the buckles have dug in after wearing the blinders all day, and the pain settles deep into my bones.

"Why?"

I ask my mother this the first time she shows me the thing I must wear. She's bought one for me and one for my sister, and laid them out on the bed. I dislike them immediately. There's no way this design can be comfortable. Yet Mother says we must wear them all the time here, except when we're alone.

"It's the law here," my mother says. "The government wants to protect its people."

"Protect people? From what?"

I hear the bitter note of Kaitep's laughter; I can tell that she already knows. "From us, idiot," she says. "They're afraid of what we can do. They don't think we can control it." She crosses her arms and sets her jaw. "You can't make me wear that thing."

From her tone, I know that she has already decided to have a fight. Mother knows it too, but she's still trying. "'Fear is the result of ignorance,'" she quotes. "The people here do not understand what we are, and so they ask for more from us. We can teach them, in time."

"Should we coddle them, then?" Kaitep says. Her gaze traces the blinders on the bed with disgust. "I won't wear them. If it frightens them, they can learn not to fear."

I leave shortly after that, when the shouting gets too loud. I know that the next morning when we leave the house, Kaitep will be wearing them anyway.

The people here are not our kind. Their eyes are cool, soft things. Until, of course, they're looking at us. Then their eyes are not so soft.

I can still remember the first time that the bumps appeared on my skull, when my blood began to hiss and fizzle in my veins, and my eyes grew sharp and dangerous. The change is one that all of my kind must go through, yet I hid between the roots of the cypress tree because I was afraid of turning my family to stone.

Kaitep was the one who found me and taught me not to fear. She cupped my cheeks and made me look into her eyes, until I knew that I could never hurt her, even by accident.

"Be proud," she had whispered. "You're one of us now."

Father has embraced the blinders wholly. He wears them as much as possible, and their imprint has become a permanent groove on his face even when he takes them off. "It's wonderful to have this opportunity," he says. "We can show the others how willing we are to cooperate. Anything we can do to make people more comfortable, we *should* do. It's our duty as citizens."

"We never had such a 'duty' back home," Kaitep mutters.

Father hears, and pretends he doesn't. He won't be able to lie so carefully if they fight. I am sure he thinks he is helping us adjust. Kaitep says he likes being blind, and I tell her she likes being cruel.

If the new blinders are meant to make the others feel safe, I do not see it working. When I walk on the street with my family, we wear our blinders as carefully and uncomfortably as warriors in armor—and that is how people treat us. They give us too much room on the street. They glare at our backs as if we've done something wrong. Most importantly, they never meet our gaze.

"Why are they staring at us?" I whisper to my mother one day. "We're doing what they want us to, aren't we?"

"Not as long as we're still here," my sister hisses back. "They don't want us blinded, they want us gone."

My mother says nothing. I wish she would deny it, even if it's the truth. It's more than the physical discomfort that bothers me, the fact that when I wear them I can hardly see. It's knowing that I wear them because someone else is afraid of me. It marks me as an outsider, and brands me as dangerous.

In school, everything is different. The things that they try to teach us are strange and unfamiliar, and when I fail to learn quickly, they label me stupid. The other children stare even worse than strangers on the street. I see them whispering behind their hands, and the whispers turn to laughter. Everything is strange to me, but from the way that people look at me, I realize that I am the strange one. I am the thing that does not belong.

"Where are the snakes?" one girl asks. She squints at my head as if I'm hiding them beneath my braids.

"That's just a myth," I say. "Only our ancestors had them."

The girl makes a face. "That's lucky. Those weird glasses already make you look like a monster."

I'm almost speechless. But not quite. "I only have to wear them because of people like you," I say, but the girl isn't listening, and she has no reason to care.

That's the first time I ever hear such a word describe me or my kind. And yet from then on, I see it in every glare a stranger shoots me through the murky tint of my blinders.

Father is always trying to find more people like us. He drags us into a different neighborhood every week, to sit down with families who have never so much as heard of the town we hail from, but who at least look the same as we do. The adults talk vibrantly about home. We children eye each other, distrustful, yet desperate. We have nothing in common but our heritage, but for now, it is enough.

Once we were all just people. Our culture was only an element of our complex being. Now, we are reduced to our origins.

There's one afternoon when they bring me to the house of a family whose son is wearing the blinders. This in itself is unsurprising, because it's expected of us all—but he does not remove them the entire time we see him, even within his own home. I tear mine off the second the door closes, like most of the adults. But the boy merely scratches at the places where they dig into his skin, and then lowers his hands.

"Aren't you uncomfortable?" I ask.

He nods. "But they say it's safer to keep them on all the time."

It did not occur to me until then that this place could make us frightened of ourselves.

Soon the children at school grow bolder in their questions. This, as it turns out, is worse than their mocking silence.

"Do you ever take them off?" they ask. "Can you look at each other? Can you look in the mirror? Have you ever killed anyone? Even by accident?"

At first, I try to be patient. Then, I simply try to correct them. And finally, I stop trying to do anything but hold my temper in check.

After a while, I start to hear the stories, the ones that inevitably come up in my presence. "I heard that where you come from people get turned to stone all the time. That the streets are just loaded with statues, but they used to be people." The girl who says this grins in a gap-toothed way that reminds me that she's making fun of me.

There are other stories, too. The ones the adults tell, when they think Kaitep and I aren't listening. In one, a person like us is beaten to death by a mob who thinks she's trying to take off her blinders. In another, a statue is discovered in an alleyway. It's a man with a knife in mid-cut, and he's staring forever at someone that is no longer there.

There's a curfew after that. Men in uniforms come to our house and ask our parents questions. My father has never broken a law in his life, but that doesn't matter to them. They look at him past his blinders as if he's already done something wrong, and in their eyes, he has.

One day, Kaitep returns from school crying, with a cut on her cheek. She tells us that two people—men, not children—started yelling at her as she walked home. Then they started throwing rocks. No one stopped them. She ran away before they could catch her.

Our mother holds Kaitep and lets her cry for hours. It's strange to be reminded that Kaitep is still a child. Father says nothing. His face is struck dumb of any expression. I wonder what he's thinking—that we will make a better life here, in a place that already thinks we are monsters?

I am not afraid of what I might do. I am afraid of their fear, and what it may lead them to do to us.

From then on, Kaitep stops fighting with our mother. This frightens me even more.

I can see her anger, seething beneath the surface, every time she puts on the blinders. Now she pulls the rage down into herself, and lets it build and build. "You know the person who designed these things wasn't even one of us," she says bitterly as she finishes the final strap. "They fear us because we're different, not because we're more dangerous. If a man can use his hands to strangle his wife to death, do you make him cut them off?"

I recognize the words in her mouth have first come from someone else's.

"Remember where our power is," she tells me one night, laying her hands over my eyes. "It comes from in here. And they can never take it from you."

I can't voice the words that rise up on the back of my tongue: can it really be power if it is the reason they hate us? Is it power if I can never use it? For doing so would mean becoming exactly what they already think I am.

I don't ask her where she slips off to, but I don't tell our parents either. When she comes back, she's quieter. The anger is still there, but it's as flat as the horizon. I hear about the marches, hundreds of people like us walking the streets without their blinders on, staring into people's eyes and leaving them frightened, confused, alive. Many of them don't know until then that a gorgon can decide whether what they see turns to stone.

The marches are quickly banned. Crackdowns are promised. And still, my sister returns home late, stuffing slogans into her pockets and pretending she's worn her blinders the entire time she's been out.

Of course our mother finds out. That's when our house becomes a battleground.

"I won't let you go to those protests!" Mother cries.

"We're peaceful," Kaitep argues. "We'll never change anything if we don't *do* anything."

"It isn't safe there!"

"It isn't safe anywhere!" Kaitep says back. "Not for people like us!"

Tears stream down mother's face from underneath her blinders. "All you'll do is get yourself killed," she says.

Kaitep bares her teeth. "If anyone tries to hurt me, I'll just look them in the eye and turn them to stone."

It all happens so quickly that I only understand it in the aftermath. One moment our mother is turned away to wipe the tears from beneath her blinders—the next she has spun around and seized Kaitep by her shoulders, and started shaking her like a doll. In Mother's eyes, I can see movement behind the pupils like a hive of bees.

"You will *not*!" she cries. "You will *never*!"

I have never seen her like this. I am more afraid than I can ever remember being. Even Kaitep's face is a mask of fear, pale and wide-eyed. I had not realized until now that our mother felt this anger, too.

"Do you understand, you foolish girl?" she snarls. "If one of us steps out of line, they will turn on *all* of us. They cannot tell the difference!"

As quickly as it started, it's over. Mother's hands fall to her sides. It seems she becomes smaller, frailer. The air, which seemed full of an electric charge, turns brittle and dead. A moment later, Kaitep runs for our room, and I know that tomorrow she will not go to the meetings, though perhaps she will the day after.

When I lay down that night to go to sleep, I can tell by her breathing that she's still awake. Just before I drift off, I hear her tiny voice. "I want to go home."

But there's nothing I can say, and so I say nothing at all.

Father is quiet at breakfast that morning. "They're suggesting a law to have us wear the blinders all the time," he says. "Something about a locking mechanism. A government agent would have the master key."

Not even Kaitep looks up from her food. The silence binds us tight.

That night, I dream of walking through the city's streets in the shadow of the Acropolis. The city is more silent than I have ever heard it, more still than a summer sky just before the first distant roll of thunder. I feel the sun on my skin, and reach up to touch my uncovered eyelids. When I lower my hand, I continue down the street, weaving my way around the statues that stand their silent watch, frozen in place, their eyes always meeting my own.

When I wake, it is still night. I sit up in bed, careful not to disturb Kaitep, who is sleeping peacefully for the first time I can remember. I stand, and go to the window. It is closed, as it always is when we take off our blinders. I open it. Outside, the street is quiet, and the moonlight makes everything into stone. If anyone were to see me, standing at my window with my hands peeling the curtains back, they would see a young girl like so many others in this city, but with eyes that cut like broken glass. I could meet their gaze. I could stare into them, and show them that we all have the capacity to do harm, and I can choose mercy as well as anyone.

Or I could turn them to stone. There they would stand forever, turned to my window, a finger of accusation.

The street is empty. No one sees me. I close the curtains again.

The next morning, I strap my blinders on with steady, practiced hands. I tell myself I am not afraid.

I tell myself I am not afraid.

THE AUTHOR of this account remains unknown. A connection has been proposed between the journal and one Kaitep Nabireh, who was among the casualties of the government crackdown at the Kimani Square Protests. Records show that Nabireh did indeed have a sister, but further information as to her identity or location was unavailable. The journal itself was discovered in a refuse pile, shortly after the names of the dead were disclosed to the public.

AMELIA FISHER graduated from Fairleigh Dickinson University in 2015 with a BA in Creative Writing. She also received her school's MFA award for her fiction. She is currently a recurring book reviewer with *The Literary Review*, and spends most of her waking hours writing, reading, and living speculative fiction. In her un-waking hours, she dreams it. She has lived in Egypt, Russia, Turkey, and the USA; these days she can most often be found in the haunted basement of her family home in Vienna, Virginia, when she isn't living out of a minivan in the woods. One day soon she hopes to embrace the minivan life full-time.

ABOUT THE EDITORS

In addition to editing *Mad Scientist Journal*, **JEREMY ZIMMERMAN** is a teller of tales who dislikes cute euphemisms for writing like "teller of tales." His young adult superhero books, *Kensei* and *The Love of Danger*, are now available. He lives in Seattle with a herd of cats and his lovely wife (and fellow author) Dawn Vogel. You can learn more about him at http://www.bolthy.com/.

DAWN VOGEL has been published as a short and novella-length fiction writer and an editor of both fiction and non-fiction. Her academic background is in history, so it's not surprising that much of her fiction is set in earlier times. By day, she edits reports for historians and archaeologists. In her alleged spare time, she runs a craft business and tries to find time for writing. She lives in Seattle with her awesome husband (and fellow author), Jeremy Zimmerman, and their herd of cats. Visit her website at http://historythatneverwas.com.